WRECKED

Blind Man's Alibi #1

Sarah Grimm

COPYRIGHT © 2016 Sarah Grimm
Print Edition
Print ISBN 978-0989936156

Shrek ® *is a trademark of Dreamworks, Inc*
Don't Let the Sun Go Down on Me © *UMPG*
Words and Music by Elton John and Bernie Taupin

Cover Art by Kari Ayasha, Cover to Cover Designs

Published in the United States of America

This book is dedicated to Amy Lillard for putting up with my insecurities. AJ Nuest for loving Gary as much as I do. And for my family for listening to me talk about these characters as if they were real.

February 15

I dreamt of an angel last night. An angel of fair skin and long auburn hair with a white gown made of delicate lace and gossamer wings that took my breath. Her arm was outstretched before her, a key dangled from her fingers. Not a car or a house key. Not a key of gold or fancy jewels. A silver key about an inch in length and of plain design. A simplified skeleton key.

I awoke before I could take her offering and immediately began to sketch my angel. To capture on paper the image so clear in my mind. But somehow I have lost the memory of her face – the angle of her cheeks or the shape of her lips – and only that key remains. That silver, uncomplicated form hanging from a basic chain. Why was she offering it to me? What did it represent? I'm afraid to speculate, for deep down, I believe I know.

I saw my oncologist yesterday. My treatment isn't working, just prolonging the inevitable. And so I made the decision to opt out of further treatment and accept my fate. Then I dreamt of an angel, and a key.

ONE

"SORRY, BUT SUCKING off a narcissistic asshole who's so damn drunk he can't recall the words to his own song is not my idea of a good time."

His bark of laughter echoed in the empty hall. "You really are a ray of sunshine, aren't you?"

God, what a terrible idea this had been. Hoping to put some distance between them, Emma Travers quickened her pace, only to stumble over the uncustomary height of the heels her best friend Alison had convinced her to wear. Her ankle screamed in protest, forcing her to skid to a halt. Balancing precariously so she didn't face plant on the concrete, she struggled against the zippers, finally succeeding in pulling the rhinestone studded stilettos from her swollen feet. She barely resisted the urge to turn around and throw them at the head of the man who'd pissed her off faster than a Bugatti Veyron went from zero to sixty, and instead tossed them aside and continued her escape in bare feet.

"Come back and see me sometime, Emma," Joe Campbell, lead singer of the British alternative metal band Blind Man's Alibi, called out to her.

Fat chance!

"I could use a bit of sunshine in my life." The murmur hit her ears like a shout, and stopped her in her tracks.

Well, shit.

Emma remained rooted in place, unable to decide if he was for real or filling her with pretty words in order to get her to stay and sleep with him. He sounded sincere enough, but the only way to know for certain was to face him. Something she really didn't want to do.

Not that he was painful to look at. Oh no, Joe Campbell was extremely pleasing to the eye, a fact he knew too well. One, she was certain, he used to his advantage whenever an occasion presented itself. Like tonight, when she'd gone against character and accepted his invitation backstage after the show.

One glimpse of the man who stood alone in the room she'd been unceremoniously delivered to and Emma went hot all over. Unable to speak, she'd allowed her gaze to take a long, slow journey over his body. His torso was bare, giving her an unobstructed view of hardened pecs, a flat washboard stomach and muscles that rippled and shifted, making the Chinese dragon wrapped around his left upper arm and onto his chest seem alive as he slipped his left hand into the front pocket of his jeans. Dear God, those jeans! The way they hung on his lean hips, the top button undone like he'd just pulled them on. They rode so low there was no mistaking that underneath them he was commando. Her gaze had locked on the obvious bulge behind his fly and, for a moment, she'd actually considered dropping to her knees before him and taking a taste.

Then he'd opened his mouth. What was that saying? *Elvis has left the building.* She was outta there.

With a deep breath for courage, Emma turned around and was greeted by the same image of the man as before. Except that the whiskey bottle he'd held in his right hand

and lifted to those delectable lips too many times to count, was nowhere to be seen. Oh great, and the hulking brute who'd brought her backstage stood leaning against the wall to Joe's right.

Gary, she was pretty certain he'd introduced himself as Gary, held his arms crossed before him, head tipped toward the floor in a pseudo relaxed pose designed to give the impression he hadn't just heard every damn word they'd said. He blew the image to shit when he lifted his head and winked at her. Winked! Was everyone in the music industry completely bonkers?

Emma did her best to ignore the brute and focused on the singer. "You're a real piece of work, you know that?"

"What did you expect?"

Good question.

"I guess I hoped the stage show was just that, a show, and that there was a decent guy behind all of that. Maybe I wanted to believe the *'I'm too sexy for my own good'* attitude was just publicity."

"Sorry to disappoint." His tone didn't sound regretful at all. He strode toward her, moved with such a fluid grace Emma's heart thumped in response. His long legs closed the distance in half the time it had taken her to get this far. She made herself stand her ground as he stepped in close, closer than she'd yet allowed him to get. Close enough she caught the subtle hint of soap on his skin and whiskey on his breath. "You're right about one thing, I'm an asshole. But it wasn't the alcohol that caused me to lose my words tonight, Emma Travers. It was you."

His chin-length brown hair was nearly dry now and hung over his eyes as if windblown, though nary a wisp of air blew from the vents above. Eyes she was surprised to learn were two different colors—one brown, the other a mix of brown and green. "You excel at telling a girl what she wants to hear, I'll give you that."

His gaze didn't flinch. "How can you doubt the truth? You were there, front row center. Close enough to touch me." The soft timbre of his voice warmed her even more than the heat radiating off his skin. He fell silent, unmoving, as if he were waiting for something. What, she wasn't certain. Unable to meet his gaze, she lowered hers and found herself transfixed by the movement of his Adam's apple as he spoke. "All you had to do was reach out."

An image of hands pawing and clutching at him whenever he'd trekked too close to the edge of the stage flashed through her mind. She swallowed hard, her mouth going dry, and shook her head. "Is that what you wanted me to do? Grope you like the other women in the audience? Do you actually enjoy that?"

"Not particularly."

"Yet you expect me to believe that, for some unknown reason, you wanted me to touch you?"

"You stood out from the crowd. Not singing, not screaming, just standing in the front row. It was impossible not to notice you. I wondered why you were at the show. You didn't seem to be having a good time. Then you smiled at me...my mind blanked."

What the hell was she supposed to say to that? Thanks for noticing me?

"I was feeding you lines and you just stood there, staring." Much the same way as she was doing now. Christ, he was beautiful. Her fingers itched with the need to trace his lips, his mustache, the little hairless spots on the outside of his bottom lip and that sexy as hell strip of facial hair that went from the center of his full lower lip down, to blend into his short trimmed beard.

Her throat went dry as dust. "Why me? I'm not actually supposed to believe you saw me and lost your place, am I?"

"That's what happened." His words were matter-of-fact, meant to be believed. "You know it's true, you were there."

Emma shook her head.

"Contrary to what you think, I was not too drunk to remember the lyrics. You see, I'm an accomplished drinker. I've been at it a long time. Long enough to know that forgetting the words to one of my songs is about as never-going-to-happen as forgetting how to please a woman."

"Why?"

"Why what, Sunshine?"

"Why are you a practiced drunk? Is that all you do, spend your free time partying?"

"Interesting. You don't question my forgetting how to please a woman?"

"Hah! You could probably pull that off if you were co-matose."

A rumble of appreciation emanated in his chest. The corners of his mouth kicked up into a smile, one so powerful it stopped her lungs altogether for a few seconds. Arrogance blazing in his eyes, he lifted his right hand.

The calloused tips of his fingers glanced off her cheek as she caught his wrist. "It's time for me to go."

"Stay." His deep voice combined with his intent gaze spread warmth throughout her body.

She forced herself to look away. Her eyes trailed a path down his right arm, over the bulge of bicep, the bend of his elbow, to where her hand circled his wrist. Beneath her thumb, which was busy making slow, gentle sweeps across his skin—*When exactly had it started doing that?*—a tattoo drew her attention. Measures of music circled his wrist once, twice, three times before ending in a large, red and black abstract G clef on the outside of his forearm.

"Tell me why you came backstage to find me if you weren't interested in, how did you put it, 'Sucking off a narcissistic asshole'?"

She felt bad for about ten seconds, then recalled the insulting way he'd treated her when first she'd entered his room.

"Why did you come backstage, Em?"

Shock? Curiosity? Because I can't wrap my mind around why someone like you would choose someone like me?

Emma wasn't sure if that was what he wanted to hear. She was certain he had no interest in knowing ever since the day her oncologist had informed her there was nothing more that could be done, she swore to pack as much living as she could into the time she had left. To squeeze every last drop of juice out of life.

She kept all of that to herself, instead releasing him and taking a step beck. With a deep breath to center herself, she met his gaze. "I'll stay."

He flashed her a crooked smile.

"But no more alcohol."

"Done." He turned and motioned toward the room in a way that told her she was to take the lead.

Emma snatched her shoes off the floor. As she skirted around the man who made panties drop across the globe, she told him, "Just so you know, I'm not sleeping with you, no matter how many pretty words you throw my way."

"You keep telling yourself that, Sunshine. Maybe you'll even begin to believe it."

CHRIST, SHE WAS something. This spitfire who drew him like moth to flame.

She wasn't at all his type. He wasn't attracted to pixies with short blonde hair and compact bodies. But the sight of her looking up at him from the audience had been like a one-two punch to the gut. His mind blanked, and for a full minute he couldn't have drawn oxygen into his lungs to save his soul. It should have scared the shit out of him, except it hadn't.

She exuded a confidence that wasn't vain, and something else, something Joe couldn't name. Happiness? Light? Vibrancy? Whatever it was, she lit up the fucking arena with it. Filling him with a sudden, overwhelming, and desperate desire to soak it up. Desire so strong he'd actually sent Gary to find her and invite her to join him backstage. Neither of them believed she would do it and, for some mind-numbing reason, that *had* scared the shit out of him.

Which was when he realized he was a bloody nutter. Who did that? Had one look at a woman and saw the answer to the downward spiral their life was on? No one sane or rational, that was for damn certain.

In a move intended to dull the unnatural connection he felt for a woman he'd never met, he'd been a third of the way through a bottle of his favorite Irish whiskey when she'd stepped into his dressing room. She'd hovered just inside the doorway and introduced herself—Emma Travers—a name befitting her all-American girl appearance. His reaction to her was swift and violent and told him in no uncertain terms that the whiskey hadn't dulled a bleedin' thing.

She'd stared at him through turquoise eyes set in a face

that was porcelain pale. Eyes that revealed her every emotion as they'd scorched a trail over his body, snagging for a long moment on his groin before returning to his face.

She wanted him. To a man like him, she was an open book. Still, something had him tipping the bottle and sipping of the whiskey instead of her lips as he'd longed to do. The women he chose to be with had an edge, a gleam in their eyes that screamed they were just as eager to be used as he was to use them. Emma Travers had a purity to her that bordered on innocence.

She was a breath of fresh air. Sunshine to his darkness.

He could probably snuff the light out of her in no time.

A sense of decency reached out and grabbed him by the balls. She deserved better than him. And so he'd done everything possible to drive her away. In no time at all, she was back out that door and down the hall so fast his head spun. Yet even though her leaving was for the best, he couldn't help but follow her so he could watch her walk away. Imagine his delight when she'd shown enough spine to verbally strip the skin from his bones on her way out.

Damn. His cock had snapped to attention and laughter—his long lost friend—bubbled up before he could swallow it back down. Sunshine and sass: now that was a truly irresistible combination.

"Pretty confident aren't you?"

Emma's voice pulled Joe out of his head. He followed her into his dressing room, closing the door behind him. "What's that, Sunshine?"

The question was barely past his lips when she turned. The hand holding her shoes smacked into the center of his chest, the pencil heels stabbed him like knives. "Is that really necessary?"

Small silver hoops with clear stones decorated her ear lobes. Her left upper ear also sported three silver rings—each slightly different from the other. A tiny tear drop gem adorned the cartilage at the opening of her ear, tying everything together.

"Joe?"

"If the door is left open it will only invite others to join our conversation and I would prefer that not happen." He looked down at the shoes boring a hole in his pec. "Now, can we dispense of these instruments of death?"

"How did you know I considered beaning you with them?"

She had? Fuck. If that didn't bring another snort of laughter. "I was referring to the spikes digging into my flesh." He curled his fingers around her wrist and pulled her hand away from his chest, releasing it at her side. "You were going to throw them at me?"

"You were rude." She was staring at his left pec, where the head of the dragon that circled up his bicep and over his shoulder rested. Mouth open in a roar, teeth bared, and forked tongue hanging out.

"I was." He wondered if tats turned her on or off? "He doesn't bite."

"What?" That brought those entrancing eyes back to his. "I'm sure the same can't be said about you."

He allowed his gaze to take a long, slow journey over her body. His cock rose to take a peek, too. "You might like it."

She arched an eyebrow then turned away, but not before he caught the whisper of excitement in her eyes. The killer heels remained in her grasp as she moved about the room, trailing her free hand over everything—the back of the couch, the side of the whiskey bottle he'd left on the table.

She caressed the fabric of the shirt beside it between her thumb and forefinger before moving on with one last brush of her fingertips.

His gaze skated down her back and landed on her perfect ass. Covered in body hugging denim, the material cupped her like a lover, showing off curves that would bring even the strongest man to his knees. Sheer ivory silk trimmed in black rhinestones stirred with her every motion, teasing him with glimpses of the lace bra beneath it. His fingers twitched. She was temptation personified.

Too bad she'd made it abundantly clear that finding relief for the ache in his balls was not in his immediate future.

"No doubt, I would." She came to a stop in front of the giant bowl of rainbow condoms. Her hand dipped in, and she filtered them through her fingers as she lifted it back out. "Though I'm not sure I could stand the competition."

"It's not what you think."

She looked him right in the eye. "It's not a ginormous bowl of condoms? Do tell."

He wondered if she realized how refreshing she was. How different her direct, in-your-face demeanor was from...*Hell,* just about everyone else in his life.

"For every show, the venue receives a contract that includes hospitality requests, including dressing room accommodations."

"And one of the items on your list is a bowl of rainbow condoms?" She had already walked away from the damn things, moving around the room again, touching everything she found.

"Yes. No. *Shit.*"

She glanced over at him, her expression seconds away

from breaking into a grin.

Joe raked his hair. Here he stood, talking about condoms when all he wanted was to tear one open so he could bury himself inside of her. He wanted her naked and panting beneath him. Or on her knees in front of him. Hell, him on *his* knees in front of *her*! Just as long as she was naked. "At the beginning of the tour a woman snuck into my hotel room."

"That actually happens?"

He pushed off the door, stalked around the end of the couch and sank into the center cushion. "More than you want to know."

Emma shook her head. "Unbelievable." She was at the dressing table, eyeing the items he'd either taken from his pockets or off his person after the show: a smattering of guitar picks, his identification, mobile phone and leather cuff bracelet. She picked up the cuff, wrapped it around her slim wrist, then removed it with a shake of her head. "Please, continue."

"I went into the room and found her naked in my bed." Something that at one time he wouldn't have hesitated to take advantage of but, that night, hadn't been tempted. "I chose not to involve Gary or hotel security, and instead, tossed her clothes at her along with the excuse that I was out of condoms, then pushed her out the door. After which I promptly forgot all about her and collapsed into bed. The next morning, we discovered one of the buses vandalized."

She absorbed that, looking like she might say more but she didn't.

"I told everyone what had happened the night previous and they thought it bloody hilarious. Steve especially, who made certain there were condoms in my dressing room before the next show. Marvin, our manager, has since written it into the backstage rider that one of my needs is—"

"A bowl of rainbow condoms." Emma closed the distance between them and sank into the corner of the couch, her knees tucked up underneath her. She set her shoes atop the coffee table before her. "What else does this rider state you require?"

"A couch like the one you're sitting on."

The sweep of her hand back and forth across the soft leather was hypnotic. "Nice."

"In a private dressing room so I can be alone when I feel the need."

"How often does that actually happen?"

"More often than you'd think."

She lifted her eyebrow in silent question.

He glanced at the pieces of paper that littered the table near her heels. "I require quiet to write. It hasn't been going well lately."

Her gaze cut to the same spot. "May I?"

"Sure." *What the bleeding hell?* He never shared his music with anyone—not until it was to his satisfaction. He'd never allowed a woman to scour through his personal items, either. However, there was something about Emma. She possessed an air of tranquility and a natural curiosity that made him comfortable with her. She hadn't pulled any fan girl moments and that was refreshing.

She picked up the top piece of paper, then the one below it. "You write lyrics before music?"

"Always."

A third paper joined the other two in her hands and Joe held his breath. A few beats passed before she set them all back atop the table. A few more before she met his gaze.

"It's…beautiful."

Beautiful was not something his lyrics had ever been called before. "Excuse me?"

"A bit melancholy and ominous but beautiful. You're a modern day troubadour."

He found himself laughing. What was that, twice tonight? Had to be a record.

"Why is that funny? What you've written here is poetry. I'm fairly certain a troubadour was a composer and performer of lyric poetry and song."

Beautiful. Christ, he'd sliced a vein and bled on the page and she thought it was beautiful? "I should use that the next time I check into a hotel – 'The Troubadour'."

"You check in under false names." It wasn't really a question, more like a realization spoken aloud.

"I had to find some way to keep naked women from breaking into my room."

She cocked her head and studied him for a minute. "You joke but…you don't find it funny."

There wasn't much about his life he found humorous. He was a broken man—not that he was going to admit that to her.

Emma pulled her feet out from under her, stretched her legs out and propped her heels near her shoes. "Not something you want to talk about, huh?"

Joe looked at her bare toes, painted bright pink, the largest two sporting tiny white flowers. "Don't like your shoes?"

She grinned and dropped her head against the back of the couch. "You know, all you have to say is 'Change the subject, Emma'."

"Change the subject, Emma."

Her smile remained, but damn it if some of the light didn't go out of her eyes. "My friend Alison convinced me to purchase then wear them tonight, a decision I've come to regret. Sure they look good, but they're ghastly to walk in."

"Alison, was she at the show with you?"

"She was. She bought the tickets. A gift for me."

"So you're a fan?" *That was a bloody stupid question, wasn't it?*

"Yes, I'm a fan. The tickets were front row center, after all."

"Did you enjoy the show?"

"I did. You've got great stage presence."

"Interesting. Most people tell me I have an amazing voice."

"You do, at least when you're not forgetting the words to your own songs." Her eyes danced with amusement. "But why would I want to be like everyone else and tell you so?"

"What can I say," he replied, staring at her mouth. "You distract me."

"So you've mentioned." She stared at his mouth in return. Her tongue rolled over her bottom lip, like she was imagining his taste.

Joe swallowed a groan. His cock pressed at the fly of his jeans, begging to be released. "It's the truth. And Sunshine, you couldn't be like everyone else if you tried."

She got to him, damn it, like no other. It was more than just her curvy body and killer blue eyes. She was easy to talk to. She didn't make demands or expect him to be anything but himself—not the superstar, just the man. Being around her gave him a true sense of peace. Something he hadn't had a lot of lately.

"Is that good or bad?"

He waited until she leveled him with those eyes. "Definitely good."

Her smile lit her face, temporarily blinding him with its brilliance. He turned his whole body toward her, not so subtly trying to get closer. Her scent invaded his lungs, fresh, floral and arousing as hell.

"What does Gary do?"

Damn, if that wasn't like a bucket of ice in the trousers. Emma Travers was hell on his ego. "He's head of my security team."

"Your bodyguard?"

"I suppose you could put it that way. He doesn't just keep me safe though, he also steps in when need be to keep fans from getting hurt."

"Has he been with you long?"

"Since the first tour. About seven years."

"So he's more than the head of your security team—he's also a friend?"

"He is."

Emma nodded. Her gaze slid around the room before cutting back to his. She was quiet a moment as she studied him, a look of contemplation on her face. "You know you never answered my question."

"What question?" There were a few he hadn't answered.

"Why are you an accomplished drinker? The Jameson— I assume it's on the rider you were talking about."

"It is." He let out a long, slow breath. "Does the why really matter?"

"Yes."

His mind raced a moment too long with a response apparently, because she pushed on.

"You know what I think?"

"I have no idea."

"You work very hard to keep your feelings hidden. And you succeed. I don't know if you've always been that way or if it's a recent thing. But you're beginning to crack and fall apart."

He took a deep breath and let it out slowly, considering his response. "Why would you think that?"

"You told me."

"I never—"

"Come back and see me sometime, Emma," she quoted verbatim. "I could use a little sunshine in my life."

He had no response that wouldn't leave him feeling exposed, so he remained silent.

"What is it you want from me? You can tell me, Joe. It's just you and me here."

You just zero right in on those difficult questions, don't you, Sunshine? "I don't know."

She reached out and settled her hand on his forearm. Her heat seeped into his skin, and he realized somewhere along the line he'd forgotten how good it felt to be touched. He honestly couldn't recall the last time it happened. The women in his life tended to grope and scratch.

"Yes you do. You've got your health. You've got friends, family and fans who love you. Yet you're drowning yourself in alcohol and meaningless sexual encounters. You get to see the world, don't have to worry about where your next paycheck will come from, but you're not happy, are you?"

The words hung in the air between them until Emma continued. "You're in a dark place. I don't know how long you've been there or if you even fully realize it, but something inside of you does. You wanted to make a connection. Not based on sex or—"

"Oh, I wanted a sexual connection. Still do."

She released a soft sigh and dropped her hand from his arm. He missed her touch immediately. "But you also want more. If you didn't, you would have let me walk away and found someone else to warm your sheets."

How could she possibly… It was as if she'd reached inside him and touched a place no one ever had before. Maybe because no one else had been looking for it. No, it was more than that. It was like she could see straight through his defenses and into his soul. It was terrifying.

"You're not a psychotherapist or something, are you?" he asked, forcing nonchalance into his voice when he felt anything but.

"Do you need one?"

"Probably."

"I'm not a psychotherapist, just speaking from life experience."

"I find that hard to believe. How old are you?"

"Why, because life doesn't kick anyone younger than thirty in the teeth?" She shrugged. "I'm twenty-three."

And she'd been kicked. She'd been kicked pretty damn hard if the flash of pain in her eyes was any indication. "You want to talk about it?"

He watched her carefully, noting her fingers shook when she reached for the skeleton key around her neck. Made of silver, it was simple in design, maybe an inch long, and hung from a silver chain threaded through the circular bow. She began worrying the key between her fingers. "God, no."

He covered her free hand with his. "I'll share if you do."

"I don't want your pity." She looked at him, startled, like she hadn't meant to give voice to the thought, then sent him a little smile. "Pretend you didn't hear that."

Pity her? Why would I pity her? His thumb brushed over the backs of her fingers. "Em?"

"It's nothing." As if to prove it, she released her grasp on the key, dropped her hand atop his—effectively sandwiching his hand between both of hers—and changed the subject. "How old are you?"

"Why do you want to know?"

She shrugged. "It seems only fair. You asked my age."

"Twenty-nine."

"Hmm. Do these music notes have significance?"

He closed his eyes at the touch of her fingertip on the back of his wrist, then opened them to watch as she traced each note. "It's the opening measures of our first number one hit."

Flattening her hand on his she ran it up his arm to the G clef near his elbow. "And this? Is the red…?"

Joe rolled his arm to give her better access.

"Is that drops of blood?"

Most people never noticed that the red was shaped like drops of blood and, in the same area, the black splotches had distinctive shapes as well. "Blood, sweat and tears."

"Yeah?" Emma took a closer look. "I suppose it took a bit of that to get where you are today."

"A bit."

"Tell me what it's like being onstage in front of thousands of screaming fans."

He let out a long breath. "It's a rush. Especially when the bass drum pounds out the opening beat. The energy at that moment is palpable. Then the guitar sings her angry melody which stirs the emotion higher."

"And you join her, softly at first, barely audible, but growing louder, stronger, until the lights go up. *Bam!*"

Somewhere during this tour, he'd lost the thrill of it, but watching her as he described what it used to be like for him brought it all back. Her gaze held him rapt. He couldn't look away had he wanted to. She was intoxicating. "The initial roar of the crowd...it's hard to put it in words. It's deafening. Your heart pounds in your chest, your blood races through your veins at speeds that make you dizzy and feel..."

"Alive," she supplied, her tone filled with reverence.

"Alive." That was as good a description as any.

Emma stared at him, eyes warm, mouth slightly curved. He had no idea what she was thinking, but hoped it had to do with him finally learning her taste.

A knock on the door broke the spell. She startled, pulling her hands away and tucking them into her lap.

Joe shook off his disappointment. "Enter."

The door opened and Gary stepped in. "Everyone's heading to the hotel."

"I guess that's my cue to leave."

It was a damn sad day when he couldn't even get a kiss before the woman beside him made a run for the exit. "Come with me."

"Nice try, but no." She bent over and grabbed her shoes.

"I didn't mean it that way." Not that he still didn't want to get her out of her clothes and into his bed. No way could he pretend that wasn't the case. "We could...talk some more."

"Maybe next time."

"Tonight."

She backed toward the door, shoes dangling from her fingertips. "What about tonight?

"We have another show. Come back and see me."

Eyes still locked on his, she misjudged and backed into the doorframe. Knocked off balance, she shot her hand out to steady herself and landed square in the center of Gary's chest. She glanced up at him before returning her gaze to Joe. "Jesus. He's built like a brick shithouse, isn't he?"

Gary grinned, but Joe shook his head. "Don't say things like that. He doesn't need his ego stroked."

Those beautiful blues left him again to settle on Gary. She poked him in the chest with the tip of her finger.

"Emma," Joe said.

"Sorry. What were you saying about tonight?"

Gary chuckled. Joe ignored him. "Come back and see me tonight?"

"I'll think about it." Then, with a parting smile, she walked out of his life.

Loneliness crept in and wrapped its cold hands around him. Joe huffed a breath, leaned back against the couch and tossed his arm over his eyes. Silence settled in, but he knew Gary still remained. "You're not going to see her to her car safely?"

A click of the radio and Gary's voice filled the room. "Blonde with short hair sporting an ivory tank with black rhinestones is headed for the exit. She's VIP. Make sure she gets to her car safely."

"Will do, boss," came the response.

"VIP?" Joe asked.

"I like her," Gary replied. The couch shifted as he leaned against the back of it. "She calls you on your shit."

"Yeah, she does."

"You're very calm. Calmer than I've seen you in a long time. It's surprising since I'm fairly certain she never did allow you access to her knickers."

"The Jameson wore off a while ago," was the best excuse he could come up with.

Gary laughed softly. "You keep telling yourself that if you want. I know it's bullshit."

Joe removed his arm from over his eyes. Gary was no longer in sight. "Gare?"

"Yeah?" The answer came from behind him, back by the door.

"You think she'll come back tonight?"

"I hope so, mate. For your sake, I surely hope so."

So did he.

February 21

Alison and I went out to celebrate today. She called it my new birthday – the day I decided to be an active participant in my life instead of just letting it go on around me as far too many people do. She even got me a present: front row tickets to Blind Man's Alibi. It's no secret I have a major fan girl crush on lead singer, Joe Campbell. That voice! The concert is about six weeks away so I should have hair by then. Perhaps not a full flowing mane, but enough that the stage lights won't reflect off my cue ball head and blind the band (no pun intended). Of course, that would be one way to get noticed, wouldn't it?

It's amazing what happens when the cold hard reality of how short life really is slaps you in the face. The changes that take place, the realizations that occur. Although alive, too few of us ever really live. I mean grab-life-by-the-balls live. I know I haven't. I've spent the last few years working and feeling sorry for myself. I have no family, only a handful of friends, and have never been in love. Tragic? I used to think so.

That was before a man in blue scrubs and a white coat told me I only have six months left to live.

I'm twenty-three years old and I won't make it to twenty-four.

Shit.

I'm terrified of dying. There, I said it. What scares me even more is the thought of dying without ever hav-

ing truly lived. So from now, until the end, I vow to embrace life. To smile through the pain, cramming as much as I can into the time I have left. I will take risks, dance beneath the stars, laugh, love, and cherish every moment. I will face each day with my head held high, focusing on today, not dwelling on the past or worrying over the future. I will LIVE.

Number of days since I decided to live: 1
Number of days until Blind Man's Alibi concert: 41
Current level of panic: 8/10

TWO

April 4

LATE. SHE WAS so very late. Most likely too late for anyone to still be hanging around. Too late to get inside.

Emma drove around the parking lot, sneaking behind the row of semis lined up in such a way as to hide the tour buses from view. She parked her truck beneath a light pole and stared at the back entrance.

Men and women moved in and out of the arena, loading equipment into the semis at a pace that made her dizzy—an endless stream of activity as the set was torn down and the show packed up in preparation of pulling out of town.

"What are you doing?" she murmured, barely able to hear her own voice over the music blasting from her speakers. Unless she could get one of these people to summon Gary, her chances of getting inside were slim to none. The smartest thing for her to do was turn the truck around and head home. But the lure of seeing Joe again was too great.

She had spent the entire day thinking about him. In two weeks, she was due to deliver her final design to her very last client, yet she couldn't concentrate long enough to get any work done. She'd boot up her computer and stare at the screen without seeing it. Seeing instead the look in Joe's eyes when he'd asked her to come back tonight.

She hadn't planned to. Not even last night—this morning, she corrected—when she'd told him she'd think about it. She'd never planned to come back. That was, until she'd found herself in her truck heading for the arena.

She had it bad for him. *But hell, you only live once, right?*

Sliding out of the vehicle, she crossed the parking lot and walked up the ramp, expecting someone to stop her at any moment. Oddly enough, no one paid any attention to her until she was about six feet from the entrance and Gary materialized in front of her.

Emma slammed to a stop so sudden, she stumbled. "Holy… You scared the crap out of me! Do you always lurk in the shadows or is it just my lucky night?"

He grinned. "I've been trapped inside all day. Needed some air."

The temperature was around forty-seven degrees with a breeze cool enough to cut through her jacket, yet Gary stood before her in a short-sleeved tee that hugged his brawn like it had been painted on. Not a single sign he was cold marred his dark chocolate skin. "You forgot your jacket."

"I did. Perhaps I could borrow yours. Appears it might fit."

Emma looked down at her outfit. Once the urge to come became too strong to resist, she hadn't worried over her appearance. Just grabbed her old army jacket and tossed it on over her favorite lounge-around-the-house top—a pale pink racer back tank with twisted shoulders. She'd traded her yoga pants for a pair of jeans and topped off the look with pink Chucks.

The jacket was too large for her, its sleeves hanging to

her second knuckle, but it was well worn and as comfortable as any sweater she owned. "It once belonged to my high school sweetheart. When I caught him behind the bleachers with one of the bitchy, popular girls, I kept it."

"Probably looks better on you, anyway." His smile widened, giving her a teasing glimpse of dimples. Dimples! "The Buddy Holly's complete the look."

"Buddy Holly's?" *Shit, she was still wearing her computer glasses!* Pulling them off, she stuffed them in the coat pocket. "I was working."

"Casual Friday?"

"Self-employed."

"Ah."

"I'm a graphic artist. I was working on a client's design." *Why was she telling him this?* "I'm not out to impress anyone."

"That's good. Most people trip over themselves to please him."

Emma frowned. "I don't even know what I'm doing here."

"He's a good man. Once you get past the—"

"Narcissistic asshole?"

His laughter was full and deep, easing a bit of her nerves. "That was brilliant!" He was still chuckling as he slipped his fingers into his back pocket and handed her the item he retrieved. "Thought you might like to have this."

A backstage pass. The plastic was cool to the touch and sported a photo of the band on one side, and their logo along with the words *all access* on the other. She stuffed it into her coat pocket with her glasses. "Thanks."

"It works better around your neck."

"Aren't you walking me in?"

He tossed her a look that said she was missing the point. His gaze moved from her face to her pocket and back again. For a moment she thought he was going to say something, but he turned for the door to the arena instead.

"What?" She had to scramble to catch up. Pulling the pass from her pocket, she slipped it around her neck. "What were you going to say?"

They stepped through the back door and started down the hall. Unlike the night previous, when she was too on edge and worried about where he was taking her to pay much attention, Emma took the time to study the man at her side. The first thing she noticed was that he walked silently. As in, she couldn't hear him move. Not his clothes, his footsteps, nothing. How was that even possible?

He was a good six inches taller than Joe, which put him around six-four, with black hair clipped short—shaved close to his head short—and the tiniest hint of grey in his mustache. His T-shirt was black, as were the cargo style pants and military looking boots on his feet. There was nothing identifying him as part of the band's security team, not even a pass around his neck. Then again, she couldn't imagine anyone trying to stop him from going anywhere he damn well wanted to go. There was an air of authority about him and, just in case someone missed it, he backed it up with a whole lot of muscle.

The radio on his belt squawked. *"Boss, we have a code one at the stage."*

Gary snatched the radio and pressed the button on the side. "I'll handle it."

He stopped before a set of double doors leading to the left and turned to her. "I have to deal with this. Look, you're going to head straight down the hall and through that door.

Take a right and about half-way down the next hall is your destination. It's a blue door on the left. It should be open."

"You never told me what you were going to say."

"What?"

"Outside. The whole backstage pass thing? Why did you give me such an odd look? You see, you just did it again, although that look could be interpreted as frustration."

His brow furrowed. "I have to deal with the code one. Just head—"

"Down the hall and through the door. I got it."

"Keep the pass in view and no one will dare get in your way. If you get lost find one of the arena security staff— they're all in red shirts—they can have one of my guys radio me. Got it?"

"No worries, Shrek."

He froze with his hand on the door. The look he gave her was one for the books. "Bleedin' hell. A cartoon character? Why not something like Heimdall? I could deal with being called Heimdall."

"Who?"

"The guardian sentry of Asgard."

"Because you're a guardian of sorts."

"Exactly. I look like him, too."

"No, you don't."

"The hell you say."

"You're much more handsome."

Gary grinned. "And you're full of it." The radio squawked again. "I'm coming," he mumbled, pulling the door open. "Shrek. *Shit.*" He glanced back over his shoulder. "Because I'm a grouchy ogre?"

"Because you're fucking huge and surprisingly charming."

He laughed as he disappeared through the door.

Emma reached the blue door in no time. It was open, just as he'd said. But unlike last night, this room was full of people. Conversations were going on everywhere, coalescing into a noise so loud she wondered if anyone could actually hear what anyone else was saying.

This was unexpected. A headache had already begun to make itself known at the back of her skull, something she hadn't worried about when she imagined it would be just her and Joe. But a room full of people would be enough to push her pain to new heights. The noise was going to be bad enough, add to that perfume, cologne, and any lingering odor of cigarettes… Now was the time to decide. Did she do this or go home?

Emma stepped into the room.

She was immediately swallowed, sucked into the mass of bodies talking, laughing, and drinking copious amounts of alcohol. She wasn't five feet into the room and she'd already been offered multiple glasses of God only knew what. Shaking her head at another offer, Emma stepped to the side and right into someone.

She turned, prepared to apologize, when a female voice full of condescension stopped her.

"Nice outfit. Who exactly do you expect to attract with that?"

Seriously? The little bitch stood about Emma's height—even with the four inch fuck me pumps on her feet. She was also so damn drunk she swayed, and…*wait a second.* Emma caught site of the pass hanging around the chick's neck. Was she for real? Before she could respond, the girl grabbed hold of Emma's pass.

"Oh my God! Your pass is all access. What did you have

to do to get this?"

"Do?"

"What do you want for it?" The acrid scent of alcohol swamped Emma's senses as the girl leaned closer. "I've never gone down on a woman before, but I'd be willing to give it a try if you'd give me that pass."

Emma took a step in retreat and bumped into someone else. Unfortunately, the girl before her had yet to release her pass, and the move damn near strangled her.

Emma reached out and pried the girl's fingers loose. The girl released a shriek that caused ears to ring and her head to throb.

"Sweet Jesus," Emma mumbled.

"Sweet Jesus!" the girl screamed, then lunged.

A muscled arm circled Emma's waist, lifted her off the ground as if she weighed nothing, and held tight as she and the owner of the arm stepped out of harm's way.

Gary swooped in, out of nowhere it seemed, and escorted the girl from the room. Her screams grew in pitch with each expletive that spilled from her lips.

"Sweet Jesus," Emma repeated right before the heat of the body wrapped around her from behind penetrated. "Put me down."

"Sure thing, Sunshine."

Joe.

She spun around as soon as he released her and, sure enough, there stood Joe. For a split second, she couldn't breathe. Surely it was both criminal and unjust for a man to look so good.

His untucked, green heather T-shirt hugged his upper body, molding the highs and lows of his muscled chest and arms. She wasn't certain if tonight's jeans hung as low as last night's, but a part of her wanted to find out. Would he allow her the thrill of lifting the shirt? Would his arms raise so she could remove it completely?

A flush of heat threaded through her veins. She forced herself to take a step back.

Unaware of the road her thoughts had traveled, Joe gifted her with a smile. "I didn't think you were coming tonight."

"Neither did I."

His eyes moved over her like a caress, down the front of her body to her feet and back again. Her pulse picked up a notch as he paused on her breasts before returning his focus to her face. He reached out and snagged the edge of the pass hanging around her neck, his eyebrow raised in question.

"Gary thought I should have it."

"Good man."

"He said the same about you."

His eyebrow slid even farther up his forehead. "You asked Gary about me?"

"No. Tell me something."

"Okay."

His immediate consent gave her pause. Emma mentally shook her thoughts loose. "That girl's pass, did I see it correctly? Was that really a blowjob smiley on the front?"

His grin turned wicked. "Those were Steve's brainchild."

"Your guitarist?"

"Yes. They are given to women who trade sexual favors—"

"Blow jobs."

"Usually, yes, for access back stage. I don't think any of us ever imagined that the women would wear them with pride."

"Gee, and all I had to do for my pass was make a man laugh. Who is it that hands those gems out?"

"The roadies. It began as a way to let everyone know the wearer made their way behind the scenes not because of who they know, but because—"

"Of who they blow?" Her eyes took in the room and its inhabitants. The women outnumbered the men ten to one, with passes like the one around her neck the minority. Indeed, most were adorned with that disturbing yellow smile.

Emma pressed her fingers against her temples. There was too much noise in this room, too many warring scents, and way, way too many women willing to do just about anything to get the attention of the man standing before her.

"Your world, Joe…" She searched for the words as she did her best to block out those around her and focus solely on him. "Do you enjoy this?"

"Some of the time."

"And these women…they're who you…" *Jesus*. She wasn't a naïve little girl. She knew the amount of pussy offered up to musicians had to be extraordinary, but to see it firsthand made her stomach turn. "You sleep with these women?"

As if choreographed, a body in a skintight red dress stepped between them and curled itself around Joe. A hand tipped with long blood red nails trailed up his chest, caressing every ridge and outline of muscle in the way Emma had wanted to do not ten minutes ago. The voice that came out of the red dress was a throaty whisper. "Hey there, sexy. If she won't fuck you, I will."

Joe struggled to extricate himself for only a short while

before a new set of hands pulled the woman off him. Gary, again? Emma didn't look to see. Instead, she spun and headed for the door.

"Emma, wait."

She knew he followed behind her, but didn't slow down. She needed five minutes, just five minutes away from this insanity so she could pull herself together. Miraculously, she was back in the hallway in a few strides.

"Emma!"

A few more and she was at the women's restroom she'd spotted on her way in. Emma pushed through the door without pause and welcomed the blessed silence. Thankfully, it appeared she had the room to herself. Peeling her jacket off, she placed it near the sink, then leaned her hands on the counter and stared at her reflection in the mirror.

She hadn't planned on coming tonight. Not when, after only a few hours of talking with him, he'd become all she could think about. He invaded her thoughts at the most inopportune moments. She'd tried to work and instead replayed last night over and over in her head—the good moments as well as those first tense moments where every-thing that had come out of his mouth was sexually charged and tinged with expectation. Now she understood why.

Her stomach rolled, the removal of her jacket not enough to cool her overheated body. Turning the faucet on, she ran her hand beneath the cold water a few times, then pressed it to the back of her neck. She closed her eyes against the knowledge that she really wasn't much different from those other girls. In all the years she'd listened to his music, how many fantasies had she spun around the great Joseph Campbell?

The door swung open. Footsteps drew closer, bringing

with them Joe's scent. How the hell she recognized his scent after one night was a mystery.

Keeping her eyes closed, Emma ran her hand beneath the water and placed it against the back of her neck again.

"I do not sleep with those women. Do you have any idea how many men they've been with before they get to me?"

The thought turned her stomach into a painful knot. "But women throw themselves at you all the time."

"They do."

"And sometimes you take them up on their offer."

Joe didn't reply until she met his gaze.

"I like sex, Emma. Quite a lot, actually."

He offered her a bottle of water and she took it, twisted off the top, and drank deeply. "Sometimes you even send Gary into the audience after a girl who catches your eye?"

"You were the first one I ever sent Gary to find."

"Why?"

"You know why."

"Not really." She took another swig of water then held the bottle out for him. His fingers brushed across hers as he took it from her in a move she was certain he'd purposefully executed. "What about passes like mine? Who gets them?"

"All Access? Only friends and family. That's the Holy Grail there. The only pass that grants access anywhere and is good for every show of the tour regardless of what country we're in."

"Don't you have day passes or something?"

"A guest pass that gets dated and initialed, yes."

"Then isn't that what I should have been given?"

He wore the same look Gary had flashed her earlier. "You really are a ray of sunshine you know that?"

"You said that before." She frowned. "Access anywhere,

huh? No wonder."

Joe raised the water bottle to his mouth.

"You don't want to know what that girl offered to do to me for this pass."

He lowered the bottle without drinking. The plastic protested as his grip tightened. "Wanna bet?"

The husky words spiraled right through her. Emma went hot all over.

Joe tossed the bottle into the trash, apparently unconcerned with the fact that it was not yet empty, and stepped closer. Awareness raced from her head to her toes. For a split second, she couldn't breathe.

"Emma."

His voice was even deeper, a gruff whisper that turned her insides liquid. The warm puff of his breath caressed her lips as his gaze bore into hers. The need to have him take her mouth with his inundated her. She couldn't deny it, but had to.

Emma looked up into his eyes, watching them darken just before his mouth lowered. In the last moment before his lips claimed hers, she turned her head.

"Fuck," he rasped, brushing his lips over her jaw, her ear, her neck, and sending her pulse into orbit. "I've never had to work so hard for a simple kiss."

"Face it, you're only interested in me because I'm the first woman who hasn't fallen at your feet."

His chuckle vibrated through her everywhere they touched. "It's refreshing, that's for sure."

"It builds character." She blew a long breath, trying to get her body to settle down. His proximity wasn't helping. Heat poured off him. His warm masculine scent washed over her and, even though she was trying like hell to ignore it, the desire to kiss him had yet to abate. "Besides, there is nothing simple about us."

"No, there isn't." Joe sighed, then stepped back just far enough she could take a deep breath without tasting him. He reached out and pulled the door open. "Come, Sunshine, meet my band."

Emma picked up her jacket and stepped forward, pausing for only a moment when his hand settled against the small of her back. Not atop the tank—beneath it. The crooked smile was back as he shifted his hand and slipped a finger through her belt loop, brushing way more skin than necessary in the process.

Her belly executed a little flutter.

She arched a brow and he shrugged. "Wouldn't want us to get separated."

He wove through the throng of people with a skill that spoke of practice, tugging her closer against his side whenever someone shifted or bumped into her. The farther into the room they went, the louder it became, until distinctively masculine and heavily accented voices alerted her to their final destination.

And what a destination it was. Dear God, talk about testosterone overload. As striking as these men were in photographs or onstage, they were tenfold up close and personal. They stood at the farthest corner, before a table littered with enough alcohol to stock a nightclub, surprisingly separate from the other inhabitants of the room.

Joe came to a stop before them and, using the damnable hold he had on her belt loop, pulled her against his side. A few brain cells fizzled at the contact. They disintegrated when, finger still hooked in the loop, the rest of his hand flattened across her ass.

"Caught her, I see," a man she recognized as one of the band's guitarists commented. Short black hair, five o'clock shadow that couldn't disguise the dimple in his chin, and eyes so dark they appeared almost black: Steve Thayer—the man behind the blow job passes.

"She's a little mite, isn't she?" This from Zach Brenner, the other guitarist, who was shirtless, tattooless, and topped his straight shoulder-length brown hair with a skull cap. "Looks to be more your type, Bobby."

"That she does." Robert Poulsen's grin could only be described as Cheshire cat. With his long black hair and dark skin, Emma guessed him to be of Mediterranean descent, but that was just a guess. "What's your name, luv?"

The arm at her back tightened and a deep rumbling sounded. Emma glanced at Joe, positive she was just hearing things because damned if that didn't sound like a growl coming from him. Low and almost...possessive?

She said his name once, softly, then bumped him with her shoulder.

"Watch out for him." Joe's gaze was locked on Bobby. "He's a shark, that one."

"And you're all honor and virtue when it comes to women?" Emma snorted. "Thanks for the warning. I'll be sure to keep on my toes."

Laughter erupted.

Joe shook his head and smiled down at her. "You probably recognize these blokes: Steve, Zach, Bobby and Kirk. You know Gary, of course. Guys, this bundle of sass is Emma."

"Hello, Emma." They responded en masse. All except Gary, who winked at her, and Kirk.

Kirk Lombardo, Blind Man's Alibi's drummer, tipped

his head and smiled. With hair that looked a whole lot like it was two weeks of growth after being bald, tattoos that covered both arms and the backs of his hands, and gauges in his ears, Kirk demanded attention. The thing is, it wasn't all of that which grabbed and held hers, it was his eyes. A silvery green, Kirk's eyes were hypnotic—hypnotic and tinged by a deep sadness.

While Emma pondered what could have caused the sadness, Kirk snagged a bottle of Jameson and a couple of glasses off the table. Palming both glasses, he filled one, twisted his hand and offered it to Joe.

Who turned it down with a shake of his head.

"Emma?"

"No, thank you."

With a shrug, Kirk placed the empty glass and the bottle on the table. Then he quietly drifted away, blending into the crowd with an ease she wouldn't have believed had she not seen it with her own eyes.

"Em?"

She looked at Joe. "I'm sorry, what?"

"You slipped away for a minute there."

No, that would be his drummer. How was it she seemed to be the only one who noticed?

Her gaze slid across the room to where she'd last seen Kirk, but he was gone.

"Did you enjoy the show tonight, Emma?" Steve asked.

"I didn't catch it. I was at last night's show."

Steve cocked his head and looked directly at Joe. A grin split his face. "Indeed."

"It was madness." Zach snatched a beer off the table, twisted its top off and tipped it to his lips. He shook his head. "Utter madness."

Steve continued to grin at Joe, who ignored him. "It's toward the end of the tour. Everyone's a little crispy."

"Even the fans?" Zach snorted. He and Steve shared a look. "That woman who snuck onstage and attached herself to Joe? Christ, she was like an octopus. I thought Gare was going to need backup to pry her loose."

"She was pretty impressive for a wee woman." Steve turned his head, and gave Emma a slow looking over from tip to toe. "Are you sure that wasn't you?"

"Pretty sure."

Joe watched as Bobby poured a glass of whiskey. "The octopus had red hair." He shifted his shoulder like he was trying to dislodge something. "And claws."

Emma frowned.

Steve smirked.

Whatever. She wasn't reacting to the news that Joe had been pawed during the show tonight, but by the way he stared at the lone bottle of Jameson like a lover. Unlike last night, he had no alcohol on his breath. From the look on his face, it wasn't for lack of wanting.

Steve's grin turned into a belly laugh. "Then Bobby got too close to the crowd and someone grabbed him by the knob. He seemed remarkably jolly about the whole business."

"She was pretty," Bobby replied.

"Is that who you keep looking for?" Zach asked, causing Bobby to shrug.

"She could find her way backstage. I wouldn't mind letting her have another go."

Steve grunted. "Too bad it was the bloke next to her who groped you."

As they started arguing about whose hand was where,

Emma glanced back at Joe, who still stared in the direction of the whiskey. Why didn't he just have a glass? Was it because of her? Because of last night when she'd told him she would only stay if he stopped drinking?

"I know who you are." Zach took a pull of his beer and pointed at Emma. "You're the bird from the front row last night. The one Joe was ogling when he was so rat-arsed he forgot where he was."

"Rat-arsed?"

Joe groaned. "Ignore him."

"Trolleyed. Arseholed. Bladdered," Zach suggested, which prompted Steve to join in.

"Tanked up. Legless. Pissed."

Emma slid Zach a long look. "Drunk?"

"Aye, drunk."

Joe was right. She should have ignored him. "You couldn't just say drunk?"

"Not as much fun, is it?"

Seeing right through him, she laughed softly. "Not as much fun as watching me scrabble to decipher rat-arsed, you mean?"

They all found humor in that and laughed aloud, even Joe.

"Excuse me."

At the sound of the female voice directly behind her, Emma startled, then did it again as Joe's hand slid across her ass and settled at her hip. His hand flexed as he turned them both to face the new arrival.

New arrivals, she corrected, noting the group of four young women. With their over processed hair, skimpy shirts and even skimpier skirts, they all looked the same... Right down to the passes around their necks. Not those disgusting smiley passes, at least. These were ones Emma hadn't seen yet. Like hers, the passes around the young women's necks where decorated with the band name, the name of the tour and the year. Unlike hers, theirs also sported a radio station call sign and the word *Guest*.

"Can we get your autograph?" the girl closest asked, which for some inane reason started the rest of them giggling.

More than a little tempted to roll her eyes, Emma was relieved when Gary stepped forward, a black marker in his hand. Joe released his hold on her in order to take the marker, which allowed Emma to step away from the crush as all four rushed forward to be the first to have their shirts signed.

Make that their breasts.

As the shirts lifted, Emma did roll her eyes. A mistake as the move made her head pound harder.

"Damn it." She pressed her fingers to her temples, doing her best to push back the nausea that churned her stomach.

"Something wrong?"

She glanced over her shoulder at Gary, which was far more pleasant than staring at breasts. "Headache."

"Would you like something for it?"

It wouldn't do much good. What she needed was her prescription, but anything was better than nothing. "Are you going to push the button on your radio and pain reliever will magically appear?"

The question hadn't made it passed her lips and an individual packet of pain medicine was in his hand. "Something like that."

"Don't tell me. You had it in one of those pockets. What else are you hiding in there?"

His only response was his signature wink.

"I don't suppose you could get your hands on chocolate milk while you're at it?"

Gary's eyes lit with a quick flash of humor. "That will be a little more difficult but, for you, I can make it happen."

"I bet you could. Don't worry about it though."

"Are you sure?"

"Yes. Thank you."

He was on the alert the whole time he stood next to her, his gaze never settling in one place for very long. Eyes on the room, on Joe, the rest of the band, and the cluster of females still hanging on their every word. Then back to her.

Emma circled around behind him, searching for a bottle of water in a sea of alcohol. "You don't miss much, do you?"

"I try not to."

Tequila. Whiskey. Scotch. Vodka. Wrinkling her nose, she went around to the back side of the table. There had to be something designed to quench thirst instead of produce a buzz. "Perhaps you know where I can find some water?"

"Beneath the table."

"No wonder." Emma flipped up the table cover and sure enough.

"Not most people's first choice."

She cracked the top off a bottle and swallowed the pills. "I'm not like most people."

"Understatement."

Something in his voice had her wishing she could see his face. Emma opened her mouth to ask just what he'd meant when the sight of Bobby walking away, a girl tucked beneath each arm, snagged her attention. Behind the trio, Zach, Steve and the remaining girls trailed.

Movement at the opposite side of the table brought her

focus back to Joe, his gaze once again locked on the whiskey as he absently held the marker out in Gary's general direction. The expression on Gary's face as he followed Joe's line of sight spoke volumes, yet he kept silent as he tucked the marker into his back pocket and turned to face the room once again.

Emma circled the table and stepped next to Joe. His left hand settled at her lower back, but his focus never wavered.

As much as she wanted him to look at her, his distraction allowed her to soak in the sight of him up close and personal. The man had the most amazing lips. Full and thick and circled by a closely cropped beard that only emphasized their beauty. Lips she had the most irrational urge to chew on whenever she looked at them. Like now. The urge was so strong, she looked away, only to find herself lost in his eyes.

The green of his shirt emphasized the green in his bi-color eye. God, if she thought the man's lips beautiful, his eyes were out of this world. "Joe?"

"Mm?"

He called himself an accomplished drinker. Yet here he stood, struggling, fighting some internal battle to resist and not fall prey to the bottle tonight. Being stuck in this room where he couldn't get away from it probably didn't help. Perhaps she could.

Reaching out, she traded her bottle of water for the Jameson and offered it to him. "Thank you for last night."

His focus remained on the whiskey as his hand curled around it. "You're welcome."

She was going to need to kick it up a notch—he was still too intent on that damn bottle. She leaned a bit closer, so close his beard tickled her lips as she whispered in his ear. "Sure it was just masturbation, but I was thinking of you.

And it was *amazing*."

That brought his gorgeous eyes to hers. She grinned, backed up a step then another, turned and walked away, weaving through the crowded room.

"What?"

She had his complete attention now. Joe followed closely behind her, ignoring those who tried to have a word with him. "The best orgasm of my life," she said, then shivered for effect.

He began to swear colorfully.

Her smile grew.

"Why are you telling me this?"

She stopped at the door and faced him. "To say thank you. Without you, it wouldn't have been the same."

"Fuck, Sunshine." His jaw tightened and his nostrils flared. He leaned closer, closer still, thrusting the bottle of whiskey into the hands of someone to his right. Oh yeah, his eyes were on her now, and they were on fire.

Her body answered the call. Her nipples throbbed. She felt them shrink to two tight points.

"You do realize that image is burned into my brain for eternity." His low, guttural voice turned her on even more. She wanted to ask if he was referring to her nipples, or the image of her masturbating. Slipping her jacket on, she hugged it around herself.

His mouth curved in a smug smile. "Yeah, that one, too."

Someone shouldered their way past them both, knocking Emma off balance. The stench of too much cologne and *Dear-God-she-didn't-know-what* assaulted her. Pain flared behind her eyes and Joe went blurry. Reaching out, she grabbed hold of his forearm. "Come on."

"Where are we going?" he asked, matching her pace.

"I could use some fresh air. How about you?"

"Outside?"

He sounded so perplexed by the thought, she chuckled. "Yes, outside." Where she could take a breath of air that wasn't tinged with the stench of sweat, sex or alcohol.

"I don't know, Em."

She looped her arm in his. "Don't worry, I'll protect you. And if we run into anyone I can't handle, there's always Shrek."

"Shrek?"

"Your shadow." A glance over her shoulder confirmed Gary was right where she'd expected him to be. "Yup. There he is."

Joe chuckled. "I'm fairly confident the ogre had a Scottish accent. We're Brits."

"Semantics."

A comfortable silence fell over them, one Emma welcomed after the noise of the room.

They were nearly at the doors when Joe broke it. "You know you didn't have to go it alone."

It didn't take him long to get back to that, did it? "It's less complicated alone."

"Best orgasm of your life." He scoffed. Reaching over her shoulder Joe pushed open the outer door then leaned in and said softly, "I bet I can top it."

This time her shiver was real.

March 14

When I was first diagnosed with glioblastoma multi-forme I wanted my mother. A typically normal reaction for any child except that mom had never been much good at comforting. At least not comforting me. She was always more interested in dad, and parties and... well, just about anything besides being a mother.

I should have been gutted by the diagnosis, but at that point I was still in denial. I couldn't possibly have a brain tumor, I had no symptoms. Sure, a migraine every now and again, but the doctor had to be wrong. He'd confused my chart with someone else's. All that was wrong with me was a small bump on the head from a fall.

They wanted to start my first course of chemo right away: a combination of two drugs I was warned would be pretty evil and have major side effects like total hair loss. I'm not a vain person, but I am a girl, and the thought of losing all of my long blonde hair was pretty hard to take. I just gritted my teeth and got on with it.

It seems like so long ago now, and I suppose it was. By this time, I've been ill for over two years and I just can't comprehend it. It's like being stuck in a time warp, watching everyone's lives move on and change, while mine remains stagnant. A constant stream of hospitals, doctor appointments, blood tests, and hope. Not that any of it made a difference.

Glioblastoma Multiforme. What kind of name is

that? Why can't doctors ever keep things simple? Call it what it is. A tumor. A monster eating away at my functional brain tissue. Ha! You'd think it would have starved by now.

The Monster is winning and I'm helpless to stop it. I get headaches. Really severe headaches like someone is digging around in my skull without the benefits of anesthesia. I've been prescribed an injectable pain med, but it knocks me out for hours, sometimes half a day. With so little time left, I can't afford to lose half a day. Instead, I ignore the monster. I pour all my energy into functioning through the worst of it while dreaming of all the glamorous and exotic places I will visit before this is over.

Number of days since I decided to live: 22
Number of days until Blind Man's Alibi concert: 20
Current level of panic: 7/10

THREE

April 4

E MMA WALKED OUT of the arena and sucked air like an addict snorted cocaine. Unable to summon the energy to endure the harsh glare of the overhead lights, she kept walking down the ramp. She needed someplace quiet and dark. She needed to breathe, to find some sort of center.

Her arm still looped in his, Joe walked at her side. He stood close, close enough she could tell that while, on the outside, he appeared relaxed and at ease, his body was fraught with tension. The muscles in his arm shifted and flexed as she steered them to the darkest spot she could find. Right alongside the tour buses.

He came to a stop, his head swiveling from side to side, taking it all in. Perhaps he was looking for something, what, she had no idea. There was no longer a flurry of activity, no people running in and out of the building. The semis where gone. They were completely alone.

Emma stared at him a moment, her eyes adjusting quickly to the darkness. "What's the matter?"

"Tell me again why we're out here?"

"I needed some fresh air."

"Ah, that's right." He let out a long breath and looked at the foremost bus. His muscles locked up tight under her touch and his feet shifted.

"Relax."

"What?"

How was she supposed to ignore The Monster when he couldn't stop fidgeting? "You really need to learn to enjoy life a bit."

"You don't think I enjoy life?"

"Not the important stuff."

"Like?"

She looked away, tipped her head back, and drank in the night. The moon was full, an illuminated circle of light set against a star filled sky. "Like take a deep breath of fresh air every once in a while. Look up and appreciate the stars. They're amazing, aren't they? The universe is so large and we're but a small part of it."

At first he didn't move, and although she couldn't be certain, Emma felt that his eyes were on her. Finally, he blew a second breath and tipped his face to the sky. "Before we were headliners we played a lot of outdoor venues. They're still my favorite."

"You don't play them anymore?"

"Not usually, no."

"What, it's a rule in the rock star handbook—no outdoor venues once fame is in hand?"

His laughter drew her gaze. He stood beside her, hands in his pockets, head tipped back, crooked smile in place. And damn, if someone were to ask her at that very moment which she wanted more, the man next to her or a few more months, she would've been hard pressed to choose. "Dance with me."

His expression managed to be shock and amusement at the same time. "What?"

"Dance with me beneath the stars."

"You're not serious."

He was looking at her now so he knew she was. She flashed him a smile. "Afraid someone may see you?"

"Yes. I can't dance."

"So sway with me to the music."

"I hate to tell you this, Sunshine, but there is no music."

"You're honestly going to stand there and tell me you're a songwriter, yet you can't imagine music where there is none?"

He didn't move.

"Think of it as an opportunity to get me in your arms. Bodies pressed together intimately, hard angles against soft—" She was pulled in so quickly, she lost the oxygen from her lungs. *Men. They are so easy sometimes.*

He hadn't lied, he couldn't dance. Emma didn't care. She closed her eyes and laid her cheek against his chest. The tempo of a firm and steady heartbeat proved incredibly therapeutic. The pounding ache in her head eased a bit.

A few ins and outs of his breath passed before the tension in his body began to abate. "You were just fucking with me, weren't you? About…going it alone?"

She stayed there in his arms, the rumble of his voice all she could hear as the rest of the world stopped existing. He was strong and solid. There was nowhere else she would rather be.

When she didn't answer, he sighed. "Either way, thank you. It was the distraction I needed."

"I'm glad I could help."

One hand on her hip, the other sliding up and down her spine, he hugged her closer. "There's something about you, Emma."

She pulled back enough to look into his eyes.

"It draws me. A light, a spark, fuck, I don't know what it is" He sighed. "Listen to me, going on like a complete prat."

"I have no idea what that is," she admitted. Then, because she couldn't stop herself even if she wanted to, Emma reached up and cupped the side of his face. His short beard caressed her palm as she slid her hand down, trailing the tips of her fingers from just below his ear to the corner of his mouth.

His hand fisted at her back, the muscles in his arms flexed.

Her pulse accelerated to where she could feel the beat of her heart in her chest.

His lips were soft, surprisingly so, as she traced the tip of her index finger from one corner of his mouth to the other. The seam of his lips parted and she dipped inside, just enough to trace a bead of moisture down the center of his bottom lip and over the strip of facial hair connecting to his beard. Oh, how she loved that bit of hair, and spent a few precious seconds running her nails over it before lifting up on her toes and taking a nip.

Before she could open her mouth for another bite she was pulled into his arms for a crushing kiss.

His mouth devoured hers as he lifted her off her feet. Her back made contact with something metallic and cool enough it brought chills. Then the heat of his body pressed against her, trapping her in place. His palms slid down her back until the globes of her ass filled each hand, tightened as she wrapped her legs around his hips.

The groan he released thrilled her, made her dizzy and wet. Her palm still cupping his face, she pushed the tip of her finger into his mouth. His teeth clamped down on the fleshy end, causing her to gasp, then he was all over her. His right hand slid up her hip, across her stomach and curled around the wrist of her left arm where it was pinned between their bodies. He lifted her arm out of the way and pressed it above her head as he moved in closer, sinking into the space. Then closer still, until there was no mistaking how aroused he was.

God, this was crazy. His taste—the very fact this was happening—blew her mind. Awareness flared through her. The press of his hand on her ass. The strength of his body. The raw scent of aroused male. Her lips fell open on a gasping moan, and his tongue slipped between, stroking, searching, exploring. Leaving her breathless.

Tightening her legs around his hips, she pulled him closer, until nothing but their clothing separated them. Even that was too much. Her free hand found his hair, soft and thick, and fisted. Her sex pulsed. She shifted as much as her position allowed, tipping her hips and pressing harder against the firm ridge of his erection. He released a sound that was nearly a growl so she did it again.

The blare of a car alarm shattered the night.

He went still. Chest heaving, he dropped his forehead to the bus. "What the fuck?"

"Red truck," came the response, reminding Emma they were not alone.

She peeked over Joe's shoulder and found Gary about thirty feet away, his back to them. In the distance, beneath the lot light, sat her pickup, lights flashing a warning, horn honking. "That's mine."

Joe had her left hand pinned beneath his above her head. Her right hand was still in his hair. When she wiggled to be let loose and came into contact with his raging hard-on she knew exactly what had happened. The intimate press of their bodies had triggered the truck's panic button.

He released her, remaining close until she got her feet back under her, then stepped back. "Yeah?" He shook his head as she dug her key fob from her front pocket and silenced the alarm. "That's your truck?"

She smiled at him. "My Valentine's present to myself. Isn't she beautiful?"

He just looked at her.

"What?"

"You continue to surprise me."

She wasn't certain how she should respond to that. Before she had to, voices sounded from the top of the ramp. She gazed toward the arena. Through the darkness, she could just make out the band stumbling toward her and Joe. "Looks like our time is up."

"Yeah. Christ."

As much as a part of her loathed the idea of his leaving, she'd known it was coming. And fast. After all, the semis had already pulled out, it only made sense that the buses wouldn't be too far behind.

Forcing herself to take a calming breath, she pressed her palm against her stomach. Her heart leapt into her throat, but she kept her features neutral. "I'm sorry. I don't know what I'm supposed to say. Is there protocol for this?"

Joe's gaze held hers, dark and filled with things. Things she had no idea how to interpret.

"No?" *Jesus, she was babbling.*

Neither of them moved. They just stood there as the band walked past them, climbing into the bus she was still leaning against the side of.

Emma ran her hands down herself, belatedly making

certain everything was covered. "Is this bus yours, too?"

He shook his head, his eyes taking her in carefully. "The foremost one is mine."

"Just you?"

"Me, Gary, and Kirk. Although it looks as if Kirk is riding with the boys tonight."

She straightened, needing to get out of there. "Okay then, I guess I'll go."

He reached for her, but she shook her head. "I'm sure you're used to this... Saying good-bye to women." As she spoke, she backed toward the bus he'd said was his. "But...it's best if I just leave."

"Emma."

"It was great meeting you."

"Emma—"

She didn't stick around to see what he had to say. Turning on her heels, she started across the lot, kicking herself with every step. The urge to look back at him nearly overwhelmed. Instead, she glanced at Gary. And stopped dead in her tracks.

Gary arched a brow.

"What am I doing?"

He started to say something then stopped.

"I—" *Damnit Emma, you can't just walk away.* Letting out a long breath, she turned and found Joe standing in his bus's open door. "Two nights with a rock singer and I don't even get a lousy T-shirt?"

He flashed a wicked, naughty grin, then reached an arm over his head, gripped his shirt at the shoulder blade, and pulled it over his head in that sexy way men do. He dangled it on the end of a finger. "Now what about me?"

Emma swallowed hard, her mouth going dry. She

snagged the marker out of Gary's back pocket and walked back to Joe. Stepping onto the bottom step put her eye to eye with the dragon on his pec. "Turn."

When he turned, she pulled the cap from the marker and wrote "*To my biggest fan*' on the back of his right shoulder with her telephone number just beneath.

He looked over his shoulder, trying to see what she'd written as she replaced the cap. "Do I want to know?"

She settled her hand in the center of his chest once he faced her, holding the marker in place. He covered her hand with his and was left with the marker when she slid free and curled her fingers around his shirt. "I don't know. Do you?"

He absorbed that, looking as if he might comment, but he didn't. Instead, he cupped his large broad hand behind her neck and hauled her up to him. On her toes and off balance, Emma curled her fingers in the waistband of his jeans as he consumed her with a kiss so aggressive and needful it left her dazed.

His release was just as quick and had her wobbling on the step, her hold on him the only thing keeping her from stumbling. Struggling to regulate her breathing, she ran her gaze down his body until it snagged on her hand, inches away from where his erection threatened to burst the buttons on his jeans.

God, he was beautiful. It wasn't fair just how beautiful. Emma opened her mouth to speak, then closed it, not sure what to say. She released her hold on him and stepped back to the ground.

"See you around, Sunshine."

Yeah, like that was going to happen. "Bye."

Heart thundering in her ears, she closed her eyes and took a deep breath, trying to ground herself. Sorrow nearly choked her. She managed to keep her composure as she passed Gary. "It was nice meeting you, Shrek. Take care of yourself."

His soft chuckle carried to her as she continued across the lot. "Believe me, the pleasure was all mine."

EMMA DROVE HOME to her two-bedroom condo just a few minutes west of the arena. She'd bought the place after stopping chemotherapy and, although the modern design wasn't really her style, the expansive floor to ceiling windows in her corner unit had been impossible to resist.

She'd slowly decorated and painted as her energy level allowed, softening the stark lines and neutral palette with splashes of color and furniture with rounded edges. Plants helped marry the interior with the exterior landscape and art placed strategically about brought it all together. As a result, the place had become her home, a haven of comfort and warmth where she didn't feel confined to a box or trapped in darkness.

She loved it here.

But at the moment, she needed darkness.

Her hands shook as she unlocked the door, nausea surged. The ache at the back of her skull had become a pounding that mirrored the beat of her heart and brought tears to her eyes. She told herself the tears were from the pain, as anything else was unacceptable. Her feelings for a certain singer had nothing to do with it.

Alison rushed forward as Emma stepped inside. She was twenty-four, willowy, with dark brown hair that hung to the middle of her back. "Emma, my God, I've been trying to reach you all day. I was afraid something happened after I left you at the concert."

They'd been best friends since middle school where they'd crushed over the same boy. Through the years they'd survived more than their fair share of highs and lows, lows that often required Alison's help to shore her up. So Emma wasn't all that surprised to find her here now. "I don't have my phone."

Alison's eyebrows drew together as she studied Emma with a worried tilt to her mouth. "It was on your nightstand. Dead battery."

She had a habit of doing that. Turning away from the glare of the living room lights, Emma stumbled down the hall.

"Emma?"

"I need my medicine."

"I'll get it. You lie down."

She entered her bedroom, where she dropped Joe's shirt and her backstage pass atop her dresser. She closed her eyes on a wave of dizziness, doing her best not to throw up what little she had in her stomach. As she stumbled for her bed, she stripped, leaving a trail of clothing in her wake. Naked, she slipped beneath the covers, the cool sheets a shock against her overheated skin.

Eyes closed, she practiced the breathing techniques she'd been learning about on the internet. Deep, controlled breaths meant to slow her body down. She'd been doing okay tonight, until the tears started. Tears were a weakness, an admittance of defeat, and they always brought a triumphant surge of victory from The Monster. And made him that much more difficult to ignore.

Alison stepped back into the room, leaving the light in the attached bath on. She pressed Emma's single dose auto-injector into her palm then shuffled away, never able to stand to watch as Emma administered the pain medication.

"I'm sorry." Emma rolled to face away from her bath and the offending light. She spotted Alison at her dresser, the all access pass in hand. "I didn't mean to worry you."

"Where... Have you been with him this entire time?"

"I was home all day." Her phone battery must have been dead the whole time. "I went back."

"You went back for the second show?"

"After the show." The mattress dipped as Alison sat at Emma's side. A cool cloth brushed her forehead and she nearly groaned aloud. She dropped her hand away from her eyes as Alison washed her face.

"Did he hurt you?"

What? "Why would you think—?"

"You're crying. You're kind of freaking me out."

This wasn't the first time Alison had played caregiver. She'd suffered through this disease alongside Emma. Through many nights filled with tears. So what made tonight different?

"Joe didn't hurt me. He..." Pissed her off, broke her heart, and charmed her all in the span of a few hours. But he hadn't stopped there. No, tonight he'd managed to worm his way into her heart just enough so that, for the first time in a long time, she was suffering a bit of self-pity. "I'm sorry I'm freaking you out."

"Oh, sweetheart, it's not your fault."

"It is. I knew when I left the house that this was coming. I went anyway."

The cloth brushed Emma's forehead again.

Alison went quiet a moment. "What's he like?"

"Sad." Her eyelids grew heavy as the medication kicked

in. "He's sad and lonely."

"Seriously?"

"Sexy." *Dear God, was the man sexy.* "Built."

"I know that mu—"

"He smells fabulous and his kisses make me want to take all my clothes off and—"

"Wow, okay, your drugs are kicking in because you are definitely oversharing."

Emma smiled wearily. "You asked."

Alison released a whisper of a laugh. "I suppose I did."

"Al?" Emma's muscles relaxed. Sleep pulled at her. "You'll stay? While I sleep?"

"Of course. I've already made up the couch."

March 27

I sat in the corner of my shower and cried today. Not out of sadness or self-pity. Not out of pain or loneliness. Joy is what brought tears to my eyes, tears streaming down my cheeks. Joy at being alive, at having an amazing friend like Alison in my life, at needing a haircut. I stood in the shower washing my hair – my hair! – and thinking I might need a haircut, and I began to laugh. Riotous laughter that quickly turned to tears.

I have hair!
Everywhere!
Eyebrow hair I refuse to wax.
Pubic hair I refuse to trim.

Pale blonde – paler than before chemotherapy – hair on my head.

I really don't want to lose any of it, but it's all one length and stands straight out from my scalp in all directions. I have hair like a helmet! Isn't that wonderful?

I cried in the salon chair, too. It was mortifying. I didn't cry when the stylist cut my hair off before beginning chemo, but I do when she trims my new growth? She patted my shoulder, which somehow made it worse. Thankfully, Alison was there to tell me what a silly bitch I was being.

After the salon, we hit the stores, searching for the perfect outfit to wear to the concert. I found it, but I wasn't nearly as excited by the clothes as I was by the necklace I stumbled upon on the way back to the car: a silver key on a delicate silver chain. I trembled as I held that key in my hand, even more as I attempted to secure it around my neck. I'd found it – the key from my dream.

What could it possibly mean?

Number of days since I decided to live: 35
Number of days until Blind Man's Alibi concert: 7
Current level of panic: 7/10

FOUR

THREE DAYS AFTER Joe Campbell and Blind Man's Alibi pulled out of town, Emma sat in her favorite spot—the all glass room of her condo overlooking the city—and watched Alison flutter about in the kitchen. She'd been doing a lot of that today, fussing like a mama hen. Not that Emma was complaining since the fussing was accompanied by baking.

Emma loved desserts.

Especially Alison's.

The most delicious scents wafted out of the kitchen, making her stomach grumble. Tempted to go see what Alison had in store for her today. She rose to her feet, picked up her nearly empty glass—which she had every intention of using as an excuse to disturb the master at work—and made it exactly two feet before Al returned from the kitchen.

Dark hair knotted at the back of her head, wearing a white chef coat over black slacks, she shot Emma a look. "I thought you were staying out of the kitchen."

"I am."

"Yeah?" Al cocked her head. "Is that why you're standing there with your glass in your hand?"

"I was having a difficult time hearing you."

"You were following the conversation just fine. You just

63

wanted to snoop. You know I prefer to present the finished product. That way you get the full effect."

When Emma frowned, Alison smiled. "You are so impatient! Now have a seat or you won't get any and, let me tell you, these Crème Brûlée cupcakes are a personal best, if I do say so myself."

She had the audacity to hold the plate of sweets high and to the right, effectively keeping Emma from getting a good look at them. But she could smell them, and they smelled heavenly.

Emma dropped into her chair.

Alison laughed softly. Then she placed her newest temptation in the center of the table and took her own seat, picking up the conversation where they'd left off. "I can't believe he gave you the shirt off his back."

Four giant cupcakes filled the plate, each piled high with what looked like vanilla frosting and caramel candy. Emma would have responded, but she was too busy salivating. She grabbed one off the plate, peeled away the fancy paper and took a bite, moaning softly as creamy custard sent her taste buds soaring.

"He really did that? You're not pulling my leg?"

"Mmmm." She nodded, then swiped her finger through the frosting and popped it in her mouth. "I think he expected me to return the favor."

Alison choked on her cupcake. "You didn't."

Emma laughed at the shock on her friend's face. She ate another bite before commenting. "What exactly is this deliciousness?"

"Crème Brûlée cake with vanilla bean cream cheese frosting, filled with vanilla custard and topped with caramelized candy. It's good isn't it?"

"Good?" She popped the last bite into her mouth and moaned aloud. "It's better than sex."

"I wouldn't go *that* far."

"Because you're getting it! It's been so long, I can't be certain, but I'm thinking these are better than the last sex I had."

Alison laughed aloud. She slid Emma a long look. "Is it better than kissing Joe Campbell?"

"How do you know I kissed Joe Campbell?"

"You told me, silly. Something about how good he smelled and how his kisses made you want to take off all of your... Oh my God! You did, didn't you? You returned the favor!"

"You're not supposed to use what I say while under the influence of pain meds against me," Emma said on a whisper of a laugh. "I didn't return the favor. You saw me when I came home with my shirt still on my person."

"And kissing Joe Campbell is...?"

"Way, way better than this cupcake."

"That particular cupcake? Or the one you already ate?"

"Good question. Let me give this one a taste and I'll let you know."

Alison rolled her eyes as Emma pinched off a chunk and popped it in her mouth. "If you were any more addicted to sweets, I just might wonder if that *was* better than a kiss, but I'm certain it's not."

"It's pretty close," Emma argued, then chased the cupcake with chocolate milk.

"Sure it is. All kidding aside, what did you do when he took his shirt off?"

"I gave him my autograph. I put it on the back of his shoulder, right above my phone number."

"You wrote on his skin?"

The shock on Alison's face was priceless. "With a permanent marker."

Shock gave way to laughter and suddenly they were both giggling like loons.

Alison sobered first. "Do you think he'll call you?"

"No. No, I don't think he will."

"You're so daring. I wish I had one tenth of your boldness."

Emma sighed. "It wasn't boldness it was...desperation."

Al stared at her. "You didn't want him to leave."

"There's just something about him. Not the fame or rock god thing... It's something else." The fact she'd gone all soft didn't escape her. Emma shook it off. "Gah! Enough of this. He's gone and I'm..." *Being ridiculous.* "Tell me about your weekend. How's Kevin?"

All the color drained from Alison's face right before Emma's eyes. "Al, what is it? What's the matter?"

"Kevin's ah...he's..."

"Did something happen?"

With tears in her eyes, she nodded. "You could say that."

"What?"

Alison pulled something from her slacks pocket and set it on the table between them. A ring. A beautiful, antique diamond ring. "Kevin asked me to marry him."

"That's great! Oh my God, Alison, congratulations, I'm so happy for you!"

Al was definitely crying, she even wiped her white coat across the underside of her nose—so very out of character for her—leaving behind a swipe of flour.

Emma handed her a napkin. "Why isn't the ring on

your finger? Talk to me."

"He wants to marry me."

"You said yes, right? Alison?"

"He took me to The Detroit Shoreway, to a darling two story brick building. Well, it's not darling yet, but it could be." She stared down at the ring as silent tears continued down her face. "It's for sale, Em. He got down on one knee right there on the sidewalk in front of it and proposed. Proposed we get married, and buy that damn building of all things. Move in upstairs and renovate the lower level for a pastry shop. Can you believe that?"

She could. Kevin was a great guy—smart, handsome, and completely devoted to Alison. After the hell Al had been through with her last boyfriend, she deserved that. Deserved to be happy. "That's beautiful."

"It's horrible!"

"Wait, what?"

"What is he thinking? We can't afford that!"

"He's a lawyer, Al. You're a chef. You won't struggle for long."

"He's a junior in his firm, just starting out. He's got law school to pay off and me...I'm..." She was starting to hyperventilate. "I don't know anything about running my own business. What if I screw it up? Then we'd have a building and a failing business and even more debt."

Shit. Emma circled the table and pressed Alison's head down toward her knees. "Breathe," she coaxed. "Just breathe for a minute."

Al grabbed a shuddering breath.

"Keep breathing." Long calming strokes up and down her back seemed to help. Emma kept at it, even as Al's breathing evened out. "You have a dream, Al. And you're the best damn pastry chef in the city."

"How would you know?

"I'm addicted to sweets, remember? And sometimes I have to feed that addiction when you're not around."

"You cheat on me with other bakers."

Emma laughed aloud at the accusation in her friend's voice. "I do. That's how I know you're the best. In fact, I believe in you so much, I'll invest in your business. Hell, I'll buy the damn building for you and—"

Alison straightened abruptly. "No."

"You can live above it just like Kevin suggested and start your life together. The rest of your life without the—"

"No, Emma!"

She shook her head, not understanding Alison's resistance. "Why not?"

Alison remained quiet, just looking at her with eyes rimmed in red and lightly swollen.

"Do you love him?"

"Of course I do!"

"You want to marry him?"

"Yes," Alison replied softly.

"Then let me help you. You know I can afford it." As a teenager Emma designed a ridiculous little app that became quite popular, earning her first million by sixteen. For some bizarre reason that was all it took to bring enough notoriety that her design work was highly sought after. With nothing but time on her hands while undergoing treatment, she was now a very wealthy woman. A fact she found both humorous and sad. "What am I going to do with all that money? It's not like I can take it with me."

Alison shook her head.

"Consider it a thank-you-for-always-being-there-for-me

gift. You told him yes, right?"

"No."

"You told him no?"

"You're not buying me a building."

"Alison, you're all I have. You're my family, my caretaker, my best friend." Her cell phone chirped, indicating the battery was nearly dead but Emma ignored it. "I never would have made it this far without you. Everything you've done for me, all that you've promised to do for me, yet—"

"Please stop. I can't... Not today."

She covered Alison's shaking hands with her own. "Let me do this one thing for you, please. You have a long life ahead of you. A beautiful man. Dreams, goals...a future."

Alison surged to her feet. "I hate this!"

Emma didn't need to ask what Alison hated. Hell, she wasn't a big fan of life's plan for her either. "It's reality."

"Reality sucks."

"*My* reality sucks. Yours is at your feet waiting for you to grab hold of it with both hands." Their gazes met and Emma sighed. "Where exactly is this building."

Alison shook her head. "Nuh-uh."

"You really like that word, don't you? It doesn't matter, I'll just call Kevin. He'll tell me."

"No, he won't."

He probably wouldn't. "Fine, I'll drive around until I find it. Or a building I believe suitable. Then I'll purchase it and leave it to you in my will."

Alison looked so horrified by the thought that Emma laughed aloud.

After a moment, Alison was laughing, too. "You would."

"I would!"

Alison fell silent. She stared down at the ring on the table, a look of such intense longing on her face that it brought a lump to Emma's throat. "Please tell me you told him yes."

She sighed. "I told him I'd think about it."

Emma stared at her. "Oh my God. Oh my dear Lord, Al, are you out of your flippin' mind? You've left that poor man hanging for two days! Two days! While you panicked and what? Baked for me?" She framed her friend's face in her hands and made sure to overly enunciate her words. "Go. To. Him. Do you hear me? Put that gorgeous ring on your finger and go to him. Now! Before he spends even one more second doubting your feelings for him."

"Kevin knows I love him."

"Yeah? Enough that he doesn't have to wonder what your answer will be?"

Alison pulled back, clearly shocked.

"Honey, he got down on one knee and bared his heart to you and you told him 'maybe'?"

"Oh, shit, Em."

"Yeah, that about covers it."

They walked to the door together, Emma's hand on Alison's shoulder, urging her to move faster. Pushing her out the door, she smiled at her best friend. "Don't forget to wipe the flour off your nose."

Alison hugged her, turned for the elevator then spun back. "Wait, I have flour on my face? Let me back in so I can clean myself up!"

Emma closed the door.

"Emma! How could you?"

"Love you, honey!" She turned the lock on the door, fighting a smile. "Tell Kevin I said hello."

Two hours later, Emma did something she never did. She remembered to plug in her cell phone.

The late morning sun had shifted, making her glass room too uncomfortable to enjoy, so she'd retreated to her office. But she didn't have the urge to work right now. So she sat at her desk, staring at her screensaver, her thoughts on her best friend. She remembered the joy on Alison's face as she rushed out the door, heading for the arms of her lover, and that brought a smile to Emma's face. She was genuinely happy for them.

And also a little bit envious.

Maybe it was time for a change. Normally, she found the quiet of her condo restful. A comfortable haven away from the noise and chaos of the daily grind. But lately it had become almost too quiet and only served to remind her how alone she was. She was nearly done with her final design project. Perhaps it was time to get away.

Away from Cleveland and the places that reminded her of her mortality.

Away from days spent locked indoors.

It was time to embrace life. To travel. See the world. Live extravagantly.

No more yoga pants and tank tops.

No more chick flick marathons with nothing but a quart of Chubby Hubby to keep her company.

Hello midnight strolls through Tuscany, afternoons at the Louvre, and topless sunbathing in Brazil!

Mind made up, she woke up her laptop and logged onto the internet, nearly startling out of her seat when her phone charged enough to restart and alerted her to a new voice message with a loud chime.

"Definitely too quiet in here," she mumbled, then picked up the phone and pushed the button to access her voicemail.

"Hey, Sunshine." She stopped the recording and stared at her phone in shock. Another push of the button started the recording over.

"Hey, Sunshine."

His voice sounded like it was pitched lower than normal, almost—dare she believe it—intimate.

Oh, God.

She felt like a teenager who'd just received her first phone call from a boy. She felt like a silly girl, something she'd never thought of herself as, because as she pressed the button one last time and his voice filled the room, goosebumps scattered across her flesh.

"Hey, Sunshine...that is if I have the right number. I had to use a bloody mirror as the wankers wouldn't read it to me. Why do you have a computer greeting as your mobile message? I was hoping to hear your voice."

She couldn't believe he'd actually called her. She needed to add his number to her contacts list. She needed to breathe, to get herself under control.

She needed to call him back!

Emma picked up the phone and punched the redial button. It rang endlessly then went to voicemail.

"This is Joe. You know what to do."

"Hi, it's Emma. I'm not sure when you called me, but this is me calling you back." *Genius.* Emma rolled her eyes. "Anyway, I'm home if you would like to call me again."

Her cell phone buzzed seconds after she set it down. She picked it back up. "Hello?"

"Emma," he said, a huskiness to his voice she didn't have to wonder about.

"I woke you."

"I was having a lie down. I've been up...I lost count...thirty-six hours or so?" There was a rustling sound followed by a yawn.

"You need your sleep. I'll talk to you la—"

"Don't ring off! I...need to hear your voice."

He'd said similar in his message. There was very definitely something wrong. "Where are you? Did something happen?" Emma allowed herself a few seconds of panic. "Are you okay?"

He murmured something too soft to catch.

"Joe?"

"I'm in California. Flew out for a party, but no one feels much like celebrating. A mate of mine got shot last night. Dominic Price?"

"Dominic Price?" She shook her head and considered pinching herself. She was talking to one rock god about another rock god like it was just everyday normal conversation. "Black Phoenix's Dominic Price? Is he—?"

"He'll recover, but it was bad."

"I'm sorry."

"Yeah," he whispered. "Gettin' pissed on whiskey sounds brilliant right now."

She took a deep breath and let it out slowly. Sure, the other night he'd admitted he had a problem with alcohol, but to start drinking this early? He couldn't be serious. "Isn't it all of eight in the morning in California?"

"Time of day means nothing."

She didn't know what to say so she said nothing.

"Emma? Sunshine, talk to me."

"How does whiskey at eight in the morning sound like a good idea?"

"Enough whiskey and the brain shuts off."

"Doesn't sound like it's working much as it is."

Silence.

Absolute dead silence.

Shit. She had a bad habit of giving voice to thoughts that were better off flitting around in her head. Alison always told her that one day she'd say the wrong thing and live to regret it. "Look, I'm sorry, I—"

Joe barked a laugh. "Not a whiskey drinker, I take it?"

"I don't drink."

"Wait, not at all?"

He sounded so appalled by the idea, she grinned. "Not alcohol, no."

"Bloody hell. A tea-totaling ray of sunshine. How the bleedin' shit does that happen to me?"

"You're just lucky, I guess," she said dryly, which made Joe laugh harder.

"I knew you would make me feel better. Tell me, anything new in your life?"

Met a rock star the other night and for some reason he turned to me instead of the bottle? "I had cupcakes for breakfast."

"Did you? What kind?"

"Crème Brûlée. They were fantastic. Better than…"

"Whiskey?"

Emma took a deep breath and let it out slowly, considering her response. Did she really want to finish her statement?

"Em? You were going to say whiskey, right? How would you know if you've never—"

"Sex. I was going to say sex."

It was Joe's turn to be quiet a minute. "Then you're doing it wrong."

"You think so?"

"I know so. The best orgasm of your life was self-induced and now cupcakes are better than sex? You need to…"

Dare she ask? "I need to what?"

"Bring your sexy self to me so I can show you how it's done."

God, his voice was all low and rough and sent heat skittering over her every single nerve ending. "I know how to make love, Joe."

"I'm not talking about making love, I'm talking about fucking. Hot, sweaty, screaming-my-name-as-you-come fucking."

"I'm not interested in—"

"Awe, Sunshine, don't start lying to me now."

He was right, she was lying. Both to him and herself.

"I saw the way you looked at me when you walked into my dressing room. If I hadn't acted like a—"

"Asshole?"

"—I could have had you naked in under sixty seconds."

Just the memory of how he'd looked in nothing but those low riding jeans had her salivating. "But you *did* act like an asshole."

"Yes. And I regretted it almost immediately. Enough that I watched you walk away from me."

"You were just checking out my ass."

"You do have a bloody beautiful ass."

Her pulse tripped into overdrive. "Joe," she said, her voice pathetically breathy even to her own ears.

A rustling sound came through earpiece followed by a grunt. "Fanfuckintastic. Did you know it's impossible to get comfortable when your cock is hard as stone and there's an ache in your balls?"

His statement was so blunt and honest, she released a startled laugh. "At least you're no longer thinking about whiskey."

"Sure I am. Only now I'm imagining sipping it off the globes of your ass."

Emma did her best to swallow further laughter, which caused her to snort. Which, in turn, sent her into hysterics.

"How can you laugh at me," he asked, his voice a combination of frustration and laughter, "knowing I am the only source of relief at this point?"

Who the hell had conversations like this? Certainly not her. Not before today at least. "I'm sorry you're going to have to self-satisfy." She pictured him. Completely alone in his bed, eyes closed as he palmed himself, and moisture pooled in the apex of her thighs. "But I'm not sorry it's me you'll be thinking about as you do."

The air hissed out between his teeth. "You're not helping."

"I know, and I'm sorry. I really am, but…"

"But you're really not."

"Not even a little."

April 1

Today is the third anniversary of my parent's death. Three years in, I still get up with the same sadness I felt on the day they died. I know I've mentioned they weren't the most caring or supportive people. But they were my parents, and I loved them.

I went to the cemetery and put flowers on their grave. Looking down at their names on the headstone was sort of surreal what with my own fate staring me in the face. Is this really my life?

On the surface, I appear to be just like every other twenty-three-year-old woman. However, I couldn't be more different. People my age don't normally recognize their own mortality. They don't sit down with their lawyer and write up their Will. Or arrange and pay for their own funeral.

People my age don't stare down at the roses they've just placed atop a headstone and wonder if anyone will care enough to do the same when they're gone.

Number of days since I decided to live: 40
Number of days until Blind Man's Alibi concert: 2
Current level of panic: 9/10

FIVE

April 17

J OE WOKE WITH a start, groggy and disoriented. He blinked to bring his eyes back into focus, trying to recall where he was. Georgia? Florida? Fuck, he had no idea. Backstage, that much he knew. Rock music boomed from speakers hidden in the ceiling, loud enough to be painful, but not enough to drown out the chatter of voices or cackle of laughter. Bodies pressed in from every side, none of them aware that seated in the middle of it all, he'd drifted off.

None except the generously breasted brunette working her way up his thighs. She seemed to be taking advantage of the fact.

"Sod off," he muttered, shifting to dislodge her. His body ached, his throat was on fire, and he was in no mood to be polite.

She gave him an obvious looking over, steadfastly ignoring his command.

Where the fuck was Gary? He pushed her hand away as she reached for his fly, only to have her outmaneuver him. "I said sod off!"

Disentangling himself from the brunette required standing, which was easier said than done. She countered his every move until he gave up being nice and simply stood, causing her to lose her balance and drop onto her ass at his feet.

He couldn't find it in him to care.

If Joe were to be honest with himself, he didn't care about much anymore. They'd played to a sold out stadium tonight—the second night in a row to be exact. He'd spent his youth dreaming of this day and now that it was here? He sure as hell wasn't enjoying it the way he'd always imagined. He was sick of it all, sick of the shit. He didn't know when it happened, but one day he'd just become disillusioned and unhappy. The music no longer brought the joy it once did. The audience no longer brought the thrill it once did. And the whiskey currently burning its way down his throat? It no longer brought the relief it once had.

Emma was right. He was in a dark place.

Joe leaned his sorry arse against the wall and took in the room. He ignored those shouting greetings or trying to get his attention and instead concentrated on drinking enough to quiet his demons. Fifteen minutes later, Gary finally made an appearance at his side, and it still wasn't working. "About time you showed up. Where the hell have you been?"

Gary's gaze went from Joe to the bottle of Jameson and back again. "Doing my job." His tone of voice made it obvious he didn't like being questioned.

Joe didn't give a shit. "Your job is to be here when I need you."

"My job is the security of both you and the fans. It is not to be your lap dog."

"Yeah, well I could have used your help getting the brunette off my lap a bit ago."

"Appears you did just fine without me."

A chime coming from his pocket stopped Joe from threatening to kick Gary's ass, which was probably a good thing since he didn't stand a chance against the man. Not with the buzz of alcohol swirling through his veins.

"You going to get that?" Gary asked, his gaze sweeping the room.

Joe took a pull from the whiskey bottle before he replied. "Didn't plan to."

"Hmm."

"What?"

Gary slid him a long look.

"Say it."

"I was just thinking it might be someone who could improve your mood."

Emma. Joe shifted the bottle to his other hand and removed his phone. He swiped his thumb across the screen to answer the call. "Hello?"

"Joe?"

His smile was instant and automatic. "Hey, Sunshine."

"Joe? I can barely hear you. Where are you?"

"We're still at the stadium. The show ended about an hour ago."

"Partying." At least he thought she said partying. He was having a hard time hearing her since the brunette had reappeared, sidling up to him and rubbing her bountiful boobs against his arm like she could change his mind.

Joe disentangled himself from the brunette with a muttered, "Sod off." Lucky for him Gary was there to make sure she got the message this time.

"Excuse me?"

"What?" He reached up to plug his free ear, and ended up smacking himself in the temple with the bottle of Jameson. "Fuck!"

"You're drunk."

Shit, add a throbbing skull to his list of aches tonight. "Well on my way, yes."

"The way you're slurring your words, you're already there." The music stopped as the song ended, allowing him to hear her sigh. "Why?" she asked softly. "You told me to call you."

"I like talking to you."

"I like talking to you, too, Joe. When you're sober."

The music started up again. Some teen queen pop star known for using auto tune. Even with the help, Joe couldn't stand her voice. It was a moment before he realized he couldn't hear Emma, not because of the caterwauling blaring from the speakers, but because she was silent.

"Emma?" Working his way through the overcrowded room, he aimed for the door. "Em?" He turned left, heading for his dressing room. "Are you still there?"

"Why do you do this to yourself?" For the first time since he'd answered the phone, Joe could hear her perfectly. "Why do you do this to me?"

The pain in her voice tore at him. It, like everything else about this day, pissed him off. "What exactly am I doing to you?"

"Reaching out to me then falling right back into the same bad habits. Why reach out if you aren't going to even try to change?"

A group of fans was making their way down the hall toward him. The bird in the lead spotted him and opened her mouth in what he could only guess was going to be a scream. Joe ducked into the first room on his right. Thank Christ, it wound up being his dressing room.

He pulled the door closed behind him with a snap, then leaned against it. "You have no idea what my life is—"

"Spare me the *'I don't know what your life is like'* crap!" Emma's tone was clipped and inflexible. "Everyone has shit to deal with, Joe. We all have demons—things we wish we'd done differently. Some of us don't have the luxury of time, but you do."

His stomach knotted with discomfort and confusion. He'd done exactly what she said he had—reached out to her then was too weak and chickenshit to resist drinking. But that last bit... "What the hell are you talking about?"

"You don't get the same moment twice in life."

"That's original," he said on a low, baffled, bewildered laugh.

"Yeah? Well, how's this for original? You want to live your life in a fog of alcohol and women, go right ahead. Just leave me out of it."

"What are you saying?"

"I'm saying I hope you're sober enough to remember this moment. Good-bye, Joe."

"Wait! Emma?" A glance at his display told him she'd rung off. "Emma? Fuck!"

Joe threw his mobile across the room where it smashed against the wall with a satisfying thud. He threw himself into the corner of the couch and tipped the bottle to his lips.

The door swung open. Gary stepped into the room.

"What?" Joe hissed between his teeth.

"Just making sure you're in one piece. Is there a problem here?"

Joe didn't respond.

"You appear to be in better shape than your mobile. That's going to make calling her back and groveling a bit difficult."

"What makes you think I have anything to grovel over?"

Gary tossed his head back in exaggerated laughter.

"You're an arsehole."

"You talk to your girl that way? No wonder she rang off already."

"She's not my girl." He barely knew her. They'd spent two evenings together and managed all of three—no four—telephone conversations since. He was in… Fuck, he didn't know what city, while she was half-way across the country in Ohio. How did any of that make her his girl? Still, an ache of emptiness ballooned in his chest as he spoke the words aloud. "She told me to piss off."

"Smart girl."

"Fuck you." Too bad his directive lacked feeling. She *was* smart. She was a bright ray of sunshine. A light that drew him because light was something he didn't have right now. He was darkness: a man losing interest in life. What would an angel like her want with a sinner like him?

The best thing for her to do was stay away before he pulled her into the shit alongside him.

"May I speak freely?" Gary asked.

"You've never needed permission before."

"You won't like what I have to say."

"Again, when has that ever stopped you?"

Gary sighed. "How long have we been doing this, Joe? Six? Seven years?"

"Seven years sounds about right."

"It used to be fun. We had some good times. Then this tour started…"

Goddamnit. Now Gary was dissatisfied? "Gare—"

"You've changed, Joe. You fell for the line of shit you're constantly being spoon fed and you believe you're something special. You drink too much, fuck too much, and all I can do is stand in the shadows and watch."

He didn't believe himself to be special. Maybe for a time there, but not any longer.

"I've watched you spiral out of control, sink lower and lower, lose your interest in the music, lose yourself," Gary said, his voice dropping in volume. "I can't do it any longer."

"You're quitting." Story of his mothereffing life lately.

"Do I need to?"

Joe lifted the bottle.

Gary snagged it from his hand before Joe could drink any more. "Get your shit together or I will!"

A crushing weight settled in his chest. Gary was the closest friend Joe had. He couldn't lose him. "I don't know how."

"Find a way."

"Don't you think I've tried?"

"Not hard enough."

"Fuck!" Joe surged to his feet, fists clenched at his side. He hadn't wanted to hit something so badly in a long time.

"Go with that emotion."

"The one that has me wanting to pound on you?"

"I'll find a local gym and we can go a few rounds if you'd like. But the one I was referring to was the emotion that has you staring at the pieces of your mobile like you'd give your left nut to be able to use it." Gary pulled his phone out of his pocket and held it up. "Call her. Beg, grovel, crawl if you have to. Promise her the moon and then deliver. Just get her here because, as far as I can tell, she is your best chance of reclaiming the man you used to be."

Joe's mind was spun with the shocked realization that what Gary said—everything he said—could be so spot on.

"Huh."

"Did you honestly believe you were the only one who could see the changes in you when she was around?" He held out his hand, offering up his mobile phone.

"Small problem…I didn't memorize her number."

"Bloody hell." The mobile went back in his pocket, the whiskey into the bin by the door. Gary pulled the radio off his belt. "Anyone have eyes on Marvin?"

"I got him, boss," came the response. "Just a sec."

Marvin's voice followed a moment later. "Yeah?"

"We need a replacement mobile. I have a singer with a bit of groveling to do."

"I'm on it."

Joe dropped back onto his couch. What more could he do?

Gary stared down at him. "Scare up some roses while you're at it. In case the wanker forgot to back up his contacts. Mayhap he'll get lucky and she'll call him."

"No," Joe mumbled.

"Lots of them," Gary emphasized. "Send them to Emma Travers, Cleveland, Ohio."

"No roses." Damn it if he was going to do this—and it was pretty bloody obvious that if he didn't, Gary was going to in his name—then he was going to do it right. "Those big yellow flowers with the brown centers."

"Did you get that, Marv?"

"What yellow…what is he talking about?"

"Sunflowers," Gary supplied. "The bleedin' sap is talking about sunflowers."

"That's them," Joe said quietly. "Sunflowers. Lots and lots of sunflowers."

April 18

"I CAN'T BELIEVE you're going through with this."

Emma handed off her credit card with a smile then turned back to Alison, who stood to her right, her attention focused on the pamphlet in her hand. "Why not? You know I've always wanted to."

"Yes, but…I guess I always thought you would have someone with you. Me, or Melody, or…*someone*."

So had she.

"I mean, isn't it dangerous traveling to all these places alone?"

Emma chuffed a laugh.

"Don't. Don't be flip about this, Em. I'm not just talking about the normal dangers of a woman traveling abroad by herself. I'm talking about your health." The more she talked, the closer Alison's face got to the pamphlet. She was either really enjoying the photos of Scotland's castles, or trying to hide. "What if something happens and there's no one around to help?"

"That could happen here, honey. You know that as well as I do."

"I just think you should wait for the next group tour."

Emma hooked a finger in the top of the pamphlet and pulled it down. The pain and regret in Alison's eyes was horrible to see. "Al—"

"Here you go!" The return of the travel agent stopped their conversation cold. Which was probably a good thing. It wasn't like Alison actually needed the reminder that six months was too long to wait, any more than Emma wished to give voice to it. "Sign here, here, and here."

With that done, Emma accepted the handshake from the agent. "Congratulations, Ms. Travers. I hope you have a wonderful trip."

"Thank you." Stuffing everything into her leather satchel, Emma gently took hold of Alison's elbow and exited the travel office.

"Don't be mad," Alison stated the moment they were outside.

"Why would I be mad?"

"It's just... I worry about you and...I wanted to be able to do this with you."

"I know, honey. I'm not mad, honestly."

"Then why are you steering me around in a way reminiscent of how mom did when she was mad?"

"I'm not—"

Alison raised a brow.

Emma let out a long breath and released her arm. She stopped walking and stood at the edge of the crosswalk, waiting for the light to change. Closing her eyes, she tipped her face to the spring sun.

"Talk to me, Em. Why is this trip something you're suddenly in a hurry to make? I mean, you can't even wait a week? You have to leave tomorrow?"

She sighed, blinking her eyes open, then using her hand to shade them from the sun. "I don't know. I guess... tomorrow just feels like the right time."

"You seriously think I'm going to believe that?" Alison dug through her purse until she located a pair of sunglasses, which she promptly pushed at Emma. "Try telling that to someone who hasn't known you for as long as I have."

Emma pushed the sunglasses into place and thought about her answer. Alison was right, they'd known each other too long for her to accept the simple answer. The thing was, she wasn't exactly sure how to explain why she felt it was time to go. Oddly enough, being a cancer patient—having to face chemo and radiation, doctor appointments and hospital stays—had given her a sense of purpose. Without it or her job to occupy her time, she was plagued by a strange sense of loneliness.

Last night's conversation with Joe certainly didn't help. She'd gone to bed feeling lonelier than ever.

"What are you running from?" Alison asked softly. Her teeth worried her lower lip as a frown creased her forehead.

"What aren't I running from?"

The little frown didn't lighten. "Running away from it won't change the outcome. It never does."

Emma had to smile. "Waxing philosophical?" She shrugged. "Facing it head on doesn't always make a difference, either."

As the walk light clicked on, they both stepped into the crosswalk.

"I'm just surprised. You're not normally a runner."

"I prefer not to look at it as running, just changing up the scenery."

"And you're sure you can't wait a week before bringing about this change of scenery?"

The clawing pain in her head told her the time to travel was now. Sure, the fact that she hadn't gotten much sleep last night most likely had a lot to do with it but, even so, this made two headaches in two weeks. They were getting more and more frequent. "I'm sure."

"Fine," Alison said as she opened the door to their favorite restaurant. "I may not be able to change your mind about leaving tomorrow, but I can damn well take you to the airport. No arguments."

"I would like that."

"Good. Now let's get you some food. You're looking a little pale today."

FOOD HELPED TO appease The Monster so that by the time Emma arrived home, she was in better spirits. Jim, her building's lobby attendant, promptly greeted her when she walked in. "Good afternoon Ms. Travers. Ms. Willows."

Since Alison had plans for the evening that couldn't be changed, she'd decided to accompany Emma home and help her pack a bag. Something small that included only the essentials, designed to make moving from city to city and country to country easier. Following Emma through the door, she nodded at Jim and signed the visitor's log.

"How has your day been so far?" Emma asked, as she slipped the key into her mail box and palmed her mail.

"Just fine."

"Good."

"Um, Ms. Travers?"

Already half-way to the elevator, Emma looked back at him. "Yes?"

"You received a delivery today that was ah...too large for the closet?" As he spoke, he motioned at the closet where most deliveries were locked until a resident picked them up. "So I let them deliver to your place. I went in with the delivery men to make certain they didn't touch anything."

"Ooh," Alison murmured. "What did you order?"

"I haven't ordered a thing. Are you sure the delivery was for me?"

"Absolutely, Ms. Travers."

Wait, was that a smirk on his lips? "Jim?"

The cart bell rang, signaling a resident needed help unloading their car. "I need to get that. Have a wonderful afternoon, ladies."

He was definitely smirking as he grabbed a cart and headed off.

Alison let out a little laugh as they stepped into the elevator. "That was odd."

"Very."

"You can't think of anything you ordered?"

"Nothing that would cause that smirk on his face. Tell me you saw it, too."

"Oh, I saw it."

The elevator stopped and the doors slid open. Passing through, they came to Emma's door. A turn of the key, a twist of the knob and they were both inside.

"Ho-ly shit." Alison moved farther into the room, turning in a circle, taking it all in.

Emma stood frozen in place, her hand over her mouth. She couldn't take her eyes off of the sight before her. Her heart took a hard leap.

Someone had bought out the entire city's supply of sunflowers. They were everywhere she looked. Vases upon vases of bright yellow sunflowers covered every available surface in her living room.

"Holy shit, Em. Someone likes you. A lot!"

Only one person she knew could have pulled this off. "More like someone is groveling."

"It's so beautiful. Like a sea of sunshine."

A sea of sunshine. In spite of everything, Emma felt herself soften. "Nice touch, asshole."

"Wait, you know who these are from? How do you know? You haven't even looked at the card?" Alison made her way to the largest vase, strategically placed in the center in the room. "How can you call someone who did something so sweet an asshole?"

"They're from Joe," Emma said as Al pulled the card from its envelope. "And believe me, he earned the title." She stuck her nose in the closest vase and inhaled. "What does it say?"

Alison stared at her.

"What?"

"The card is completely blank except for two words written in the middle. 'The Asshole'."

Emma laughed as she carried a vase across the room and set it on the mantel, just below her angel sketch. "Yup, it's Joe."

"Joe? As in Joe-sex-on-two-legs-Campbell?"

She laughed again. "That would be the one."

"What are you not telling me? Why is Joe Campbell sending you... Jesus, there have to be fifty vases of flowers here! That concert was like ten days ago."

"Two weeks ago," Emma corrected, pulling her cell phone from her pocket and taking a shot of the vase on her mantel. With the press of a button, the photo was sent.

"Who did you just send that to?" Alison wove her way through the room, snatching the phone from her hand before Emma could put it away. "You've got his phone number? Emma Mae Travers you'd better start talking." The broad smile on her face softened her command. "I'm going to take a wild stab here and say your act of desperation paid off. He called you, didn't he?"

Emma couldn't contain her own smile. "Yes. We've spoken four times since then."

Alison shook her head, her eyes full of wonder. "This is

amazing. You never said a thing."

"I was…getting used to the idea."

"You were hoarding him. Not that I blame you."

Emma gave a rough laugh as she crossed to another vase. The flowers smelled sweet, like candy, but she had to get her nose up close. "You make it sound like I have him tied up in my closet."

"Do you?"

"Of course. I let him loose this morning just long enough to order me flowers. A girl needs to feel important, you know."

"Looks to me like you're pretty important to him."

"It does, doesn't it?" Emma said softly.

Alison sat on the couch and attempted to prop her feet on the coffee table, which was impossible due to the vases littering the top. She gave up, crossing her legs instead. "So, Joe's groveling, which is what you said the flowers were for. That means he hurt you." She fell silent, studying Emma for a moment. "Is he who you're running from? Because I've got to tell you, Em, if a man cared enough about having hurt me that he filled my house with flowers? Well, I'd be running toward that man, not away from him."

April 4

I can't sleep. My mind is whirling and bouncing around like a kid on a sugar high. My heart is racing. It's two o'clock in the morning and I'm staring at the ceiling of my bedroom, thinking it's going to take an act of God to get me to relax. Last night was the Blind Man's Alibi concert, and not only did my dream of seeing Joe Campbell, live and in the flesh, come true, I got to meet him. One thing to note: he is nothing, and everything, like I imagined he would be.

I expected him to be more beautiful in person than any medium could suggest. He was.

I expected him to be confident and a tad arrogant. He was that, too.

What I never expected, and was wholly unprepared for, was how lost he seemed.

Sad.

Lonely.

Adrift.

Sure he hid it well, but I have the unique advantage of not only being sick, which makes me more aware of the people around me, but of being an outsider to his world. I looked into his eyes and all that nonsense about being able to see into someone's soul began to make sense.

We talked for hours. I can honestly say I have never felt such an intense connection to another person in such a short amount of time. I ached as I walked out of the stadium and away from him. It wasn't an extension of my total fan girl obsession with Joe Campbell the rock star but, instead, a visceral reaction to Joe Campbell the man.

He felt something, too, for he invited me back tonight – his last night in Cleveland.

No matter how tempting the offer, how desperately I want to see him again, I don't dare go. His lost soul calls out to me. Tempts me to show him what I've only just begun to learn myself: How to embrace life.

Something that can't be taught in one night.

Yet one night is all it could ever be.

Number of days since I decided to live: 43
Number of days until Blind Man's Alibi concert: 0
Current level of panic: 6/10

SIX

April 18

Somewhere in the distance a phone rang. A shrill, persistent tone just loud enough for her to hear it, yet soft enough she couldn't tell from what direction the sound came. The fog surrounded her, consumed her, causing her limbs to feel heavy and weak. It was dark. So dark.

A sense of urgency swelled within her. She had to get to that phone, no matter what it took. She never questioned the why, because the urgency was there, twisting and spinning at the back of her mind. Until the pain smothered it.

So. Much. Pain.

The Monster.

Run. Run away. Hide.

She didn't have the strength to fight.

She gave herself up to the fog. Surrendered to the darkness.

EMMA LAY IN bed, ignoring the nagging ring of her phone. It didn't matter who kept calling her. Nothing mattered until her mind cleared and she could reacclimate to her surroundings.

It was always like this after having to use her injection to chase The Monster away. A struggle to quiet the panic enough to allow her heart to settle. An even bigger one to figure out how much time she'd lost.

Opening her eyes, she blew a sigh and chose the fastest way to get her answers. "Hello?"

"There you are." *Joe.* At least she still had enough brain cells to recognize his voice. Then again, he was pretty hard to forget. "I've been trying to reach you for hours."

She blinked to clear her vision. When nothing came into focus, she stretched out her arm and turned on the lamp. There, that was better. There was nothing wrong with her eyes except the shadowed darkness of night. "What day is it?"

"What day? Sunshine, did you go on a bender tonight or something?"

Or something. She'd spent an untold number of hours under the influence of some pretty heavy duty narcotics. "Is it Saturday or Sunday?"

"Saturday."

Saturday. That was a good sign. Saturday was the day she'd bought her tickets for a tour of Europe, and laughed over lunch with Alison. "What time?"

"Half past eleven in the evening, my time. What's going on with you? Are you okay?"

She should do something to allay the fear in his voice but, it was still too soon. She'd yet to alleviate her own worry. "I'm okay, I…just give me a minute. It takes a minute."

"What takes a minute? Emma, do you need me to ring someone for you?"

"I'm okay," she repeated. "Call me back in ten minutes." Ten minutes was all she needed to pull herself together. "Ten minutes, Joe. Please."

He was silent a moment, like he was thinking about it. "Okay. I'll ring you in ten minutes, but if you don't pick up…just make sure you pick up the phone."

"I will. I'm fine."

"Right. Fine."

"It's just…ten minutes and I'll explain."

Emma waited just long enough for Joe to concede, then disconnected. She pressed her fingers against her closed eyelids and stretched, testing her muscles. It took a focused effort to get them to move. With a grimace, she rolled off her bed, landing with a thud on her hands and knees beside it. Not exactly her most graceful moment, but hey, at least now she was fully awake.

Good God, she'd never had that much trouble pulling herself out of the drug's clutches before. Climbing to her feet, she stumbled to her bath. A splash of cold water helped the gritty feel of her eyes, and a toothbrush the nasty taste in her mouth. Making her way to her bed, she relaxed in a semi-upright position, her back supported by a jumble of pillows.

Emma had barely gotten comfortable when her cell ping-ponged. She pressed the button and accepted, then fumbled the phone in alarm as Joe's face appeared on her screen.

"Shit!" Her expletive was immediate and automatic. Her mind still fuzzy, she hadn't recognized the difference in ringtone or paid much attention when accepting the call. Which is how she suddenly found herself in a video chat.

She was barely dressed, certainly in no condition for Joe to see her. Thankfully, her phone landed face up, giving him a view of her pristine white ceiling, and not much else. With a breath to center herself, she picked it up.

If she thought she'd prepared herself to see him, actually *see* him, she was wrong. The missing him had been bad enough with only his voice in her ear. Now, it was a growing ache inside of her. "Hey."

"Hey yourself. You want to tell me what that was all about?"

She was staring. She knew she was staring, but was helpless to stop. His mismatched eyes and overlong hair. Those lips circled by his short-trimmed beard. God, it was like being punched in the stomach, and all she could do was try to catch her breath.

"Emma?"

What had he asked her? Oh, right. "I dropped the phone."

"Before that. The first time you picked up."

Emma shrugged. "I was asleep. Couldn't wake up."

"And the first time I called? Were you sleeping then, too?"

"Did you call earlier today?"

"Yeah, before the show."

That would explain the weird feeling of having struggled to pull herself from quicksand only to fail. "Yes. I...vaguely remember a ringing phone."

Joe cocked a brow at her. His dark hair fell into his face and her fingers itched with the impossibility of reaching through the screen to brush it back. "You sleep that soundly?"

"Not normally." Since her lungs appeared to be working correctly again, she drew a deep breath to steady herself. "I get headaches sometimes. Pretty severe ones. The medicine I take for them usually knocks me out for hours."

"You had one of these headaches today?"

"I did."

"Which is why you needed ten minutes. Because I woke

you and you weren't sure what day it even was?" Joe rubbed the back of his neck. "Sounds like some pretty potent stuff."

"It is."

"Is your headache gone now?"

There was an underlying note of concern in his voice. Emma smiled, and did her best to reassure him. "Yes, it's gone. I'm glad you called. Although you did catch me off guard with the whole video chat thing. That's a first."

"You worried me with the whole *'what day is it'* thing."

"I suppose that would be a bit unsettling."

"A bit, yeah." His eyes dropped, lingered on her lips, then made a slow leisurely journey across the rest of her face. "Look at you. Christ, you're even more beautiful than I remembered."

"And you still know how to tell a girl what she wants to hear." There it was—his crooked smile. Emma hadn't realized just how much she missed it until that very moment. "You're looking pretty good yourself."

He grimaced. "I look like five kilometers of bad road."

"Now that you mention it," she said, and was rewarded with another smile. "You look tired. Which makes sense if you just finished a ninety-minute set.

"The crowd tonight was fierce. We fed off their energy and pushed harder, played longer."

As he told of his night, Emma shifted this way, then that. It had nothing to do with not being interested in what he had to say; and everything to do with finding a comfortable position.

It was a moment before she realized he'd gone quiet. Her gaze returned to his image on her screen.

"Emma? What are you wearing?"

There was something in his tone. Something she

couldn't name. "Don't get overly excited, it's nothing sexy. Just a t-shirt."

"*My* t-shirt."

She glanced away.

"It's my t-shirt, isn't it? The one I gave you outside the stadium. You're wearing my t-shirt." His grin turned cocky. "Were you missing me tonight, Sunshine?"

"Yes." Her answer pushed the teasing light from his eyes. "I didn't feel good and was looking for some comfort."

"How does my shirt bring you comfort?"

"It smells like you," she admitted softly.

Joe swore. "Now I feel even more like a piece of…" His words ended in a sigh. "About last night. I'm…I'm sorry."

Emma grinned. "Was that painful? Because it looked like it caused you actual physical pain."

He shrugged.

"You're not used to having to apologize for your actions, are you?"

"No. But that's not it…" He shifted a little then scrubbed his hands over his face. A move that told her he'd propped his phone against something, instead of holding it as she was hers. "Look, Em, I was a righteous shit last night and when you rang off, I…Well, I smashed my mobile to bits."

"Because you were mad at me."

He hissed a breath then locked his gaze with hers, an intensity in his eyes that had her heart skipping a few beats. "I wasn't. Not with you. I was angry with myself. I had driven you away and that's the last thing I ever want to do."

The ache inside her grew. The calls and texts that brought them closer in spirit, only amplified the physical distance between them. That distance was never more apparent than right then, as she wished, above all else, she could touch him.

"I'm sorry," he repeated, the words coming easier to him this time. "Forgive me."

Her heart climbed into her throat. "I already did," she admitted softly. "Earlier today, when I came home to a condo filled with flowers. How did you manage to round up that many in less than a day?"

"Marvin. He's the reason I have a new mobile, as well."

His manager. Of course.

Joe's mouth curved in a slow smile. "Were there lots of them? I asked for lots of them. A few lots actually."

"I think you went overboard."

"Probably. Everything past threatening to kick Gare's ass is a bit of a blur."

"You didn't!" She burst out laughing. "He'd fold you in half and stuff you in the luggage compartment of your tour bus."

"I'll have you know I can hold my own in the sparring ring." His expression suggested she'd somehow questioned his manhood.

"Maybe in a sparring ring." She left out the part about him needing to be sober.

"Damn. It's a good thing my ego is—"

"Inflated?"

"—healthy. You know how to wound a man."

"Gary's bigger, looks to be stronger, and has a completely different skill set than you." One that included hand-to-hand combat, if the way he held himself was anything to go by. "He's obviously more level-headed than you, too or, believe me, you'd be in the luggage compartment."

"And to think I sent you flowers," he said with a laugh.

"Yeah, you did." She smiled, her gaze holding his. She seemed to have no control over how her voice had gone all soft on her. "Thank you for that."

"You're welcome." His had gone all soft too. Wasn't that interesting? "Are you going to show me?"

Her mind skittered in a million different directions. "Show you what?"

"Your flowers."

"Right! The flowers. Of course. I sent you a photo earlier."

"Man, I would love to know where your mind just ran off to."

"I bet you would," she whispered under her breath.

"What was that?" When she didn't answer, his mouth curved in a knowing smile. "You sent me a snap of one vase. I did better than just one vase."

He most certainly did. Easing out of the bed, Emma turned her phone around so he was looking in the same direction as she. Without a word, she exited her bedroom and headed down the hall, flicking on lights as she went. Once in her living room, she made a slow sweep left, then right so he could get the full effect.

When Joe made a comment she didn't quite catch, she turned the phone so the camera once again faced her. "What was that?"

He didn't answer. He didn't say a word, just closed his eyes. He kept them closed for a good thirty seconds while his nostrils flared and his jaw tightened. Finally, he snapped them back open to reveal a look so hot, it scorched her through the phone.

"Fuck me dead," he muttered harshly.

Caught off guard, Emma gasped. "What?" His gaze was

locked on something to her right and behind her.

Trying to figure out what he was reacting to, she looked over her shoulder, and was met with a reflection of her lace and silk covered ass. Thanks to the oversized mirror leaning against the wall and the fact all her shifting around on her bed had caused his shirt to become wedged in her waistband, Joe had the perfect view of white floral undies trimmed in turquoise lace. This particular pair was cut high in the back, designed in a way that left the bottom half of her cheeks exposed.

"Shit!" Emma slapped her free hand over her butt and turned so the mirror was no longer in view.

"Don't you dare," Joe whispered, his voice low and rough. "Turn back around, give me another look."

She hesitated.

"Come on, Sunshine. Don't make me beg."

She turned.

"Awe, Fuck." His gaze locked onto the mirror behind her. His eyes were completely on fire.

Her nipples hardened. And thanks to her wearing nothing but his shirt there was no mistaking it. Good thing he was still focused on her ass.

"You're not wearing pants," he said with just a hint of accusation.

"You woke me from a sound sleep. What did you expect?"

He looked down, leaving her staring at the top of his head. There was a rasping sound, followed by a sigh.

Holy shit, did he just unzip?

"Christ, now I'm going to spend the night with the imprint of my zipper permanently tattooed on the side of my cock."

His voice, deep and full of arousal, was the stuff fantasies were spun around. Her fantasies, at least. She squeezed her thighs together in response.

A low groan ripped from the back of his throat. He leaned in, closer to the screen, and said gruffly, "Sunshine, it's time to move away from the mirror and prop me on the side table so we can end this night the right way."

"Why do you want me to prop you on the side table?" she asked, her voice almost as hoarse as his.

"So I can watch you touch yourself."

Her breathing hitched. His gaze held her prisoner. More tempted than she ever would have imagined, she whispered, "Why would I need to touch myself when I've got your voice?"

"Christ."

"You have a voice made for sin, Joe. If you ever give up music, you could make a killing as a phone sex operator. Men do that, too, right?"

The look he gave her was priceless and went a long way in distracting her from her own arousal. "Better yet, for your next release, just make a record that is nothing but sex talk. Naughty words of encouragement and promise in that sexy as hell accent. My God, you'd have a platinum seller overnight, with just the single women snatching it up to masturbate to. I bet even the ones with lovers would get on board. Just pop their earbuds in and get naked with their man while your voice drives them to the best orgasm of their life."

He scowled, and she had to laugh. "Are you blushing? It's hard to tell with your beard but...You are! You're blushing!"

"I don't think so."

He most definitely was. "I'm serious. The accent, that growling sound you make when singing that has every heterosexual woman who has ever heard you wondering if you make the same noise while having sex. Your voice alone could…" Emma shivered in delight.

His eyes burned. His crooked smile made an appearance. "My voice alone could what, Sunshine? Bring you to climax?"

She was already halfway there. "Yes."

The growl he released curled her toes. He turned away, Adams apple bobbing, then with a muttered curse, he remet her gaze. "We'll be in Baton Rouge tomorrow. The Capital Center Hilton."

"Joe?" He couldn't possibly be asking her to come to him. Could he? Her heart turned over in her chest. It was a moment before she could draw enough oxygen into her lungs to speak. Telling her what city they would be—or currently were—in was nothing new. But he had never, not once, told her what hotel he was staying at while performing in that city. "I'm leaving for New York tomorrow."

"Work?"

"No." During one of their first telephone conversations she'd told him she was a self-employed graphic artist. What she hadn't told him was that she'd completed her final design. "From there I catch a flight to Scotland."

"Why the fuck would you want to go there?" Suddenly he was walking, she could tell by the way the scenery behind him kept changing.

When he finally stopped, Emma caught the flash of a bottle as he raised it toward his lips. "Joe."

He sighed and set the bottle down. As he looked back at her, the wounds she'd glimpsed that very first night were there again.

Tell me you don't want me to go.

She'd change her plans in a heartbeat if he asked. Which was crazy, really, but being with him, even if it wasn't in a foreign destination she'd only dreamt about, was better than being alone. She was tired of being alone, of wanting something—him—and not being able to have it. If the look in his eyes was any indication, he was tired of it, too.

"When will you be back?" he asked, his voice completely devoid of expression.

"I don't know."

Tell me you want me to come to you. Say it.

He just watched her silently. Minutes ticked by and still, he said nothing.

"Joe." She repeated softly.

"You should…"

Oh, God. Her heart actually skipped a beat.

"You should go to England. Far classier lads to be found there."

Disappointment nearly choked her. No worries. She was being foolish, thinking this thing between them could be anything more.

"Yeah. I will." It was hard to get the words past her dry throat. "I have to get up early tomorrow, so…"

"Right. Sure." A shadow fell across his face, but he still didn't give voice to the words she was so desperate to hear. "Have a good trip, Sunshine."

Joe disconnected.

Emma returned to her bed and cried herself back to sleep.

ALISON STOOD BESIDE Emma in the airport check-in line, fiddling with her phone. "I can't believe you're really going through with this."

Emma sighed. "Didn't we go over this yesterday?"

"Yes, but that was before you received enough flowers to brighten the day of patients all over the city."

The line moved forward two steps. Alison's attention was still on her phone so Emma took hold of her elbow and pulled her along. "Thank you for doing that, by the way, for delivering them to the local oncology wards."

Alison shrugged like it was no big deal, but Emma knew otherwise. Gifts of any kind helped to lift patients' spirits. But those most appreciated were the ones that brought beauty to a drab, white-washed hospital room.

"I'm serious, Al, thank you."

"You know I would do anything for you. And what is the alternative, just leaving them in your condo?" She was quiet a moment, still staring at her damn phone. "Just so you know, I'm not giving them all away. I'm taking one or two home with me."

"Good." The line shifted again. Emma looked back at Alison with a frown. "Ahem."

Alison glanced up and stepped forward.

"What is it with you and that phone, anyway?"

"I'm looking at pictures of us." Al tipped the phone so Emma could see the screen. "Look! Here we are at high school graduation." She flipped to the next photo. "At my twenty-first birthday party." One more flip and Emma's stomach dropped to her toes. "And here we are at the Blind Man's Alibi concert."

"I'm coming back, you know," Emma reassured, her throat tight. "You're going to see me again."

"It doesn't feel like it. It feels more like..."

"More like, what?"

"Listen to me," Alison commanded softly. "Okay?"

"Okay," Emma agreed.

"Don't just say okay, *hear* what I'm saying to you."

"All right. Yes."

"I know you've always wanted to travel—"

"That's what I'm doing."

"—but I'm not convinced that's what you're doing."

Emma raised a brow.

"I think you're running. Heck, I know you are because you admitted it to me just yesterday. Running from your prognosis, from your feelings for Joe. Emma, you said you were going to live. Instead you're running away to die."

What the hell? Where did she get that from? Emma stood in stunned silence for a moment. "That's not true."

Alison shoved her phone in Emma's face. "Look at him, Em. Look!"

Joe onstage, staring down into the audience. Staring at her. While she had been busy feeding lines to him, Alison had obviously been snapping photos. Emma couldn't help herself. She curled her fingers around the phone and brought Joe's image closer.

"You don't even want to go to Europe. It's written all over your face."

Alison was right, she didn't want to go. Emma had spent her morning re-packing her bag over and over while surreptitiously checking her phone. But no matter how much she wished he would, Joe hadn't called.

It was hard to pack a bag while crying.

Even harder to ignore the truth while it was staring her in the face.

"I'm so damn tired of being alone," Emma whispered.

"I know you are," Alison replied with terrifying gentleness. "Here's the thing, you don't have to be alone. Not if you choose to live."

Emma shook her head.

Alison shifted to stand at her side, pointing at the photo. "Look at the picture, Emma. Do you see his expression?"

"He looks…" She had no idea how to describe it.

"He looks like he's been waiting his whole life to find you and suddenly there you are."

"No."

Alison sighed and rested her head on Emma's shoulder. "I've looked at this picture over and over these past few weeks. That is exactly what his expression says." When Emma didn't respond, Alison continued. "Do me a favor."

"What?"

"Go to him. If you want to travel, travel with Joe. If you want to grab life by the balls, grab—"

"Joe by the balls?"

Alison snorted. Then she glanced at the people around them, all of whom had suddenly fallen silent, and snorted again.

Suddenly they were both laughing and it felt good. It felt really, very good.

Emma sobered first. "And if he turns me away?"

"Then you hop a flight to Scotland and see the world. Just…don't stay gone too long."

She was tempted. So tempted. "God, Al."

Alison raised her eyebrow, challenge gleaming in her eyes. "One thing about you that has never changed, not since we first met, is the way you run headfirst into any situation no matter how complicated it is. You don't back down. You've never backed down, Emma! Why would you start now?"

Heart double-timing in her chest, Emma shoved her ticket into her satchel. She turned to the woman behind the counter. "I need a ticket to Baton Rouge, please."

"That's my girl," Alison whispered. She took her phone away from Emma.

The attendant smiled. "First class or—"

"Whatever is available on the first flight out."

"We've got a seat in coach on flight 1226 which departs from Concourse B Gate 3 in ninety minutes."

"That's fine." Emma handed over her credit card.

Alison started bouncing on the balls of her feet. "I'm so happy you're doing this. You're going to send me lots of pictures, right? So I can live vicariously through you?"

"You have Kevin," Emma said pointedly.

"Right. Sorry." She cleared her throat then grinned. "I still want photos."

"Fine."

"Lots of them."

Emma took her ticket from the attendant and started walking. Alison matched her pace, which wasn't difficult to do since she stood only three inches taller than Emma's own five foot five. They moved to Concourse B and stopped just outside the line waiting to go through the security scan.

Alison gave her a fast hug. "I'm going to miss you. More than you know."

"I'm going to miss you, too."

"Nah, you'll be too busy living the rock star lifestyle."

Emma grinned and dug through her satchel. "I have something for you." She pulled out the gift she'd purchased only three days ago. "For you and Kevin. Sort of a…wedding present, I suppose."

Alison looked down at the white box wrapped in a red bow and her smile faded. "A wedding present? It couldn't wait until you get back?"

"No."

Alison didn't move.

"Open the box, Al."

"I'm afraid to," she said shakily. A quick tug and the ribbon fell away. Alison lifted the lid and made a sound that was half laugh and half sob. "What did you do?"

Nestled inside, tied together by a second bow, was a set of silver keys atop an embossed card. The card belonged to Larry Bowerman, Emma's attorney. The keys belonged to a building in The Detroit Shoreway.

"It needs some minor repair," Emma warned, "but it's structurally sound. A corner building, which I think would work best for getting noticed."

"Emma."

"Larry has all of the paperwork. You and Kevin need to go see him. He's got something for you to sign."

"Em," Alison's voice broke.

"You can't say no." Her voice sounded like gravel, even to her own ears. Tears burned the backs of her eyes. "It's already yours."

Emma was suddenly pulled back into Alison's arms and hugged so tightly she could barely breathe. "I should have known you would do this," Alison managed through her tears.

"You should have."

"I didn't want this. But I'm not giving it back."

Emma chuckled, the air whooshing from her lungs as Alison clutched her tighter before releasing her. It was a moment before she could speak. "You can't give it back. I told you, it's already yours."

"It's really too much."

"It's not," Emma said fiercely. She cupped Alison's face in her hands so they stood eye to eye. "You want me to grab life by the balls? Well, guess what? I want you to do the same. I love you. You know that, yes?"

"Yes. I love you, too."

"Good. Now go get Kevin and make a call to Larry. I have a plane to catch and a rock star to grab."

April 7

Alison is engaged! Sometime in the last three days, while I was having the experience of my life, Alison was having the experience of hers. Kevin got down on one knee, offered her an absolutely, beautiful diamond ring, and asked her to be his wife.

I can't begin to imagine how incredible that must have been for her.

I was blown away when she told me her answer had been maybe. Maybe? What was she thinking? She needs to grab that man with both hands and live! Not tell him maybe.

I fear I may be a part of her non-answer. A reason she is dragging her feet about moving forward with her life. She was here the second night I spent with Joe, even though she had no idea I would need her. Seems as if she is always here, ready to catch me when I fall.

The emotions that played through me when I realized I was holding my best friend back, no matter how unintentional, are indescribable. Pain, sadness and guilt are only the tip of the iceberg. It has to stop. I will do whatever it takes to make it stop.

I have to leave Cleveland. Get far enough away that Al will no longer feel the need to mother or care for me. It is crippling her, and that, I just can't have. Maybe Europe – I've always wanted to see Big Ben and The Eiffel Tower. Or South America – I hear Rio is nice this time of year. I never planned to see it all

alone, but Alison's life is moving on, moving forward.
Who am I to stand in her way?

Number of days since I decided to live: 46
Number of days since I met Joe: 4
Current level of panic: 7/10

SEVEN

I T WAS MORE than seven hours after her decision to go to Joe that Emma arrived at the 1927 art deco style hotel in Baton Rouge. It was lovely. Though she barely gave it a passing glance as, nerves wound tight, she approached the front desk.

A man who resembled her grade school gym instructor flashed her a lukewarm smile. "Welcome to the Hilton. How may I assist you?"

"I'm looking for Joe Ca—" His name had nearly passed her lips before reality struck hard and fast. There was no way this man was going to give her Joe's room number. Not even if she begged.

Blind Man's Alibi had played the convention center adjacent to the hotel. Emma knew because her taxi had passed in front of the building, giving her a view of the banners hanging just inside the glass entrance. Although it was clear the concert had ended, hundreds of people wearing souvenir t-shirts still lined the sidewalk, spilling out into the street, presumably waiting to get a glimpse of the band.

Standing at the front desk, stumbling over Joe's name, Emma feared she looked like just another groupie. "Shit."

The gym-instructor look-alike raised his eyebrow. "Miss?"

"Just a minute, I'll call him." Setting her carry-on at her side, Emma fished her phone out of her satchel. She pushed the button on the side to wake it up. Nothing happened.

"No, no, not tonight." She sent up a silent prayer that she'd turned her phone off before take-off, as she'd been instructed to do, then held down the button longer, to turn it on. Still nothing.

Her battery was dead.

Perfect.

The man gave her an obvious looking over. When he met her eyes again, his gaze seemed curious, but not unfriendly. Of course, it was his job to be polite.

Placing her phone atop the desk, Emma dug through the contents of her satchel once more. She had her all-access pass tucked into her journal. Joe had said that allowed her to go anywhere at any show worldwide. Perhaps it wasn't too late for her to get into the convention center.

She curled her fingers around the soft brown leather, careful to remove only the journal and nothing else. Unhooking the leather ties, she quickly flipped through the pages, causing the pass to slip free and slide to the floor on the opposite side of the desk.

"I'm so sorry," she said as the man—Terri, his nametag read Terri—collected the pass.

He blinked down at it a minute before he set it alongside her phone. "That's perfectly all right, Miss...?

"Travers," she answered automatically. "Emma Travers."

"Emma Travers," he repeated, typing on his computer keyboard.

"Oh, no, I'm not a registered guest I'm—"

"In room 1056."

Terri pulled a key card from the stack next to him,

clicked a few more keys on the keyboard, then ran the card through the programmer. "If I could see some identification, please?"

"I believe there's been a misunderstanding."

He gave her a polite smile. "Not if you are, indeed, Emma Travers and can provide identification."

What was going on? Emma hadn't a clue.

She pulled out her passport and handed it to Terri. He looked at it, then up at her, then back to the i.d. one last time before appearing to be satisfied. He added it to the growing pile of items on the desk before her, then placed the key card he'd just programmed next to it. "Welcome to the Hilton, Ms. Travers. You are in room 1056 on the top floor." He motioned across the room. "That bank of elevators is the one you need. Do you require any assistance with your luggage?"

"I... No, thank you."

"You're very welcome. Enjoy your stay, Ms. Travers."

At a complete loss for words, Emma stuffed everything back into her satchel, picked up her carry-on and headed for the elevators. She pushed the call button, her mind running back through the conversation she'd just had. How could her name have possibly been in that computer?

Turning on her heel, she headed back to the desk to find out. "Terri?"

He looked up, surprised to see her standing there again. "Ms. Travers?"

"How am I...? Can I see my reservation?"

His brows drew down and his forehead wrinkled. "Excuse me?"

"How am I listed in your computer? May I see it?"

He didn't say anything for the longest time. Perhaps he

thought she would change her mind and walk away. Emma stayed rooted to the spot.

With a sigh, he typed on the keyboard once more, glanced around the room to make sure no one was looking, and turned the monitor in her direction.

Sure as shit, her name was right there on the screen. Right beneath...

Emma laughed. "Of course."

Right beneath, *'The Troubadour'*.

Terri turned the monitor back to its original position. "Is there anything else I can do to assist you?"

"No. Thank you, Terri."

"You're very welcome."

It wasn't until the elevator doors slid closed that it hit her. The only way her name could be listed on the room, was if Joe put it there. Her heart raced within her chest. The sensation wasn't an unpleasant one. As each floor ticked off on the panel, her anticipation grew, until her body literally vibrated.

Hallways spread out in each direction on the top floor. Emma went right, noting the room doors were much farther apart than normal. About halfway down, she reached her destination. A swipe of the card turned the little light green. A twist of the knob and she stepped into a room so large, it had to be a suite. The entertaining area, or whatever a person wanted to call it, went off to her left. An L-shaped couch sat near a slider leading to what she assumed was a private balcony. On the wall opposite hung a flat screen tv above a wet bar. There was also a dining area, a desk, and a very comfortable looking recliner. Everything in the spacious room had been done in neutrals, which was kind of a letdown, really. They could have at least added some color or contrast somewhere.

Voices drew her farther in, to an open door along the wall at her right. Emma wandered through. A luxurious king size bed sat dead center, a chaise lounge at the foot. Topped with a white duvet and piled high with pillows, the bed was meant to be the focal point of the room. But it was the couple at the far side of it that drew her gaze.

The man was standing with his back to Emma, jeans down around his thighs. He wasn't wearing anything else—except a smile it seemed—for there was a tinge of laughter in his voice as he said, "Happy to be of service."

She swallowed hard, trying to dislodge the rock in her throat. Joe. That was Joe's voice.

Which meant it was Joe standing bare-assed, pulling his pants up.

The strawberry-blonde at his side smiled. Dressed in jeans and a blouse, she looked at Joe like him standing half-naked while she was fully dressed was completely normal. Her hair was long, curly, and artfully piled atop her head. She was beautiful.

Pain. All encompassing, all consuming filled Emma up. Not the kind of pain like her headaches. This pain was surprisingly more crippling. For a moment, all she could do was stand there and absorb.

Emma must have made a noise, some sound to alert them to her presence, because the woman looked up and frowned. "I swear I closed the door."

Joe turned, hands still working his button fly closed. "Emma."

"You know her?" the woman asked.

Emma's gaze ping ponged between the two of them, finally landing on Joe. The first thing that popped into her head came out of her mouth. "You stupid sonofabitch."

She had no idea if she meant him or herself.

"It's not what it looks like," Joe argued.

"It looks like you were pulling your pants up over your naked ass."

"Okay, I was doing that."

The woman threw Joe a look of disbelief.

Yeah, well join the club, sweetheart. Emma couldn't believe it, either. "You're a real piece of work, you know that?" She turned and headed for the door as fast as her feet could carry her.

"Emma!"

Out of the suite and back in the hallway, she made straight for the elevator. She needed to get away from him. Fast. Before she did something stupid like break down and cry.

"Damn it, Emma, stop!"

"What was I thinking? I should have known better than to fall for a goddamn rock star."

A hand wrapped around her arm gently. Emma pulled against it, but to no avail.

Joe tugged her close, looking into her eyes. "How about you give me a chance to explain what you just walked in on?"

"How about you spit it out for Christ's sake?" the woman commented.

"Beth," Joe warned.

"I just think you should be aware of the fact that you're already drawing a crowd. This hotel is full up with people trying to catch a glimpse of the band. It would be wise to either get to explaining, or move your ass back to the suite."

Emma shook her head. "I'm leaving."

Joe sighed. With a heavy frown, he stared down at her. "The woman behind me is Beth, my wardrobe mistress."

"The *band's* wardrobe mistress," Beth corrected. "I swear to God, men are so stupid." She moved closer, stopping beside Emma. "Emma, may I call you Emma?" She didn't wait for a reply. "What you saw back there was nothing more than me hounding Joe here for his stage clothes. He ran out of the venue after the show like all the hound's in Hell were hot on his tail. Dumbass didn't even change first. I need to get everything cleaned and put away before we pull out of town in a few hours, so I tracked him down and ordered him to strip."

Emma looked her over. Sure enough, Beth was carrying a pair of jeans and a shirt. Both looked like they could be Joe's. As explanations went, it was a good one and seemed to fit the situation. The anger and hurt flowing through her veins just a second ago vanished.

"It's nothing that I don't do after every show," Beth continued. "I know it looked bad but, trust me, you don't have anything to worry about."

"I'm not her type."

Beth nodded. "True. I'm not into men."

Emma smothered the smile that threatened to tip up the corner of her mouth. Yeah, that news made her just a little too happy.

A chime sounded, signaling the arrival of the elevator. As the doors slid open Beth stepped in, settling her free hand on the side to hold them open. "So, now that that's out of the way, you have about two minutes to decide if you're staying or leaving. Because, seriously you two, that crowd is damn close."

Emma noticed them then, a group, hell a throng, of

young women coming down the opposite hall. They talked excitedly, heads tipped together, eyes wide and locked on the trio by the elevator. Their target became clear as they drew closer, close enough Emma clearly heard the frontrunner exclaim, "I told you it was him! That's Joe Campbell!"

Shit.

Joe didn't move. He didn't turn to see what was coming up on him; didn't even appear overly concerned about it. He did ease Emma even closer and level her with his bi-colored eyes. "Stay with me," he commanded, his voice a husky whisper.

For a moment, Emma forgot to breathe. Her heart was suddenly doing calisthenics. "Yes."

Without another word, Joe released her arm, settling his hand at the small of her back.

One of the women pulled out her cell phone and started taking pictures. Suddenly multiple phones were out.

Joe ignored them and started down the hallway leading to his room. He didn't speak until they were back inside the suite, door closed firmly at her back.

The room didn't seem anywhere near as large this time, not with Joe so close she could feel the heat coming off his body, catch the scent of his skin. He smelled pretty damn good, too, even if he had just finished a show. Warm and musky and male. Not at all unpleasant.

He took her carry-on from her and set it aside. Then slipped her satchel off her shoulder, and placed it on the floor. He stepped closer, flattening his hands against the door on either side of her head. "You're here."

His voice washed over her, deep, rough, and arousing in the most delicious way. Her toes curled in her shoes. Her breath caught in her lungs. It whooshed out of her a second later when he continued. "I left the venue to ring you. I didn't want an audience when I begged you to come to me." He was careful not to touch her, even as every inch of her, every part of her mind and body craved it. His heated gaze moved over her face. "You didn't answer. I feared I was too late."

"My phone is dead."

"You forgot to charge it again?"

"Don't I always?" Her nerves tingled and her heart stopped when his lips curved in a smile.

Leaning in so his mouth brushed her ear, he asked, "Why aren't you on your way to Scotland?"

The hot breath of air across her skin caused a shiver. "I hear English lads are much classier."

"Fuck, yeah, we are," he growled coarsely and she laughed.

A pulsing need hummed through her body. The need to trail her hands over every inch of him, then follow the same path with her mouth. But first...

Her hand shook as she reached for him, brushed the hair out of his eyes then cupped her palm on his cheek. "They gave me a key to your room. I told them my name and they gave me a key to your room. Why?"

"You're listed as my guest," he said simply. "Have been since—"

His words fell away as Emma stroked her thumb over his lips. His breathing grew erratic.

"Since when?" she encouraged.

"A while now. I always hoped you would find me again. I can't get you out of my head."

The words shot a shiver through her.

This close to him, she could make out the fine details of

his Chinese dragon tattoo. It really was exquisite. But it was the body beneath the art she was most interested in. Unable to resist any longer, she ran her free hand down the front of his chest. From his shoulder to his stomach, then back up again. Everywhere she touched he was warm, soft skin over taut muscle. It was intoxicating.

She slid her hand lower, over the waistband of the jeans barely staying on his hips, and pressed her palm to the bulge of his erection. His cock jumped. Loving the reaction, she worked her hand up and down the length of him, outlining every glorious inch.

"Emma."

She was instantly wet.

His hard gaze swept down her body just before he pressed in close, pinning her against the door. One hand holding her head, the other slid down her spine, to settle over her ass cheek, squeezing and caressing, pulling her hard against his erection. Then his mouth covered hers, his tongue stroked her bottom lip and pushed inside. There was nothing teasing about his kiss. It was hard, rough, and overpowering. She whimpered into his mouth.

Desperate to get closer, Emma reached for the hem of her shirt and tugged it off. Her bra came next, landing on the floor at their feet. She didn't have much up top, but it was enough to fill his palm as his hand left her ass to close over her breast.

"God, yes," he mumbled, his thumb slowly rubbing back and forth across her nipple.

A shuddery breath escaped her.

He dove back in. His lips met hers over and over in a kiss that had her stomach tumbling. She'd missed the taste of him and, wanting more, she caught his tongue between her teeth, and bit down lightly. His fingers clenched in her hair. Tugging her head back, he kissed her deeper as a groan rumbled from his throat. The sound shot through her, electrifying every cell in her body.

As good as his mouth felt against hers, it felt a hundred times better fastened on her nipple. She breathed his name on a helpless whimper then arched her back, pressing her more firmly against his mouth as he licked and sucked her flesh. Her other breast got the same treatment until her head fell back against the door with a thud and her knees went weak.

His mouth skimmed lower, kissing her ribs, her stomach. His beard brushed her skin, the touch almost as arousing as his mouth. He slipped his hands inside her pants and, with his palms brushing over her ass, stripped her jeans down her legs. She stepped out of them, leaving her in nothing but her panties.

In her most intimate fantasies, and there were quite a few that featured Joe, she'd never imagined this one. It was usually her on the floor and him standing mostly naked before her.

He started a trail of kisses up her thigh, stopping to give the highly sensitive spot where leg met torso a lick before pressing his mouth to her fabric-covered mound. Already half gone, she panted his name.

"Turn around, Sunshine."

Blood rushed through her veins and thundered in her ears. "What?"

"Turn."

Emma did as he asked, resting her forearms against the door. With no idea what he had planned for her, she braced for anything. She expected the stroke of his fingers across her flesh. Instead, he gave her his mouth.

"You are so damn pretty," he breathed, then sank his teeth into the globe of her ass. Pain mixed with pleasure, and she sucked a desperate breath and whimpered. It turned to a groan as his tongue soothed tender flesh.

She was wearing the same style panties as last night, the kind that left the lower half of her cheeks exposed. By the words of appreciation Joe continued to whisper, he liked what he saw. Her breathing grew unsteady, ragged, making her breasts brush the door with every breath she gulped. She startled when his hand replaced his mouth, fingertips caressing as his palm molded her shape. "So damn pretty."

He rose to his feet, his right hand smoothing up her side to palm her breast. The move brought him closer. His erection pressed against the cleft of her ass and a groan ripped from between her lips.

"I haven't been able to get your knickers out of my head." The sound of his breathing fell around her. A tremor played in his voice. "Do you know how many times I've had a wank in the shower over them?"

Dear God.

"In the middle of sound check, the image of your ass slipped into my head and I was hard as a spike. I had to take a break for a tug. Thankfully, all I need to get off is to imagine you on your knees, lips around my cock as you take me to the back of your throat and suck me dry."

The cock he spoke of pulsed. The hand resting on her ass slid higher, over her hip and down, teasing over the front of her soaking wet panties. She squeezed her thighs together and shuddered, tilting her pelvis in an attempt to get him closer to where she needed him most.

"Tell me," he whispered. "Tell me what you want."

"Touch me."

"I am touching you, Sunshine. And you feel fucking amazing." His finger was back, teasing her with the briefest flick before slipping away.

"Joe!"

"I'm thinking we should test your theory…see if my voice really is all you need."

"Don't you fucking dare."

His laughter vibrated through her. The fingers slipped beneath the elastic waist of her panties and slid into her pubic hair. He teased and taunted her for a moment, then pressed the heel of his hand against her clit.

Deep inside she was shaking. A shuddery breath escaped her. "You," she gasped. "Inside me. Now."

"My fingers?" he asked, then slipped two deep inside her. "Or my cock?"

She didn't care, didn't have enough in her to care. His naughty mouth had done its job and her orgasm was there, right there, just waiting to break free. All she needed was a little more pressure.

She bucked her hips, forcing his fingers even deeper. The room spun as hammering need filled her. Like a woman crazed, she rocked back and forth, riding his hand. Her breathing hiccupped. Her body tightened. Light and dark exploded inside her and her pussy clenched.

Desperate for his mouth, Emma reached back, fisted her hand in his hair and used her hold to bring his face to hers. She sucked his tongue into her mouth as greed drove her hips to a frenzied pace. Almost there, she was almost… Spots swam in front of her eyes and her body bucked as she exploded. The climax ripped through her, every muscle inside her pulling tight. Her body throbbed. Her blood roared in her ears.

Joe continued to kiss her, slowly, softly, nothing like the feverish passion of a few moments ago. Aftershocks pulsed every few seconds, squeezing against his fingers. Her grip on his hair went lax as the pleasure faded.

"Fuck, you are sweet," he muttered against her lips and she released an embarrassed laugh. Then he slipped his hand from her panties and into his mouth and the feeling fled. The sharp bite of arousal returned, shocking her even more than the site of him licking his fingers clean.

She wondered what she tasted like. Whatever it was, he was enjoying it. Turning to face him, she took hold of his wrist, and guiding his fingers to her mouth, found out for herself. "Mm, I taste good on your skin."

Immediately his eyes homed in on her mouth. His nostrils flared, his body went taut. "Fucking great if you ask me," he said, his voice low and fierce. Then he picked her off her feet and carried her to the bedroom.

April 11

Today was the second time I spoke with Joe on the phone and I still struggle to wrap my mind around it. Why me? Out of all the women he has met in his life, what is it about me that keeps him coming back? I wish I knew the answer, but in the end it doesn't matter. Because he does keep coming back to me, and talking to him brings a joy like I haven't experienced in so very long. After years of always worrying about tomorrow, I am finally satisfied to just live in today.

Okay, so the fact that today I got to hear Joe's voice helped. Today's conversation wasn't much different from our last. Somehow, no matter how innocent they begin, our talks turn sexual. Call it pent up frustration or a natural part of his personality, whatever it is, it takes my breath away. Joe is damn good at dirty talk. Good enough to have me squirming. And when he says my name? My brain shuts off. God, if he ever talked to me like that in the flesh… I shiver just thinking about it. I'd most likely lose my damn mind.

Seven days. It's amazing how much can change in such a short amount of time. A week ago I was grieving the loss of a man I'd only just found. Feeling sad and alone and sorry for myself. Today I'm feeling content, a little bit horny, and a lot less lonely. All because of one man. One voice. And a connection I can't explain.

Number of days since I decided to live: 51
Number of days since I met Joe: 8
Current level of panic: 5/10

EIGHT

J OE HOPED LIKE hell he didn't drop Emma before they got to the bed. Between kissing her and sliding his hands over her ass, it was close. She wasn't making it any easier on him, either. The one time he left her mouth long enough to keep from tripping over the chaise, she leaned in and bit his lower lip. Growling, his dipped his head and kissed her again.

At the side of the bed, he slowly let her slide down his body. She kept going until she sat on the edge of the mattress. A quick swipe of her hand pushed the pillows to the floor then she was working on the button fly of his jeans.

He pushed her hands aside. "Not yet, Sunshine." No, first he was going to peel her panties off and look his fill. Then he was going to part her thighs, bury his face in her curls and get a proper taste of her. He was starving for another taste of her. "Lie back."

Her eyes went glossy with arousal as she lowered her back to the bed.

He hooked his fingers in the material at her hips, sliding her panties down and off before parting her legs. Fuck, she was beautiful. Pale blonde curls covered her mound, and he could see moisture gleaming there. She didn't try to hide herself from his eyes, just lay back. "Don't move."

Knowing once he had his taste of her there would be no

slowing down, Joe left her long enough to dart into the bathroom. When he came out, he tossed the string of condoms onto the bed and sank to his knees before her.

Cupping her ass, he pulled her closer to the edge and lowered his face until his mouth hovered just above her folds. Her scent enveloped him. He breathed it in with a groan.

She wiggled, trying to get closer.

He held her in place.

"What are you waiting for?" she whispered, settling her hand on his head.

Although he longed for her flavor on his tongue, he waited, making sure she felt his every breath against her core. Her legs shifted and her hips left the bed. The fingers in his hair fisted. When her body began to tremble uncontrollably, he knew she was ready. Pressing his face closer to her heat, he licked her.

Satisfaction surged through him when her back arched off the bed and a whimper slipped from between her lips. Sweet, she was so sweet. He groaned as he repeated the action, covering her clit with his tongue, and slipping his middle finger inside of her. She whimpered again, but he didn't stop. He kissed her, flicking his tongue against her clit in time with the stroke of his finger. When she began to thrash, he added another finger.

Deep, slow strokes turned faster and harder as he worked her closer and closer to orgasm. Her body went taut, her thighs pressed tightly against his shoulders, and when he knew he had her right on the edge, he lightly clamped his teeth down on her clit.

A scream worked its way up the back of her throat and broke loose as the orgasm hit her. Her stomach dipped, the muscles inside her contracted and clenched.

Blood pounded in his cock, need screamed inside of him. His hands shook as he shucked his jeans and ripped a condom off the strip. Somehow he managed to roll it on without exploding, then crawled up the bed, pulling her with him. Wrapping an arm around her waist, he braced himself on his other elbow near her head. He pushed his fingers into her hair, the strands like silk against his palm as he settled the tip of his cock against her entrance.

Face turned to the side and eyes closed, she didn't move. Beneath him, her body pulsed.

He pressed his lips against her cheek and groaned. "Put your legs around me and hold on."

Her legs circled his hips, the shift in position opening her wider and allowing him to dip inside. Through the thin barrier of the rubber he could feel her heat. It called to him, promising release. He pushed against her entrance and her nails dug into his shoulders. Fuck, she was tight. He retreated, then pressed in again, this time sinking a little farther. She arched against him, propping her heels on his ass, urging him deeper. As she closed around him, slick and hot, he surged forward, burying himself to the hilt.

Emma's eyes opened, her gaze locked on his face. Sliding a hand into his hair, she pulled his head down and pressed her mouth to his. Held him there while she kissed him like she was starving for him.

He pushed and retreated. Pushed deeper. Her nipples rubbed against his chest, her pussy tightened around his cock. She tore her lips away from his and stared up at him. "Harder."

That was it. That was all it took for his brain to shut off and his body to take over. He took her hard, took her deep.

He caught her right leg behind the knee and pulled it up. Opening his line of sight so he could watch himself slip in and out of her. Harder and faster he drove, his climax bearing down on him. He was like a man possessed. Some part of his brain recognized it, even as he was helpless to do anything about it. His frenzied strokes pushed her body up the bed until she pressed her palms against the headboard to hold them in place.

He dropped his head into her neck and inhaled her. His balls pulled tight. Fuck, he didn't want to go without her.

"Emma," he growled, and that was all it took. She arched against him, crying out as her pussy clenched and tightened around him. His cock jerked, his balls pulled tighter and he lost himself to her, shuddering and shaking as he climaxed.

It took a few minutes for Joe's breathing to return to normal. He lifted his head and looked down at the woman he was still buried inside. Her eyes were closed, head tipped slightly away from his. She wore a soft smile on her face, a flush of color on her creamy, pale skin, and a hint of whisker burn on the tops of her breasts. She took his breath away. "Em?"

Hands still pressed against the headboard, she stretched, flexing every muscle in her body, including the ones deep inside her. "Mm. I can say for certain that your sex growl is way hotter than your stage growl."

He choked a laugh. "Good to know."

Turning her head, she locked her turquoise eyes on him. "I'm never going to be able to watch you perform again without recalling that growl as you came inside me."

Christ, how was he supposed to resist her? "Do you always say what you're thinking?"

Her hands came down to frame his face and she kissed him softly. "Usually, yes. I don't have much of a filter."

He liked that about her. He also liked the way she was touching him, tracing around his eyes, down his cheeks, like she was memorizing the shape of his face. She stuck the tip of her finger into the hair below his bottom lip, trailing her nail lightly back and forth. Then she arched up and nipped the same spot.

His cock stirred back to life. His hips jerked reflexively, pushing deeper, then he froze. *Shit.* "Condom."

"What?"

She was nibbling his lips, doing her best to keep him close. Her internal muscles tightened as he began to withdraw. *Sweet hell.* "Sunshine."

"Where are you going?"

Out of my damn mind. "Give me a minute. I have to dispose of the condom."

When he came back, he found her sitting up, her legs crossed in front of her, a satisfied smile on her face. Her gaze followed him as he crossed the room, trailing over his body from head to toes before stopping on his groin. Enjoying the attention, his cock stood up and said hello.

Heat flared in her eyes. Her tongue danced across her bottom lip. "Come here," she whispered, shifting to her knees. "I want to kiss you."

She didn't mean his mouth.

"No." Joe wasn't sure who was more surprised by the denial that passed his lips, him or Emma. His footing stumbled and he stopped just out of her reach. Every cell in his body cried out for him to step closer and let her have her way. Just the thought of her hot, wet mouth taking him deep was enough to make him beg. But she deserved better.

He held out his hand, fingers beckoning. "Come with me."

"Where?" Her wanting to know didn't keep her from crawling to the edge of the bed and placing her hand in his.

He pulled her in, then stopped with his lips a whisper from hers. He absorbed the way her breath caught, the way his own did the same. He'd wanted her since the first time he saw her, standing motionless in the audience, blue eyes watching him. The passing of time hadn't diminished the wanting. Neither did having just been balls deep inside of her. He couldn't get enough. "Shower."

"You want to shower with me?"

"God, yes." Her fingers danced across his flesh, a light touch on his chest, his pecs. When she raked her fingernails across his stomach, he lost his concentration. "Emma."

"Yes?"

What the hell had he been saying? "I spent ninety minutes onstage beneath the lights. Do you have any idea how goddamn hot it is up there?" Unable to stand the torture, he covered her wandering hand with his own. "Listen, I may not have had enough control to stop myself from taking you the first time, but I damn well have enough not to do it a second time. Not without showering first."

A slow smile curved her lips. "Are you afraid you smell bad?"

"I know I do."

"I don't think so." Pressing her face into his neck she inhaled, her voice dropping to a whisper. "I love the way you smell: male and earthy."

He barked a short laugh. "Earthy, huh? I guess that's one way to put it."

Her mouth was on the move, licking and sucking her

way to his pec. Her tongue on his nipple spurred him into action. Cupping her ass, he lifted her off her feet, groaning as her legs came around him instantly, pressing her wetness against his lower abdomen.

"You're really into this macho show of—"

Her words ended in a gasp when he danced his fingers down her crease and kept going, using them to open the lips of her pussy then circle her clit. He rubbed against her, each circle making her breath more and more ragged. When he finally slid his fingers inside, she sighed.

"What were you saying?"

"I…oh…there, right there."

"You like that?"

She didn't have to answer, the slick wetness coating his fingers said it all. So did the way she melted against him. Their lips were all but touching and, unable to resist, he leaned in, covered her mouth with his. She opened for him, slipping her hand to the back of his head and sliding her tongue against his. And like every time he kissed her, an engulfing heat swept through him.

"Shower or bed?" she whispered against his lips, before coming at him from a different angle.

He couldn't think past the way she was mimicking the thrust of his fingers with her tongue. Tearing his mouth away, Joe blinked her face into focus. "Huh?"

"Shower or bed? I don't care which it is, but for the love of all that is holy, quit teasing me and choose."

He started walking. Straight into the bathroom where he flicked on the water without setting her down, then tipped his head toward the counter. "There."

She looked down and a smile played across her lips. "The counter works for me."

Christ, she'd be the death of him. "I meant the box of condoms. Grab one."

For someone who'd just told him to stop teasing, she sure did take her own sweet time pulling a string from the box. When the tip of her tongue poked out from between her lips like she was thinking hard on which one to tear off first, Joe stepped in the shower and beneath the spray.

She gasped, then started climbing his body to get away from the water. "Jesus! It's freezing!"

Laughing, he tightened his grip on her, which was difficult to do with her wet and squirming. "Hold still."

She thumped his shoulders with her fists. The string of condoms still in her hand flew up, slapping the side of his face. "Turn around! I swear to God, Joe, if you don't turn—"

He turned, his laughter dying as the water poured onto his head and back. *Shit.* "It's not that cold," he lied.

"Sure." Her tone of voice told him she knew he was full of shit. "Put me down macho man, it's all yours."

The minute her feet hit the ground, she shifted to the far side of the tub, curling into as small a ball as possible to remain out of the spray.

He smiled, squirted shampoo into his hand then washed his hair and face. Under no circumstances would he give her the satisfaction of shivering.

"You know," she said, laughter in her voice. "You might be more convincing if there wasn't any...shrinkage."

"There isn't."

She laughed aloud.

He grinned despite himself. "If you're so concerned about my so-called shrinkage, why don't you come over here and help reverse the situation?"

Working shower gel into a lather, he soaped his shoulders and pecs, his abdomen, then lower. Her eyes followed his movements. Her nipples hardened into two tight peaks.

"Emma?"

She didn't move.

Wrapping his hand around his cock, he stroked from base to tip once, twice, then again as he watched her every reaction. A flush covered her chest, just below her key necklace. Her breath came faster.

Straightening, she took a step in his direction. "Looks like you're doing fine all by yourself."

No matter how arousing it was to have her watch, this wasn't somewhere he wanted to go alone. Lucky for him, she was beginning to crack. Her tongue swiped across her lips. A few more strokes of his hand and she was trembling.

Suddenly she was there, adjusting the temperature of the water with one hand as the other covered his hand on his cock. She pressed her lips to his chest, dragging her tongue over his nipple as she followed his lead, learning his pace. He let her take control, groaning as her hand replaced his, squeezing, stroking.

"Is this what you want?" she whispered, then dropped to her knees and looked up at him through her lashes. "Is this what you think about while you—what did you call it— have a wank?"

"Yes." He cleared his throat when his voice began to fade. "You're what I think about."

The slow slice of her mouth over his cock was better than any fantasy. She sucked and kissed, working her mouth up and down his length as her hand caressed his balls. Pleasure shot straight up his spine. His hands shook.

In less than three minutes she had him ready to beg.

"Fuck, Sunshine...your mouth....more..."

Bloody hell. She not only has me begging, I'm stuttering.

She hummed, sending flashes to senses already overloaded. She curled her fingers around him at the base, stroking, pumping, as her mouth continued to work his tip. Heavy breathing filled his ears and he didn't know if it came from him or her. He didn't fucking care.

"Emma." He couldn't last much longer and he wanted to be in her pussy when he came. Still giving him the more he'd begged for, she drew him in until she deep-throated him. He slammed his hand against the wall as his knees started to buckle. "Stop," he whispered. "*Emma.*"

Snagging her beneath the arms, he hauled her to her feet. Thank Christ, she let go of the important bits as he did. They faced off, both of them gasping like they'd just run a marathon.

Joe shook his head. "Not in your mouth. Not this time."

"Okay."

"Condom."

She looked around, then squatted at his feet. He closed his eyes and held his breath, sending up a silent prayer that she was going for the condoms. He teetered on the edge. If she touched him, he would snap.

"Here," she whispered.

She held the strip of condoms, water dripping off the foil wrapper. With no way to hide the tremble in his hand, he scooped them up, tore one off and dropped the rest. Rolling the rubber over his cock caused the rigid flesh to jerk and he hissed a breath. His self-control shattered.

With an animalistic growl, he dropped his hands to her hips and spun her to face the wall. He caught one of her wrists, and pinned it above her head, then the other, shackling them in place with one hand. Then he pressed his knee between her thighs, forcing her to spread her legs.

"I'm sorry," he whispered, as he dipped his knees and used his free hand to line the head of his shaft even with her core. "I won't last if you touch me." He pushed inside, working past her initial tightness. "Fuck, you're so wet...so soft...let me in."

She hissed, shoving her ass back against him, allowing him greater penetration.

"That's it...relax."

"Can't," she gasped. "Going to come."

Her pussy convulsed around his cock and he drove deep, crowding her against the wall. He withdrew and did it again.

"More," she commanded. "Give me more."

"Fuck yes."

He dipped his knees lower, lifted her hips higher and found an angle that made her gasp. He held her tightly and hammered into her, driven by his own urgency. He thrust harder and harder until the sound of their flesh slapping filled the room. Until her body shuddered and shook, her pussy clenched, and she cried out.

His own orgasm bore down on him and, with one last thrust, he gave himself up to it. Exhausted and spent, he collapsed against her.

This time it took longer to get his heartrate under control. He wasn't even close when she spoke. "Joe?"

"Mm?"

"You can put me down now."

He opened his eyes and looked first to where his hands continued to hold her hips, then to where her feet dangled a few centimeters in the air. "Right. No problem." He pulled out, then settled her, leaving his hands on her until he knew she had her balance. Once she did, he pressed his back against the cool tile next to her, and pulled her into his side. He switched off the shower.

She placed her head against his pec and sighed. "You may have to carry me to bed."

"Sorry, Sunshine, I'm not sure my legs will hold me up much longer."

She was leaning more and more against his side, as if all her bones had melted. He knew the feeling. "Where's your bodyguard? I bet he could help."

"You seriously want me to call Gare to help us back to bed?"

"I'd call nine-one-one but my phone is dead."

He chuckled. "It's also farther away than the bed." He closed his eyes, trying to recall the last time he'd felt this at peace. He was calm, centered, his mind focused on nothing more than the soft press of her body against his and the question of how he was going to make it to the bed without falling flat on his face.

"Good point." She stirred, shifting out of his hold. "All right, let's do this. I could use a nap."

He cracked an eye open and checked out her ass as she stepped from the tub. He liked what he saw. "My mark looks good on you."

"What?" Standing at the sink, she faced him, her eyebrow raised in question. Then she followed his line of sight and brushed her thumb over the imprint of his teeth.

"Sorry about that," he mumbled, removing the condom. Tying the end, he disposed of it and stepped out of the shower.

She handed him a tissue. "No you're not."

"Not really, no." Pulling her close, he pressed a quick kiss to her lips, smoothing his hand down her back to rub the spot. "I may have gotten a bit carried away."

"Ya think?"

"You obviously don't understand the sweet temptation that is you." How could she, when even he didn't? Sure, she was beautiful. She had a smile that could brighten his any mood and a body that brought him to his knees. But none of that explained this relentless hunger for her. He couldn't fucking get enough of her. Not once tonight had he thought about losing himself in the fog of alcohol. Instead, all he thought about was losing himself in her. Even now his cock was rising to the occasion.

She felt it, too, for she pressed her pelvis against him, tearing a groan from the back of his throat. God, he needed another taste. Unable to resist, he kissed her. Not simmering hot and full of passion this time, but slow and soft. He couldn't deny the surge of satisfaction that swelled as she melted against him.

He wasn't sure how long he'd been kissing her when they came up for air.

She swayed a little as she stared at his mouth. "It must be all the vocal exercises."

"What?"

"You're really skilled with that tongue."

Joe threw his head back and laughed. Christ, she was something. "How long can you stay with me?"

She ran her thumb across his bottom lip, then pushed it into his mouth. "How long do you want me?"

Instead of an answer, he scooped her into his arms and carried her to the bed. It was going to be a long, long time before he was ready to let her go.

EMMA CLOSED HER eyes and sighed, the lazy circles Joe was tracing on the base of her spine enough to tempt her to sleep. Joe was on his back, his arm thrown over his eyes. She was on her stomach, using his right ankle as her chin rest. They were sideways in his bed, naked and sated.

She shifted, groaning as muscles not used to lovemaking protested. It had been a long time for her, and never had it been like it was with Joe. Propping herself on her elbow, she looked up at him, wondering why he got enough sheet to cover his essentials, while she wasn't allowed any.

Cool air blew from the ceiling above them, causing her to shiver. "Joe?"

"Mm?"

"Where are the blankets?"

Still drawing circles on her back, he lifted his other arm and motioned over his head. "Floor."

On the opposite side of the bed.

Too tired to move, Emma decided it wasn't worth the effort. Sleep pulled at her. She was just beginning to drift off when someone pounded on the wall outside the bedroom.

"Time to go," a male voice called out. "You decent?"

"I am," Joe replied. "But Emma—"

Gary walked into the room.

Emma scrambled off the bed and to the floor. Shit, she still didn't have anything to cover herself with. Reaching up, she snaked the sheet off Joe and wrapped it around her body.

"Okay, now I'm not, but Emma is."

Gary just stood there, a small smile on his face. Apparently, the state of Joe's undress was something those around him were used to as Beth hadn't reacted to it, either.

Joe tossed his arm back over his eyes. "Give us twenty, Gare."

"You've got ten."

"Shit. It'll have to do." And just as easy as you please, Joe fell asleep.

Emma knew, because a soft snore slipped from his lips. Giving in to the temptation, she trailed her gaze over him. Even in sleep he was larger than life—built and beautiful. He stole her breath. She wanted to crawl back in the bed next to him, rest her head on his shoulder and curl into his heat.

Blinking away the thought, she returned her gaze to Gary.

His smile widened, giving her another tease of the dimple she'd first glimpsed weeks ago. Then he reached into the thigh pocket of his military-style black pants and pulled out a pint of chocolate milk, which he tossed at her.

Emma caught it and returned his smile. "You knew I was here."

He tipped his head.

"Let me guess—"

"Beth," he supplied. "She's made certain everyone has learned of your arrival."

"Great." Cracking the top on the milk, she took a drink. "So it's like high school all over again. Where everyone gossips about everyone else's secrets."

"It can be difficult to keep secrets when you're stuck together 24/7 for eighteen months."

"Wow, is that how long you've all been touring?"

"This time, yes."

She couldn't imagine. Day after day, show after show,

the buses, the crowds. It had to get tedious. After a while, wouldn't they all begin hating each other?

"It's not about secrets."

"What?"

"The news of your arrival spreading like wildfire through the members of the band and crew?" Without taking his eyes off her, Gary tipped his head toward the bed. "It's about him."

"Joe?"

"He's not drunk, he's not being an unbearable ass." Gary's voice softened a bit, telling her without words that he cared for Joe. "You calm his demons."

Emma sat on the edge of the bed near Joe's feet, tucking the sheet tighter around her breasts. "I don't know how," she admitted.

"It doesn't matter how, just that you do. Thank you for…being here." Gary's gaze glanced off Joe, still snoring on the bed. He shook his head. "Twenty minutes," he said, then walked out of the room.

April 17

I've never been good at letting go. Honestly, I've not made that many connections in life, so learning to deal with the loss of those I care about isn't something I have much experience with. Growing up, I was the odd kid – the one parents didn't want their child to hang around. I was too loud, too hyper and way, way too good at blurting out the first thought that popped into my head.

The last one I've never been able to shake, which is why I don't connect easily. Most people don't like being a party to your thoughts. I've been called a bitch more times than I can count. But I don't apologize for who I am. Why should I? I'd rather be someone's shot of whiskey than everyone's cup of tea.

I suppose that is why my pain is so great. We connected, Joe and I. He didn't seem to mind my bluntness. I threw it in his face the first night we met and instead of driving him away, it brought him closer. In return, he brought me closer. Joe drew me into his life and I was happy there. I looked forward to the phone calls that lasted for hours. The moments we were so excited we talked over each other as well as those when we would lapse into silence; not feel the need to fill the space just…be together.

Now I have to let him go. I always knew one day what we had would be gone. Not because I'm sick. No, Joe growing tired of me and moving on was bound to happen long before my illness played into it. I thought he would drift away slowly, the time between calls would grow longer and longer and one day it would be over. I was prepared for that. What I wasn't prepared for was losing him to the bottle.

Which is utterly ridiculous since I've known about his love of alcohol for as long as I've known Joe. I was naïve to think a few phone calls could keep him from falling back on old patterns and behavior. I know that. But knowing it didn't keep me from being blindsided. I was completely unprepared for angry Joe, drunk Joe, enjoying the groupies and the after party Joe. Maybe that Joe has been here all along, but he never showed him to me. Not until tonight.

I'm so angry I'm shaking. I don't know if it's with him or myself.

That's not true, I do know. I'm angry with him. Life is precious. How can he just throw his away like this? I can't watch him do it, I just can't. God, the pain of putting that on paper is even worse than the pain of giving voice to it. How can that be? Maybe it's just beginning to sink in. I told Joe good-bye and now…now I have to learn to let him go.

If only I knew how.

Number of days since I decided to live: 57
Number of days since I met Joe: 14
Current level of panic: 7/10

NINE

April 20

AN HOUR AFTER Gary delivered his twenty-minute warning, Emma found herself in the hotel freight elevator. Joe was on her left, his hand at her back, beneath her shirt. Having slept the entire time, he was still a bit groggy and she was certain the moment he was prone, he'd once again be out like a light. On her right Gary looked the exact opposite: alert, aware of his surroundings, and ready to take on whatever the hell they were sneaking out the back door of the hotel to avoid.

"It's two-thirty in the morning, you know," Emma said to neither man in particular. "Isn't this a bit of overkill?"

No comment. Obviously she was talking to herself.

"You could have pulled those big black buses up to the front entrance and no one would notice."

Again nothing.

She sighed and did her best to breathe through her mouth. It wasn't that she minded sneaking out the back of a hotel so much as the elevator smelled. She couldn't quite place it; some sort of spicy food or maybe it was strong cheese? Either way it wasn't pleasant. Not when combined with the fact it was hotter than Hell's waiting room in there.

Feeling a bit queasy, she stepped forward, shifting closer to the elevator doors as they neared the first floor. She had to get out of here. Mechanical boxes with no view of the outside world were bad enough when they didn't stink. Too enclosed, too locked up, too tight a space. It all started with her cancer treatments—day after day, hour after hour trapped in a windowless room of the hospital while her chemo was administered—and culminated in a dream of being buried alive. *Trapped. Locked in a dark, dank coffin with no way out.* Just the memory of that dream was enough to make her sweat, cause her stomach to turn over.

Like it was churning now.

Shit.

It wasn't that she was claustrophobic, the size of the space wasn't always an issue. Whether or not she could see outside was. She had to be able to see outside. Had to.

The moment the doors began to open, she slipped out, sucking untainted air into her lungs. She skidded to a stop, as two young women got up close and personal.

"Is he in there?"

"We didn't miss him, did we?"

Gary stepped out behind her and Emma pictured his wide shoulders taking up the space between the open doors. "Who are you looking for?" she asked, already knowing what their answer would be. *Guess I was wrong about no one noticing the band's departure.*

"Joe."

"The lead singer of Blind Man's Alibi."

Did these two always talk at the same time? As usual, Emma said the first thing that came to mind. "Joe Campbell, right? I hear he decided the lobby was safer. If you hurry, you can still catch him."

She waited, ignoring the unease in the center of her gut, and leaned against the wall opposite the elevator as soon as the two ran off. When neither Gary nor Joe exited the elevator, she looked up. Sure enough, Gary stood centered between the open doors, the barest of smiles on his face.

Emma sighed. "Don't say it."

"Say what?" Gary asked all innocent-like.

"I told you so."

"That's not at all what I was going to say." He glanced up and down the hall, then stepped out, Joe right behind him.

Joe slipped an arm around her, tugging her close enough to kiss her temple. "Quick thinking."

"*That* is what I was going to say."

Emma smiled. "It doesn't take much to distract a rabid fan."

Joe snorted.

Gary raised a brow. "You'd be surprised."

Then they were walking again. Down the hall and to the left, then right, another left. How did Gary find his way around these places? She'd just opened her mouth to ask when they pushed outside, right next to two tour buses sitting nose to rump, their diesel engines idling. The two black beasts shone in the moonlight and she wondered exactly what they looked like, since she'd never seen them in daylight.

Like the first time she'd laid eyes on the buses, Joe walked to the front one and boarded. He switched the duffle he carried to his right hand, then reached out his left, a broad smile on his face. "Come along, Sunshine."

Instead of taking his hand, Emma handed him her carry-on luggage. Joe's smile broadened. She followed him past the driver, whom she nodded at, and into the living space. Emma didn't know what she'd expected, but what she stepped into was gorgeous.

The front of the bus was a combination lounge and kitchen. Beneath the large window on the right wall was a black sofa—leather of course, since he seemed to have a penchant for it—with built-in drawers beneath. At one end a small table was placed; the other left open. Next to that was a full size refrigerator surrounded by mahogany cabinets. Mahogany! On a tour bus.

On the left were more cabinets, the lowers topped with black granite. There was also a stove, microwave, one of those single serve coffee makers, and the couch's smaller twin. Settled atop the twin, watching a flat screen on the end wall nearest the entrance, was Kirk. He gave her a wave. Emma waved back.

Joe shifted both bags to his left hand, using his right to point things out to her. "So, this is the bus. As you can see, this is the front lounge and kitchen. The cabinets are fully stocked but if there's something special you want, just tell Gare or Marvin."

She hadn't met Marvin yet so that was going to be a bit difficult.

"Just past the kitchen here is the front bath, nothing much to see there. But right here is where the day sheet is posted."

"The day sheet?" She stepped closer to what he was pointing at—a printed sheet of paper that showed things like 'Load In – 1 p.m.' and 'Doors Open – 7 p.m.'. It even stated the time the bus was to pull out of town. Too bad they'd missed that one by a long shot.

As if reading her mind, Joe continued. "We refer to it as the 'sheet of lies' because around here things change pretty quickly so it's normally wrong."

They headed farther into the bus, through a narrow hall with three curtains stacked on either side of them. Emma wondered about them as Joe kept up with the tour. "We have full internet and satellite television at all times, so if there's something you need to get done or want to watch, you can."

"Is it password protected?"

"Gary will make sure you get it."

She glanced over her shoulder, expecting to find Gary shadowing them as always, and instead spotted him back in the front lounge chatting with Kirk.

Joe walked through an open doorway and into the room at the back. Another lounge, complete with a curved black built in couch and sleek coffee table. Floor to ceiling mahogany cabinets lined the left side of the room, with one lone cabinet on the right wall where five guitars hung behind glass doors.

"This is the back lounge," he explained unnecessarily as he placed their luggage on the couch. "There's also a second bath there."

Emma stuck her head inside the room he pointed out. "Seriously?"

"What? It's a bath with a shower."

"A travertine shower."

He shrugged. "We spend a lot of time on the buses. Comfort is essential."

True enough.

He was standing close, which seemed to be the norm if they were in a room together, and she couldn't resist pushing his hair out of his eyes. How could he stand it hanging in his face all the time? "Where do you sleep?"

He brushed past her, grabbing her hand as he did, guiding her back into the hall. At the curtains, he stopped. "These are the bunks. Mine, Gare's and Kirk's." He pointed to two spots on the wall to her right and one on the left. Then he pulled open the curtain just below the bunk he'd identified as his own. "You can have this one."

A hole in the wall. Joe wanted her to sleep in a hole in the wall. A three-sided box with a mattress and pillow, small enough she had to wonder how Gary even fit in one. Dark wood, dark curtain, dark linens...darkness.

No light.

No window.

No escape.

"No," she whispered.

He took in her expression. "Emma?"

Cold sweat trickled down her spine. The tremble started in her knees then worked its way up to her stomach, her shoulders, and down her arms. Dear God, it was tiny. Too small, too dark and way, way too much like...

Emma shook her head, pushing the thought away. There had to be a real bed in this place. There was no way she could climb in that space and relax. Hell, she couldn't even *look* at that space and relax. She pulled her hand from his, edging toward the front lounge.

"Emma." Joe said softly.

Too softly. Damn it, she couldn't lose her shit in front of him.

Too late.

Her breaths came too fast. There was nothing she could do to level them out.

His fingers circled her wrist. His eyes gentled. "Em."

With a shake of her head, she took a step just as the bus pulled away from the hotel with a lurch. Knocked off balance, she reached out for a handhold, only to be tugged into his arms. Automatically her hands shot out to slow her forward momentum. As they came into contact with his chest, her fingers involuntarily fisted in his shirt.

"I can't," she said with a shudder. "I'll...I have work to do." It was a lie, but she'd find something to do. Just as long as no one made her climb into that coffin in the wall. "I'll sit in the front lounge."

"Sunshine, are you claustrophobic?"

She couldn't look at him, couldn't let him see the irrational fear coursing through her veins. The risk of coming unglued was too great. Focusing on her white-knuckle grip on his shirt, she shook her head.

His big hand cupped the nape of her neck. "Look at me."

While her heart was racing with adrenaline, his was an even, steady beat beneath her hands. He was strong, solid and, as she looked into his face, she wished she could absorb some of that strength.

"Everything okay back there?" Gary called.

"No worries." Joe never took his eyes off her, softening his voice before he spoke again. "Breathe. Breathe with me, Em." He drew in a slow, deep breath that she copied. "Keep breathing."

"I can't...Joe—"

"Just breathe."

She was trying to. A slow breath in, even slower exhale. A shiver.

His hand slid to her back, delivering long, leisurely strokes that set the rhythm for her breaths. "Christ, you were edgy in the elevator and I thought it was just the temperature." Emma closed her eyes as his lips pressed against her temple. "You should have said something."

"I'm not claustrophobic."

He smiled against her skin but didn't comment, just continued those comforting strokes on her back. "You can sit up front. No one will stop you."

Opening her eyes, she blinked him back into focus. "Okay."

"Better now?"

"Sure."

He kissed her softly. "I'm drained. You wore me out, Sunshine. I'm going to get some rest, okay?"

"Yeah." The minute he released his hold, she darted to the front lounge and took the couch opposite Kirk. She sat on the end nearest the table and removed her turquoise Chucks, setting them aside. Emma turned to face the front of the bus, pulled her knees to her chest and wrapped her arms around them. Then watched the scenery go by as she worked to pull herself together.

God, she was embarrassed. Completely horrified by her reaction to the sleeping arrangements. Thank Christ, Joe hadn't teased her about it. Instead he'd just done his best to sooth her. Rubbing against the chill in her arms, she wondered how long it would be before she got any rest now.

Someone stepped beside her and placed something on the table. She glanced over and found a pint of chocolate milk. Lifting her head, she met Gary's gaze. "The frig is stocked. Make yourself comfortable, okay?"

The man missed nothing, so she didn't need to ask if he knew she'd flipped out. "Thanks."

He winked at her then headed to the back of the bus.

Emma removed the top from her milk and sipped, scanning the room, checking out everything she had only glanced at earlier. Did bands own the buses they toured with or rent them? She thought she'd read somewhere that they were rented. Either way, it was an impressive set up. All the comforts of home in a mobile package. All but a proper bed.

Stop. Don't go there again.

The television on the wall across from her drew her attention. Some sports event was being broadcast, rugby if she wasn't mistaken. The volume muted, players in bright shorts and uniform shirts ran around the field carrying what she would call a soccer ball. The game held her attention for a short while, especially when a player from one team tackled the other team's player, then the man watching it drew her gaze.

Kirk Lombardo, drummer, sat in a position that mirrored her own. His beat up jeans were faded and torn, and topped with a black shirt that appeared just as old and comfortable. Tattoos peeked out above his collar and down the lengths of both arms to his knuckles. Not tribal or the uncolored black type men wore nowadays, these were brilliant blues and greens, bold yellows and bright red: wings, possibly a raven, a serpent, music notes and skulls. The black gauges in his ears were just large enough her pinky could fit through the hole and his hair was super-short, shaved close to his head short.

She wasn't usually a fan of so much body art, but the look worked for him. Really well, actually. He was quite handsome and the ink only added to his attraction. But it was his eyes that held her spellbound as he turned his head and looked at her. Pale, silvery-green and full of something she couldn't name. What was it with these men and their eyes? Was there something in the water in England?

"Are you okay over there?"

Despite being the one who beat the hell out of his drum set, providing the thundering force behind Blind Man's Alibi's sound, Kirk was surprisingly soft spoken. Maybe his unique look drew the eye enough he didn't fear not being heard?

"Emma?"

"What? Sorry. I'm fine, thank you."

He flashed a smile then went back to watching the television. "I can't stand those bunks. That's why I'll get on the other bus every now and again. It has a rear lounge with a bed. Of course, that has its own set of problems, mainly Bobby." Kirk slid her a long look. "Whatever you do, don't confuse the two buses. That's the last place you need to be."

"Um…okay?"

"Trust me. You want nothing to do with that bus. But don't worry, it's easy to tell them apart, even in the dark."

"How?"

His gaze returned to the television once more. "The other pulls a trailer. Just look for the one without a trailer."

She nodded, turning her attention to the game. "What's in the trailer?"

"Lots of things. Mainly Bobby and Zach's motorbikes."

"They bring their motorcycles on tour with them?"

"Yeah."

"Everywhere you travel?"

He shrugged. "Pretty much."

Interesting. How much free time did they get to roar around the city? Or did they prefer the back roads and quiet stretches of countryside? Did they ever ride the bikes instead of the bus? Talk about freedom. The open road, the wind in her hair. It must be thrilling. The rush of adrenaline, the rumble of the bike beneath.

"Zach."

Kirk's voice snapped her out of her fantasy motorcycle ride. "What?"

He smiled at her. "You look like you would love to go for a spin. Make sure you ask Zach, not Bobby."

That was the second time he'd warned her away from Bobby. Then there was the night Joe introduced her to his band...what had he called Bobby? A shark? "Do you have a serial killer in the band or something?"

"Or something."

Emma frowned. She picked up her milk and took a swig, the whole time watching Kirk.

"You are exactly what Bobby goes for—blonde and petite. Joe isn't normally into that, but Bobby...the more innocent the better. Then he corrupts them, uses them up and spits them out."

There was a story here. She could hear it in his tone; see it in the flash of pain in his eyes. Looking to lighten the situation, she smiled. "Interesting. So I'm not Joe's type at all, huh?"

"No. Sweet and innocent has never been his thing."

She laughed. "You've got me all wrong."

"Maybe."

Something in his voice had her reassuring him. "I have no interest in Bobby."

"He won't care. At some point, he'll make a move on you. It's best if you don't get caught alone with him or Joe will feel the need to remind him that you are his girl by planting a fist in Bobby's face."

"You're messing with me, right?" He glanced at her and she could see that he wasn't. "Fuck."

That brought a smile to his face. "Maybe you're not

quite as innocent as you look," he noted. "Welcome to the tour, Emma."

"Gee, thanks. I can tell it's going to be...interesting."

"Won't it?"

For a moment she pondered what lay in store for her on this adventure, but then the day caught up with her. Scooting around for a comfortable position, she finally gave up and watched the scenery outside the window. Soon her eyelids grew heavy.

"Emma?" Kirk. His voice even softer than normal.

"Mm?"

"The lower drawer on the far side—the side opposite you?"

"Yeah?"

"There's a blanket and pillow in that drawer."

Too tired to stand, she crawled down the couch, pulled the items from the drawer and crawled back. She settled on her side, facing the interior of the bus and pulled the blanket over her. Once covered, she shimmied out of her jeans and dropped them atop her shoes. Sore muscles began to unwind. She blew a deep breath.

"You good?" Kirk asked.

"Yes. Thank you."

He turned out the light, bathing them in darkness but for the soft glow of the television and some sort of LED rope lighting worked into the design of the ceiling.

Emma closed her eyes and allowed sleep to claim her.

SHE AWOKE TO voices—terse and angry—one of them Joe's. Still blinking sleep from her eyes, Emma sat up and focused on the room around her. The first thing she noticed was Joe and another man standing near the stove, arguing. Joe looked to be fresh from a shower, his hair damp and pushed away from his face. A blue denim shirt, sleeves rolled back to expose his forearms, hung open and topped jeans and boots. A multi-strand black leather cuff circled the wrist of the hand holding a mug of what she assumed was coffee. The other hand fisted at his side.

"Watch yourself," he said to the man on his left.

Whatever response the man made was lost to her as Kirk crossed in front of the pair without giving them a second glance. Kirk was also dressed complete with shoes, as was Gary, whom she discovered at the foot of her couch, texting.

"Morning," Gary said, glancing up from his phone.

"Is it?" A check out the window verified the sun was indeed shining. It also told her they were parked. "I guess it is. Where are we?"

"Lake Charles, Louisiana. Parked behind the arena."

"What time is it?"

"Seven a.m."

That explained why she felt like she had sand in her eyes. If it was seven in the morning, they had all managed maybe four hours of sleep. Emma blinked a few more times and pushed her hand through her short hair. Wait a second, why was the stove farther away than last night? She glanced around once more then realized the couch she and Gary shared was part of a slide out someone had opened while she slept, making more room in the lounge.

The volume of Joe's voice increased and the man next to him matched it. The man crossed his arms and turned a cold stare at her.

"That's Marvin," Gary supplied, slipping his phone into the thigh pocket of his pants.

Ah, the manager. "What are they arguing about?"

Gary returned the man's stare, forcing him to glance away. "You."

"Me?"

"Marvin strolled on the bus this morning, discovered you in what he likes to consider his spot and started up with his typical theatrics."

"I'm awake now, I'll move."

"Ignore him." Gary shot the 'him' he was referring to a look that spoke volumes. Emma wondered about the details, as there was obviously some bad blood between them. "The boys have an interview this morning. We'll be leaving in a few."

She wasn't lazing about in her panties and tee while everyone else was dressed and ready for the day. Especially if she was already the topic of conversation. Tossing off the blanket, she stood, turned her back to the arguing pair, and pulled her jeans on. The fact that the room went quiet was impossible to miss. Emma ignored it. She folded her blanket and set it atop the pillow, then slipped her satchel over her shoulder and grabbed up her Chucks just in time to hear Marvin mutter, "Jesus, your piece of ass isn't shy, is she, Joe?"

"Shut the fuck up, Marvin," Joe growled. A warning.

Kirk cursed softly.

Gary rose to his feet. "Marv..."

Joe's shirt hung to mid-thigh on her. Women showed more skin at the beach than she'd just flashed so she knew Marvin was trying to rile her. She refused to give him the satisfaction.

Emma curled her hand around Gary's bicep—as much of it as she could—and gave tense muscles a squeeze. When he glanced down, she winked.

Every eye in the room was on her as she crossed to Joe, but she only had eyes for him. His free hand still fisted at his side, he appeared only seconds away from using it to pound his manager's face. Not good. She flashed him a smile meant to reassure. It didn't appear to work.

She stepped closer, close enough she could slide her left hand down his arm and work her fingers into his clenched fist, while curling her other around his mug. The look on his face was a cross between anger and concern, as if he wasn't sure how she would handle the situation. Did he think she would dump the contents of his cup on Marvin's head? Tempting, but under no circumstances was she wasting caffeine. Even if she wasn't much of a coffee drinker.

Staring into his eyes, Emma lifted the mug to her lips as the fingers of her left hand drew patterns on his palm, encouraging him to relax. The too hot liquid hit her tongue, causing her to wince. Not coffee. Tea. She made a face then noticed the mug itself—white and blue with the word 'wanker' painted on the side in big cursive letters.

Emma laughed as she handed the tea back to him. "Nice. A gift from the band?"

Joe flashed her a smile, albeit a small one.

"Good morning, Marvin." She faced the man, her voice giving no hint to her irritation. "My name is Emma Travers, which you should know since you arranged a delivery for me just the other day." He had beady eyes, a bit too much around the middle and a sour expression on his face. Emma didn't like him, and it wasn't because of the insult he'd flung her way. No, there was something else; a negative energy that emanated from him. It was uncomfortable enough she nearly stepped away. "Remember it. Use it. Derogatory comments are unprofessional and unnecessary. Perhaps if you learned some decorum, you too, could have a piece of ass accompany you on this tour." *You nasty sniveling bastard.*

Laughter followed her down the hall until she stepped into the back bath and closed the door. Dropping her satchel and shoes, she stared at her reflection in the mirror. "Well, that was fun." Not.

The man didn't warrant a second thought. With her habit of saying the first thing that popped into her head, she'd been called much worse than a piece of ass. But, damn it, he'd bothered her just enough she'd forgotten to find her luggage and dig out her toiletries.

A quick check assured her there was shampoo and soap. With a sigh, she turned on the shower, stripped off her clothes and stepped beneath the spray. Hot water beat down on her shoulders and back, soothing tense muscles, calming her nerves. She smiled when she squirted soap into her hands and discovered it wasn't too masculine a scent. Soaping herself down, she squeezed out shampoo and washed her hair. Absently, she wondered if everyone had left for the interview. It would be nice not to have to face anyone else when she went in search of clothes. Because, yeah, she'd forgotten those, too, in her rush to escape.

With a shake of her head, she turned off the water, ran her hands through her hair and turned, startling at the sight of Joe leaning against the closed door. Eyes ablaze, he tossed a towel at her, large smile in place.

She caught the towel and snapped it open. "I won't apologize."

He shifted and drew in a deep breath, his gaze on her hands as she dried herself. "I won't ask you to. That smart mouth of yours is one of the things I like most about you."

"Yeah? Even when it's you I'm telling off?" Done with

her arms and chest, she moved the towel lower. His gaze followed. Her pulse fluttered.

"Especially then." Still leaning against the door, he watched her every move. "I meet a lot of fakes in my line of work." Immediately his eyes homed in on her mound. "You, on the other hand, are genuine."

She let out a shaky breath. Although he was staring at the pale blonde curls that matched her hair, she was certain he wasn't talking about people whose carpet didn't match their drapes. "Fakes?"

He shifted, flexing every muscle in his back like he was trying to shake something loose. "It doesn't matter." His gaze never left her mound. "I brought your luggage."

She gave the bag at his feet a quick glance as she secured the towel around herself. "Thanks."

He grunted and pushed off the door. Removing his shirt, he dropped it atop her bag, then started working the buttons on his jeans. "I have an interview this morning. We're leaving in five."

Her stomach leapt. Her body grew wet. "Yet you're removing your clothes."

"I am." The timbre of his voice made her shiver.

"Have something on your mind?"

His eyes filled with so much fire she nearly had an orgasm on the spot. "Giving you a proper 'good morning'."

He wasted no time backing her against the vanity. Tugging the knot between her breasts, he watched the towel drop to the floor before lifting her and sliding her butt onto the countertop. Desperate to touch him, she helped him shove his jeans down his thighs. As his cock sprang free, she curled her hand around it, stroking the long, smooth length. Tightening and releasing, her every caress ratcheted he-excitement as much as his. It was crazy, how much she wanted him. They'd had each other so many times last night, she'd lost count. How could she still want him like this?

He let out a groan, then leaned in and kissed her. Hard. Hard enough he had to grab her hips to steady her as she lost her balance and nearly slid into the sink.

She pressed her face to his throat and laughed. "We can't do this. They're all out there."

"Who cares?"

His mouth fastened on her neck and sucked on her skin. Her hand squeezed reflexively. "You're going to substantiate Marvin's opinion of me."

Pressing a condom into her palm, he cupped her jaw, tilting it up to his. "You're more than a piece of ass to me, Emma." He kissed her lips and she slid her fingers around his biceps. She held on, tightening her hold as his hands left her face to stroke down the front of her body and close over her breasts. He massaged her, teased and tormented her until she was panting, her pulse throbbing.

She lifted her right leg until her thigh pressed against his hip, opening for him. The move brought his gaze to her lower half, then his hands. He brushed his fingers over her wet flesh, a light touch of skin to skin. "Tell me you know. Say it. I need to hear the words."

"I'm more than a piece of ass," she whispered.

His thumb slipped inside her, slow at first, then insistent. He let out a low sound as if touching her suffused him with pleasure. "You're wet."

"Pavlovian response to you..." Her mouth fell open as his thumb brushed just the right spot and she lost her breath.

"To me what? Taking off my clothes? Playing with your breasts?"

He dragged his thumb across that magical spot again and she couldn't suppress her whimper. "Saying my name."

His grip on her hip tightened. His thumb stopped moving. "You're shitting me," he said, voice husky.

"You like my sass," she gasped, tilting her pelvis, rocking against his hand. "I like my name on your lips."

His mouth came down on hers at the same time his finger joined his thumb, twisting, stretching her opening. He swallowed her moan as she pressed closer, urging him deeper. No amount of coaxing sped him along. He held her in place, controlling the depth and angle of penetration. In complete control of her pleasure, he worked her body, driving her desire higher and higher. She lifted her hips off the counter and he slowed.

Emma slid her hands into his hair. "Joe."

Her voice, full of frustration, brought his gaze off his hand to her face. His arousal mirrored her own. He curled his finger and the assault on her senses was enough to wring a cry from her lips. She fisted his hair, tugging.

"Sunshine, you're the one holding the condom."

"Shit."

A smile tipped the corner of his mouth. He pulled the condom from the death grip of her fist and rolled in on. Then he was there, right where she needed him to be. He pushed inside her, slow and even, stopping as her inner muscles began pulsing. "Are you?"

"God, yes." She clutched his shoulders and kissed him as her orgasm began, triggered by the pleasure of his body joining with hers.

"Fuck," he ground out. Then his hand was back on her

breast while the other grasped her hip. "Hold on." He pushed deeper, lifting her ass off the counter. The change in penetration ratcheted her orgasm up a notch and she came in a flash of blinding light, bucking, grinding against him and chanting his name.

His grasp on her hips tightened, dug into her flesh. He withdrew then thrust, once, twice, again and again, his rhythm hard and fast. God, the way he moved, like her release had pushed him beyond reason, leaving him struggling for control as he raced to find his own. He hammered into her, pulling her closer, holding her as tight against him as he could get her. Suddenly his muscles went rigid and he released a growl, watching her as he pulsed inside of her, always watching, letting her see what she did to him, allowing her to experience the pleasure she brought him.

It was the most erotic thing she had ever witnessed.

Those eyes. She'd never get tired of looking at those eyes. She traced the tips of her fingers around them, down his cheeks, over his lips. "I like the way you say good morning."

"Yeah," he whispered, then kissed her, leisurely this time, kissed her until she was grasping his shoulders again. "Good morning, Emma."

At her name on his lips, her body clenched hard, making him groan. "Christ."

She kissed his throat, his collar bone, trailing her tongue over the shell of his ear as he withdrew. "You're going to be late."

"You're not helping." Voice full of frustration, he disposed of the condom and pulled his pants up, fumbling with the buttons.

With a soft laugh, she trailed her fingers across his abs,

along the smooth stretch of skin just below his navel and above his waistband. "Everyone will know what you've been up to. You smell like sex."

He reached down and snagged her wrist, removing her hands from his body. "No one will get close enough to notice. Besides, I'm pretty sure it's the room more than me."

"Fantastic."

His mouth curved into a slow smile. Snagging his shirt off her luggage, he pushed his arms into the sleeves, this time buttoning it and tucking it into his jeans. "Don't worry, everyone's going with me. You're okay with being alone? We shouldn't be gone long."

"I'm fine. Don't worry about me."

He tipped his head, backing toward the door. "Don't forget to charge your mobile."

Shit, she'd forgotten all about that. Alison was probably trying to call her.

"You forgot again, didn't you?" He grinned, not waiting for an answer. Hand on the doorknob, he raked his gaze over her body. "I don't suppose there's any chance I can convince you to stay just like that until I get back?"

"Sorry."

"Can't fault me for trying." Then he was gone, closing the door behind him.

April 18

The Monster is alive. Clawing against the inside of my skull. Scratching and snarling; doing everything he can to break me down, just break me. I won't let him win. I can't. There's still too much to do, too much life left to live. I finally did it. I booked my European vacation today. All of the places I've yearned to go: Scotland, England, France, Germany, Italy. They're all on the agenda. My tickets are purchased, my bag packed. I'm ready to catch the first of many flights tomorrow and begin my adventure. It's what I've always wanted, and yet…there is a sadness inside of me knowing I'm doing this alone.

Always alone.

I should be used to it. After all, I was the only child of absentee parents. Lately, however, alone is a pain-filled thing to be. He changed that for me. Joe. Only after meeting him did I truly understand how much I was missing.

How very lonely I am.

My motto is to live in the moment. Forget the past, don't worry about the future, and enjoy the day I'm in. I do my best to live by this dictum but sometimes, sometimes it's difficult. Today, it's impossible.

I came home to flowers. Sunflowers. From Joe.

After the way our conversation ended last night, the last thing I expected as I walked through my door was a room filled with vases upon vases of the happiest flower on the planet. I told him goodbye and I meant it. Then I spent a restless night mourning his loss, only to decide it was for the best. There is no future for us. I can only bring him pain.

It's advantageous that I go now, before he becomes even more important to me. The irony of it is impossible to miss. I'm finally setting out on the trip of my dreams, and the man of my dreams sends me the sweetest apology ever – a room filled with sunshine.

Sunshine. He's called me that from the beginning. As if I have a light that somehow makes his life brighter.

Sunshine...my stomach summersaults every time he says it.

Here I go again, breaking my rule, worrying about tomorrow and wishing for something more. More time. Time I could spend with Joe.

I hate this. The doubt. The fear.

The Monster.

The way it forces me away, to move faster, run farther. To see everything I can before it wins.

I leave for Europe tomorrow – a sunflower pressed between the pages of my journal, my only companion.

I no longer fear the end.

I fear being alone when it comes.

Number of days since I decided to live: 58
Number of days since I met Joe: 15
Current level of panic: 9/10

TEN

April 20

A FTER THE STEAMY dampness of an overheated bath-room, the warm spring air that greeted Joe as he stepped off the bus was exhilarating. Or maybe it was the flood of endorphins swimming through his system. Either way, he stood there with a ridiculous grin on his face and enjoyed the rush.

Emma.

She got wet when he said her name.

Fuck, that bit of information was going to wreck him.

The blare of a horn drew his attention to the black SUV idling a few feet away. One SUV, where there were supposed to be two.

"Hurry the fuck up!" The back window was down and Steve's head popped out of it at an odd angle, indicating he was sitting in the third row, leaning over the seat before him in order to holler out the window.

"Where's the other SUV?" They always had two for this exact reason, so no one had to climb all the way into the back.

"Marvin took it."

"Bastard." Joe should have fired him long ago, but he was a damn good manager.

Slipping his sunglasses on, Joe opened the door closest

to him, palmed Steve's face and pushed him away. He took the seat behind the driver and next to Kirk, closing the door with a snap.

"'Bout bloody time," Bobby groused from the back seat. "What the hell you been doing?"

"His girlfriend if the just-been-thoroughly-fucked look on his face is any indicator." Steve said, cracking Zach up.

Joe smiled. Turning so his back was to the door allowed him to see everyone in the vehicle. And they were all there: Gary in the front passenger seat, Kirk and Zach on the middle bench seat with him, Bobby and Steve in the back. Everyone except for Marvin, who'd taken it upon himself to leave without them.

Bobby looked at Joe for a long moment then shook his head. "Wanker."

"No, actually, that would be you," Joe corrected.

"Pfft. I prefer the hands wrapped around my dick to be my girl's."

"You don't have a girl, Bobby." Zach pointed out.

"Au contraire, I have many, many girls."

Steve shook his head and smirked. "Yet you're not the one wearing a just-been-thoroughly-fucked grin, are you?"

Bobby shrugged and flipped him the bird. Steve smiled unapologetically.

"Rumor has it," Zach said, dropping his ankle over his opposite knee and glancing at Joe, "Marv called your girl a piece of ass."

In the front seat, Gary muttered a suggestion for Marvin that was a physical impossibility.

The comment caused Kirk to chuff a laugh.

Joe smiled. For months now, Kirk had been distant and quiet, moving through each day like a ghost. He would attend sound checks, do his bit for the shows, then slide away again. Sometimes for hours on end. No one knew for sure where he would go. Joe had an idea—because lately he'd been the shell of the man he used to be. But where Joe would drown his troubles in alcohol, Kirk would drown in fear. Fear for the woman he'd been raised with, the cousin who was more a sister to him. Who had disappeared exactly ten weeks ago and was presumed dead.

Christ. Joe wrapped his hand around the back of his neck and squeezed. He couldn't wait for this damn tour to be finished. Too much shit had gone down on this one. Too many of them affected in ways that weren't good. Yet Kirk was laughing, and everyone seemed to notice it. Even as none of them commented.

Steve smiled at the back of Kirk's head, relief crossing his features. "So how'd she take it, Joe? Being called a piece of ass, I mean. Is that why we're running late? You have to *sooth* her?"

"She didn't require soothing, no."

Bobby jumped on Joe's admission with both feet. "So it was you who needed it?"

If Bobby thought he could bait Joe, he was mistaken. Joe was feeling far too mellow. He'd been bloody furious when Marvin struck out at Emma verbally. Sure, she put Marv in his place, but that didn't mean his words didn't sting. Worried about how she'd take it, Joe had gone in search of Emma to do just as Steve suggested, but in the end, it was indeed he, who had needed soothing. She did that for him—calmed him—and he didn't care who knew it.

His reply dried up in his throat when Kirk laughed again. "You missed it. Emma told Marv she preferred to be called by her given name and if he had better manners maybe he'd have a piece of ass, too."

Everyone dissolved into laughter.

Steve gasped for breath. "Are you serious? Bloody hell that is fantastic."

"I need to meet this woman," Bobby said. "Sounds like my kind of girl."

"You already met her in Cleveland," Joe clarified.

"Shit, like I'm supposed to remember Cleveland."

Kirk sobered. "She's too good for you, Bobby."

"The hell. But she's not too good for Joe?"

Without a moment's hesitation, Kirk replied, "She's too good for Joe, too."

Isn't that the truth.

"She likes him though, so leave her alone."

"I haven't done a thing to the girl," Bobby argued.

Zach cocked his head, taking Joe in with a cool glance. "He must like her, too. I've never known you to bring a bird on the bus before, Joe."

Coughing out a laugh, Bobby tapped the back of the seat near Kirk's head. "Watch out, Joe, looks like Kirk is into your girl."

"Piss off, Poulsen," Kirk growled.

"Now kids," Steve chastised. "Let's not argue the whole trip."

Joe closed his eyes and tipped his head back, resting it on the door. "Kirk and Emma have a bond." Christ, he was relaxed. The rumble of the tires on the road was hypnotic. Sleep pulled at him.

"Jesus, Joe, you're not nodding off are you? It was that good?"

Joe smiled at the exasperation in Steve's voice.

"I still don't get it," Gary piped up, confusion evident in

his voice. "She's sexy, funny and warm. You're grumpy, have zero social graces and drink too much. I never thought you stood a chance with her."

Pushing his sunglasses to the top of his head, Joe cracked an eye. "Neither did I."

Zach straightened, holding his hands like he clutched a pen and paper. "So Mr. Campbell—"

"Please don't let the interviewer this morning refer to me as Mr. Campbell. I hate that."

He hated interviews in general, which is why Zach was giving him shit. It never failed, every interview, every bloody one of them, Joe would say the wrong thing and it all would go to shit. Then, as if looking like an ass in one country wasn't enough, the clip would circle the globe at warp speed, playing over and over on all social media outlets so he could relive the moment ad nauseum.

"Mr. Campbell," Zach repeated and Joe sighed. "How did you woo Emma into your bed? Tell us your secret."

"She likes my dragon."

"Jesus!" Bobby flung out his arms, forcing Steve to duck and dodge or take one to the face. "Can we stop talking about your happy dick?"

The SUV came to a stop in front of the radio station, but Joe didn't spare a glance at the throng of people who began calling out greetings. He smiled at Bobby. "I was referring to my tattoo, ya twit."

"Let me get this straight." Zach gave up the pretense of holding a pencil in order to make a cupping motion below his pec. "You showed her your man-boob and all her clothes magically fell off."

Kirk snickered.

Joe shook his head in exasperation. This farce was the

perfect example of how his interviews always went sideways. "Yes. That's exactly what I did."

"Hell, yeah!" Zach pulled his shirt off over his head as he reached for the door handle. "I'm giving this a try."

"Brenner," Gary growled. "You open that door and I'm breaking your fingers."

"You wouldn't dare! How would I play the guitar?"

"Better than if you stir up this crowd and they get out of hand." The crowd he spoke of appeared controlled, but one never knew. "No way I can hold them all off and, trust me when I say this, you'll be my first sacrifice."

"Harsh," Zach mumbled, pulling the shirt back on. "That's harsh, mate."

Steve chuckled as if he hadn't been ready to follow Zach's lead only moments ago. "Where are we, again?"

"Lake Charles," Gary supplied, his eyes scanning the crowd.

"Louisiana," Kirk said at the same time.

Apparently liking what he was seeing, Gary pushed his door open and stepped out.

His smile in place, Joe followed, doing his best not to wince as the temperature change from air conditioning to hot humid air shocked his lungs.

"Bleeding hell," one of his band mates muttered. Joe had no idea which since the roar of the crowd increased tenfold with each band member who climbed out of the SUV. "Half past seven in the morning and already muggy as balls."

"Typical." Steve pitched his voice to be heard over the crowd. "All Bobby can think about is his balls."

They were nearly to the door of the radio station when a cute little redhead grabbed hold of Zach's arm and screamed, her pitch the stuff that could break glass. Zach jumped, appearing for a moment like he just might scream right back, then grabbed hold of her face and pressed a kiss to her lips.

The redhead fainted into her friend's arms.

Joe stared in shock. "What the fuck, Zach?"

Zach shrugged. "She scared me. What else was I supposed to do?"

"At least we know which one of us will be trending on social media tonight," Steve muttered, slapping Joe on the back. "And hey, whatever crazy shit gets said in the interview, it's not gonna top that, is it?"

Oh look, a fucking bright side. "Tell me the girl is okay. She didn't hit her head or anything, did she?"

"Nah," Bobby assured him. "She's coming around. Course Zach looks like he's thinking of trying it again."

"For the love of Christ." Reaching out blindly, Joe snagged the back of Zach's shirt and pulled him away before he could make another bone-ass move. He sighed with relief as the station doors closed behind them, Gary moving in to keep the fans out.

AFTER THE MELODRAMA of the morning—specifically Martin throwing a fit over her being in his spot—Emma sat in the back lounge, watching the latest trending video when Joe walked in.

"How did it go?" she asked, pausing the video.

Joe leaned against the wall just inside the lounge and sighed. "I hate those things. The interviewers never stay on topic and usually shift to personal questions. My life is boring. Who gives a damn what I had for breakfast?"

She smiled. "He didn't ask you what you ate for breakfast."

"You were listening."

"And here's something to note, your life is only boring to you. To your fans it's fascinating."

Joe shook his head. Pulling his hand out of his front pocket, he scratched his beard, then tipped his head to the coffee table before her. "What's the book?"

Her handmade leather journal lay open just to the left of her laptop. She'd been writing earlier, before the broadcast interview, and forgot to put it away. She gave it a look, absently wondering if he could read any of it from his distance before giving in to temptation and shutting it. "It's my journal."

"Yeah?" He grinned. "Do you write about me in there?"

"Sometimes," she answered honestly.

"What do you say? Do you mention how handsome I am?"

"Nope."

"How talented I am?"

"Nuh-uh."

He narrowed his eyes at her as if he didn't appreciate her answers.

Her smile broadened.

"What about," he began, then pushed off the wall and started in her direction, "how I make your panties wet just by saying your name?"

She held her breath as he slid onto the couch next to her.

"Do you write about that, Emma?"

Her gaze went to his hand as it settled atop the brown leather. She did her best to appear indifferent to hearing her name fall from his lips. Setting her hand next to his on her journal, she pulled it closer. "No."

"Well then, it sounds boring."

"Doesn't it just?"

He grinned, leaning in until his mouth was a whisper from hers. "You're messing with me, aren't you? You really do write those things about me."

She kissed one corner of his lips, his jaw, the tip of his nose. "You'll never know."

Her words brought a teasing smile to his face. "Do you have any idea how adorable you are, even with those bloody awful glasses on your face?"

"Shit." She'd forgotten she was wearing her glasses. She only needed them when working on her computer as they helped reduce glare and keep her headaches under control. Since she was self-employed, the look of them never concerned her. Until now.

Pulling them off, she placed them on the table.

He chuckled then caught sight of her laptop screen and his humor faded. "What is that?"

She turned the screen in his direction and pressed the play button. The clip of Zach kissing a young woman who then fainted started over. "It's trending on Twitter right now."

Frown in place, he closed the lid.

Emma giggled. "The look on Zach's face when you grab him by the collar and drag him into the radio station is priceless."

"Fuck." Shifting away from her, he reclined on the couch, his head on her thigh. "At least it's not me this time."

She straightened in her seat.

He closed his eyes. "Don't you dare. If you search my

interview blunders I'll…"

"You'll what?" she asked, settling her hand on his chest.

"Just don't. I'm not sure I could handle the humiliation."

"You got to see my glasses. It seems only fair."

"No."

"They can't be that bad."

"Wanna bet?" He rubbed at his eyes before lacing his hands over his abs.

"Tired?"

"How did you guess?"

"The droop to your shoulders and dark rings beneath your eyes as you walked in was my first clue." Add to that the weight of his head on her thigh. The fact that none of his muscles seemed to be anything but lax, and the truth was hard to miss. Slipping her hand into the open collar of his shirt, she began rubbing his chest in long, slow strokes.

"Mm, that's nice." His voice had already softened, each word drawn out.

"Yeah?" She slipped a few more buttons through their corresponding holes, allowing her better access, keeping up the gentle strokes from one pec to the other and back again. It wasn't long before his breathing evened out.

His skin was warm and soft. Her hand made another gentle pass before stopping atop his tattoo. The vibrant blue eye of the dragon peeked out from between her ring and middle fingers, his orange tongue near her thumb. She traced the lines and shadows, admiring the artist's skill. The saturation of color, the depth, and the fluid movement as if the beast was actually alive. It took talent to create such a convincing image on paper, she couldn't imagine inking it onto a living canvas.

Her fingers itched to sketch it, see if she could replicate the dramatic image, its living, breathing appearance. Flipping open her journal, she put pencil to paper. Pencil drawing was her passion, with charcoal a close second—creating light and shadow without the assistance of color. She had an aptitude for people, an innate talent at creating visually breathtaking portraits. But animals and mythical creatures? She didn't seem to have the eye for them at all.

"I'm not even going to ask."

"Jesus!" Emma jumped, spilling the pencil off her lap. It rolled under the coffee table and stopped halfway between her and the door. Struggling with the dragon's body, she'd been busy shifting Joe's shirt as she tried to get a better look at his arm, and hadn't noticed Gary's arrival until he spoke. "You need to wear a bell or something!"

Gary's dimple flashed.

Joe muttered in his sleep. She replaced her hand on his chest and he calmed.

Gary's brow lifted. "Joe's asleep." he said, his tone a mix of accusation and confusion.

"He is. Is that so strange?"

"Actually, yes. However, I'm wondering more about why you were molesting him while he's sleeping."

"I wasn't." Heat suffused her cheeks and she knew she was blushing. "I thought you weren't going to ask?"

His grin widened. "I changed my mind."

"It's not what you think."

"Your face is the color of an apple and it's not what I think?"

Emma blew a breath and offered up her journal, thumb in the center, keeping it open to the page she was sketching.

Gary's brow slid farther up his face, but he stepped forward, crossing the room in a few strides. He curled a hand beneath the soft leather and placed his other atop the open pages, then took it from her and turned it around.

"His dragon," he said his eyes alight with humor.

"Is it that bad?"

His tongue played behind his cheek, his smile huge. "It's damn good actually." He sounded sincere, but what was with that look on his face?

She shrugged. "I like his dragon."

He started to laugh. A deep, rich, belly laugh as he pinched the bridge of his nose.

Emma stared at him.

He was still laughing as he sank to the empty space on the short end of the curve to her right, setting her journal atop the table.

"I'm missing something here, aren't I?" she asked.

"Yup." He took in her hand smoothing across a sleeping Joe and shook his head.

"No one got more than four hours of sleep last night. Why is it odd that he's resting?"

Closing his eyes, Gary leaned his head on the wall. "He never rests. I told you, you calm his demons."

"The ones he normally drowns in alcohol?"

"Or tries to." He let out a slow, careful breath. "I have to walk the arena. Interested in accompanying me?"

"Walk the arena?"

"Learn the layout. Check the dressing rooms, the entrances and exits."

To say she was intrigued would be an understatement. "Sure."

He grunted. "Give me five."

"Gary?"

He was asleep. Sitting up. One minute he was making normal conversation and the next he was out. There had been no clue he was about to drift off, no warning at all, just...asleep. Like flicking a switch. How was that possible? Even Joe usually started slurring words before he tuned out, and he fell asleep at record speed, too.

She gave Gary ten, then said his name again and touched his hand where it lay atop his knee. His eyes popped open and his hand closed around her wrist, moving so fast she never saw it coming. The grip was strong, but not painful. Until she jerked instinctively and his hold tightened.

"Shit." He released her as quickly as he had grabbed her. His gaze went to her wrist before rising to her face. "Did I hurt you?"

"No."

"Are you sure? I...it's best not to touch me when I'm sleeping."

"I'll remember that." When his dark gaze drifted back to her wrist, she reassured him. "I'm fine. You didn't hurt me."

"Okay." He dropped the subject, even though she wasn't certain he believed her. A glance at his watch and he blinked. "Let's do this. That is, if you still want to."

"Sure."

Gary stood, stepping away so she could slide out from under Joe's head then scoot across the spot where he had been sitting and out from behind the table.

Emma stuffed her cell phone into her back pocket. She flipped through the pages of her journal until she found her backstage pass. Slipping it around her neck, she closed the book. "You can stop looking at me like that."

"How am I looking at you?"

She scanned him from top to bottom. Ubiquitous black

tee and cargo pants topped military-style lace front boots. Instead of his usual relaxed self, his muscles were tight, hands shoved into his pockets. "In case you've forgotten, I'm brutally honest." Most of the time, anyway. "So believe me when I tell you that if you'd hurt me, you wouldn't have had to ask."

The look on his face didn't change so she poked him in the chest with her finger. Which wasn't smart because he was built like a tank. "Okay, that *did* hurt."

He smirked.

"That's better," she said, smiling up at him. "Shall we go?"

"After you."

Emma stepped off the bus and froze as the warmth swirled around her. She tipped her face to the sun, inhaled deeply and smiled. "This is fabulous." The weather in Cleveland had been mid-forties when she left. Much too cool to even consider a trip to the lake, but as the seagulls cried out as they circled above her, she thought about it now. "Lake Charles. I assume it is named after an actual lake?"

"I wouldn't know."

She pulled out her phone and Googled it. "Holy shit, we're not far from the Gulf!" He didn't comment. "You know, the Gulf of Mexico?"

"I've heard of it, yes."

"Can we go?"

"You can. I'll even call the car service for you."

"But I'd have to go alone." She had checked the sheet of lies after everyone left that morning and knew the bus pulled out of town tonight. "Is that all you guys do? Arenas, buses, and hotels? What about sunshine and fresh air, the surf and the sand?"

"A hat and sunscreen," he added.

"What?"

"I recommend you add a hat and sunscreen to your list or you'll regret it."

Damn it, he was right. She would redden like a lobster in a pot of boiling water if she wasn't careful. "Not all of us were lucky enough to be blessed with beautiful dark skin."

He grinned, but kept his eyes on the man walking down the loading dock at their right.

"Hey, Gary," the man said.

"Jim," Gary replied.

She cocked her head and studied him for a minute, pondering everything she knew about him, which wasn't much, and all that she'd seen. There was something off about him. Something she couldn't put her finger on. "Your name's not Gary, is it?"

He miss-stepped, then blamed the concrete incline. "Watch it there."

"Is it?"

"Of course it is. That's what everyone calls me."

"Pfft. I could start calling you Shrek again—"

"Please don't."

"—you could even begin answering to it. That wouldn't make it your name."

Silence.

"I'm right, aren't I?"

"How did you come to the conclusion that Gary isn't my name?" By this time, they were at the rear entrance to the arena. He grabbed the handle and pulled the door open.

"You don't look like a Gary."

"Not everyone looks like their name."

"Of course they do."

He rolled his eyes.

They had yet to walk into the arena. "Look at me."

He did.

"Do I look like an Emma to you?"

"Actually, you do."

Emma smiled.

Gary frowned, sliding his hand into his back pocket and pulling out a folded piece of paper, which he handed to her. Taking hold of her elbow, he guided her into the building.

She blinked at the sudden change from bright sunlight to interior lights, waiting for the spots to clear from her vision before focusing on the paper he'd given her. "This is cool. Do you get a layout of all the venues?"

They turned to the left and started walking. Emma had to skip to match his steps. Good thing she wasn't wearing heels.

"About a week before each show," he said, slowing his gait. "I'll make sure you get a copy of each one."

"Um, thanks, but…" She turned the map, already lost.

He straightened the map for her, then pointed. "We are here. We'll be circling all the way around first, checking to make certain all the doors are as marked—I need to know where to place my team."

They were in the oval outside of the actual arena, the area where the restrooms and concession stands were located. It felt much larger than normal since it was empty, and reminded her a little bit of a racetrack. The urge to ride a bike or rollerblade around the place struck, bringing with it a smile. "Why do you have a team if the arena has its own security?"

Gary lifted his head, his expression incredulous. "Are

you always this chatty or am I just lucky?"

"You're just lucky." Her answer didn't appear to make his day. "I'm also running on little sleep and a whole lot of sugar right now. I inhaled a couple of apple fritters right before you all returned from the interview so…yeah, you're just lucky."

"Fantastic."

"Forget I asked," she whispered, enjoying herself.

"Wait." They were moving again, circling around the northeast corner of the building, coming up on a bunch of doors according to the map in her hand. He didn't stop, so he obviously hadn't meant to literally wait. "Where did you get apple fritters?"

Then he did stop, frowning down at her. "You didn't walk somewhere, did you?" The thought must have triggered his protective side because he puffed up a bit and adopted a look that would scare away men twice her size. "Because that wouldn't be wise—a woman who looks like you, walking around a strange city by herself—that would not be good."

"How do I look?"

His furrow deepened. "Did you run off by yourself this morning?"

When she didn't immediately answer, he puffed up even more and, sure enough, one of the arena workers who was coming around the corner took one look at him, turned and headed back the way he'd come.

Emma burst out laughing. "Did you see that? I think you just made that poor man pee himself."

This did not help his mood. "Emma."

She grinned. "You need to bring it down a notch. You're scaring the staff."

"But not you?"

"Nah. I know you're not a big scary ogre, you just act like one."

He didn't respond.

"Jees, Frank, don't get your panties in a wad. I didn't go anywhere by myself, okay? Beth brought them to me, said she thought I might be hungry."

His left eye started to twitch.

She flashed her most innocent smile.

"I don't look like a Gary to you, but somehow I look like a Frank?"

"Now that you mention it, I guess you don't."

He cupped his hand around the back of his neck and muttered. "Give me strength." He skimmed his hand up the back of his head, over his short hair and down his face. A sigh broke loose. "Here's the first door. Mark it."

She assumed he meant on the map. "How?"

A red pen appeared in his hand, most likely slipped from one of his many pockets. Taking the map, he marked the door and offered the map and the pen back to her.

She looked at his chicken scratch. Seemed easy enough. "Got it."

And they were off once again.

Just as he'd stated, when they finished the circling, they moved to the dressing rooms, then into the arena. Emma managed to keep her thoughts to herself for most of it, succeeding in not puffing him back up. Shame, really. It was rather humorous watching people stumble over themselves to get away from him.

The set was going together. Onstage one man assembled Kirk's drum kit, pulling each piece out of the storage cases as if he were handling T.N.T. Not surprising, since just behind him and to the right stood the drummer himself, twirling a stick in hand before tapping out a rhythm on one of the speakers. His feet were moving to a different beat. Emma took a moment to stop and stare, absently wondering what song was playing in his head.

The arena staff was busy setting the rows of folding chairs on the floor, while others placed the temporary fencing around the front and sides of the stage to keep fans from getting at the band or into areas off limits. Some of them tipped their heads in greeting, but most worked without paying attention to anything else around them. Same old, same old, she guessed.

In the center of it all stood Gary, map in hand, eyes scanning across everything as he jotted down notes. She followed as he circled the floor, continuously scribbling on the paper. When they returned to the place they'd begun, Emma took a seat in a lower bowl section on the side of the stage.

She kicked her heels up on the bars separating her section from the floor seating. "You're ex-military aren't you?"

Standing in the aisle next to her, Gary didn't spare her a glance. "What makes you say that?"

"The way you look, the way you move—all silent and sneaky like. Those damn pants."

He did spare his pants a look. "How do my pants scream ex-military to you?"

"They just do."

He chuffed.

"You appear relaxed, but you're always alert and taking in everything around you."

"Like I said before, it's my job."

She scooted lower in her seat until she found a comfortable position. It was fun watching everything come together, but she couldn't imagine doing it day after day. "It's more than your job, it's an ingrained part of who you are."

Gary didn't comment.

His silence spoke volumes. "I thought so. So what were you, Royal Navy? S.A.S.? A merc?"

His brow went up. "You have quite an imagination."

"You have no idea," she mumbled, stacking her hands on her belly. "It's okay. You don't have to tell me. I'll create my own backstory for you."

"Spare me the details. I'm certain I do not want to know."

He had yet to look away from his paper. She flicked the back of it. Nope, not even that got him to look down at her. "What's the matter big guy, scared?"

"Terrified." he replied, sounding as if he meant it.

Emma laughed. She laughed long and hard. Right up to the moment Kirk slid behind his drum kit. He pressed his feet on the pedals, tapped each drum as if he was testing the tone, and rolled the cymbals. Then he spun his sticks—both of them at the same time—and bam! The sound of his drums poured over the arena, the thump of the bass echoing in her chest.

She straightened in her seat, feet planted firmly on the floor and watched. Completely enthralled, entranced by the frantic motion of it all, the way each limb seemed to move out of sync with the rest yet the sound he produced was smooth and steady. Sitting at the back of the stage, with Joe before him, she'd honestly never paid too close attention to how he created his sound. Alone onstage, she couldn't take her eyes off of him.

"Emma?" The tone of his voice told her that it wasn't the first time Gary had said her name.

"What? Sorry." His dimple made an appearance and she couldn't help but smile back at him.

"I'm meeting with the rest of my team. Are you coming along or staying here?"

Her gaze drifted back to the stage. "Staying."

"Give me your phone."

Pulling it from her pocket, she passed it to him.

He pushed a few buttons, his thumbs dancing over the screen with a speed that would make teenage girls envious before handing it back to her. "Get a hold of me if you need anything, okay?"

He'd added his name to her contacts list. The name everyone called him, at least. "Okay."

He moved away on those damn silent feet of his, crossing the arena and disappearing backstage.

Emma kicked her heels back onto the rail, returned her focus to the stage and settled in to enjoy the show.

Forty-five minutes later, she was still there when Joe found her. He'd swapped out his long sleeved denim shirt for a short sleeved cotton one. The tee was snug across his shoulders and chest and loose across the abs. He had a dark pair of sunglasses pushed to the top of his head, keeping his hair out of his eyes, and looked so damn sexy walking across the arena, smiling at her, she actually sighed.

"Here you are." He stepped over her legs and took the seat next to her. "What are you doing in here?"

"I helped Gary with his check, then stayed to watch Kirk play the drums."

"Kirk was playing?" he asked, raising a brow, gaze landing on the empty drum kit.

"For about half an hour while the crew built the set. After he finished, I started texting Alison, sending her some of the pictures I've taken. She wanted pictures, so..." Emma shrugged. Alison was a big believer of documenting every memory and storing it away so she could pull it back out at a future date and time. Not much about Emma's recent past was worth documenting so she'd never gotten into the habit.

"Did you send her any of me?"

"No."

"No?" He shook his head in mock despair. "You wound me, Sunshine."

She rolled her eyes and nudged him in the chest. "I don't have any pictures of you."

"No? We'll have to remedy that then, won't we?"

He took her phone from her and held it out selfie-style, leaning into her in order to get them both in the shot. "Smile."

His scent—so undefined yet so male—engulfed her and she lost her focus. She was supposed to be looking at the phone in his hand, but instead stared at his mouth as it curved and he flashed her favorite of his smiles—the slightly crooked one that always made her want to remove her clothes. Her skin heated, her heart raced.

Noting her distraction, Joe turned his head, his gaze slowly sliding over her face. His smile faltered, replaced by a fiery look of desire that stole her breath.

"Emma," he said very softly.

He kissed her, a long, lingering touch of his lips against hers and she sighed. Opening her mouth for him, she invited him in. He licked his tongue across her bottom lip then accepted her invitation, kissing her until they finally had to come up for air.

Staggered, she murmured the first thing that popped into her head. "Damn."

He laughed softly.

She returned his smile then realized she had the shoulder of his shirt fisted in her hand and was using it to pull him closer. Releasing her hold, she smoothed her fingers across the fabric. "Sorry."

"Don't be. You won't hear me complaining." Joe returned his attention to the phone. "So, which one of these should we send her?"

"What do you mean? Oh my God, you were snapping pictures the whole time?"

He flashed a wicked, naughty grin, and stopped on one that bordered on being indecent. Heat skittered across her belly. There was no way she could send that to anyone, not even Alison. "No. Not any of those."

"Mm...I like this one."

Emma reached for the phone and he snatched it away before she could connect, tipping the screen so she could no longer see it. "Joe," she warned.

He pushed the button to attach the photo he had chosen to a text, then started typing.

"Please, don't."

One more button pressed.

"Shit. Tell me you didn't."

The phone in his pocket chimed. He winked at her. "I didn't."

"You sent it to yourself?" This time when she reached for the phone he let her have it.

Emma looked down at the screen, at the photo he'd sent himself and smiled. By its place in the timeline, they had just broken the kiss and were pulling away from each other. By shear accident, he had managed to capture them with their lips a bare inch from each other, her hand fisted in his shirt as she stared at him in awe. There was no other way to describe the look on her face. She'd been blown away by his kiss.

"Your cheeks are turning red," Joe said softly. "Is that embarrassment or excitement?"

"A bit of both, I suspect." When she looked up from the phone, the heat was back in his gaze.

From somewhere on the arena floor came a loud crash, followed by raised voices. Joe blinked once, twice, then palmed his fly and adjusted his erection, shifting a bit in his seat and clearing his throat. "I don't need to be thinking about you getting wet while we're surrounded by hundreds of people."

There was so much frustration in his voice, Emma giggled. She was still smiling as she flipped through the photos, discovering a shot of them she could actually share with Alison.

Joe squirmed again, finally kicking his feet onto the bars in front of them. "So this is what it's like to be on this side of the stage."

"You've never sat out in front of the stage before?"

He shook his head.

"Have you ever been to a concert where you weren't the performer?"

"Nope."

"Really? What age were you when Dominic discovered you? How is he, anyway?"

Joe let out a slow, careful breath and settled a hand on her leg, running his thumb absently back and forth along the inside of her knee. "He's doing better, thanks for asking."

Her cell alerted her to an incoming message. Emma read it and laughed.

"What did your friend say?"

She turned the phone so he could read it.

OMG, Em! He's so freaking good looking!

"Freaking?"

"Al doesn't swear, at least not in every day conversation. You'd most likely cause her eardrums to explode." She scrolled through her photos until she found one of her and Alison. "That's her."

"And you." Using his free hand, he took the phone from her. "I know that outfit."

"You should. That was taken the night of your Cleveland concert."

With his right hand smoothing up and down her leg, he used his left to sift through the rest of the concert photos. There weren't many. Finding one he apparently liked, he texted it to himself.

The phone in his pocket pinged in time with her startled, "Hey."

"That's a good memory. I should have that photo."

"My calling you a narcissistic asshole is a good memory for you?"

His mouth twisted into a wry smile. "Maybe not that part but the night overall, yeah." He slid his hand higher up her thigh.

Emma inhaled deeply and took hold of his wrist, stopping him from shifting even higher. "Hundreds of people are here with us, remember?" She lifted his arm and draped it across her shoulders instead, linking their fingers.

Joe tugged her closer. "I was nineteen when Dom found me and the boys playing a pub in Brighton."

"Only nineteen?"

He shrugged. "Is this all the photos you have?"

It was her turn to shrug. "I'm not a big photo taker. I prefer to live in today and not worry about the past or the future."

"And photos are memories and therefore the past?" he asked, voice filled with confusion and disbelief.

"I guess so." Unsettled, she took her phone back and held it in her lap, looking out over the arena instead of at him. "It sounds stupid when you say it. I haven't had much I felt like documenting is all."

"What about your parents? Your family?"

Even though her eyes were on the stage where the finishing touches were being added to the set, she could see him looking at her out of the corner of her eye. "I was an only child. My parents passed away three years ago. Car accident."

"Christ, Em, I'm sorry."

"It's life—none of us are getting out of it alive." Some people had long lives filled with family and friends. Others never really had a chance to live. It was a fact she had come to terms with years ago when fate took her parents from her then bitch-slapped her with the cold, hard reality that was cancer. The problem was, that cold hard reality never stung quite so much as it did now, as she sat next to a wonderful man with whom she shared a connection. Because no matter how much she wished otherwise or how powerful the bond, there was no future for them.

"Damnit, I prefer to live in today," she whispered, and because he was still watching her and she didn't want him to see the tears in her eyes, she rested her head on his shoulder.

He pulled her just a little bit closer to his side. "Most of the photos on my phone were sent to me." The gentle swipe of his thumb back and forth across her fingers was comforting. "I'm not much for selfies. I see myself in the mirror every day. Why would I want my phone filled up with my own mug?"

"You're very good at it."

"At selfies? I have to be. For the fans, you know? Sometimes they're a bit overwhelmed and I have to take the shot for them." He stood, stepping over her legs and into the aisle. "Come with me."

Disappointment settled in her belly. She'd enjoyed being held by him. Settling for holding his hand, she took it and walked with him.

They went around the stage, through the security gate, and up a set of steps, coming out right next to Kirk's drum kit. She took the lead, walking counter clockwise around the edges of the stage, trailing her fingers over the stands of guitars, the microphones, the speakers. Stopping briefly to read a set list taped to the floor, she followed his lead when he gave a light tug and moved center stage.

"This is my view," he said, looking out over the arena. "My world."

There were just enough lights shining on them that she had to squint to see out over the stadium. Everything looked so much different from this angle, larger, more daunting. Rows and rows of seating spread out before her, wrapped around from one side to the other in a lower and upper bowl. She tried to imagine what it would look like when all the seats were filled with screaming fans and couldn't wrap her mind around it. "I can't imagine."

"Hit it, Leo," Joe called and the spotlights flared to life. Twirling and dancing, spinning from one side of the stage to the other. A bright beam of light honed in on them, blinding in its intensity.

She turned her face away, blinking until her eyes adjusted. "How do you see anything?"

"I don't. Not much, anyway. You don't have to see it to experience the rush. The crowd is an energy that is palpable."

"I prefer the view from the other side. This one would give me a headache."

He smiled at her and pulling his sunglasses off his head, slipped them on her face. "Better?"

"Much." The bright spotlight centered on them went dark. No longer needing them, Emma pushed the glasses to the top of her head.

Joe stared out at the arena again, focused on a spot in the far back. "This used to be my favorite place to be."

"Used to?"

A few strides, and he stood at the front edge of the stage. "You were right there."

She looked out to where he was pointing and wondered how it could look so much farther away than what she recalled. Her memory was that she could have easily reached out and touched him, but from this angle that seemed impossible. Whether from the darkness of the rest of the arena or the glare from the lights above, she couldn't see the front row very well, which probably didn't help her judge the distance.

"I don't remember what I was singing."

"Because you weren't."

"Smartass," he said on a laugh, then pulled her closer.

"You were singing *Alienation*."

"Was I? I like that one."

She made a face. "It's terrible."

"What?" He stiffened in surprise. "It is not."

"*Solitude creeps like the mist, charring your soul, consuming the light.* That is horrible. It's so depressing."

The left side of his mouth tipped up in a grin. "That's what I was singing?"

"That's the last line you sang before going silent and standing there not moving. It was like you just turned off."

He threw back his head and laughed. Laughed so hard he almost doubled over. "Christ, that's brilliant! No wonder I forgot my words."

His laughter was contagious, though she had no idea what he found so funny. "What are you talking about?"

"I was singing about being consumed by darkness when I looked into the audience, and found you smiling up at me like a ray of sunshine."

"That's corny."

"Yeah, it is. It's also true." He trailed his fingertips from her cheekbone to her chin, flipped his hand over and used the backs for the reverse trip. Then he started singing it, that terrible depressing song, in his incredible sexy voice.

It pinged a memory.

"Wait." She had to cover his mouth with her hand to get him to stop singing. "You said that to me."

When he licked her palm, she pulled her hand away, wiping it on his shirt.

He grinned. "What did I say?"

"*You really are a ray of sunshine, aren't you?* You said that after I stormed out of your dressing room and told you off. I thought you were being sarcastic."

"Well, Sunshine," he said, reaching for her hand. "You thought wrong."

Damnit, she didn't know what to say. She fell silent as her brain struggled to come up with the proper response. He just stood there and looked at her.

When her stomach chose that moment to rumble, the spell was broken. He arched a brow, and she shrugged. "All I've had to eat today is a couple of donuts."

"Let's get you something to eat."

Not letting go of her, he tugged her hand, leading her toward the back of the stage. Glancing over her shoulder, Emma looked into the audience, to the place where she had stood front row center. With the lights swirling and dancing around...how had he ever spotted her? The conditions would have had to be perfect; the chances of it happening slim. But it had. Somehow it had.

"Joe?"

He held open the curtain and stepped aside so she could pass through first. "Yeah?"

"If the stage is no longer your favorite place to be, where is?"

The look he gave her caused her heart to skip a beat. It stopped altogether when he replied softly, "With you, Sunshine."

April 19

Remember that boy in high school every girl wanted to date? The handsome, charismatic one with the smile that melted hearts? The boy who somehow, for some inexplicable reason you never fully understood, wanted you? Sure, it was fleeting and didn't last, but for a moment he was yours and you were happy?

That's what I have with Joe.

I'm supposed to be on a flight to New York. Instead, I'm bound for Baton Rouge. He didn't ask me to join him, not in so many words. I had to look deeper, to the pain and vulnerability in his eyes. I had to see more; the truth that I'd been hiding from.

I need Joe and he needs me.

I want him and he wants me.

It is as simple and complicated as that.

I may not understand the why's and whatfor's, but I've decided it doesn't matter. I don't know how long it will last, be it two days, a week, or six. It does not matter. For a moment in time – this moment – he wants me and I'm going to grab hold with both hands and enjoy.

Life – with all its ups and downs – I'm running headfirst into it.

There's no time for anything else.

Number of days since I decided to live: 59
Number of days since I met Joe: 16
Current level of panic: 4/10

ELEVEN

April 20

B LIND MAN'S ALIBI was about to take the stage. They'd
gathered in Joe's dressing room, the entire band plus
Gary and a few of his security team packed into the room,
putting off an energy Emma couldn't help but absorb. A
high she'd never experienced before—like a drug, but with
fewer side effects.

Everyone talked non-stop, laughing and joking. Everyone but Joe. He'd grown more and more quiet the closer the
time came and switched into business mode the moment he
stepped into the hall. It was fascinating.

Gary led the way to the stage, Joe and the boys trailing
behind him. The rest of the security personnel spread out
around them, keeping any fans who broke through the
barricade from getting too close. There were a few of them:
girls hollering about love and destiny, men tossing around
words like hero. Flashes went off, panties were thrown—
seriously, she had always thought that was a myth—but the
band walked on, ignoring the chaos around them.

The crowd was restless, their energy palpable, just as Joe
had said. It hit Emma like a wall as she stepped to the back
of the stage and up the short flight of stairs. One of the
security team keyed his walkie and alerted that the band was
ready.

The arena lights went out.

Emma's heart began to race as she was drawn into the excitement of it all.

Disguised by darkness, the band took the stage and got in position. Joe remained behind. A roadie handed him an earpiece, which he placed in his right ear. He tilted his head as if listening to someone or something, then gave a thumb up and a nod. He rolled his shoulders, bounced on the balls of his feet and shook his arms—loosening his muscles.

The audience grew restless, their volume increased.

Kirk pounded the beat on the bass drum and Bobby joined him.

People whistled, women screamed. It was intense, the noise level deafening.

Even with the stage lights so low, Emma could see Joe's body begin to vibrate. Steve and Zach began the opening chords of the song, their guitars melding together perfectly. Joe moved forward, taking the wireless mic someone held out to him and gliding across the darkened stage with a skill born of practice.

Emma's heart synced to the beat. Anticipation built slowly, painfully, until the band's haunting melody was the only sound. Everyone could see the shadow at the front of the stage, and waited anxiously for what was to come. The music trailed off and everything went silent. Then, just when she thought she could wait no longer, all the lights in the house went on with a flash; from pitch black to blinding in a nanosecond. The band leapt into action, flipped on with the same switch that lit the arena. The crowd roared and launched to their feet.

Center stage Joe smiled at his audience then released one of his trademark growls.

Emma's toes curled in her shoes. She shivered in delight. Just last night she'd had that sound in her ear as he'd moved between her legs—the rumbling that seemed to start at his feet, vibrating through his entire body before releasing from the back of his throat. She shifted, more aroused than she wanted to admit. Her nipples hardened, aching in the worst way possible.

Sweet Jesus, how was she going to make it through the whole show when just the first sixty seconds made her wet?

The man knew what he had done to her, too. He glanced over his shoulder, focused his attention to the spot she occupied, and flashed an arrogant, gorgeous smile before breaking out in song.

"Asshole," she whispered affectionately.

Seventy minutes later, Emma remained glued to the same spot. A little less horny than she'd been in the beginning, but still having a wonderful time. Watching a concert from backstage was a new experience for her, and while she enjoyed it, it wasn't something she would recommend for everyone. First, it was painfully loud, something she hadn't expected. With all the speakers aimed toward the audience, she thought it would be quieter. Yet her ears were ringing more than the night she stood front row center. The second reason for not recommending her current position was the view. There wasn't much of one. All she could see of any of them was their backs.

Not that Joe's backside was painful to look at. She just preferred his front, which she had an amazing view of whenever he stepped out for a clothing change. When Joe traded sweat-soaked shirts for dry ones, he did so not three feet from her. This allowed her to watch him: the flex and play of muscle, the shimmer of the lights on his skin. It provided her a front row seat to half-naked Joe. Not that she didn't already know what full-naked Joe looked like.

Damn. She began to salivate just thinking about it.

As if summoned by her thoughts, Joe stepped off stage. He removed his earpiece and took the towel Beth handed him, rubbing it over his head and face. In a move choreographed by time and practice, Beth pulled his soiled shirt over his head and replaced it with a fresh one without any awkwardness, even as he towel-dried his chest. Joe shoved his arms through the sleeves, released the towel into Beth's hands and replaced his earpiece. The entire process took seconds and, fascinated by it, Emma watched every time.

Joe never seemed to notice though, always returning to the stage as quickly as he'd stepped away. But not this time. While Zach continued his guitar solo, Joe drank greedily from a cup he'd been handed. Then he turned and met Emma's gaze.

He grinned, crooked his finger, and mouthed "Come here".

She stepped toe to toe with him.

Without warning, his right arm snaked around her, warm and taut with muscle, pulling her in tightly as he pressed a hard kiss against her lips. Stunned, she didn't react quickly enough, and was left standing there with a stupid grin on her face as he returned to the stage.

"I wouldn't get overly excited."

"Sorry?" Emma asked, turning to the woman on her left. People had been moving about, in and out of the area throughout the show, which by her guess was nearly complete. This girl, however, she hadn't seen before.

"That kiss?" The smile she gave Emma seemed less than sincere even though it was blindingly bright. "I wouldn't get overly excited about it. You're not at all his type."

"Really? I suppose you are?"

"Of course," she replied with a nod, running her fingers through her long curly hair. She had beautiful bottle-blonde hair and ginormous fake breasts. Breasts she appeared very proud of, as she made a show of positioning them in her low cut dress as she smacked her glossy lips.

Emma smiled. All petty jealousy aside, this chick didn't stand a chance with Joe. He didn't like fakes.

She turned back to the stage.

Which seemed to set the woman off. "I mean seriously, why would he go slumming with you when he could have me?"

Emma wore her typical jeans and a tank—this one sporting the band's name and tour dates—her favorite pink Chuck's on her feet. How did that equal slumming?

The chick's eyes went to the stage. "Or her for that matter. Even that skank is classier than you."

The skank she was referring to had managed to make her way over the barrier before security could grab her. She ran across the stage and launched herself at Joe, literally taking flight. Gary snagged her mid-air before she could body slam Joe but, hell bent on wrapping herself around him, she grabbed at his shirt, scratching and clawing before being hauled off the stage.

Fake tits began to laugh, snorting like it was the funniest thing she had ever seen. Emma found it disturbing. As a fan, it was one thing to appreciate the band members, another to want to meet them. It was a completely different story to paw at them as if they were a piece of meat.

"Face it, sweetheart," the chick said with a flip of her hair. "You are completely out of your league."

Emma skimmed her gaze over the woman. Dressed in a barely there scrap of lace—*was that a dress or a tube top?*—that barely covered the essentials, the chick's entire purpose for being backstage was unmistakable. This woman was looking to bang a rock star, and she didn't care what she had to do to make it happen. It was too bad, really, because beneath the bleached hair and over the top boobs, she was a pretty girl. But the slutty dress and desperate gleam in her eyes screamed cheap. The yellow blowjob smiley hanging around her neck cinched it.

Emma bit the inside of her cheek and told herself not to comment. When the woman arched her brow and flashed a smile that could only be interpreted as her believing she'd won the verbal battle, Emma broke her silence.

"Nice pass," she said, flashing her best social smile. "You've got a little something right...." She rubbed at a spot on her bottom lip.

Fake tits actually rubbed at her own lip before Emma's meaning seemed to sink in. "Bitch!"

"As if you're the first person to ever point that out." Fed up with it all, Emma walked away.

What a petty beast. God, people sucked.

She massaged her temples as she headed for the rear steps, nearly running into Beth in the process. Beth gave her a big smile and a thumb up but Emma returned neither. Putting the bitch in her place had been far too easy. Not falling for her line of crap in the first place would have been the better move, but her lack of sleep over the past forty-eight hours was catching up with her. And fast. A dull ache had started at the base of her skull, and she was feeling tense and abrasive.

The man minding the barrier gave her a nod as she

passed through, heading left. She considered hitting the concession stand for some water, but that meant circling back the way she had come. Instead, she ducked into the first room after turning into the hall leading to the band's dressing rooms. Long tables covered in booze lined the left and back walls, and a couple dozen people already milled about. Last time she'd been in a room like this, the water had been hidden beneath the table at the back. Emma headed for it.

No one gave her a second glance as she crossed the room, not until she flipped up the table covering and pulled a bottle of water from the cooler.

"You look like you know your way around here," came a male voice from behind her. Too close behind her. Emma took a step to the side, startled.

"Maybe you could help me." His smile made her skin crawl. "Where can we go that is private?"

"Who?" Him and his imaginary friend? There was no one else there.

"You and me."

She slapped his hand away as he reached for her breast—correction, the all access pass hanging between her breasts. "Personal space, learn it."

Heads turned and soon more people joined Mr. Grabby Hands in a half circle around her. The first was a redhead who regaled her with tales of Joe and how she was going to fuck him. Then came the questions: What relationship did she have with the band? Could she get their autographs? How about an introduction? One guy even tried to shove his CD into her hands while promising to get her fuck drunk if she would pass it to the band.

Sweet Jesus, these people were fucking insane.

She headed across the room, weaving through the crowd as best she could, finally hugging the wall before she made any headway. She stopped short when Bobby stepped in front of her.

"Hey," he said, Cheshire cat grin in place. "You're Emma, right?"

She had been re-introduced to the members of the band during their sound check, so he knew exactly who she was. "Yeah, that would be me."

"You're cute."

"Ah, thanks, you are, too?" Big mistake, for he stepped in closer. Close enough she could smell the booze on his breath and the sweat on his skin. Unlike Joe, whose post-concert scent drove her wild, Bobby's turned her stomach. "Excuse me."

Emma stepped right.

Bobby stepped with her. "Cute, but not really Joe's type."

"Not the first time I've heard that today."

"No?" He shifted closer.

"You're really going to want to back off."

"Why would I do that? Maybe you're just playing hard to get."

"I don't think so."

His gaze flitted over her body. "We could have a little fun, Joe won't care. We've shared before."

Jesus, what kind of people lived like this? Fakes and takers—users treating people like pawns on a chessboard, a means to an end. It all made her sick to her stomach. "Listen up, Poulsen. If you don't get the hell away from me, you're going to be singing soprano for the rest of the night. Why don't you take your lame ass lines and arrogant bullshit and use them on someone else? Hey, you know what? There are a couple of yellow smiley babes standing behind you right now. I bet one of them would be interested in a man drunk enough he probably can't even get it up."

Someone started laughing. *Great, because I wanted an audience.* A glance over Bobby's shoulder told her it was Steve.

Bobby took advantage of her distraction. He curled his hand around her upper arm and leaned in, making sure she felt his erection by pressing it against her side. "Make no mistake doll, I can get it up."

And one swift kick to the junk would get it back down. "Take your dick off me," she growled.

"Fuck's sake, Bobby, you have a death wish?" Steve pulled Bobby away from her, his gaze bouncing off the man's groin. "You did not just... I've seen the way Joe looks at this one. He's going to beat the shit out of you for touching his girl."

The dumb ass didn't appear concerned. He flashed his teeth in a big smile. "Like hell. If Joe's that into her, why is she out here with us while he hides away in his dressing room?"

"Walk away, Bobby," Steve said, voice tight and furious.

Thank Christ, he did.

Emma took a deep breath and rubbed her temples. She popped the top on her water bottle and scanned the room. In those few minutes of tense conversation, the crowd had grown exponentially. Bodies were everywhere, mostly women. Tall and short, anorexic and plus size, blonde, brunette, and everything in between. Most with the same abhorrent pass. "Does this go on after every show?"

Standing a respectable distance away, Steve sipped his

drink, ignoring the hopeful glances of the girls nearby. "You have to be more specific. I'm not sure what *'this'* you are referring to."

"The booze, the party, the massive amount of women with yellow smiles around their necks?"

He grinned—no teeth from this one. "Mostly."

Emma frowned and swallowed some more water. "I'm guessing your roadies see a lot of action."

"I suppose they do. I take it you object."

"It's disconcerting, seeing as over half the women in the room are sporting those smiles."

"That's the life, babe," Steve replied with a shrug.

She cringed at the derogatory term. It certainly wasn't an endearment. "Using people is your life? If so, *babe*, your life sucks. It's not bad enough that nearly everyone in this room wants to use you, you have to return the favor?"

"Women want to get close to us," he replied, no longer so cocky about it. "So they seek out ways to make that happen."

It was more likely that his crew had learned to seek out women willing to do anything for the promise of getting close to the band. "That's really the type of women you want to surround yourself with?"

"It's a party. We want party people."

A couple of girls were making out on the far side of the room, mouths and hands all over each other. Next to them two guys held their cell phones aloft, videotaping the action. A man sat slouched against a wall with a woman in a tiny sparkly dress in his lap. He fondled and kneaded her breasts, pinching at her nipples while she deep throated the tongue of the dude on her right.

But the exhibition that captured and held her gaze, was

the girl rubbing herself against Bobby, tugging at his waistband, working his zipper down. Jesus, was she really going to drop to her knees and blow him in front of everyone? Charming.

"I can honestly say that your idea of a party and mine are worlds apart."

Steve followed her line of sight. "Fuck." He stepped over to the pair, muttering more expletives, pulling Bobby away from the girl before she could get more than one hand into his pants. "Whoa, mate, you color blind tonight?"

Color blind? Emma glanced back at the girl, noting for the first time the bright yellow blowjob smiley around her neck. Jesus. She was going to throw up.

She gave the group a wide berth as she bolted for the door and headed for the exit. She had to get out, away from it all. It was disgusting, the way they treated women. Hell, the way these women treated themselves was demoralizing. Her hands began to shake. Fresh air was a necessity.

"Emma."

At the sound of her name, she looked up and spotted Joe, bottle of Jameson in his hand, standing outside the door of his dressing room with Gary. Fantastic. As if this night didn't suck ass enough, she had drunk Joe to deal with. No, no, and oh, hell no. Emma walked right past them.

She rounded the last corner at a near jog. Just up ahead, at the end of the hall, was the exit. Her skin crawled. Her stomach rebelled. If one more person grabbed at her or offered sexual favors, if she witnessed just one more act of depravity, she was seriously going to lose her shit. Or hurl, it was still a toss-up which one would happen first. The door drew closer, she was nearly there, almost free.

A hand hooked her elbow and, God help her, she came

out swinging. Still holding her elbow, Joe caught her fist with his other hand. The bottle of Jameson clattered to the floor at their feet, soaking her shoes. Fucking perfect.

The stench of whiskey engulfed them.

"Christ, Emma, what the fuck?" Since she was still struggling to break free, he used the weight of his body to stop her, pinning her against the wall.

"Let me go," she snarled, gaze locked on that exit sign. "One drunken mauling is all I can take, thanks."

The body pressed against hers went taut. "Someone touched you?"

"I need to leave." She stared at her escape, so close yet so far away. "You have to let me leave."

"Not until you talk to me. What happened?"

Emma focused on him for the first time. His mouth drawn tight, concern darkened his eyes. "So far tonight I've been told I was out of my league, someone offered to get me fuck drunk of all things, and oh, I was also asked if I'd be willing to arrange a hook up between you and a lovely redhead named Ginger of all things. Ginger was even kind enough to tell me she would start your evening of debauchery by sucking you off. She included a verbal description of how she imagined you would taste."

"Christ."

"Twice I was told how I'm not your type. Twice. I've been propositioned more times than I care to think about, and assured by the one that you have no problem sharing women, so hey, having a dick pressed against my hip wasn't something I should get so upset about."

His body tightened, his nostrils flared. "Who told you that? Give me a name."

She pushed against his chest to no avail. "It doesn't matter because I've had enough of this fucking place and everyone in it." Her voice escalated to a near shout. "So, if you don't mind, get off me!"

This time when she pushed him, Joe released her.

She made a beeline for the exit, slamming the push bar as hard as she could and shoving the door wide. The cool night air welcomed her and she sucked it in, forcing the smell of sweat soaked bodies from her nostrils. Sickening it was all so very sickening. Unable to control the flood of adrenaline racing through her veins, she began to pace.

Joe followed her outside. Choosing a spot beneath the light, he leaned against the building, wisely keeping his distance.

"You want to fuck me, too?" she asked, her tone sounding foreign to her own ears. "How about right here? Beneath this light is as good a spot as any, right? Not like anyone around here seems to care if they have an audience."

"I care," he replied softly. "That's not my thing."

Emma stopped in her tracks and faced him. Hands in his front pockets, wet hair hanging in his eyes, his face all shadows and light...he was so damn handsome it hurt to look at him.

"And I don't share. Maybe once or twice in the very beginning—"

"Stop, please."

"—when I was young and stupid and we were just starting out."

His admission didn't help. "I never needed to know that," she whispered, clutching her stomach. There was a very good chance she was going to be sick. "I don't want that image in my head."

"I would never share you. You're mine, Emma. Do you

hear me?"

The trembling started—adrenaline tinged with a boat-load of disgust. "Is it always like this?" She wasn't exactly certain why she was asking. Hadn't Steve already told her it was? "How can you stand it, Joe? The petty jealousy runs rampant in this place. I mean, how do you know who your friends are?"

"I don't. There's no way to know who is here because they care about me and who just wants to use me. The options are endless—money, forge a friendship with me so I can introduce them to someone else, bragging rights."

"Bragging rights?"

He shrugged. "Fuck a superstar, maybe you can eat off it for a week. Tell their story to the rag magazines or, better yet, manage to get pregnant and you're set for life."

"That's repulsive." She twisted the top off the water bottle still clutched in her hand and chugged. It wasn't enough to remove the sour taste in her mouth. What was wrong with people? "Jesus, it's too bad you dropped the whiskey. I could use some right now."

"You don't drink."

"I could start." If this was the kind of shit that went down night after night, it was no wonder he was an accomplished drinker.

"No," he said softly, adamantly. "And to clarify your earlier statement, I am not drunk."

She took a long hard look at him. He was right. Nothing about him said he'd had anything to drink. His damp hair could be from being onstage, but she would guess it was from a shower, as he hadn't smelled like anything but soap as he'd pinned her to the wall. His words weren't slurred in any way like they'd been that night on the phone. His eyes weren't vulnerable and sad like they'd been the first night she'd met him. She didn't know for certain, but imagined hiding emotions was far more difficult when drinking. Tonight, as he stood beneath that light not three feet from her, she couldn't read him for nothing.

"Your world, Joe…I had no idea. How could I have even imagined?" He stood there, his dark eyes on her, silent and assessing. Her throat tightened, her eyes burned. "No wonder you seem so sad and lonely sometimes. You need me."

"Yes." He didn't deny it, didn't shy away from it, or pretend her words weren't true. "But I think right now, you may just need me more. Come here, Sunshine. Let me hold you."

JOE DIDN'T REALIZE he'd been holding his breath until Emma stepped into his arms and pressed her face against his chest. Christ, she was upset. Enough she had taken a swing at him. She'd meant business, too. If he hadn't dropped the whiskey bottle, she would have connected with his jaw. Sick bastard he was, the thought made him smile. She had spirit, his ray of sunshine. He liked that about her.

Wrapping one arm around her middle, he eased her closer, snugging her against his body. She released a shuddered breath and he curled his other hand to the back of her head and pressed his cheek to her hair. He did his best to school his breathing, but it wasn't easy. There was more than just anger flowing through her veins, riling her up. Someone had hurt her.

"Who manhandled you?" Pressed his dick against her hip is what she'd said. *Fuck.* He was going to break it off.

Emma shook her head then buried her face in his neck.

Her arms tightened around him.

He was going to kill the bastard. Tear his balls off and shove them down his throat. Joe had firsthand knowledge of what it felt like to be mauled and pawed at. He was sporting the claw marks on his chest to prove it. It was bad enough when the women came after him, but at least he could get away. Emma wasn't very big, and a man could overpower her fairly easily.

His body tightened at the thought. Bile crawled up the back of his throat. "Tell me who touched you." There was no disguising the anger in his voice.

"Joe," she whispered, her hands stroking his back, soothing him as she'd done after his interview. Her soothing him, instead of the other way around like it was supposed to be. "It doesn't matter anymore."

Her breathing leveled out, the trembling eased. Not wanting to stir her up again, Joe didn't argue.

Her hands skimmed his body, almost like she couldn't help herself. Not clawing desperation or groping, but the brush of her fingertips, a gentle caress. Christ, he needed it.

He'd walked off stage, stupid grin in place, knowing he'd find her waiting for him. Desperate to see her, touch and be touched by her. Only her: Emma. After a mere twenty-four hours, he was addicted. To the way she made him feel, how she made him complete. She was his new drug. And when she hadn't been there, he'd gone in search of his old drug. This had done nothing but make him feel unworthy. He hadn't lied to her, he wasn't drunk. Not on whiskey, as he hadn't consumed enough of it. But, as he stood outside that arena, sunshine in his arms, the brush of her hands over his chest, he knew he could get drunk on her. He was desperate for it.

"Come back inside," he whispered, need making his voice husky. "We'll go to my dressing room."

"No! I'm not going back in there." She pushed out of his arms, leaving him empty.

He tucked his hands into his pockets to keep from reaching for her.

The wind picked up, the smell of rain in the air.

She shivered, reaching out, her fingers brushing his jaw. "The bus."

He opened his mouth, then carefully closed it, not wanting to misinterpret her meaning.

She dropped her hand to his shoulder, smoothed it down his chest where she fisted the front of his shirt and tugged. "We'll go to the bus."

He licked his suddenly dry lips. "Okay."

"Okay," she repeated with a smile. Then she turned and headed for the bus, the sway of her hips in the moonlight drawing his gaze.

"Gare?" He didn't need to look away from Emma to find the man. Gary was there somewhere, far enough away to allow their conversation to remain private, yet near enough to step in if anyone tried to interrupt. Sure enough, Gary materialized out of the shadows and walked to Joe's side.

Joe met his gaze, no longer worried about keeping his emotions in check. "Find out who put their hands on her."

"It'll be my pleasure."

"Just don't touch him. The bastard is mine."

April 20

Two days ago I wrote about my dream trip to Europe and how I would have to make it alone. But how quickly things can change! Yesterday, instead of getting on that flight to Scotland, I got on a flight to join Joe. Today I sit in the rear lounge of Blind Man's Alibi's tour bus while the band is away at an interview. We're in Lake Charles, Louisiana, and while alone at this very moment, I am no longer alone.

No longer alone.

Just writing that makes my stomach flutter. I've been lonely for so long, it's still a shock to my system, near impossible to imagine. I'd pinch myself to make certain I'm not dreaming, but the ache in my body does that for me. Oh, the aches! I never could have imagined. My body isn't used to the workout I got last night. Or the one again this morning. Wow. He... It's hard to explain, but I'll try.

I imagined that sex with Joe would be incredible. Off the charts, even. What I never expected was how it would change me. I know that sounds cliché but, something inside of him speaks to me on a level I've never experienced before. His focus on me was complete, leaving me no room to hide. Not from the way he made me feel, or even how I made him feel. We laughed and made love, then did it all over again. The things... In the hard light of day I should be embarrassed, but how can I be? I can never be embarrassed by the things I do with Joe. He draws out my every desire, even the ones I kept hidden from myself. Not just my sexual desires, but also my desires for life. He makes me...happy. He makes me the person I was before cancer.

Joe makes me want to follow through with my promise to take risks, make love in the rain, dance beneath the stars, and cherish every moment. He makes me want to embrace life for however long I have left. And as I swear to follow through on this promise to myself, I'll make one other promise. Along the way, I will teach Joe how to do the same.

I'll find a way to drive away the darkness and replace it by light. Do away with the sadness and bring back the joy. Life is precious; you can't treat yourself like an afterthought. If we're going to dance, let's dance.

Number of days since I decided to live: 60
Number of days since I met Joe: 17
Current level of panic: 4/10

TWELVE

April 20

JOE PROPPED HIS back against the couch in the rear lounge and watched Emma. Her eyes were closed, her face relaxed. She was asleep, sprawled across the blanket he'd tossed to the floor before having his merry way with her. Facing him, her head propped on her hands, not a stitch on. Her body glowed in the soft light. With every curve highlighted, every part of her on display, he sat and looked his fill.

Christ, what this woman did to him. She was terrifying.

He'd meant to take her slow and gentle, savoring every caress, every touch of her hands across his skin, every stroke of their bodies coming together. It had taken only the barest brush of her lips against the scratches the stretched from his right collarbone diagonally across his pec to throw those good intentions out the window.

He was sick of the shit, sick of it all. The so-called friends she spoke of, the fakes and fanatics. He had told her the truth today on that stage; she was his favorite place to be. With her. Anywhere with her. In ten years, she was the only one who had ever touched him. He'd needed that, needed her. To help chase away the demons. To do the job the whiskey no longer could. So he had taken her hard and fast—taken her six ways from Sunday—and she'd let him.

Anything he'd asked of her, she'd given. Anything he gave, she took. He'd wanted to forget and he had. Lord, he had. He'd lost himself in her.

He had no control where she was concerned. She wove a spell around him, brought him to his knees. Even now, need pounded through him. He wanted nothing more than to roll her beneath him and bury himself inside her again. Experience the sensation of her warm, wet heat closing around him, taking him deep. The sweet friction of her lean body pressed against his.

Sweet hell. And someone had told her she was out of her league. They had no bloody idea.

Joe stood and grabbed his jeans where they lay across the back of the couch. In her sleep, Emma said his name. Just his name and he was squatting at her side, pulling the blanket over her and whispering words of comfort. Words he couldn't hear over the rush of emotion flooding him. Christ, he was a goner.

Pulling up his pants, he walked away from her, shutting the door behind him.

He discovered Kirk and Gary in the front lounge, talking quietly while on the muted television the boys of Top Gear played rugby with cars and a giant ball. Joe grabbed a mug from the cupboard and filled it with hot water from the coffee maker. He added a tea bag and honey. No one spoke until he had sipped the brew, soothing his tired throat. Eighteen months of near nightly performances—vocally, he was at his limit. "What did you find out?"

Gary stood. Not a good sign.

Shit. Gone was the contented bliss of a few moments ago, replaced by tight muscles and a burning sensation in the pit of his stomach. Joe sipped his tea, waiting for the ball the drop.

"Bobby cornered her at the after party."

Kirk swore.

Joe tightened his grip on the mug.

"Told her she wasn't your type," Gary continued, his hands opening and closing at his sides like he wanted to hit something. "That they could have a little fun, you wouldn't care, you were into—"

"Sharing." Of course, it had been Bobby. "Fucker." Joe set the mug aside instead of throwing it against the wall as he wanted to. Anger burned like acid until he clenched his teeth so tightly his jaw popped. The temperature in the room seemed to rocket.

The bus started to move, slowly pulling away from the arena. Joe moved faster. He whipped open the door and was forced to hold on or lose his balance as the bus slammed to a halt with a squeal of brakes.

"Remember what I taught you," Gary called out as Joe vaulted into the parking lot.

He'd taught him to inflict pain, and that's what Joe planned to do.

The second bus sat idling a good thirty feet away. Rage fueling his every step, Joe closed the distance in record time. Flinging the door wide, he stomped up the steps, the slap of his bare feet the only sound.

Three sets of eyes stared at him as he rounded the corner and stepped into the front lounge. Joe only cared about one of them. "You motherfucker."

Bobby launched to his feet. "Fuck. Look, I'm sorry man, I just—"

Joe plowed his fist into Bobby's face, welcoming the shock of pain that burst through his hand.

Bobby stumbled back, blood gushing from his nose. "Goddamnit!" He covered his bloody face, voice muffled and thick. "You had to hit me in the face?"

Joe couldn't recall the last time he was this angry. His body shook with it, heart pounding a furious beat in his chest. His own band mate—his brother. This was the man who'd put the haunted look in Emma's eyes, who'd pressed his dick against her while propositioning her. "I could fucking kill you right now, Bobby. You ever put your hands on her again and I'll go for more than your face."

His meaning was unmistakable as he glanced at the bass propped on the end of the couch: a hand-carved sapele and ebony fretless five string. The thing Bobby loved most.

"You wouldn't!"

Joe lowered his voice, tone menacing. "I will not only destroy it, I'll shove the pieces so far up your arse it'll require a surgeon to remove them."

"What the shit, man, she's just a—"

"Shut the fuck up, Bobby," Steve warned.

Too late. Joe already had him by the front of his shirt, fist pulled back and ready to swing.

Zach caught him by the elbow before he could follow through. "Whoa, Joe, he doesn't know what he's saying. He's drunk."

Steve stepped between them, pushing Bobby back, putting distance between him and Joe. "That's no excuse and you know it, Zach."

"Yeah, I do, but you really want to watch Joe pound him?" He released Joe's arm. "Seriously, Joe, he's not worth breaking your hand on his face."

"No, but Emma is." Joe wiped the back of the hand in question across his mouth. "He knows better than to go after what's mine."

"Do you see this?" Bobby said to Steve. "He's lost his damn mind."

"I see it," Steve replied. "And I'll advise you to shut it."

"Lost his damn mind," Bobby muttered, pinching the bridge of his nose then staring at his bloodstained fingers. "Hey, Joe, did you leave it in your girl's snatch?"

"You are a stupid bastard, Bobby," Steve hissed, then hopped onto the couch and out of the way. "He's all yours, Joe."

Joe took two steps in Bobby's direction, who was smart enough to evade, then snagged the bass instead of pounding in his face the way he really wanted to.

Bobby sobered. "No!"

Zach began to swear.

Steve sat back down. "He asked for it."

"Joe," Bobby pleaded. "Don't. Don't hurt her. Not my baby."

God he was sick of Bobby's bloody bullshit. The man had no boundaries, no moral sense at all. He went after anything and everything he wanted, most times on a whim, and didn't care who he hurt in the process. This time he had crossed the line. Hurting Emma was the last straw.

A crack of thunder shook the ground beneath the bus. The skies opened up, the sound of pounding rain against the roof near deafening.

Joe turned and headed for the exit. He leapt from the bus, welcoming the cool drops against his overheated skin. Winding up like a discus thrower, he flung the instrument as far as he could. The resounding crack as it hit the asphalt wasn't near as satisfying as bloodying Bobby's face a bit more would have been, but the roar that followed was close.

Gary and Kirk stood in the door of their bus. Joe squeezed past them, shaking the rainwater from his hair. "Let's get out of here, Clay."

His driver nodded and shifted into gear.

"Feel better?" Gary asked, no expression on his face.

Joe rolled his shoulders, attempting to dislodge the tension. "Fuck, no."

"I do." Kirk took his usual seat and looked out the window to where Bobby was scooping his bass off the parking lot. He smiled broadly. "He's been asking for it for months."

Joe began to pace, which wasn't easy to do in the small confines. He rolled his wrist, opened and closed his aching hand.

"Head or gut?" Gary asked.

"His nose is bleeding like a bitch."

Gary's eyes lit with a quick flash of humor.

Joe grinned. "It felt good. Satisfying."

"All that adrenaline and endorphins coursing through your body, I don't doubt it." Gary tipped his head to where Joe was cracking his knuckles and shaking his hand. "They're starting to wear off and it doesn't feel so hot anymore, does it? Let me have a look. It's easier than you think to break the small bones in a hand when hitting someone. Especially when you go for the face."

"Bastard's got a hard head," Joe mumbled. "I'm fine. Nothing's broken."

"Except Bobby's nose, I hope." Kirk was still smiling. It looked good on him.

"Take a seat." Gary pointed at the corner of the couch nearest the table, upon which a first aid kit rested.

Joe circled the table and sat down sideways, his back against the wall. One foot on the cushion, the other on the floor, he faced the front of the bus, resting his right hand on the table. He closed his eyes. "What's with the first aid kit? Did you think I was going to let him land a punch?"

"You were pretty pissed off." Gary began scooping ice into a bowl. Joe didn't need to see it. He could hear it. "People get sloppy when fueled by rage."

He was still pissed off. "You taught me better than that."

"Maybe. The kit is for the scratches on your chest, though. They're not pretty, the one looks a tad bloody, make sure you clean them good."

Joe had washed them with soap in the shower, but opened his eyes and pulled the kit closer. Removing an alcohol swab, he tore it open and scrubbed his skin.

Gary placed the bowl of ice on the table. He picked up Joe's hand, flexing it, moving it this way and that, pressing his fingers between the knuckles. "The scratches are curtesy of the girl who climbed the barrier?"

"Yeah." Joe winced when Gary hit a sore spot. Gary tortured him by working his fingers even deeper. "Christ."

"Your hand's fine," Gary pronounced.

"Told you."

"Best to be certain. Ice it, you don't want it swelling too much. You have to perform for the masses again tomorrow."

Their current number one hit had Steve and Zach on electric guitar, and Joe playing acoustic. Joe tore open another swab before pushing his right hand into the ice. "Sure thing, mom."

Gary frowned. He took his place at the end of the couch and crossed his legs at the ankles. "Your girl has a decent swing of her own. For a split second there, I thought she was going to mar your ugly mug."

"So did I," Joe admitted, setting the alcohol swab aside.

He'd managed to break open the one scratch. It oozed a bit.

Kirk straightened. "Emma took a swing at you?"

Gary and Joe smiled.

"She did. Gare here didn't even try to protect me."

"What do you think I was doing, taking you sparring all these months?"

"Trying to give me a release other than whiskey," Joe replied honestly.

"It helped your reflexes, too. She damn near connected."

Kirk crossed to the refrigerator and removed a bottle of beer. On his way back to his seat, he picked up Joe's mug, holding it in a manner that asked if Joe wanted it.

Joe tipped his head.

Kirk handed it over. "I wish I'd seen it."

"No you don't." All the humor left Joe.

Gary shook his head. "Her eyes were wild, like a cornered animal."

"Bobby," Kirk guessed.

"I get the feeling he was just a small part of what had her running out of the arena like all the demons in hell were hot on her tail."

Joe frowned at Gary. "He was the one who pushed her over the edge."

The rear toilet flushed. They fell silent and waited to see if Emma was coming out of the room or not. The door opened and she stepped out wearing a tank top and tiny shorts, wrapping the blanket around her as she walked.

She was an exhausted and tousled mess. Joe couldn't contain his smile. "Hey, Sunshine, did we wake you?"

She shook her head. "I got cold."

He motioned her over. She took the spot between his legs, turning onto her side to face the others, her legs curled up next to her. He wrapped his arm around her as she snuggled against his chest.

"What were you all talking about before I interrupted?"

"Taking you to the gym with us tomorrow," Gary replied. "I think you'd make one hell of a sparring partner."

"I got a bit carried away, didn't I?"

"You took a swing and missed. There are worse things." Kirk's gaze settled on the table. "Wait until you find out what Joe did to Bobby."

"What?" Emma sat up and narrowed her eyes at his hand soaking in ice. "What is it about men that they think they have to pound the shit out of each other?"

"Says the woman who took a swing at me."

She grinned. "You've got me there, but—"

"He touched you," Joe stated matter-of-factly.

"Who told you?" His refusal to answer her question caused her to frown. "Now you're hurt. Because of me."

"He's fine," Gary informed her, making it sound like she was overreacting. "You know rock stars, all delicate and soft."

Kirk jumped in. "Joe lives for the attention, why do you think he sings? Standing out front like *'look at me, I'm all fabulous and shit'.*"

Joe glared at both of them, but it worked. Emma laughed, relaxing against him. Her thumb made slow sweeps across his ribs.

"I'm fine," he reassured.

"What about Bobby?"

"He'll heal." Joe tipped his head back and rested it against the wall, soaking up her touch. "I'm not too sure about his bass, though."

April 30

"GARY, IT'S EMMA. I…need a ride. I don't have any money for cab fare because…I was…robbed. I was robbed."

Beautiful, Em, way to trigger his protective side. She'd start the voice message over, but what would be the point?

"Don't get all scary ogre on me, I'm all right."

Except for the headache making itself known, her second in ten days. Probably due to lack of proper rest which, ironically enough, is why she'd fallen asleep at the beach and had her bag stolen. At least she'd had her cell beneath the edge of her towel or she'd really be screwed. As it was, she was out her laptop, bankcard, about fifty bucks cash, shirt, sunblock and favorite pair of Chucks. Oh, and her backstage pass as well as her passport. Because hey, as if replacing everything else wasn't going to be problematic enough, she had to try to refill a prescription without proper identification. Perfect.

Two uniformed police officers stood a few feet away, waiting to take her report, but she had to call Gary first. No way was she pulling up to the arena in a cop car. She wouldn't be allowed in, anyway, not without her pass.

"I'm at…" Emma pinched the bridge of her nose and wracked her brain. "North Beach. Near the entrance. My head hurts and I have nothing but my bikini and a towel." *Why was she telling him this?* She glanced at the two officers, the younger one staring at her in a way that made her uncomfortable. Wrapping her towel around her waist, she admitted, "I'm feeling a little bit vulnerable right now so…if you could send a car to pick me up, that would be great." *Shit.* "Okay, I'll…wait. I'll wait right here."

She disconnected.

The officers asked her a billion questions, including if they could see her I.D. Yeah, because a woman who had just had her belongings stolen would have that. Really? What made it worse, the entire time the older officer typed the information into his iPad, the younger ogled her breasts. He was obviously not a size-based guy, as there were much larger specimens on the beach, but hers happened to be right there in his face, highlighted by her turquoise bikini top. He was skeeving her out so bad that when the big black SUV pulled up alongside of them and Gary stepped out—not normal, everyday Gary, but puffed up, scary Gary—she damn near cried with relief.

He did his bodyguard thing, scanning the area around him, then stepped to her side, gently taking hold of her elbow. "Emma, are you all right?"

"Sir," skeevy cop said, not allowing her to answer. "The young lady has reported that she was robbed this afternoon—"

Gary gave the cop a look and he shut up. Yup, big scary ogre Gary was that terrifying. He even made a man with a gun on his hip take a step back.

"I'm okay, Gary," Emma answered, bringing his attention back to her.

She sighed with relief when he produced a shirt for her to put on. She didn't even care that it was a man's shirt and three sizes too large. Trading her straw fedora for the shirt, she pulled it on.

"Why are you fidgety?" There wasn't a single ounce of happy in his eyes as he dropped her hat back on her head. "What aren't you telling me?"

Emma didn't answer. Didn't want to answer.

Gary narrowed his eyes. "Emma?"

She slid the officer a look, confirming he was still staring at her, even with a shirt covering the view. When Emma crossed her arms over her chest, Gary straightened. Damn if he didn't puff up even more before facing off with the officers.

"Stop it." She hadn't even had to point out which man was making her uncomfortable for the guy wasn't quick to evert his gaze. When Gary shifted forward, she curled both hands around his bicep. "No."

Of course, he ignored her. "You get off disrespecting helpless women?"

Shit. She might have argued being called helpless if she wasn't feeling so exposed. "Gare, please, my head is pounding and I have so much to do yet before we leave tonight." Tugging on his arm was pointless, so she settled her hand in the center of his chest. "Dial it down a notch, big guy. Let's just get out of here."

Without taking his eyes off the officer, he curled his fingers around her elbow. "Are you done with her? Your report is complete?"

"Yes, sir." The older officer replied.

"Good." Gary walked her to the SUV, opening the door for her. She didn't miss the fact that, as he did so, he made sure his big body obstructed the young officer's view. Hero material, her big scary ogre was.

Emma leaned her head against the headrest and closed her eyes, expecting him to take the front passenger seat where he'd been seated when he arrived. Instead, he circled the vehicle and slid into the seat next to her.

"Please don't lecture me," she said softly. "I dozed off in the sun. I know better, but…"

"But you haven't been getting enough sleep." He nudged her hand and she opened her eyes to find him offering her a bottle of water and package of over the counter pain reliever.

"Thank you," she whispered, swallowing the pills.

"What did you lose?"

"My favorite satchel, my laptop, bankcard…" The rest was inconsequential, with the exception of, "my passport. I need to refill my medication, but I don't know how I'm going to pull it off without any photo I.D." She pinched the bridge of her nose. "Shit, my back stage pass was in there, too. I'll need a new one."

"No worries."

She bowed her head a moment and picked at the label on her water bottle. "I'm sorry."

"Why are you apologizing to me?"

"You had to come get me."

He pulled her sunglasses off, studying her face. "I didn't have to. I could have just sent the car. I *chose* to come get you."

"Why?"

He didn't answer.

"Why?" she repeated.

He looked her over slowly, then stared out the wind-shield. "I didn't like how you sounded in your voicemail. And, before you ask, you admitted you were feeling vulnerable. That is completely out of character for you, Emma."

It was.

"You draw out my protective side."

"Really?" She teased. "I thought that whole non-verbal intimidation thing you did back there was just a natural part of your charm."

His dimple flashed, and she smiled. He still wouldn't look at her.

"In case you haven't noticed…" He was quiet a moment, then blew a breath. "I'm fond of you."

"Thank you. I'm fond of you, too." Emma reached for him, hovering her hand above his arm as she wondered if she would be crossing a line, stepping over some invisible boundary. Deciding she didn't give a shit if she was, she placed her hand atop his.

He startled, glancing from her hand to her face.

"Thank you," she repeated. "Seeing you was…" She chewed her cheek, searching for the right word, finally going with the easiest one. "Comforting."

"Because you were feeling vulnerable."

"Yes."

"How bad is it? The headache?"

She removed her hand from his. "Pretty bad."

Concern colored his brown eyes. "You should lie down when we get back."

"I can't. I have to get to the pharmacy and then the laundromat. I have no clean clothes."

"Beth can—"

"No," she said with a shake of her head, regretting the move immediately as the ache increased.

"You won't use the car service. You won't use Beth's services, even though both are at your disposal. Why?"

How to explain it? "Beth doesn't need to wash my clothes. She's got enough to do."

"And the car service?"

"You have enough to do, also. You don't need to be calling for a car for me whenever I want to go somewhere. I can take care of myself, you know." Most of the time, at least.

"I'm not a charity case."

His eyebrow slid up his forehead. "No one said you were. Joe would—"

"No," she said more adamantly. "Just drop it, okay?"

He tipped his head.

"Good. You didn't tell him you had to rescue me today, did you?"

"And trigger *his* protective side? You know what happened last time."

She did. Bobby was still sporting the faded green reminder of two black eyes. He also made sure never to get too close whenever they were in the same room with each other. Emma almost felt bad for him. Almost.

As soon as the SUV pulled into the arena lot and stopped next to the bus, Emma jumped out. She headed straight for the rear lounge, where she had left all of her things. Somewhere back there was her credit card, which she needed in order to get cash to do her laundry and pick up her prescription. Her journal sat atop the low table. She flipped through the pages—thank God she hadn't taken that with her today or she would have grieved its loss more than anything else—but came up empty. She dug through her carry-on luggage. Nope. That left only one place to look.

Dropping to her knees she began digging through her bag of dirty clothes, checking the pockets of each item as she removed them. Discovering a pair of jean shorts that didn't appear too dirty, she added the towel to the stack of clothes needing washing and pulled the shorts on.

Gary hovered in the doorway. There was no other word for it.

"Damnit, I had it the other day, where did it go?" She whipped out a pair of jeans and a pale yellow thong came with them, landing on the toe of Gary's boot.

Muscle ticking in his jaw, he closed his eyes, as if the sight of that yellow scrap of lace pained him.

"Oops." She stuffed them back in her laundry bag. "You act as if you've never seen women's panties before. But they're tossed at the band damn near every night."

He let out a long, slow breath as if struggling for control. "Yes, but those don't belong to the woman sleeping with my best friend."

Emma grinned.

"I already hear more than I want to, I don't need visuals—"

"Stop." Horrified at the thought, she covered her face. "Oh my God."

"Emma."

"No, seriously. There's no privacy around here, is there?"

"Um…is this what you're looking for?" In his hand he held a black American Express card.

"You found it!"

"I thought you were a graphic designer."

"I am." She snatched it away from him, tucked it into the back pocket of her jean shorts and scooped up her bag of laundry. "I don't think I'll make it back in time for start of the show, but I'll be back before it's time to leave, okay?"

He nodded, the oddest look on his face. "The car is waiting for you. Use it."

"Gary."

"Just…humor me, okay? You're not feeling well. The driver will take you anywhere you need to go and he'll wait for you."

She nodded. "Okay, but only if you stop looking at me

like I have two heads."

"Just trying to figure you out," he admitted.

"Well, stop it. You know me. Nothing's changed." Patting him on the arm, she darted out the door, pulling her phone from her pocket as she went. "Al, it's me. I need you to do me a favor. I lost my passport today, but my driver's license is in my safe at the condo. Can you overnight it to me? I'll text you the address. Oh, and I'll also need a snapshot of it sent to me as I have to hit the pharmacy. Call me when you get this message, okay?"

JOE STOOD AT the end of the couch. From his position near Emma's head, he watched her chest rise and fall on slow, even breaths. She was turned away from the door, facing the back of the couch, her left hand covering her eyes. The presence of her injector pen on the coffee table confirmed what her body language had already told him. She'd been suffering from a headache tonight, one bad enough she'd needed her medication. She was down for the count, and wouldn't rouse for hours.

No wonder she hadn't made it to the show. He'd wondered where she was when he'd come offstage and discovered she still hadn't returned from her errands. Panicked by the thought that something had happened to her, he'd had Gary call the car service and learned she'd been dropped off hours earlier. Joe had taken the time to shower and collect his things then headed straight to the bus, where he found her just a few moments ago, asleep in the rear lounge.

Gary walked in and glanced at Emma, then the room around her. "She asleep?"

"Headache." Joe let out a slow, careful breath, then sank

to the couch. "The second in days that she's needed her medication to treat."

Gary nodded, looking over Emma again, concern evident in the tight set of his brow. "She's not getting enough sleep."

Joe sighed. "I know." He stroked Emma's arm with the back of his hand, his gut tight. "We have a three-day stretch with no shows coming up. We're all more than ready for the break."

"Yeah. She had the headache earlier today, when I picked her up at the beach."

"Where she was robbed. Which you failed to tell me about until after she'd come back then left again."

Gary took in Joe's expression and shook his head. "I didn't need your help or the logistical nightmare your arrival at that beach might have caused." His gaze settled on the coffee table, and he stepped farther into the room. Pushing her auto-injector off her open journal, he picked it up, looking back at Joe with a raised brow.

"What is it?" Joe asked.

"She ever talk to you about what she does for a living?"

"Design work, why?"

Gary shrugged and handed Joe the journal. "She's very talented."

She'd drawn him. Joe stared at the page in the dim light, speechless, completely blown away by what he was looking at. Not that it was his own mug, but the realism of the sketch. Using nothing but strokes of her pencil, light and shadow, she'd captured him so accurately it reminded him of a photograph—his eyes, the shape of his nose, shit, he could even differentiate the individual hairs in his beard. "Bloody hell."

"When did she catch you playing?" Gary asked.

"This morning." Gary's odd expression made sense now. It had been a long time since he had played for the sheer enjoyment of it. A long time. Sitting with Emma that morning, her smiling in that heart-stopping way she had while the pleasure of their love making still infused his body, he'd been filled with the need. Taking up his acoustic had felt natural, familiar, and for once in longer than he cared to admit, the joy of creating returned.

Joe placed the journal on the table and looked down at a deeply sleeping Emma. She did that for him, drew out the music buried inside of him, brought back the joy that had been missing for so long. He looked down at her and his heart took a good hard leap, crawled right up into his throat so that it was difficult to draw a deep breath.

"Fuck." He scrubbed his hand over the back of his neck and closed his eyes to the emotion rolling through him. "What am I supposed to do with this now?"

Gary grinned, as if the bastard knew exactly what Joe was struggling with. Probably did. Hell, he'd always been good at reading people.

Joe sighed. "What's so damn funny?"

"You," Gary replied simply. "Welcome back to the land of the living."

April 22

Alison is angry with me. She wasn't exactly thrilled when I gifted her and Kevin a building, but she accepted it. After all, the deed was already done – literally inked in her name. She has never really had a problem with the fact that I have money. She does have a problem when I try to spend it on her. Al is proud like that, wanting to forge her own way in life, including the up and down struggles that can arise when money is tight. She says it builds character and makes her a better person.

I already know she is one of the best damn people on this earth.

Which is why, although I respect her feelings, there are times I do things my way. Buying her that building was one of those times. Arranging to pay for all of the repairs and renovation expenses, another.

I just hung up the phone after speaking with her. She's so upset with me, she swore and Al doesn't swear. I'm truly sorry I made her that angry. I feel even worse that I brought her to tears with the reminder that she is the only family I have. Best friends. Forever.

With my forever and hers being so utterly different, I have no regrets over what I did. Building a business, making it a success as she starts a new life with Kevin, together as man and wife, is stressful enough. She doesn't need the added pressure of worrying over the cost of remodeling, or bakery equipment, or making certain her building meets code. I can give her those things. It's no worry for me.

I need her to be happy. After everything – my diagnosis and treatment, the resulting depression – she was there for me, always there for me. At times, to the detriment of her own health. Hers is a debt I can never repay. I don't have enough time. All I have is money. So I used some of it to comfort her, the way she has so often comforted me. Instead, I made her angry. I made her cry.

It tears me up, shreds me.
She is my closest friend.
My family.
The best damn person on this planet.
Maybe someday she will understand.

Number of days since I decided to live: 62
Number of days since I met Joe: 19
Current level of panic: 8/10

THIRTEEN

May 8

E MMA ENTERED THE arena, a broad smile in place. They were in Chicago, a huge change from the warmth of the Gulf of Mexico only a week ago, but she wasn't complaining. How could she, when they'd checked into a hotel in the wee hours of the morning and had a three day break from everything, even bus travel, at the close of tonight's show? She was more than ready for some time away from the chaos. Three days with nothing to do sounded like heaven to her. As heavenly as the box of cupcakes she carried smelled.

With the schedule Emma had sent her in hand, Alison had taken it upon herself to whip up and overnight a baker's dozen. Good God, they smelled good. No one baked like Alison. No one. Emma couldn't wait to get her hands on Al's newest creation—The White Russian. A vanilla bean cake with a hint of Kahlua and vodka, topped with vodka buttercream frosting and a dark chocolate curl. Alison had promised to send a couple of them, along with a variety of other flavors.

Emma turned left, heading for the dressing rooms. She'd begun memorizing the layout of the venues prior to their arrival, recognizing how much easier it made getting around the places since she wasn't always surrounded by security personnel and others who could help guide her the way the band was.

After sharing her sweets with the boys, she intended to catch a taxi to Michigan Avenue. She'd replaced her laptop—actually, Joe had—something she still wasn't comfortable with. Since she had yet to replace her satchel, she was hoping to hit Coach, as well as a few other shops, before the show. Her Am Ex was in her back pocket, calling her name, just begging to be used and abused along the Magnificent Mile.

One more left brought her to her destination—Joe's dressing room. The door was wide open, voices drifting into the hall.

"Bloody hell."

Joe, his back to the door.

Wearing jeans that hugged him like a second skin, a brown leather belt and black sleeveless T-shirt that showed off his tats, he looked like the rock god he was. He was talking to Marvin or, more accurately, Marvin was talking at Joe as Gary and the rest of the band lounged around the room.

"I don't understand why she needs to be here, is all," Marvin said, his voice far from warm.

"Because I want her here."

Marvin shook his head. "Your dick wants her here. Your brain is just along for the ride."

You little weasel. Emma snapped her spine straight.

"Marv, Jesus, quit being such an asshole," Gary snarled. "What does any of it have to do with you?"

"I prefer Joe be focused on the music instead of his pseudo-relationship. He has writing to do, another album to—"

"Fuck me." Joe's hands gripped the table in front of him, the muscles in his arms flexing. "Can we at least get through this shit storm of a tour before you start riding my ass about the next album?"

Gary cursed quietly. "He *is* focused on the music. Now more than ever."

"He's focused on his piece of ass and blind to everything else, including the fact that she's using him."

Sniveling piece of shit. "How exactly am I using him?"

Joe whirled around, surprise on his face.

Marvin smiled maliciously. "Eavesdropping?"

"You can't really call it eavesdropping when you're talking loud enough to be heard half way down the hall." She stepped out of the doorway, crossed to the table and placed the box on the center. "Premium cupcakes from my friend in Cleveland. Thought you guys might like one since she is a fantastic pastry chef. You won't be sorry."

No one moved. All conversation had stopped and, although she didn't check, it felt as if all eyes had turned to her.

So let's do this. Emma gave Marvin her sweetest smile. "Enlighten me, Marv. How am I using Joe?"

By his startled expression, her refusal to ignore the accusation took him by surprise, left him with no reply.

"I've never asked a thing of Joe."

Marvin recovered quickly enough. He looked down his nose at her. "Free travel. You get to see the States."

"Out the window of a bus that only seems to move in the dark of night?" She laughed. "I gave up an European tour to be here. Try again."

"You said Scotland," Joe said, his voice flat, strange.

"Followed by England, France, Germany and Italy."

"A lie, most likely," Marvin hissed.

Emma didn't spare him a glance. She kept her focus on Joe. "The tickets are in my journal."

Joe stared back at her, clearly shocked. "Why didn't you go? Why come here?"

"For you," she replied softly.

"For his money. You're just after his money, like all the others."

"Marv," Gary warned.

Joe said nothing.

Emma's throat went dry as dust. "Do you want to see a statement of my net worth? Would that make you happy?" She pulled her phone from her pocket. "I'll call my accountant. Does Monday work for you?"

Marvin showed his teeth. "Like any good gold digger couldn't print up a false statement."

This couldn't be happening. Marvin was coming after her with a vengeance while Joe just silently stood there, not even trying to deflect the attack. "You can't believe what he's saying, Joe. You know me better than this."

His gaze skittered away and she had her answer.

Jesus. This whole scene was horrific.

"Maybe you're just looking to hook him," Marvin rushed on. "Have a baby."

"Yeah, because all of this screams marriage and children and happily-ever-after," she replied sarcastically.

"All it takes is one child and you're set for life."

Emma sighed, scrubbing her face with her hands. "I'm already set for life, thanks."

Marv coughed a laugh.

She really wanted to hit the bastard, wipe that smug smile right off his face. His insinuations were making her ill.

Her stomach clenched into a painful knot. "What, don't I meet your idea of a woman with wealth? Let me guess. Because nothing about me screams money, I'm automatically a gold digger? How about if I have my lawyer draw up a contract stating that no pregnancy will occur and on the extremely rare possibility it does, I will not come after your client for support. Will that suffice?"

"It's a start."

"Fuck you!"

"Classy. You're real classy."

"Okay, that's enough," Zach mumbled. "This isn't funny anymore."

"This has been fun for you?" Emma asked, incredulous. "Well, I'm so glad I could entertain you all." *Shit.* She blinked and, for a terrifying moment, she thought she was going to cry.

"Joe." He couldn't possibly believe that she was anything like the women who hung out at the after parties. That she wanted—*what had he called it?*—bragging rights. She wasn't a user and she sure as hell wasn't a gold digger. As if she would ever be with him for any other reason than the fact that she cared for him. "I've never asked you to buy me anything."

"Why not?"

"What?" Jesus, she couldn't believe this. He actually looked as if he would've preferred it if she had. What was going on here? He'd shut himself down so tightly she couldn't read him. Not at all. "Fine." If this was how he wanted it. She held out her hand, palm up. "Give me your wallet."

Without hesitation, he reached into his back pocket and handed it to her.

"Did you see that?" Marvin preened. "That's exactly what I'm talking about."

She'd seen it, all right, and it only confused her more. "You think I'm using you, so you hand me your wallet?"

"I need you, Em. I may not understand why you want to be with me, but I know you make me a better person." His complete honestly surprised her, seeing as though they had an audience. "If keeping you with me means I buy you a little something every now and again, so be it."

"That's the dumbest thing I've ever heard." She could have laughed, if it wasn't also the saddest thing ever. "You want to keep me so, if that means throwing money at me, you will?"

Joe shrugged. "I have more than enough."

Damn idiot. "And if I want a Bugatti Veyron?" she asked, throwing out the most ridiculous thing she could think of. "Would you buy me one?"

He made a face. "Not the best looking car, but if that's what you really want."

"Are you fucking serious?" She shouted, and a shadow of doubt crossed his face for the first time. "A one point five million dollar supercar?" Jesus Christ, she was hyperventilating. What the hell? Did he think so little of her? "I'm not a prostitute. You can't just buy my company."

Marvin snorted.

"Shut the fuck up, Marv," Gary snarled, his face lined with fury.

"I don't think you're a prostitute," Joe said softly.

"No? Just a gold digger, then?" She looked at him and her heart broke a little. Pressing his wallet against the center of his chest, she released it, not caring if he caught it before it hit the floor. "Keep your money. If I want a supercar, I'll buy it myself."

"As if," Marvin snarled.

"Joe," Gary said sternly. "Stop this. You're not going to like where it ends."

Joe's nostrils flared. "What do you know, Gare?"

"I know in thirty seconds you're going to be the sorriest son of a bitch in this room." His gaze bounced off Marvin. "And that's saying something considering the company."

Zach laughed softly.

Fury flashed in Marvin's eyes. "Watch yourself, Gary. I can have you terminated."

"Bullshit. I don't work for you, Marv, but good try." A muscle ticked in Gary's jaw. "Go ahead, Emma, show him. Lay your cards on the table."

He meant literally.

"Damnit, it's none of his business."

"No, but your boyfriend here made it Marv's business when he failed to step up and stop this before it even started. The asshole is on a roll now. He won't stop unless you shut him down."

Marvin's back snapped straight. "Fuck you Gary. At least I'm looking out for Joe. Isn't that supposed to be your job?"

Gary scowled. "Play your card, Em. Put him in his place before I have to. I'd rather not have to resort to violence."

"Did she promise you a piece, too? Is that why you let her at Joe?"

"Jesus Christ, Marv!" Kirk exclaimed.

"She must be an amazing lay to keep Joe's attention—"

His movements a blur, Gary grabbed Marvin by the throat. Gare didn't even have to take his eyes off her to do it.

Marvin squeaked.

"STOP!" She couldn't take it anymore. Marvin's biting hatred, Gary's ferocious anger and Joe, standing silent through it all. It was time to end it. Slipping her card wallet from her back pocket, Emma slapped her black American Express on the table.

The crack echoed in a room gone quiet.

"Are you satisfied," she asked Joe. "Are we done now?"

Gary released Marvin with a light shove.

Joe stared at the card on the table.

Marvin cursed beneath his breath. "How the fuck? Who are you?"

"Hang on, I have to see this." Zach was on his feet, rushing over. "Shit, Marv, even you don't have one of these." He snagged the card off the table and flashed it at Steve, Kirk and Bobby.

"Pisses him off, too. Look at his face," Kirk snickered.

"Bloody hell," Steve exclaimed. "Joe found himself a sugar momma."

"You're all fucking assholes." She was looking at the biggest one.

"Sunshine—"

"Don't you dare," she whispered, snatching her card away from Zach. She shut her eyes tight, but a tear escaped anyway. "What have I ever done to deserve this from you? Tell me, Joe. *You* asked *me* backstage. *You* called *me* the first time. You *told* me where you were staying, essentially inviting me to join you. Now, because I did, I'm a gold digger? A user, just like everyone else you surround yourself with? Guess what? If you have nothing but users in your life, that's on you. Make a change." She turned for the door. "You can start with me."

"Where are you going?" he asked.

"Away from you."

Bobby's laughter followed her out the door. "Christ, I love your girl, Joe. If she's done with you, can I keep her?"

Emma flipped him off and kept walking. Goddamn fucking rock stars.

To hell with them all.

"IS SHE BACK?" Joe looked past Gary, glanced around the backstage area but didn't spot her. He didn't have to define the "she" he spoke of. There was only one woman he wanted to see. The same one he'd driven away that morning in his dressing room by not calling off Marvin. She'd been gone for hours, longer than ever before, and he was beginning to fear she wasn't coming back.

Gary tipped his head. "She showed up about twenty minutes ago."

Relief filled him. Joe released a breath he hadn't realized he'd been holding, then stripped his shirt off and handed it to Beth. Eager to talk to Emma, he chugged water from the bottle Beth handed him, then bent at the waist and poured the rest over his head. He pushed his dripping hair back from his face and studied his friend.

"Why do you have that look on your face? Still want to knock me on my ass for hurting her this morning?" Friend or not, there was still a bloody good chance Gary would do it.

Beth handed him a towel. Joe dried himself then pulled on a clean shirt.

"You don't have to worry about me, but if I were you, I'd brace myself. Pretty sure Emma's planning to knock you on your ass." Gary's face warped into an all-out smile.

Shit. Joe had the good sense to be nervous. She'd been working out with Gary lately, which meant she wouldn't miss. He rubbed his chin. "I should probably let her get a shot at me, huh?"

Gary laughed. "You'll never see this one coming, mate."

Seeing him in this mood stunned Joe for a second. Gary was always so serious at work. Not tonight. He was paying attention to what went on around him, but did so with a smile on his face. There was something about it which caused a kick of fear in Joe.

He wasn't ashamed to admit it.

At least not to himself.

He followed Gary out of the stage area and down the hallway, stopping to sign a couple autographs on the way. Joe's shoes echoed in the enclosed space. As usual, Gare didn't make a sound. "Is she in my room?"

"No."

Surprised, Joe slowed as they passed his dressing room and glanced inside. The room was empty. His surprise grew as they turned a corner and Gare tipped his head in the direction of the after party. It was no secret Emma hated them, did everything she could to avoid them, choosing instead to slip away and go for a walk. Usually outside, beneath the stars.

Joe crossed to the room. Centered in the doorway, he scanned for Emma, found her on the opposite side, standing with her back to him. At the sight of her, he damn near swallowed his tongue. "Fuck me dead."

Gary patted him on the shoulder as if to say 'nice knowing you'.

Joe blinked, then once more. It had to be her. He would know that ass anywhere. But...

Was she trying to kill him? She wore black leather. *He had a thing for black leather.* "Fuck me."

Gary chuckled. "You said that already."

Black leather stilettos adorned her feet, the heels high enough he wondered how she didn't lose her balance just standing in them. They had a strap across her toes, and two around her ankles that cinched with silver buckles. Shit, the shoes alone screamed sex and that was before he laid eyes on the pants.

They hugged her body, highlighting everything a man could want highlighted with the addition of silver zips in strategic locations. The way the leather cupped her ass was downright indecent. He broke out in a cold sweat.

A fitted jacket topped the look, also with silver zips. He had no idea what it was made of, just that it wasn't leather. She'd buttoned it in front, but fat lot of good that did since whatever she wore underneath was cut low enough to show off a swatch of pale skin that extended from her neck to the silver key dangling between her breasts.

Christ, she was beautiful.

She'd cut her hair; a bit shorter on the sides and back with the length left in front. Her eyes were done up the way women did them—all smoky like—and she had painted her lips the color of raspberries. Joe loved raspberries about as much as he loved Emma's smile. Too bad her smile was for the bloke who looked like he wanted to take a bite out of her.

She *was* trying to kill him. That much was obvious. He'd barely gotten his pulse settled from the show and she sent it right back into orbit. She was so fucking hot, his head almost blew off. The watch and silver bracelet on her right wrist, her nails painted a deeper, richer shade than what was on her lips. It was too much. Gary's comment about her knocking him on his ass suddenly made sense.

Without a word, Joe started across the room, blind to everything but her. She glanced his way just before he got to her and her smile faded. He wondered if it was because of the predatory look he was certain he wore or the words they'd shared so many hours ago.

Stepping between her and the man she spoke with, Joe settled his right hand on her hip and kept walking, backing her against the wall. He rested his left forearm next to her head and leaned in.

Her hand on his chest stopped him.

"What are you doing in here?" he asked.

"Talking to your friends."

"Those aren't my friends."

That brought the hint of a smile to her lips. Not as bright as the one she'd flashed that tool who'd been hanging on her every word. He felt a kick of jealousy, something he'd never experienced before. He didn't like it.

"You need a shower," she said softly.

"I thought you loved the way I smell after a show. Earthy, wasn't it?" Her heels brought them damn near eye to eye. Joe leaned a little closer. "Tell me you're wearing something beneath that jacket."

Her smile broadened.

Joe swore softly.

"Uh, Emma?" A man's voice. Most likely the one she had been speaking with.

Emma ignored him.

"What does your friend want?" Joe asked.

"To fuck you."

Jesus. His body bucked as if she'd slapped him. He was

pretty sure that's what she'd wanted.

"He's hoping you swing both ways. Do you? I didn't know the answer to that question."

"Fuck, no," he growled.

Her smile grew wider, brighter than the one she'd flashed the man still trying to get her attention. It stole Joe's breath.

The hand on her hip flexed. He used his hold to ease her closer and, when her mouth dropped open, he knew he had her. He pressed his lips to hers softly, and she sighed.

"I missed you at sound check, Emma." Since she'd been a part of his life, sound check had become one of his favorite times of the day, if only to see what kind of crazy stunt she came up with next. From dancing in the aisles with one of the crew to acquiring one of the arena security's golf carts and holding drag races, there was always something that made him smile.

"Did you?" She dragged her thumb across his lips.

He nipped her.

"Stop that. You're wearing my lipstick."

"I don't care. I need to talk to you." The lapels of her jacket shifted as he fisted his hand at her side, stretched across her breasts, causing more and more skin to peek out from beneath.

"Yeah?" She placed her finger under his chin and urged his head up. "My eyes are up here. It helps to look at them when we talk."

"Who the hell wants to talk?" Christ, he could barely breathe and his jeans were damn near strangling his cock.

"You just said you did."

Her sexy clothes combined with that smile just about did him in. "You're killing me with this outfit, Em."

"Mm, I love the way the leather feels against my skin." His gaze tracked her hands as she smoothed them over the globes of her ass. His breathing shifted. Actually, he wasn't sure he was breathing at all. "And my butt looks spectacular in them." Yes, yes it did. "But I wonder, does it show my wealth? I wouldn't want you to mistake me for a gold digger."

Shit. She knew how to throw a punch. He'd give her that. It hit with unerring accuracy. He shook his head, trying to clear his thoughts. "I know you aren't a gold digger."

"Really?" She stepped to the side, just out of his reach. "What did you think I was after then? Do tell."

Instead of giving him a chance to respond, she walked away, crossing the room in those impossibly high heels, her sexy hips swaying. He wasn't the only who noticed, either. More than one set of eyes tracked her as she walked out the door.

"Fuck." If her plan was to torture him, drive him out of his bleedin' mind and pay him back for being an asshole this morning, it was working. Not giving a shit who gave witness, Joe cupped a palm over his groin and adjusted his erection. He flashed a smile at anyone who happened to notice, then followed Emma out of the room.

Her scent filled the hall, something light, fresh, and completely new. She didn't normally wear perfume. Joe drank it in along with the rare beauty of her ass shrouded in leather. His head swam. Blood roared through his veins. As she disappeared into his dressing room, he paused, right hand on the wall for support.

"Be strong," Gary said from behind him, voice filled with humor. "Her death blow can't be too painful, right?"

Joe shook his head. "You're enjoying this way too much."

"I admit watching you struggle puts a smile on my face. Women have always come too easy for you."

"Those were the days, right?" Now there was a big fat fucking lie. He wouldn't trade now for those days no matter what sweet torture Emma had in store for him.

Gary chuckled, knowing he was full of shit.

Joe took the final steps to his dressing room. "Wish me luck."

"It wouldn't do you any good, mate."

Joe closed the door on Gary's continued laughter. Resting against it, he looked up at the ceiling and shook his head. Then, because he didn't have the strength not to, he focused on Emma as she walked around the room, trailing her fingers over everything as she went. She stopped in front of that damnable bowl of condoms and dipped her left hand in.

He caught a flash of black circling her wrist. "Is that my cuff?"

"Yes." She didn't look up, just continued flipping through the condoms like it was a bowl of candy and she was searching for her favorite flavor. What happened to eye contact while talking?

"I was looking for it earlier. Where did you find it?"

"In my luggage."

"You stole it?"

"Of course." She shrugged, shifting away from the condom bowl and to his duffle, which sat on the table near the door. "Just like you steal my panties all the time."

It happened often. They'd be cramming clothes into luggage, either to take to or return from their hotel suite, and wind up with odds and ends that belonged to each other. For him, it was always her panties. Imagine that.

"I like to wear them on my head when you're not around," he teased and she laughed.

"Gross."

His wallet was in her hands. She opened it, flipped through what cash he carried and checked out his identification. He would have commented, but he was sure that's what she wanted from him.

Goddamnit, he'd screwed up—allowed Marvin to plant the seed of doubt. He knew why he was with her. She brought him joy, pushed away the darkness, made him smile, laugh. And the sex. The sex was out of this world! Emma was comfortable with her body, her sexuality, open to just about anything he wanted from her. But why was she with him? What did he really have to offer her? If not his fame, his fortune?

What a colossal fuck up his silence had created. Silence, hell, it had been fear. It seemed that every day he needed her more. She bewitched him, crawled under his skin, into his bloodstream, until he couldn't imagine having to face each day without her. He'd yet to figure out what to do with that.

With a toss of his wallet back into his bag, she turned, pinning him in place with her bright blue eyes. "Listen to me, because I'm only going to say this once."

He tipped his head. "I'm listening."

Her fingers worked the buttons on her jacket loose and she peeled it off, tossed it atop his bag. *Dear God.* He swallowed past a suddenly dry throat, completely entranced by the shirt she revealed. Whatever the fabric was, he wanted to sing its praises. It draped across her skin, molding itself to her breasts like a lover in a way that told him in no uncertain terms she was braless beneath. The vee in the front dipped damn near to her waist, far lower than the jacket she'd topped it with.

"Christ, Sunshine." When he groaned and had to shift to find comfort, she smiled.

"That look right there." She moved closer, her gaze holding his, but didn't finish her thought. "I went to the after party without you. I wanted to talk to people. I needed to understand how you could believe I was anything like them." She rubbed her finger over the tip of the dragon's tail peeking out from beneath the sleeve of his shirt. "Do you know what I discovered?"

His concentration took a nosedive along with his breathing. He shook his head.

"They're not your friends."

"I told you that."

Her hand slid under his sleeve and curled over his shoulder, smoothing back down to his bicep. "And I'm telling you, they all want something from you. Not a smile or a glance. Not a moment of your time or to make small talk. They want…bragging rights."

He'd told her that already, too.

"This is why you don't trust anyone, Joe." She nuzzled her nose against his temple. Her breath brushed his ear. "Because you surround yourself with takers. I wonder why that is?"

Speech was becoming difficult. He placed his hands low on her hips and tugged her in until his erection fit in the notch between her thighs. "I never chose those people, Em."

"No? Because they looked like they were wearing your pass." Hands on his biceps, she spun, swapping their position. Instead of resting against the door as he had, she walked him backward across the room, stopping once he stood before the couch. "You know what else I noticed?" She took hold of his hand, running her fingertips over the callouses on the ends of his fingers, his thumb. "None of them know me."

When she licked the callous on his ring finger, he nearly choked. "No?"

"They have no idea that I know the taste of you, the feel of you. The hitch in your breath as I take you into my mouth or the way you whisper my name as you come."

"Emma." *Christ, she was seducing him with just her words.*

"They don't know that you have a thing for black leather and if I wrapped it around my ass, I'd have your eyes on me tonight." She leaned in and pressed a kiss to the bottom of his chin.

His breathing grew labored.

"Don't you find that odd, since all *I* want from you is bragging rights?"

There it was, her death blow. All of the oxygen left his lungs like he'd taken a physical hit to the solar plexus. She curled her leg behind his and shoved. Completely off balance, he landed on his ass on the couch.

"You said you don't know why I want to be with you? Here's a hint." She no longer looked at him like she wanted to crawl inside of him, more like he'd broken something inside of her. His gut knotted painfully. "It's not so I can tell my friends about sleeping with a rock singer and it's not so you can buy me things. I don't want your damn money. If I want a supercar, I'll buy my own. Got it?"

"You were supposed to go on a tour of Europe and instead you came to me." He was still so utterly confused by that fact, it sounded in his voice.

She softened. "I did."

"You traded castles and wine tours for a cramped bus, not enough sleep and what? Post-concert stench?"

"I love the way you smell."

"Fuck." He closed his eyes and rubbed the pad of his hand across his forehead, startling when she straddled him.

"Look at me." She cupped his face. "I traded being alone for being with you. I'm tired of being alone and suddenly I don't have to be." She scooted closer, shifting until her heat pressed against his erection. His hands hovered over her hips. "Do I have your attention yet?"

Shit, she had it the first time he laid eyes on her and every time she walked into the room since.

Emma leaned closer—like she was trying to become one with him—and stopped as her lips hovered over his. "I don't want your money," she repeated. "I don't want to take pictures of you and sell them to the press, have your baby so I'm 'set for life' or write a tell-all book about how amazing you are in bed."

She kissed him and he couldn't help running his hands up her back and molding her torso to his. Her hardened nipples pressed into his chest and he groaned. She changed direction of the kiss, nipping at his lips before delving deep and he groaned again.

Pulling away, she stared at him through heavy-lidded eyes. "Look at you." In a move that always drove him crazy, she rubbed her thumb over the hair below his bottom lip. "You're so sexy when you're vulnerable."

"I'm not vul—" He couldn't say it because they both knew it would be a lie. Instead, he gave her the truth. "You scare the shit out of me, Emma."

"Good."

He smoothed his right hand around to cup her breast and glide his calloused thumb over her nipple. It hardened into a tight bead and his mouth went dry. He looked down at his hand, thumb rasping back and forth, working the opening of her V-neck wider and wider until her nipple peaked out.

"Joe."

The way she said his name...fucking damn.

"Do you know what you do for me?" She cradled the back of his skull, clenched his hair, and tugged until his focus was on her face and not her bare breast. "You make me laugh. And for some reason I don't completely understand, you like my sassy mouth. You could have any woman you wanted—there's a room full of beautiful women out there— yet you're in here with me. Looking at me like... Do you know how empowering it is to have you look at me the way you are right now? You make me feel special, as if I'm important to you."

"You are important to me," he whispered, and was re-warded with a smile that could've melted glaciers.

"That's what I *do* want from you, Joe. It's all I want. To be important to you."

Those women she spoke of paled in comparison to her. The way she looked at him, like she didn't see him as the sinner he was even though he knew she saw everything. The way she smiled at him, touched him. She could almost convince him he was worthy of her.

She crawled off his lap and it was all he could do not to grab hold and pull her back. One quick flip of her wrist hid her breast from view. "Come on," she said, offering him her hand.

He took it and stood. "Let me guess. You want to go for a walk."

"I was thinking more along the lines of going someplace where we can't be interrupted. How private do you think the balcony on our room is?"

"Not private enough."

"That's too bad. I've always wanted to make love in the rain. The contrast of the cool water and your hot mouth on my skin."

The look on her face nearly had him swallowing his tongue. "My shower is ten feet away."

"Nice try," she said with a laugh, "but not at all the same thing."

She picked up her jacket and slipped into it, situating the collar just so. Sexy—the whole damn outfit was sexy. He couldn't take his eyes off her as she opened the door and told Gary they needed a car. "Make it a sporty one, if you can. I've been feeling the need for a fast ride all day."

Joe choked a laugh at her double entendre. "You like fast cars, Sunshine?"

She closed the door and smiled. "I do. You?"

"Bobby and Zach can keep their motorbikes. I prefer four wheels over two. Raw horse power, the growl of a powerful engine and a spectacular display of G-force at acceleration." With each reference, her smile grew. "Never been a fan of the Bugatti, though."

"No?"

"I prefer the Koenigsegg."

She let out a slow, appreciative breath.

"That's why I have one."

"Shut. Up."

He smiled.

She pushed off the door and stepped closer. "Which one?"

"The Agera RS."

Her hand settled on his chest. Her breathing was unsteady, ragged, making the rise and fall of her breasts more pronounced. "You're not messing with me, are you?"

"No."

She closed her eyes and hummed. A mild tremor worked through her and her fingers curled into his shirt. "I think I just had an orgasm."

Christ. She did look a little flushed.

"You'll take me for a ride in it, right?" A shuddery breath escaped her. "Lie to me if you have to, just say you'll take me for a ride."

Un-fucking-believable. All over a car.

"Better, yet." The gruff rumble at the back of her throat had his brain misfiring. "I'll ride you in the car."

This time it was his breathing that accelerated. "Sorry, no sex in the Koenigsegg."

"On the garage floor next to it, while I touch it?"

She wasn't kidding. He threw his head back and laughed. She was hot over a car. Not that the Agera RS wasn't one hell of a car. "I'll give you something to touch," he said as his cock hardened even more.

"Do you have a picture of it?"

"Why would I have a picture of my cock?"

Her mouth dropped open. She shook her head in what looked like confusion. "Your car."

"No." Of course he did, but he wasn't going to tell her that. "I'll make growly noises at you while you ride me, though."

Her head tilted as she smirked. "It would help if I had a

photo to go along with it."

A rap on the door let him know Gary was back with a ride to the hotel for them.

"Bloody minx," Joe muttered, then bent at the knees and scooped her over his shoulder.

He was nearly at the door when she said, "Your bag, you forgot your bag."

He spun her around and squatted so she could snatch it off the table. There was a rustling like she was rummaging through his bag for a picture of the Agera. "Em," he warned

"This," she said with a sigh. "I might be tempted to re-think my gold digger status if it meant getting my hands on this car."

He slapped her on the ass. Hard.

"Dear God, I think I just came again." Her voice went all throaty as he opened the door.

Standing in the center of the doorway, Gary arched a brow. His gaze moved from Joe's hand on Emma's ass—which was damn near in his face, what with her still over Joe's shoulder—back to Joe. "The car is here, but you've got company."

Joe nodded. "What kind of company?"

"The kind with cameras."

"Shit." He set Emma on her feet. "Behave yourself."

Emma's smile was of the oh-so-sweet variety. "I'm not the one playing macho man."

"No, you're the one having orgasms over a car." Sure as shit, she'd pulled his mobile out of his duffle and found a picture of his Agera on it. He made a grab for it. "Give me that."

"No." She dodged his reach as she typed on the screen.

"You can't seriously be—"

Her phone, hidden somewhere on her person, chimed to alert an incoming message. Eyebrow raised in challenge, she dropped his mobile into his duffle.

"You forwarded it to yourself."

She smiled, the tip of her tongue playing with her lip.

"Unbelievable." He slid his hands over her body, focusing on the zips, until he found the bulge that had to be her phone. Slipping his fingers inside the pocket, he ignored her startled protest as he pulled it out and handed it to Gary—who wasn't shy about checking the message.

Gary released a laugh.

Joe handed over his mobile as well. "Sorry, Sunshine, no car porn. I can promise, you won't need it."

April 28

I was watching Joe today. I do that a lot, actually. Watch him when he's working, talking with fans, or even when he's sleeping. (I try not to think about how creepy that makes me sound.) I compare who he is today with the man I met backstage that night. Even the man I imagined him to be before we ever met. He is so much more.

He has a gift – a way with words and music. Joe brings joy to so many people's lives, I wonder if he even realizes it. I was one of those people – I know he doesn't realize that. Whenever I was down, struggling more than usual with the hospitals and doctors, the chemo and radiation, I would turn his music on, let the words wash over me and feed my soul. Let it bring me the strength I was lacking. I would turn the music on and tune out the world.

I was watching Joe today, and wondering how I could do the same for him. Should I tell him what his music has meant to my life? If I do, it opens up so much more that needs to be said. I'm not sure I'm ready to explain it all. Would it help drive away the sadness? Or bring him even more? I can't know for certain.

When we met, the music inside him was dying. I saw it in his eyes. Read it in the lyrics that littered the table in his dressing room—those beautiful, pain-filled words that haunt me still. Somewhere along the way, no matter how much joy he gave to others, he'd lost his own. Darkness was his friend, his mistress, and music doesn't survive in darkness.

Today Joe was smiling. He smiled at me when he caught me staring. I had decided to risk it, attempt to explain to him the series of events that brought us together. Then he smiled. And whatever had brought him that moment of joy, be it me or the fact that the sun was rising and, with it, a new day, I couldn't take that happiness away from him.

Number of days since I decided to live: 68
Number of days since I met Joe: 25
Current level of panic: 6/10

FOURTEEN

May 8

IT WAS RAINING, the night air chilled, as they stepped outside. Joe set his hand on the small of Emma's back and used his body to block as much wind and rain from her as he could. Pointless when she stopped at the side of the limo and tipped her face to the sky. A smile of pure pleasure curled her lips before she looked back at him and pressed in for a kiss. The warmth of her mouth on his, the cool water; he suddenly knew exactly why she fantasized about making love in the rain. "Maybe we will check out the balcony on our suite."

Her gaze lit with something that looked like both heat and laughter. Turning back to the car, she nodded at the driver and slid in.

"Mr. Campbell," the man said as Joe stepped to the door. "Where would you like to go tonight?"

"Our hotel." He didn't need to specify which one, for the car service always had that information on hand. "Can you make it fast? She was hoping for something with a bit more horsepower than a limo."

The man tipped his head, closing the door behind Joe as he slid onto the seat next to Emma.

Emma placed his duffle on the floor then switched to the seat across from him. Her gaze bounced off everything, hand not far behind as she checked out the interior of the limo. Unlike most people, Emma never seemed satisfied with just a visual check of anything. She always added the tactile, as well. It was just one of the things that made her unique and different from nearly everyone else he knew. Another was her inability to keep most emotions off her face. He wondered what she was thinking about as they pulled away from the arena, moving through the crowd gathered outside the loading area.

She glanced at the smoked glass separating the front from the back, ran her hand across it then looked back at him, her face flush. Whatever it was, it must be good.

"Can the driver hear or see us?"

"No. Why?"

She dropped to her knees and went for the buttons on his jeans. "You promised me a ride. I guess this will have to do."

Before he had time to process her words, she popped his buttons and took out his cock, brought her mouth to the tip and gave it a lick. Unable to stop, he buried his right hand in her hair, hips lifting toward her sweet mouth. She blew a warm breath over him, and then the head disappeared into her wet heat.

"Fuck," he growled and reached blindly for the intercom button. "On second thought..."

She pumped him. Swallowed him. Those delectable lips swept over him, licking and kissing. He closed his eyes against the pleasure, a hiss slipping free as she took him to the back of her throat, right down to the base.

The driver's voice piped out of the speaker near his head. "Yes, Mr. Campbell?"

Joe had to swallow twice to get the words out. "On second thought, take us around the city a few times."

"Certainly."

Her grip increased with each stroke, sliding up and down, her speed growing faster with each pass. Primed and ready before he ever left his dressing room, he nearly lost it right then. "Fuck, yes."

She worked him until he was ready to beg, her name rolling off his tongue. Her lips smacked against him as she lifted her head and he slid free. He bit back the call to bring her back to him.

"I have a surprise for you." Her voice sounded breathy, letting him know she was as excited by her actions as he. She spent some time touching her finger to the wetness on the tip of his cock before leveling him with her eyes.

"Tell me."

She swirled her tongue over the head of his cock and smiled when it twitched in response. "It's more of a visual thing."

She was giving him quite the visual already, peeking up at him as she slid her hand up his length. A bead of pre-cum pooled and she licked it away. A groan rumbled in his chest. The hand he had in her hair fisted.

"It'll wait," she whispered, her lips brushing him with each word. "I don't think you will." He could only watch as his cock disappeared into her mouth again and his body slipped into freefall.

His head dropped back against the headrest. "Sweet Jesus." The feel of her mouth on him, all hot and tight, had his mind shutting down, need swamping him. He got lost in the sensation of her lips and her hand, lost in her. The orgasm slammed into him, knocking the air out of his lungs, her name from his lips. He filled her mouth and she took it all. "Fuck."

She'd reduced him to a panting, boneless mass capable of only monosyllabic words.

"Christ, Em."

When the pulsing stopped, he looked down at her.

Her smile spoke of pure feminine power. "Feeling better?"

He hoped to Christ she wasn't expecting an answer because he'd lost the ability to speak. Goddamn, she had brought him to mind-melting orgasm in record time.

Slipping out of her jacket, she tossed it on the seat behind her. Her 'fuck me' stilettos followed, then she was sliding her hand to the waistband of her leather pants and working the front zip open. "Ready for your surprise?"

Smooth skin gave way to more smooth skin. He tried again to speak but it came out as a whimper he might have found mortifying had he not been in the middle of a bloody heart attack. She scooted her ass to the seat behind her, slowly working the leather lower and lower before stepping out of it. Straightening, she leaned back and spread her legs wide, giving him an intimate look at her bald pussy.

"Fuck me," he whispered reverently.

She lifted her foot onto the seat and pressed her heel to her ass, smoothing her hand down to slide between her lips. "You like it?"

There wasn't a hair left—everywhere he looked, there was only beautiful, bare skin.

"I swore I would never do it, but they say it increases sensitivity. I'm dying to know how your beard feels on my clit."

His cock twitched, letting him know he wasn't down for the count yet.

"Mm," she licked her lips. "But first..." Her hand slipped into his duffle and pulled out a condom. Not his preferred brand. No this was one of the rainbow ones from the bowl in his dressing room. She tossed it to him. "Hold onto that. You're going to need it."

Joe laughed. It turned to a groan when she straddled his lap and her wetness pressed against his balls. "You have to give me a minute, Sunshine. I haven't recovered from the first round yet."

"You will," she promised, her right hand sliding into his hair while her left toyed with the low neck of her shirt. With a little smile, she slowly slid the fabric aside, exposing her breast.

Joe licked his lips.

She ran her hand over herself, squeezing, cupping the weight then flicking the nipple. It hardened at her touch and his mouth watered.

"You're stirring again," she whispered, a breath away from his lips.

He was. She was so fucking sexy. The way she played with herself while she rhythmically rocked against him.

Desperate to touch, he settled his hands on her hips, slipped one down and trailed his thumb over her wet flesh. "You feel incredible. So smooth and wet."

The grumble deep in her throat spurred him on.

He circled her labia, spreading her lips, opening her to his touch. Her hips lifted, pressed against his hand. Her thighs began to tremble, her hand fisted in his hair. The noises at the back of her throat as he tapped her clit stirred him even more.

She skimmed her lips across his temple, clutched at the back of his neck. "Tell me you're ready for me, Joe. I need you inside of me."

That fast heat inflamed again. Wiped out every thought but giving her what she wanted as quickly as possible. He kissed her, his tongue flicking across hers as his fingers plunged deep. He matched the strokes of his tongue to the strokes of his fingers. She matched his rhythm with the rocking of her hips. *Fuck, he was ready all right.*

She tore her mouth away from his, panting. "Condom."

In a few quick moves, she had the condom out of his hand and rolled over him. He pushed his jeans farther down his thighs as she guided his cock to her center. The press of him sliding against her wet heat had him seeing stars. He waited for her to sink down. Instead, with her hand on the back of his head, she brought her nipple to his mouth.

Joe brushed his jaw across it, back and forth, dragging his beard over her flesh. She gasped, pressed closer and he obliged, pulling her into his mouth. He flicked his tongue over her nipple, alternating between sucking and licking. Her staccato breathing filled his ears.

Just when he thought she would never take him into her body, she pushed a finger into his mouth, breaking the suction on her breast. Fisting her hand in his hair, she pulled his head back and kissed him as she impaled herself on his shaft.

She was so fucking tight. Every time he slipped inside of her, the clench of her body around him nearly sent him over the edge. He grabbed her hips and held her in place, waiting, keeping her still until she growled into his mouth. Then he lifted her until just his tip remained and slammed her back down. Their mouths broke apart. She buried her face in his neck and he did it again, then again.

She chanted his name in his ear. Over and over as he

drove into her. When her muscles began to tremble and she gulped a deep breath, he closed his mouth over hers and, swallowing her scream, followed her over the edge.

Foreheads pressed together, they sucked each other's oxygen as he struggled to control his breathing. Emma wasn't doing much better.

"You've completely destroyed me," he admitted. Her head fell to his shoulder, where she licked him from collarbone to ear. A chill ran up his spine.

"You're welcome." She pressed her nose to his neck and inhaled. "God, you smell good. Like sex and sweat and man."

"Only you would find my scent, at this very moment, appealing."

She skimmed her fingertips across his forehead, down his cheek and over his lips. Then she straightened, looked at him with heat in her eyes, and something else he couldn't name. "How is it possible that every time we have sex, it's better than the time before?"

Good fucking question. "You inspire me."

Her smile lit up her face. "I could stay here all night, with you inside of me."

"At some point the car will run out of gas." Or arrive at its destination—as it just did, pulling up to the front of the hotel.

"Shit," she hissed, lifting her weight so her body separated from his.

He already missed her warmth.

One press of the intercom button chased away the panic in her eyes. "Once more around the block, please," he requested.

The car slipped away. Joe pulled his jeans up over the

condom—what more could he do—and enjoyed the show. Emma, in her frenzy to cover herself, struggled to slide the leather up her legs. A near impossible task what with her body covered in a light sheen of sweat.

"Stop smiling," she ordered, then laughed in frustration.

"Now you know why I don't wear leather during shows."

"Help me!"

"Sorry, Sunshine, no can do." He couldn't hold back a laugh as she twisted and contorted, cursing under her breath with every tug. This brought the deep V-neck dipping down to her stomach, sliding off her shoulder until her breast popped out.

"I'm going to get you for this," she growled.

His smile grew. "You're the one who wanted a ride."

"You weren't complaining a few minutes ago."

"Neither were you." Firsthand knowledge of how difficult it was to slide into leather pants once water or sweat was involved had him moving closer. Perched on the front edge of his seat, he curled his fingers into her waistband, shifting, pulling her in until her breast was a hair's breadth from his mouth.

"Relax," he soothed. "You have to relax and stop fighting it."

"Joe."

"Trust me." He kissed the side of her breast, her collarbone, her throat. "Put your hands on the ceiling and relax."

When she obliged, he pulled up on the pants. They didn't budge.

"Stop holding your breath," he said softly, licking the shell of her ear. "I said relax."

She turned her head. "Why does this feel even more

sexual than having you inside of me only a moment ago?" she whispered against his mouth.

He kissed her, waiting until her body went fluid, one hand dropping to mold the back of his head. As she sighed into his mouth, he pulled up on the leather. Her pants slid into place. "All that work just so I can strip them off you the moment we get to the room."

She blinked at him a few times, as if he'd actually sizzled a few brain cells, before zipping in record time. Straightening her shirt, she picked up her shoes and jacket just as the limo returned to the hotel. "Hurry," she demanded.

"Greedy," he replied, grabbing his bag and opening the door.

In a move he was sure was calculated, she shifted forward, giving him an unobstructed view down her shirt as she whispered, "only for you" and exited the limo.

Joe laughed aloud as he followed her out, not at all concerned about how they looked as they scurried in the front of the hotel, Emma carrying her shoes instead of wearing them.

He smiled at a couple who appeared to recognize him and settled his hand on Emma's lower back. As the elevator doors closed behind them, he pressed her into the corner and kissed her. He dove into the kiss, taking her mouth roughly, stroking his tongue against hers as he trailed the knuckles of his free hand up and down the strip of skin between her breasts. She gave as good as she got, crossed her lips over his, nipping and biting until his breath hammered in his ears.

The earth moved, or maybe it was just the elevator stopping. Neither interested him enough to cease his assault. He smoothed his hand higher, cupping her face, tracing his thumb back and forth across her chin.

From behind him came a gasp and a low whistle, followed by another voice, this one not so appreciative. "Well, I never."

Groaning, he glanced over his shoulder, spotted a younger man wearing a broad smile and an elderly woman with a frown. Her frown deepened as she stomped her foot once as if to emphasize her disgust.

"No? Your loss," Joe muttered, then pressed the 'door close' button.

Emma giggled. "Did you see the look on her face?"

He was looking at the only face that mattered. Jesus, she was like a drug. Every minute with her made him want another. The sensation scared the shit out of him. Then her hand slipped beneath his shirt to touch skin and grounded him.

This time when the elevator stopped, it was on their floor. The doors slid open, but he didn't move. "Em?"

"Hmmm?" She skimmed her fingertips over his abs and he sighed. It turned to a groan as she drifted south to his waistband and beneath it.

"Christ, Emma."

She popped the top button and snaked her hand lower. "Are we going to go to the room and play on the balcony?"

It was a moment before his breath started flowing again. For the life of him, he couldn't remember why he didn't already have her down the hall. Naked. Beneath him. "I...was going to apologize."

She ducked her head and kissed his throat, popped open another button. "For?"

"Hurting you." Jesus, if she didn't stop she was going to get them arrested. "I hurt you this morning."

"Yes, you did. I've already forgiven you."

"Why do you forgive so easily? I don't deserve it."

"Life's too short to hold grudges or stay angry," she replied simply.

There was something in her voice, a flash of sadness in her eyes. Then it was gone.

"Now," she whispered, sliding her hand around his hip to cup his ass. "Are you going to stop the door from closing or are we going for another ride?"

He shot his hand out and slammed it against the retractable door edge. "Oh, we're going for another ride, all right." She liked the idea, if her shiver was anything to go by. "First we're heading to the room and I'm going to shower while you get naked."

"Then you're going to ride me in the rain?"

"No."

"No?"

She sounded so disappointed. He cupped the back of her head in his palm and treated himself to a taste. "Once you're wearing nothing but a smile, you're going to put those sexy fucking shoes back on. *Then* I am going to ride you in the rain."

Her lids fluttered, her entire body trembled. "You want my shoes on."

He nodded. "And you naked."

"I can make that happen." She swiped her tongue across her bottom lip. "Race you to the room?"

"No need. After you."

"You just want to stare at my ass."

"Fucking right, I do."

She laughed, leading the way out of the elevator. His duffle in one hand, the waistband of his pants in the other, he followed her, hoping like hell there was no one in the hall.

The minute they stepped into the room, Emma started stripping. Joe barely had the door closed before she ripped her blouse over her head. He dropped his duffle and toed off his shoes then choked back a groan as she pushed the leather pants down her legs, bending at the waist and treating him to an intimate view of her ass and lips as she slipped one foot free, then the other.

Desperate to touch, he made it exactly three steps before he tripped, snagging her around the waist as he caught his balance.

"What the hell?" Shopping bags littered the floor, most bulging open, contents spilling out. He laughed. "Give your card a workout today, Sunshine?"

"I did." She straightened, pressed her ass back against his erection and wiggled her hips. "We can play show and tell later. I picked up a few things I know you'll like."

"Mm." He slid his hands up the front of her body and closed them over her breasts. "I like what you're wearing right now."

"Yeah? Wait 'til I get my shoes on. By the flash of excitement in your eyes when you requested them, I think we're both going to like what comes next."

He pinched her nipples and her head dropped to his shoulder. "Joe." His name on her lips was more of an exhale. Reaching up, she curled her hand around the back of his neck. "Joe, you're wearing too many clothes."

"Damnit."

Her laughter vibrated against him. "Take your shower, but make it quick. If you're not back out here in five, I'm starting the party without you."

"Like hell you are."

He was done in four. All the lights in the suite were off when he stepped out of the bath and spotted her standing in the open sliding door that led to the balcony, wearing nothing but her 'fuck me' shoes. She was half inside the room, half out, her arm stretched to the side, catching raindrops. There was barely enough light to see her, so he angled the bathroom door to cast its glow across the room and promptly swallowed his tongue.

It wasn't her body or even those sexy shoes that took his breath. It was the smile on her face. She was watching him as she drew her arm back and trickled the rainwater over her breasts. And the smile she gifted him, so warm and full of life, if he hadn't already been completely under her spell, that smile would have done it.

"It's pretty private, actually," she said. He assumed she meant the balcony. "The building walls off both ends and overhangs the top, so the only view is straight out front and we are facing the lake."

He grunted and started in her direction, yanking the comforter off the bed as he passed.

"Of course, there's a minor risk of being spotted since the front railing is glass but…What are you doing?"

He tossed the comforter onto the balcony and set his hands on her hips. "I want you on your back, outside. We're going to need a little padding."

"Yes, but—"

His lips stopped whatever she'd been about to say. She melted against him, wrapping her arms around his neck and rubbing her chest against his. Not wanting to waste time, he backed out onto the balcony, bringing her with him. His breath hissed as the rain hit his back. "Shit."

"It feels incredible, doesn't it?" she murmured against his lips.

The wind whipping off the lake was cooler than he had expected, the rain against his overheated skin a shock to his system. It was a moment before he adjusted but, once he did, he had to admit it felt pretty fucking spectacular. Especially with her heat pressed against his front. "Lie down, Sunshine. Arms over your head."

She squatted, taking a moment to stroke her hand along his length as she eased down on the comforter and stretched her arms over her head, pressing her palms flat against the wall. "What do you have in mind?"

He sank to his knees, held his cock in his hand and rolled a condom on. She watched his every movement.

"I think you'll enjoy this." He tested her readiness by trailing a fingertip through her folds. Back and forth until her hips rose and fell with each stroke and dampness coated his fingers. "I'm going in deep. You won't be able to control the depth." He slid his fingers inside and she clamped down on them. He waited for her to relax before moving again, plunging in and out of her. "You'll tell me if it's too much."

She trembled. He wasn't sure if it was excitement or something else.

"Emma?" He stilled as he waited for an answer.

"Yes," she whispered, arching her hips, forcing his fingers deeper. "I'll tell you."

He stroked her again, thumb flicking her clit. His name slipped from between her lips as he bent first one leg, then the other, setting her heels against his shoulders. The view was incredible; she was wide open to him, unable to hide. He could see every inch of her, from the top of her head to the heels on her feet and everything in between. He could go deep. Feel her tightness all around him as he watched every emotion, every sensation cross her face.

"I've wanted to fuck you like this since I first laid eyes on these shoes." He curled his fingers inside her and her entire body trembled. "Are you ready for me, Em?"

"God, yes."

Using one hand on her ass to lift and steady her, he guided his cock to her entrance, rubbed himself along her lips then pressed forward until his tip disappeared inside of her. He withdrew and did it again.

"Mm. You like to watch, don't you?" She let her legs fall farther open, giving him an even better view.

"Watch my cock disappear into your body?" As promised, he pressed forward, went deep, until his balls slapped against her ass. "Fuck, yeah. Your lips turn rosy when you're aroused. Did you know that?"

She trailed a finger over her mouth.

"Not those lips, Sunshine." He found his rhythm, the one that had her eyes glazing over and her breath hitching. "Play with your breasts for me. Let me see you."

She immediately complied, cupping and squeezing them, pinching and tugging her nipples. Her head shifted from side to side, her back arched.

He groaned and pressed harder, deeper. The cool rain against his back, the bite of pain where her heels dug into his shoulders and the heat of her body—it all combined until the pounding in his chest matched the throbbing in his cock. He didn't think he could take much more. "Look at me. Open your eyes and look at me."

Her eyes popped open and locked with his.

He pressed deeper, faster. The pressure inside him built. "I want to watch you come, Emma."

"I'm close. I need you to…"

"Tell me." Like every time, the feel of being inside of her, the clench of her body, stole his control. She held him in the palm of her hands and she didn't even know it. He'd do anything, give her anything to get to this place only she could bring him. "Tell me what you need."

Gasping for breath, she reached between their bodies and fingered her clit.

"Fuck," he muttered. One hand on her breast, the other her clit, she pleasured herself as he pounded into her body.

"Joe," she whispered, her body tightening.

His gaze snapped back to hers so he could witness her gulp in air. Her body trembled and she cried out, pulsing, tightening around his cock as she came.

"So sexy," he whispered, then couldn't speak as his orgasm roared through him.

THIRTY MINUTES LATER, dry and sated, they lay crosswise in the bed, Emma draped on Joe's chest. He stroked his fingers along her spine as she propped herself on one elbow and pressed her lips against his sternum. Exhaustion pulled at him. Every muscle in his body cried out for sleep. But his mind wouldn't shut down.

He'd had good sex in his lifetime. Hell, he'd had great sex in his time. But sex with Emma was heart-stopping, mind-blowing and draining on more than a physical level. She engaged him emotionally, too. Something completely new and unnerving for him. His need for her shook him to the core, had him stumbling, and left him exactly what she'd called him in his dressing room—vulnerable.

He didn't like the feeling one bit.

Tilting her head, she met his gaze. "What's the matter?"

"Nothing."

She traced a finger over his lips. "You think after weeks spent wrapped up with you, half the time literally one with you, I can't tell when something is wrong?"

He sighed, lifted his head to get a better look at her. "This morning when you left?"

She shifted, moving her body higher up his. "Yeah?"

"I didn't know if you were coming back."

"And that made you feel?" She ran her mouth over his jaw to his ear, the key she wore teasing his neck.

"It made me feel," he agreed, knowing full well that wasn't the answer she'd been after. He rolled, pinning her beneath him. "Tell me about your necklace. You never take it off. Why?"

"Nice subject change."

He didn't even try to deny it. "Thank you."

Her answer didn't come immediately. He waited as she danced her fingers over his collarbone, frowning at the marks left by her shoes.

"You're going to have bruises," she whispered.

"I'll wear them with pride." He pressed his lips to the hollow of her throat, savoring her swift intake of air as he traced the delicate chain lower, across her breast, before easing the key from between their bodies. The metal was warm. He stroked his thumb down the stem, over the bow and back again.

Her eyes searched his face. "It's difficult to explain."

Joe had to laugh. "Really?"

"Why is that surprising?"

"You don't usually have a problem speaking your mind."

She winced. "True." She fell silent again, staring at his hand still holding the small silver key. "I was struggling with something."

Some of the light left her, letting him know it was something big. "You don't have to talk about it if you don't want to."

Her gaze returned to his as she ran the backs of her fingers over his shoulder, down his arm. "Have you ever had a dream that felt so real it stayed with you for days?"

"Yes."

"She had red hair and this…glow about her. Big, sad eyes and, in her hand, she held a key, on a chain."

A strange ball of disquiet formed in his stomach, which made no sense since she was talking about a dream. "The key you wear."

"Exactly like it, yes. She was offering it to me. No, that's not right. She was adamant I take it. I couldn't hear what she was saying, but I knew it was important. Then I woke up."

Her story triggered a memory. He reached back for it, trying to recall how he knew the image she described. "She was an angel."

"Yes!" She blinked and shot him a confused look. "How did you…the sunflowers."

"That's it." The memory solidified. Him standing center stage, head pounding from his wicked hangover, while the guys argued over the upcoming show. A text alert, the sound piercing as he'd yet to do anything with his new mobile besides turn it on. "You sent me a snap of sunflowers sitting on a mantel. Next to the vase there was a sketch of an angel."

She nodded. "I drew it when I woke up. Then a few

weeks later, I found the necklace in a jewelry store and…"
She curled her fingers around his, clutching the key in both
of their hands. "I don't know what it means, but I can't get
myself to take it off." The body beneath his went taut. The
sound she released similar to a laugh, only it felt strangely
more like pain than humor. "It's probably a hallucination
from…"

"From what?"

"Stress. I was struggling."

"Maybe it's the key to your future," he offered, trying to
lighten whatever had come over her.

Her gaze skittered away. Her breath hitched. He had the
terrible feeling something was very wrong as she blinked
rapidly, finally hiding behind closed eyes. "Maybe."

"Sunshine?" He propped his elbows on either side of her
head and cupped her face. His concern ratcheted up a notch
when his thumbs stroked her cheeks and found them damp.
"Em, you're scaring me."

She looked up at him with eyes a little too bright and
trailed her finger down his bottom lip. "I'm sorry." She
traced her fingertips over his brow, his temple, ran her
thumb over his cheekbone. "It's been a long, emotional day
is all, and I'm exhausted."

"Okay." There was more going on than exhaustion. The
pain in her eyes tore a hole inside him, but the thought of
pushing her for the truth filled him with a fear he couldn't
explain. One he was too chickenshit to explore. Instead, he
allowed her to keep her secrets, rolling to his side and
tucking her head beneath his chin. "Sleep. I've got you."

She snuggled closer, until her chest pressed flush against
him, and sighed. "Don't let go," he thought she whispered,
but then the tension left her as she drifted to sleep.

"Never," he said, his voice echoing back at him in the silent room. It was a long time before he relaxed enough to follow her.

May 3

I'm exhausted. Barely two weeks on the road and already I'm so tired – physically and emotionally wiped out. How do the guys do it, day after day after day? Sure, they don't have a monster in their head but, they've been at this for eighteen months. A year and a half! It doesn't seem plausible.

I imagine it helps that none of them seem to mind sleeping in the bunks. Climbing into their dark shelf, drawing the curtain and tuning out the world. It's getting so bad I was staring at those holes in the wall the other day, wondering if I could take enough sleep aid to not mind the dim coffin-like space. My inability to snag more than a few restless hours on the bus is catching up with me. I'm the youngest person on this tour and the most drained. It terrifies me. My time is running out faster than predicted, yet I have so much left to accomplish.

The headaches are getting worse. I no longer make it weeks between attacks, but merely days. They're not all bad enough to require medication, but it's not a good sign. I'll have to make a call to my oncologist soon. The medication dosage will need to be adjusted, maybe add another drug to my daily routine. When last we spoke, he mentioned a time would come when I would need that. Won't he be thrilled when I make that call, when he discovers I'm not sitting at home waiting for the end, but on the road with my rock star

SARAH GRIMM

lover and his band. Hah! Who could have ever imagined. The doc will lecture and scold. He'll tell me what I already know – that this lifestyle isn't good for me, it's speeding my progression. I need more rest, but rest just feels like time lost. Time I can be laughing and living.

Time I can be with Joe.

He smiles more now than he ever used to – the sadness once so evident in his eyes, is fading. He spends less and less time staring at a bottle of whiskey like a long-lost lover and more time writing, walking with me beneath the stars, or making love. He's letting go of the darkness a little more each day and I want that even more than I want sleep.

I want that more than anything.

Do you think it's the same for everyone, no matter how long a life they get? Do the elderly wonder where the time went? Question why they can't have just one more day, one more month, hell, one more year? Or is it just an affliction of the young? I imagine, for everyone, there is always one last thing they want to do. One final moment they long to experience.

Listen to me, getting all maudlin. God, if I could kick my own ass, I would! I've been in this damn bus for too long. It's time to get outside and find a thrill. Time to stare death in the face and tell her to kiss my ass!

There's a golf cart sitting outside, left behind by one of the arena staff after Gary called them away.

I wonder….how fast does that thing go?

Number of days since I decided to live: 73
Number of days since I met Joe: 30
Current level of panic: 6/10

FIFTEEN

May 9

"YOU SOUND HAPPY, Em."

Emma had been in the bathroom applying her makeup when Alison called. Startled by the ringing of her cell phone, which had been handed off to Gary last night, she'd darted into the lounge area and snagged it off the table before it could wake Joe. She preferred not to wonder just when Gare had returned both phones to the room, for Joe's sat there too, and instead, stood in front of the wall of windows overlooking the city and smiled.

"I am happy."

"You also sound tired. Are you getting enough sleep?"

Emma let out a long breath. "Yes, mom."

"Stop it. You have few days in Chicago before heading out again, right? It looks that way from the schedule you sent me."

"We do."

"And how do you plan to spend your time?" Alison asked, her tone teasing.

Emma smiled. "Sleep, make love, repeat."

"Sounds heavenly."

"Doesn't it?" Three days. She and Joe had three days with nowhere to go and nothing to do. Emma planned to spend as much of that time as possible in bed. Long uninterrupted hours of sleep followed by lovemaking. Because it wasn't just sex anymore. Sure, Joe could call it fucking, and often did during his dirty talk, but it was more than just a quick pleasurable release of sexual frustration or tension. So much more. Their chemistry had always been off the charts but, now that emotion played a role, every touch, every caress meant so much.

"Emma, did you just sigh? You did, didn't you?"

"I did not!" She totally did.

"You've already admitting to only being up for twenty minutes and yet you're dreaming about crawling right back in bed, aren't you?"

"Can you blame me?" Emma tipped her head against the window and ran the tips of her fingers across her stomach, imagining it was Joe's touch causing her quick intake of breath. "He makes my body stand up and sing the Hallelujah Chorus."

It was Alison's turn to sigh.

"Why are you giving me shit, anyway? It's not like you can't crawl back into bed with Kevin."

"I can't, actually. Kevin's at work."

This was new. "It's Saturday. Since when does Kevin work weekends?"

"Since he was assigned a big case. It's fabulous for him. It is, I just…we were supposed to spend the day together and now I don't know what to do with myself. I would bake, but my main consumer is two states away."

"You could always send me more. I mean, I'd choke them down if it meant giving you something to take your mind off being alone."

"You're a true friend," Alison said with a laugh.

"I know, right?"

Alison laughed harder. "You and your addiction to sweets. They were that good?"

"They smelled fabulous. The boys got to them before I could, though."

"Seriously? That doesn't sound at all like you. You're not very good at sharing."

She wasn't.

"I'll see what I can do." Al drew a deep breath and exhaled. Her tone turned serious. "How have you been feeling? Any headaches?"

"No." An outright lie, as she had one currently brewing, but she didn't need Alison worrying over her. "I haven't needed to medicate in a week."

"Good. You're telling me the truth, right?"

"I'm fine, Al."

"That's not really what I asked though, is it?"

"No, but that's the best you'll—" Emma caught a flash of movement reflected in the window and turned. Her body went hot. Her heart took a good, hard leap. She had no idea what she'd been about to say.

Joe leaned against the doorframe between the two rooms. He smiled at her as he sipped from one of the insulated cups the hotel stocked. Tea, she now knew, never coffee. Fresh from a shower, he was shirtless, shoeless, and once again wearing a pair of jeans barely staying on his hips. With his bi-color eyes and his full lips, the dragon roaring across his chest just below the imprint of the heels she'd sported last night, he was a thing of rare beauty.

"Em?" Alison questioned. "Let me guess. By that little shuddery breath you released, Mr. Sexy just walked into the room."

Emma sighed again. Al was right, her breath shuddered.

"He did."

"Is he naked?"

The question was so out of character for her friend, Emma laughed. "No!"

"Too bad."

"Says you. He looks pretty damn hot in nothing but his jeans."

Joe straightened away from the doorframe, moving across the room. His eyes never left her face as he closed the distance between them, each step making it more difficult for Emma to draw a deep breath. Would she ever get used to what the sight of him did to her?

"Tell me something, Sunshine." His sleep-roughened voice slid over her, danced across her nerve endings like a caress. He dropped his free hand to the small of her back, bending at the waist to brush a kiss along her neck. "As much as you've had your mouth and your hands all over me, how is it every morning you look at me as if it's the first time?"

"Good God, Em." Alison whispered.

Emma's heart took another hard leap. "Close your ears, Al, you shouldn't be hearing this."

His hand skimmed up her side, his eyes a beat behind. "Mm, not that I'm complaining, mind you. It's a huge boost to my ego."

Fingers brushed the bottom of her breast, teasing until her nipples throbbed. She felt them shrink to two tight points. "Your ego doesn't need boosting."

"So you say. But that look you give me in the morning? That look sets my mood for the entire day."

"And what mood would that be?"

He flashed her a wicked smile. "Horny."

Emma released a startled laugh that quickly turned to a gasp as he cupped her ass and pulled her flush against his body, sucking the skin on her neck in the process. "Quick, give me a kiss before the boys get here."

She pressed her nose into his throat and inhaled him, tipped her head up, her eyes already sliding closed. She snapped them back open. "Wait! The boys are coming here?"

"Any minute now."

"Shit! I'm not dressed yet."

"I noticed," he growled. "Believe me, I noticed."

"Crap." Emma pushed free of his hold, her eyes darting to the door of the suite as a knock sounded. "You could have warned me."

"I was distracted."

The door started to open which meant one of them had a key. Gary, most likely.

Emma took off like a shot, jumping into the bedroom and closing the door with a snap. She leaned against it and gasped for breath. "Asshole," she mumbled affectionately.

It was a minute before she realized Alison was still on the line, laughing softly. "Let me guess. You're the one who is naked."

Emma sighed. "Not completely, I'm wearing panties."

Alison lost it, laughing so hard she snorted.

"Al, I'm going to hang up if you don't knock it off." Emma looked around for something to wear. She needed clothes, fast, before one of the idiots decided they needed the bathroom. Dumping her shopping bags out on the bed, she dug through her purchases.

"Right, sorry." Al cleared her throat. "So, Joe calls you Sunshine?"

"He does." Somewhere in the pile there was a pair of medium wash destroyed jeans she'd fallen in love with. Sure, she'd spent way too much money on something with holes in them, but they fit as well as the leather pants and were so darn comfortable they justified the cost.

There, a swatch of blue denim beneath the pile of silk lingerie. Emma snapped the tags off and shimmied into the jeans.

"And your pet name for him is?"

"You just heard what I usually call him," Emma replied, digging back into the pile for a shirt.

"Seriously? You whisper that in his ear when he's..."

In the middle of hooking the front clasp of her bra, Emma froze. "When he's what, Al? You can't even say it, can you?"

"When he's inside you. See, I can say it."

She'd whispered it, as if lightning would strike if she said it any louder. Emma tried to swallow her laughter and failed.

Not wanting to damage the delicate fabric, she bit off the tag on her cream blouse—a bit over-sized, flowy and slightly see-thru, which was why she needed the bra. Slipping into it without dropping the phone was more complicated than hopping into the jeans had been. "Why are you suddenly so interested in my sex life?"

"I just think it's sweet that he calls you Sunshine. And awful that you call him asshole. He must like it, though, since he keeps you around anyway."

"Yeah, I've yet to figure out that one myself. What do you call Kevin when he's...inside you?" she asked, mimicking Alison's whisper.

"Nothing." Al sounded embarrassed by the very idea.

"No? What does he say to you?"

"Nothing!"

"Seriously? No naughty talk? No whispered words of encouragement?"

"No," Alison said on an expelled breath. She was very definitely embarrassed. "None of that."

"God, really?"

"You make it sound like a bad thing."

"No, I just… He's *inside* of you. The sensation of that alone is…" Emma shivered just thinking about how good it felt to have Joe inside her. "There aren't words. Then, once he's moving and hands are involved, mouths…" She sighed. "How can you keep quiet?"

"How can you not?"

"I'm too busy feeling to care that I'm making noise. Usually, I'm chanting his name. *'Joe, Joe, oh God, Joe!'*" she teased, giving Alison the absolute truth because she knew it made her friend uncomfortable. And hell, if she could break Al out of her sexual boredom, that was a bonus. "Other times, I just scream as he drives me to orgasm."

Al had gone quiet.

"Seriously honey, you've got to open your mouth and encourage Kevin. He'll thank you for it."

"I know I'm always appreciative as hell."

Shit. Emma spun to discover Joe in the bedroom with her, casually leaning against the door. At least he'd had the decency to close it since she'd been changing. "Joe! I was just—"

"Chanting my name. Why do you think I'm in here?"

Emma rubbed the back of her neck. "Alison, I have to go. I'll talk to you soon, okay?" Disconnecting, she tossed the phone on the pile atop the bed and remet Joe's gaze.

"You shouldn't sneak up on people like that."

"Sorry."

"No you're not."

He smiled. "I take it your friend isn't as vocal as you?"

"I was just teasing her."

"I heard. We all did."

Her face heated. "Spectacular."

"You are an interesting woman, Sunshine. You can talk to her about something as intimate as what you say when I make you come, but you blush knowing I overheard part of your conversation?" He pushed away from the door and stepped close, ran the backs of his fingers over her hot cheeks. "You got it wrong."

"I...got what wrong?"

"Would you like to know what you were chanting in the limo last night?" His voice went all husky in the way that made her panties wet. "What you were whispering in my ear as I drove you to orgasm?"

Her lungs locked. Breathing became impossible.

He bent closer, pressed his mouth against the shell of her ear and whispered her words back to her, complete with panted breath. *"Joe...God, you feel so good...Fuck me, Joe...Harder...Joe. Joe!"*

Emma shivered and pulsed once at the memory, the rough timbre of his voice in her ear. She splayed her hands wide across his chest, touching as much of his skin as she could.

"You got the scream part right. Hell, you screamed so loud that even though I was muffling you with my kiss, they heard you outside the limo. All while pulling my hair so hard I though you would tear it out by the roots."

She laughed softly, more aroused than she cared to admit. "I didn't hear you complaining."

"You never will."

Cupping his face, she kissed him.

He dropped his hand to her hip, slid it around to palm her ass then pulled her closer. Diving into the kiss, he took her mouth roughly, tangling his tongue with hers, teasing her with the press of his erection against her stomach.

"Nice," she murmured against his lips. "One of my favorite ways to say good morning."

"Strip and I'll give you your favorite."

"No-o-o." She drew the word out as she retreated a step. "No way, They've already heard enough."

He released a sigh. "You're killing me, Sunshine."

"Tough. You invited them to our suite, now you get to suffer in discomfort." She looked down at his jeans, his erection straining his button fly, and couldn't help but run her fingers over his length.

His abs contracted. "Christ, Emma."

She smiled. "Why are they here, exactly?"

"We're planning to make some noise."

"Really?"

"Come on," he said reaching for her hand. "You'll enjoy this."

She expected to find the band plus Gary scattered around the lounge area of the suite, but what surprised her was how they'd brought instruments. Joe's acoustic guitar sat atop an empty seat at the far side of the room. Steve and Zach were on his left, each with their own acoustic in their laps. Bobby sat on Joe's right, tuning his electric bass sans amplifier, Kirk next to him, twirling his sticks. Gary occupied a lone chair in the corner closest to the door, face buried in a magazine. Apparently, the noise Joe spoke of was music.

He was right. She was going to enjoy this.

Emma let go of his hand and watched Joe walk to his chair and take a seat.

"Morning, Emma." Kirk greeted her with a big smile on his face.

She returned his smile.

"What's the matter, Em?" Steve asked. As the one who teased her more than any of the others, she knew before he finished his sentence he was about to comment on what they'd all overheard. "Joe doing such a pitiful job of pleasing you that you had to take matters into your own hands?"

Joe scoffed. "More like she was bragging to her friend about my sexual prowess."

"No one gives a bleedin' shit about your so-called prowess." Zach looked up from the chords he'd been playing and focused on Emma. "I want to know about those bruises on Joe's chest."

Her face flamed again. Some days, she really hated having such pale skin.

Zach laughed. "See, now we're getting somewhere."

Ignoring him, she pulled the straight back wooden chair out from the desk and placed it next to Gary, sinking into it with a sigh. She stretched her legs out in front of her and wiggled her toes, smiling down at her deep raspberry polish, her big toes sporting bright neon butterflies with rhinestone accents.

Gary tipped the top of his magazine and followed her gaze. He looked at her feet, back at her, then shook his head and went back to reading.

"What? You don't like it?"

Steve smacked the body of his guitar. "I've got it!" He

turned his attention to Joe. "She took the flogger to you for being a righteous shit yesterday."

"You'd better hope not," she replied, crossing her ankle over her knee and poking Gary with her toe just to goad him. "Or I owe you all a flogging."

"Wrong thing to say to a room full of men," Gary muttered with a smirk.

From a seated position, Zach launched up and landed on his feet on the couch. He thrust his hand, along with the guitar still in it, into the air. "I volunteer as tribute!"

"Jesus." Emma snorted a laugh. She didn't know which surprised her more. Zach's astonishing feat or the mood of the room. Everyone began talking at once, chattering right over the top of each other. Laughter soon followed, then someone—she honestly wasn't sure if it was Steve or Zach or whether they all somehow began at once—started playing. The talking ceased and the music began. Joe's voice filled the room.

One song coalesced into another, then another. By the fifth, Emma couldn't wipe the smile off her face. She glanced at Gary, who'd closed his magazine and was watching as she was. "This is new."

He tipped his head. "They used to do this all the time. It's been months, though. At least ten."

"Yeah? They don't play their own music?"

"That's one of the rules. Sticking to anything and everything but their own music keeps it friendly and fun. No arguments over style or tempo. Just them doing what they love most."

Gary got up, retrieved two bottles of water from the refrigerator and handed her one. He followed it up with a packet of pain reliever.

She took it from him and sighed. "How did you know?"

"You keep rubbing the back of your neck."

Did she? She swallowed the pills. "Thank you."

"You're welcome. Food will be here any minute. That should help." He stayed standing, glancing at his cell every few minutes.

"Gare?"

"Yeah?"

"I have to ask about the phones. When did you bring those back?" Emma didn't look at him, finding the wrapper on her bottle safer than what she might see in his face, depending on his answer. "It wasn't last night, was it?"

"You look a little apprehensive there, Emma."

"I'm wondering if I can ever look you in the eye again," she admitted.

He threw his head back and laughed.

Emma swore. She stood and turned for the bedroom.

"Hold up." He flashed a smile her way. "It was this morning, okay? I figured it gave me the best odds of catching you both asleep."

Thank God.

Food arrived and everyone ate—no two people at the same time. When one walked away to fill a plate, another took over their part. The music never lulled though, at times, it continued without lyrics. Inspired, Emma retrieved her journal and began to sketch.

She'd just started on Kirk's hands, the way he held his sticks as he tapped out a rhythm on the arm of the couch, when Zach called, "Emma? Have any requests?"

Her answer was instant and automatic, her all-time favorite song since the night she and Alison had done an eighties vampire movie marathon. "Don't Let the Sun—"

"Oh, hell no." Joe groaned. "That's a terrible song."

"It is not!"

He just looked at her.

"Fine. Dust in the Wind."

"Kansas!" Zach exclaimed. "We can do that."

Joe looked at her, torn between amusement and irritation. "What is it with these depressing ass songs? I don't ever want to hear you call one of my songs horrible again."

"What song?" Kirk asked.

"Alienation," Joe answered for her. "She hates it."

Gary looked up from his magazine. "It is a bloody downer."

"And Dust in the Wind isn't?"

Gary shrugged.

Zach and Steve both started playing, two instruments, blending to sound like one. The melody wrapped around her, washed over her, stirred her soul. She'd loved this song since first she'd heard it. It spoke to her on a level she knew Joe, in all his teasing, couldn't comprehend. The small hairs on her arms stood at attention.

"How does it go again?" Joe asked with a smile.

Emma started singing and his smile faded. He didn't take his gaze off her, and his eyes were filled with fascination, surprise and so much hunger, she didn't know whether to laugh or cross the room and kiss him senseless.

Kirk took over for the second verse. God, he had an amazing voice. She could carry a tune, stay in time and correct pitch, but she had nothing on Kirk. Then Joe joined him in the harmonies and her world shifted.

He was right. It was a damn depressing song. Nothing lasted forever, no matter how much a person wanted it to. Life ended. Everything eventually crumbled and turned to dust. It was a truth she'd accepted long ago. But hearing those words from the voice of the man she loved…suddenly she wasn't okay with that truth. She never would be.

Shit. Now what am I going to do?

She started to hyperventilate. Like need a bag to breathe, hyperventilate. Her heart pounded in her chest. Her lungs constricted. She was in love with Joe. When had that happened?

Emma launched to her feet and would have run for the bedroom if common sense hadn't won out. She didn't need any attention, just to get out of there. Outside, where she could breathe.

Escape was the only answer.

Her trek to the bedroom was accomplished at a half jog. She tossed her journal atop the sea of clothes spread across the bed, then perched on the edge to pull her new brown suede boots out of the box and shove her feet into them. Grabbing the matching jacket, she headed for the door, rubbing her hand over her face as she went. What little breath she had left her as she slammed into a hard wall of muscle. *"Joe."*

He curled his hands around her upper arms. "What's wrong?"

She wanted to laugh. Hell, she wanted to cry. What a seemingly innocuous question and yet it invoked the oddest reaction in her. She stared at his chest, wondering how long she could stand to be locked in this room with all of them. "I need to go for a walk."

"Outside."

"Yes."

"Right now?" he asked quietly.

"Yes, right now." He had to hear her quick intake of

breaths, feel the slight tremble in her arms.

"Look at me." Adding an assist, he tucked a finger under her jaw and tilted it up to his. "Something spooked you."

"Yup," she admitted. There was no use lying about it.

"I'll take her," Gary volunteered.

Emma rubbed the back of her thumb across her forehead. When had this happened? She wasn't even allowed to go for a walk by herself? Have an *'oh shit, now what?'* moment in private? "No. I've done fine on my own for years. I think I can handle a walk in the sun without a big strong man to protect me."

Joe arched a brow.

"She doesn't seem to get what could happen to a woman who looks like her in a city like this," Gary muttered.

"What the hell does that even mean? How do I look?"

Steve and Zach started offering opinions. Emma only half listened.

"Female."

"Petite."

"A bit fragile."

"Weak."

"Beautiful." Now that voice was different, and there was no way it belonged to the man she was positive it belonged to.

Emma peaked around Joe and focused on Bobby.

He shrugged. "You want to know what Gary means, that's what he means. A beautiful woman like you, walking alone in a strange city, is dangerous. I don't know why he can't just come right out and say it."

Kirk nodded.

"Sunshine, what are you going to do if a man Gare's size comes after you?"

"Knee him in the balls. Which is what I'm going to do to you in about five seconds if you don't let me go."

Joe sighed. "Guys?"

They stood en masse and left.

"No! You..." Damnit, this isn't what she'd wanted. "What are you doing? You were enjoying yourself. Spending time with the guys."

"I'm with the guys every day. You want to go for a walk, we'll go for a walk. Just give me a few minutes, okay?"

"No." She added a head shake. "I don't want you to go with me."

"Why not?"

Because that was exactly what she *did* want. To spend time with him. No buses or sound checks or confined spaces with too many sets of eyes and ears on them. No rabid fans or squeezing in five minutes before there was somewhere else he had to be. Just the two of them. Alone.

"What is going on with you?" he asked with terrifying gentleness. "This is the third time in two days you've teared up on me. I mean the first time, I get it. I was being a bloody bastard, but... Are you going to start your—"

"No."

"—period, because I understand female hormones. I do have a sister, you know."

"God." She pressed her face into his chest. How could he be so sweet, yet so damn frustrating at the same time? "I feel sorry for your sister. You were probably a terrible brother to grow up with."

"Nah, I'm a fantastic brother." He smoothed his hand up and down her back. "Do you need anything? Tampons or whatever, ice cream, chocolate covered potato chips... Me, naked?"

She tried not to laugh and failed. "Will you stop it. It's not hormones. I'm not going to start my period. I don't have those."

"Ever?"

He sounded so flummoxed, she laughed again. "Not if I have anything to say about it."

"Is that even healthy?"

"Ahh!" She didn't know which was stronger. The desire to choke him in frustration or take him up on his offer of him, naked. "Just...go get dressed." It was obvious the only way she was getting a walk was with Joe. Now, if they could just pull it off without him being recognized. "And try not to look so...you."

One side of his mouth tipped up in a smile. "I'll do my best."

Five minutes later, he came out of the bathroom sporting a long sleeve black thermal that hid his tattoos from view. He'd tucked the shirt into his pants, a pair of sunglasses into the collar, and pulled his hair away from his face. Emma opened her mouth to comment, closed it when no words would come, then opened it again. "Is that a man bun?"

He shook his head.

"It is." She stuck her tongue in the side of her cheek and then grinned. "Look at you, all metrosexual and shit."

He sighed. "I believe the word you're looking for is hipster."

"Is it? Or is that one just less abrasive to your masculinity?"

"You're the one who wanted me to not look so me."

"Yes, but you're the one who knew how to make the man bun." She tipped her head. "Is there something you need to tell me?"

"Yeah." He stared at her. "You make me crazy."

"I feel your pain, macho man. I really do."

"Christ." He shook his head and dug through his duffle, stuffing his wallet in his back pocket and a black beanie atop his head.

Her laughter died. "Damn."

"What now?"

"You're kind of cute."

He flashed her an unreadable look, slipping his sunglasses on without comment.

"Sexy."

"You are too much." He held out his hand for her and she took it as they headed for the elevator. "Where would you like to go?"

As long as it was away from the hotel for a while, the where didn't matter. "We could hit the Magnificent Mile."

"The what?"

"The Magnificent Mile. It's *the* place for shopping in Chicago."

His brow furrowed as he pressed the call button. "You've got a pile of clothes on the bed from yesterday's outing and you want to go again?"

"I need a new pair of heels. Last night's *rain* destroyed the pair I have." The smile that curved his lips was naughty. Emma suddenly wished he hadn't put the glasses on yet. She would've loved to see his eyes. "Or, if you prefer, we can go to the salon and get you a manicure. It would really bring together this whole metro thing you have going on."

"Hipster," he muttered, pressing the call button again.

"Whatever."

"Jesus." He pulled his glasses off and scrubbed his hands

over his face. "Let me guess. You think I should get manscaped, too."

"Hell no!"

The elevator doors slid open.

"That's good, because no wax is coming near my balls. Ever."

"Neither is some other woman's hands," Emma growled. Which would happen if he ever got waxed.

A broad smiled curved his lips. "Wow." He backed her into the elevator and to the corner, using his body to block her view of everything but him. "Someone is feeling a bit possessive, today."

She was, and she didn't much like it. That didn't stop her from running her palms down the front of his shirt, from pecs to abdomen and lower. "This is mine." She whispered the statement as she cupped his groin, relished his quick intake of air and the way he pulsed at her touch.

"You won't hear me argue."

A soft sound had her spine snapping straight. She stared up at Joe, then heard it again.

A snicker of laughter.

Her face flamed. "Joe?"

"Yeah, Sunshine?"

"Are we alone on this elevator?"

His smile said it all. "A little late to worry about that now, isn't it?"

"Shit." She pressed her face into his chest and laughed. Because really what else could she do?

JOE WOKE TO pitch darkness. Alone in the bed.

After spending the afternoon with Emma in his arms as

they walked through downtown Chicago uninhibited, they'd returned to the suite and spent the rest of the day laughing, loving and sleeping, only to wake up and start the cycle over again. He'd never known anything like it. Being buried inside a woman and caring more about bringing a smile to her face or wringing a sigh from her lips, than getting off. It was a completely new and terrifying occurrence.

He was desperate to experience it again.

Of course—he blinked at the clock, 2:30 a.m.—it would help if he knew where Emma had run off to. "Sunshine?"

Joe rolled out of bed and stretched. There wasn't a speck of light anywhere to aid in his visual search or give hint to her whereabouts. Even the curtain over the slider leading to the balcony was pulled. She never did that. Emma needed light—a window to the outside world. She didn't do dark, enclosed places well, no matter how large the space.

Something was very wrong. "Emma?"

The bathroom door was closed, the shower running. Now that he'd picked up on the sound, he wondered how he'd missed it. But as he walked across the room and reached for the handle, he noticed there was no strip of light beneath the door. He stepped into the room, and thanks to the fact that he'd woken to the same darkness that greeted him now, he had a perfect view.

Emma sat on the floor of the glass shower, knees pulled tight against her chest, head bent so the water beat down on her shoulders. She was visibly trembling, her arms shaking so hard they kept slipping down her wet legs.

"Here you are." He whispered the words as he reached for the light switch.

"Don't." She curled her arms over her head. Not like

she didn't want him to see her distress, but like she was protecting herself from an unseen enemy.

He really wanted it to be claustrophobia triggered by the complete lack of light, but the curtain hadn't been closed when they'd drifted to sleep, wrapped in each other's arms and sated. No, she'd closed that curtain before barricading herself in the bathroom. Her pain wasn't emotional, it was physical.

"Hold on, Sunshine." Yanking the glass door open, he stepped inside and immediately lost his breath as the freezing cold water pelted his chest. He turned off the shower and scooped her into his arms. "I've got you."

Jesus, how long had she been sitting here? Her skin was like ice. She shook so hard, her teeth chattered as he carried her into the bedroom and set her in the middle of the bed, pulling the comforter they'd kicked to the floor long ago over her for warmth.

He wasted no time returning to the bathroom, where he grabbed a towel and her makeup bag. Dumping the contents of the bag onto the towel, he searched, shoving each item aside until he located her auto-injector and headed back to the bedroom.

"Em." He looked down at her and felt something catch deep inside. Fear for her and whatever was going on, for himself because he'd never felt so helpless in all his life. She was sitting up, the blanket pooled around her hips as she quietly sobbed, rocking with her arms once again covering her head. He'd never seen her this bad before—in so much pain, she couldn't function. The medication she needed lay in the palm of his hand, but having never actually witnessed its use, he had no idea how to help her. "How do I do this? I don't know how to help you."

"Help me sit up," she whispered, her voice so low he barely heard her.

"You are sitting up."

A whimper escaped as she dropped her arms from her head, pressed her palms into the mattress and shifted in his direction.

She'd meant sit on the side of the bed.

Placing one arm around her back and the other beneath her legs, Joe lifted her, setting her on the edge of the bed with her feet on the floor. He sank to his knees before her.

Fingers like ice closed around his, grasping, guiding his hands. She shifted his thumb off the blue button, curled his hand around the length of the tube, then guided the other to the cap on the opposite end.

"Pull." Her broken whisper brought his gaze to her face, where he found her eyes open, rapidly blinking tears down her cheeks. "Don't twist. Straight out."

He nodded and did as instructed, removing a cap with a metal tube attached.

"Here." Hand atop his, she pushed the open end of the injector onto the skin of her lower thigh. "Hold it...don't let up...two clicks."

"Two clicks," he repeated.

She pushed the blue button. A click sounded, then, about five seconds later, another. Her hand slid off his, her head dropped to his shoulder. "Don't leave me."

Tossing the injector aside, Joe wrapped his arms around her. He crawled up the bed, bringing her with him, and pulled the comforter over them both. "I'm right here, Sunshine. I've got you."

It didn't take long for her tears to dry, her breathing to ease. However, the trembling of her limbs continued. As did the clenching pain in his gut.

Unsure what else to do for her, he started to sing, his voice barely above a whisper. She sighed and snuggled closer so he kept at it, not stopping until long after she'd given herself over to sleep.

May 8

The tremors have started. They've been going on for a few days. Not every day. Maybe two or three times, now. They don't last long. Thirty seconds to a minute, usually. Just long enough to remind me that worse things are coming. Seizures and blackouts to name a few. It's all pretty terrifying. Oh, I act tough. I smile and pretend it doesn't bother me, pretend I'm too strong to break down and cry.

It's a lie.

I'm a fake.

Joe hates fakes. I've known this for a long time now, yet... I'm the biggest of them all. I honestly never thought I would still be with him. That he'd stay interested in whatever this is that draws us together. But here I am, still lapping up every moment I can while lying to him about myself. Okay, so I've never come right out and lied to his face, but not being upfront about something, choosing to keep silent instead of sharing is the same thing as lying, isn't it? I'm a fake and...I don't deserve him.

I know he would disagree. For some reason, Joe doesn't believe he deserves me. A fact made glaringly apparent this morning when I found myself on the pointed end of accusations and slander from Marvin, while Joe stood silently by – waiting, wondering, and doubting.

I left him today. Walked right out that door, the

pain in my heart the perfect excuse for saying goodbye. I left him, knowing it was the best thing to do. My tremors have started. Soon, so will the seizures.

I made it all the way to O'Hare before I broke. I stared at those planes taking off and landing, whisking people to far away destinations and bringing them home to loved ones. I stood there and thought of what I was going home to and was suddenly filled with so much fear, I couldn't breathe. I had a panic attack in the middle of the parking lot, fell straight to my knees while my body shook uncontrollably. I was angry and hurt and so damn scared of what the end of my life without Joe would mean, that I cried. Cried and wailed and screamed at the injustice of it all. Then I returned to him.

I'm too weak to walk away. Too weak to face the end alone.

I'm a fake. A woman who only pretends to be strong and tough. Who smiles and laughs as if everything is okay.

Even as my arm trembles so badly I can barely write.

Number of days since I decided to live: 78
Number of days since I met Joe: 35
Current level of panic: 8/10

SIXTEEN

May 20

E MMA ZIPPED AROUND the outer oval, past the concession stands and tables lined with memorabilia. Past the shocked faces and muttered curses of the staff. She laughed aloud when she reached the far end and was forced to enter the arena, tearing down the ramp, around the racks of chairs waiting to be placed and back out the other side. No one could stop her. No one dared.

God, it was good to be alive!

The stage was set for tonight's show, the guys in the middle of sound check. She didn't know why the schedule had been moved up, why everything was happening hours earlier than normal, but the pounding rhythm of the band and throaty growl that was Joe provided the perfect soundtrack to her mood. Like the driving beat of the bass, Emma pushed harder, moved faster, zipping through the arena at speeds that made her giddy.

She was smiling as she flew up the ramp and into the outer oval, laughing even as her body took flight.

"Jesus Christ!" Gary snagged her around the waist, scrubbing off speed by spinning them in a complete circle. Her world tilted, stomach dropped to her toes as he held her without difficulty, her rollerblades dangling off the ground. "What are you up to this time?"

"Put me down before you hurt yourself." He'd basically clotheslined her about the waist and snagged her off the floor like parents did with a small child, leaving her hanging from his right arm.

"As if! What do you weigh? All of a hundred twenty soaking wet?"

"A hundred and ten, actually."

He frowned, his gaze sliding over her. "You need to eat a donut. Or six."

She hadn't had much of an appetite lately, even for sweets, and as a result she had dropped a few pounds. The reminder dimmed her smile. "I'll go find some right now if it means you'll put me down. Or do you plan to wear me as an arm dressing all day? If so, I'd like to go that way, please."

He didn't bother to glance in the direction she pointed as he set her down, curling his hands around her upper arms to steady her as she wobbled a bit. "Nice rollerblades. Where'd you get them?"

"Thanks." They were hot pink and turquoise. Just obnoxious enough, she loved them. "And what do you mean where'd I get them? Where do I get anything I decide to tear around arenas in?"

"You stole them?"

"What? I've never stolen anything."

He crossed his arms, muscles rippled and bunched, strained the seams of his shirt. Jesus, even those muscles by his neck, what where they called—traps—locked right up. The man was seriously tense and she didn't think it was all because of her morning fun.

"There was the incident with the golf cart," he reminded her.

"Technically, I didn't steal that. I only borrowed it. I

gave it back as soon as I was done with it!"

He arched a brow.

"They're the ones who lined up the other golf cart alongside me so we could figure out which one was faster."

Someone snorted a laugh. A female someone.

Emma shifted to get a look around Gary and found the source of the laughter about ten feet behind him. A tall woman with raven hair, sharp cheekbones and a gracious smile. She was rocking a black pantsuit that showed off enviable curves, a chunky gold necklace and killer heels. Her hair was down. Long, smooth and parted in the middle, with bangs that darn near touched her eyelashes. Their length made her eye color a mystery, which drew Emma's gaze straight to her full, thick lips.

She was stunning. Honestly, one of the prettiest women Emma had ever laid eyes on. But the most interesting thing about her was the way her gaze kept sliding over Gary in a manner that expressed interest.

"Wow," Emma whispered, looking back at Gary. "Who's the hottie?"

Gary sighed. "You've been hanging with men too long."

"You're right. I apologize. Who's the woman checking out your ass?"

His spine snapped straight and he got this look on his face like he was torn between throttling her and checking over his shoulder to see if the woman really was looking at his ass. Which she totally was.

When he sighed and started to lower his arms, she stopped him. "No, keep them crossed. She is loving the whole bulging muscle thing you have going on. Trust me." Emma peeked around him again. "Totally loving it. So, you never answered my question."

"What question is that?"

"Who is she?"

"Her name is Vivian Johnson. She's from the record company."

Emma nibbled her lower lip. "Why is she here? It's pretty late in the game for a record exec to show up, isn't it?" In fact, there was barely a month left of the North American tour before they wrapped.

"The album went multi-platinum."

"That's fantastic!" Gary's brow furrowed. "What's the look you're wearing? Isn't this a good thing?"

"Marvin's been pushing Joe to write more, write faster."

She recalled Marvin saying something along those lines when they'd been in Chicago. Although Marvin didn't put it so nicely.

"Now that the label is here..." Gary shrugged. "I don't know. I try to stay out of these things. Can I put my bloody arms down yet?"

"No one is stopping you, big guy."

He cupped his hand around the back of his neck and muttered below his breath.

Emma flashed him her most innocent smile. God, she loved poking the ogre, and he made it so damn easy. "Well, for whatever reason Vivian is here, she's beautiful. A bit young for you, but I say go for it. Ask her out. I mean, you have been a bit tense lately. Maybe she could help you with that."

"What makes you think I am interested in—?"

Emma laughed, effectively cutting off his denial. She laughed so hard she lost her balance and made a grab for Gary, who steadied her with a hand on her elbow. "You do have a pulse, right?

He frowned down at her, his frustration evident in his voice. "And where would you have me ask her to? The bus? Not that many options open to me right now, are there?"

Setting her hand on his bicep, she gave it a squeeze. "All I'm saying is she's obviously into you. And I believe if you think real hard on it, you'll come up with a great big room in this place that has an even bigger couch in it."

Gary sighed.

Emma winked at him. "Oh, she's coming over here." She patted his arm. "Behave yourself."

"I could tell you the same thing."

A smile on her face, Emma offered the woman her hand. "Hello, my name is Emma." She flashed Gary a *'see, I can be good'* look.

Gary frowned.

"Vivian Johnson," the woman replied. She had a bit of an accent. One Emma couldn't place. "I'm with record company."

"So I've heard."

"Emma is Joe's girl," Gary volunteered.

"That's me." Deciding to see what would happen if she did, she dropped her hand back to Gary's arm and gave it a squeeze. "I'm also the thorn in Gary's side."

Vivian's gaze zeroed in on Emma's hand. "He does seem a bit perturbed."

"I have mad skills when it comes to riling Gary. Of course, if he wasn't already so tense it wouldn't be so easy."

Gary cleared his throat. "Emma."

"I got this." She patted him. "You see, Gare here—"

"Don't."

"—finds you very attractive." Emma waited. Stayed quiet as Vivian's gaze shifted from Gary to her. "Which you are, by the way."

Vivian's smile lit up her face. "Thank you."

"You're welcome." Emma glanced back at Gary, whose furrow deepened. "See, Gare, I don't have a problem telling a woman she's beautiful. Why can't you do it?"

He didn't say anything, just stared and frowned. Then his left eye started to twitch.

"Shit, that's my sign it's time to leave. Don't worry though, Viv. He's pretty harmless."

Vivian ran her gaze over him, from head to toe and back again. She nibbled her bottom lip, a small smile on her face. "Is that so?"

Emma shrugged. "He hasn't throttled me yet."

"The day is young," Gary muttered.

Emma cracked up. God, he was great! "I can't stand still any longer. Gotta get moving. It was nice meeting you, Vivian."

"You, too."

Emma turned and pushed off.

"Slow down before you hurt yourself!" Gary called and she laughed again.

O———

JOE STEPPED TO the front of the stage, trying to recall what the hell he'd been singing as he waited for Emma to return to the arena. She'd been zooming around on those damn rollerblades all morning, wearing nothing but jeans and a concert tank, leaving all that soft pale skin exposed to damage should she fall. Dodging left or right as workers shifted in an attempt to avoid her, she whipped past at speeds that had his stomach clenching, a broad smile on her face and laughter in her wake.

Up until two songs ago, when she'd zipped up the ramp and disappeared, leaving him to wonder if she'd run into an obstacle she couldn't avoid. Joe considered his options. Wait for her return, have one of his crew check on her, or go find her himself.

The decision was made for him when she came flying into the arena and straight to the stage. She climbed through the barrier already in place to keep fans back and tipped her head.

The smile she shot him could power the city. "Hi."

Leaning with his arm resting atop the mic stand, he stood there and absorbed. For a moment, he couldn't draw enough oxygen into his lungs to save his soul. Happiness emanated off her—hell, she was nearly vibrating with it— filling him with a desperate desire to soak it up.

Placing the mic in the stand, he reached down for her. "Come here, Sunshine."

She raised her hands and he grabbed them, lifted her up until her butt was on the stage. Then, before she could try to stand on her own, he snagged her beneath the arms, pulled her up and kissed her.

Joe molded her body to his and inhaled her, soaking up her warmth, the joy that called out to him. He kissed her until she sagged against him, gripping his shirt in two tight fists and whimpering into his mouth.

"Damn," she gasped as he set her back on her feet.

His breathing was unsteady, ragged. He'd thought he was used to the way she affected him but, as she smoothed her palms down his chest and took his hand, tracing the G clef tattoo on his forearm with the tips of her fingers, the shock of excitement took him by surprise. A simple touch, and he felt himself stir with arousal. She might as well have had her hands in his pants.

He blinked away the mental images floating through his brain. The one about ordering everyone to vacate the arena so he could lay her out on the stage and have his way with her was especially persistent. He'd never given that kind of performance while behind the mic and he suddenly wanted it more than he wanted his next breath.

Too bad he had a meeting with someone from the label. The woman Gare just walked in with if Joe were to hazard a guess.

"It's gorgeous outside." Emma's fingers smoothed up his arm, slipped into the sleeve of his shirt to rub his shoulder. "What are we all doing in here?"

"I'm trying to work." Christ, he was gone over her. He was never going to get enough. The reality of that was as obvious as the soft smile on her face. "You, on the other hand, seem to be hell bent on driving me out of my bloody mind."

"I didn't get to give you my look this morning."

"What look is that?" He asked the question, even though he knew exactly what look she was referring to.

"The one that sets your mood for the day."

He smiled at the memory. "Consider my mood set."

"Yeah?" She glanced between them, at his obvious erection, and licked her lips.

He groaned. "Jesus, what am I going to do with you?"

"Take me..." Her emphasis was on the word 'take' as she leaned closer and kissed the shell of his ear before whispering, "outside."

The pounding in his cock told him his lower half was completely on board with the idea. His brain kept going back to how the hand she held on his arm had been shaking for at least thirty seconds now. Concern for her wrapped itself around his heart, made it hard to breathe. Whatever was going on, he didn't think a mad dash outside for a quickie was the answer. "I can't, Em. Work."

She pushed away from him so fast he had to reach out and grab her arms for fear she'd roll right off the front of the stage.

"Um, guys," Gary called. "You do realize you're standing next to an open mic, right?"

He hadn't. Joe rubbed the back of his neck and swore. He'd completely forgotten that the moment she'd come gliding up to the stage.

Emma's eyes threw fire and she skated away.

Joe actually felt like a pile of ash right then.

"What the hell?" Confusion sounded in Steve's voice. "I can't believe you turned her down."

"Yeah, what the fuck was that?" Bobby asked.

Before Joe could reply, Emma returned. Spinning in a circle center stage, then facing Zach. "Hey, Zach, interested in taking me for a ride?"

Son of a bitch. No way had he heard her correctly. "Excuse me?"

"Um." Zach was smart enough not to answer, his gaze ping ponged between Joe and Emma.

Emma had her hands on her hips, spoiling for a fight. "Motorcycle ride, me and Zach. What part of that did you miss?"

"The part where you mentioned a motorbike." Jesus, she was a raw ball of emotion today. First, so damn happy she glowed and now so upset he feared she'd start throwing things any minute. Joe pushed his hair out of his face, considered the best way to handle this situation. "You can't steal my guitarist."

"Why the hell not? You have two."

"I'd love to go," Zach piped up.

Joe pitched his voice lower. "Sunshine."

"Don't Sunshine me," Emma growled. "You had your chance."

"Man, you are so fucked, Joe," Steve mumbled.

Ba-dum tish. Kirk did two fast thumps and a cymbal splash as if Steve had made a cheesy joke.

Joe ignored them, keeping his focus on Emma, who shrugged. "If I can't get any sexual satisfaction, at least I can satisfy my need for speed. These blades don't go near fast enough."

Zach grinned. "I'm ready whenever you are, Em." He moved swiftly across the stage as Joe's eyes narrowed, and wisely slipped out the back curtain.

Emma followed him.

Bobby barked a laugh. "Joe, seriously, I love—"

"Shut the fuck up, Bobby," Joe growled, which only made Bobby laugh harder.

"Emma's in quite a mood today," Gary said from his front row seat.

"Yeah, she is." Joe nodded and headed in the direction she'd disappeared.

He found her by the loading dock, her discarded rollerblades occupying the chair next to her as she leaned against the wall and tugged on her suede boots. Zach was at her side, holding a leather jacket.

Emma shook her head. "It's too warm for that, Zach."

"No, it's not. You need it on the off chance something happens and I have to lay the bike down. It'll protect your skin from the road."

325

Fuck. Joe blew a long, hard breath.

Behind them, one of the roadies maneuvered Zach's red custom chopper out of the trailer. Zach glanced at Joe, gave him a nod, then went over to help with the bike.

"Emma." She looked up at him for the first time since he'd stepped next to her. "Maybe you should rethink this." Even as he said it, Joe helped her into the jacket, snugging the buckles tight and zipping it for her.

"I need the fresh air."

"You need the thrill." He'd noticed that about her. Whenever she'd had a headache bad enough she had to medicate—and she'd had two since the one in Chicago that had scared the hell out of him—she followed it up by doing something outrageous the next day. With her last headache being just yesterday, her need for speed made sense.

"That, too." She flashed him a smile that morphed into confusion. "Your forehead is creased and your jaw is popping. Stop clenching it before you break a molar."

Zach started the chopper. At least Emma hadn't asked Bobby to take her. His bike couldn't carry a passenger safely. Zach's could.

"Joe." Her hand on his arm brought his attention back to her. "What are you so worried about?"

You. How damn fragile you look lately.

"Is Zach a safe driver?"

Joe shrugged. "I suppose. He's never been hurt. Not yet."

At his response, she moved in closer and shifted her hand to his chest. "Okay, so it's the fact that my arms will be around him, my breasts pressed against his back that bothers you?"

He covered her hand with his. "When you put it that

way."

She burst out laughing and he couldn't help but grin. Excitement showed in her eyes. She couldn't wait to jump on the back of that bike.

Shit. He sighed. "Just make sure you bring him back in time for the show."

THEY RETURNED HOURS later, screaming into the parking lot at breakneck speed. Even from his spot inside the loading dock door, Joe could plainly see the broad smile on Emma's face. She was laughing as she removed her helmet and handed it to Zach. Animated and talking a mile a minute.

Tom, the crewmember in charge of maintaining Zach and Bobby's bikes and the man Joe had been speaking with, pushed out the door and started across the lot. Joe followed.

The closer he got to her, the more he relaxed. The ride had apparently done her some good. Her color was up. The circles of fatigue beneath her eyes, so evident that morning, faded. His steps slowed as he watched her strip the leather jacket off, greeting Tom with a smile and another flurry of conversation.

She was happy. Hell, she was more than happy. She glowed.

He stopped altogether as she turned her smile on him. Five seconds ago, he would've said there was no way she could look more vibrant. He'd have been wrong. The minute she noticed him standing there she lit up then launched herself at him. Two steps, and she was off the ground and in his arms, legs around his hips, mouth fused to his.

Joe caught her effortlessly, even though the move took

him by surprise. She wasn't one to jump into his arms and usually wound up wrapped around him only because he lifted her off the floor. He dropped his hands to her hips as she cupped the back of his head and deepened the kiss, fisting her hand in his hair. Electricity crackled between them. Her taste exploded on his tongue.

"Christ," he muttered as they came up for air, both of them panting. "You had a good time."

"I had a great time! My God, you have to try that. There are no words."

"You want me to ride bitch on Zach's motorbike?"

Her eyes lit with humor. "I do. It's exhilarating."

Her second kiss tasted as good as the first. He could drown in her. Just happily let himself go right under, but she broke away from him and left his head spinning.

Her hand brushed his cheek. "The wind in your hair. The rumble of the bike. Do you have any idea how good it feels? The vibrations…Jesus, it's so titillating."

"I believe you're still vibrating."

She quivered, pressed her lower half against his stomach. "Oh, I am. I'm so turned on I can't stand it."

"I can tell."

She nuzzled below his ear. "The bus is right behind you." The words whispered between them. "Hurry."

Zach's laughter echoed behind them. "You can thank me later, Joe!"

Yeah. Later. Right now, he was too busy trying to get up the steps without dropping Emma. She was on fire, rubbing against him as she sucked on his neck. Fuck, he could feel her heat through both layers of denim. His cock pulsed, desperate to get closer.

"Hurry," she mumbled between kisses. "God, please

hurry."

She was killing him. Setting her on her feet, he closed the door and flicked the lock. He went to work on his pants.

Emma pulled off her boots and shucked her jeans in record time. Then she was on him again, crawling up his body, legs closing around his hips. He barely had his pants to his thighs, but she didn't care. She took him in hand and held him at her entrance, wiggling, shifting, loosening her grip around his neck until she sunk down on him, taking him deep.

Fuck! She didn't even give him a moment to recover from the shock before she was kissing him again, sliding up and down his cock. His bare cock.

He wasn't wearing a condom.

"Christ, Emma." She clenched down on him and he hissed a breath. "Condom."

"I won't get pregnant. I can't."

He hadn't gone bareback since he was a teenager. The sensations made him crazy. She felt so good, so fucking amazing.

"I'm clean." He pinned her between his body and the refrigerator. "Routine health checks." He couldn't believe what she did to him, how quickly she made him lose control.

"Joe." She tugged her tank over her head. "Shut up and move. I need you to move."

He dipped his head and pulled a nipple into his mouth.

She let out a soft sound that ended in a groan. "Now, Joe."

"God, yes." Curling an arm under her ass, he dropped his other hand between them and worked her clit with his thumb. Flexing his hips, he filled her then retreated, tipping his head to watch his body slide in and out of hers. "You're so tight and wet. Are you wet for me or the motorbike?"

She laughed and he felt it throughout her body and into his own. Her muscles tightened around his cock, pulling a groan from the back of his throat.

"It's for you," she whispered, pressing kisses to his neck, his temple and ear. "Look at me. Look at me, Joe."

He did. Looked into her eyes and saw something she hadn't allowed him to see before.

"It's all for you," she repeated, holding his gaze prisoner. "I love you."

Then she came, her entire body contracting, milking him, taking him over the edge with her in an orgasm more powerful than ever before.

May 14
I'm in love with Joe.

I love him so much it hurts. I knew all along it would happen. Hell, I was halfway there when I left Cleveland to join him. But I never knew, could never imagine that it could feel this good to feel this bad.

I have to tell him. Dear God, I have to.

I've tried a few times. Started the conversation about what drove me to go against character and accept his invitation backstage. Why I was willing to be just like the women at the after parties I hate so much. How I would have done anything and everything he asked that night just for the memory. For that moment in time when he saw me, wanted me, and turned to me to satisfy a need.

For the chance to have him smile at me.

The way he does now.

More than once, I've tried to explain my need to suck everything I can out of life. To experience as much as possible in the time I have left. Every time I do, every time I start, Joe stops me. And because I'm scared, so damn scared to witness the affection in his gaze change to pity, I let him.

I can't bear the thought of his smile fading.

It would destroy me.

Number of days since I decided to live: 84
Number of days since I met Joe: 41
Current level of panic: 9/10

SEVENTEEN

May 20

JOE STOOD IN the middle of the after party, bottle of Jameson in his hand. All around him people were laughing and carrying on, generally having a good time. People who tried to engage him in conversation eventually moved on. He had no desire for small talk. The only thing he wanted was to consume enough whiskey to be numb. To feel nothing where, right now, he felt everything—the incredible sense of joy coupled with a deep, all-encompassing panic. This was where Emma had found him so many weeks ago. In this place he hadn't returned to since. This was where he'd been before her, drowning in whiskey and nameless, faceless women.

Could he survive returning here?

She loved him. Emma loved him. God, it was the most incredible feeling he'd ever experienced. Also the most terrifying.

Because he loved her more than his next breath. More than the music that fed his soul.

And he was losing her.

In that place deep down inside of him, buried so deep he'd hoped to never have to deal with it, Joe knew he was losing her. When she was gone, where would he be? Right back here with the fakes and the liars? With his old friend darkness?

Emma slipped away from him more and more each day. She was losing weight, appeared tired and drawn. Her arms trembled and pain showed in her eyes. It was there, buried behind her smile, her laughter. Pain—colored with fear. He didn't even have to look too hard to see it. His ray of sunshine was afraid. And her fear crippled him.

Raucous laughter sounded to his left, grating his already raw nerves, mocking his pain. Some guy Joe didn't recognize telling stories about the band like they were the closest of friends.

He shifted farther away, took another slug of whiskey and frowned when it didn't dull the ache. He shook off the nameless blonde sidling up to him, unable to take his gaze off the one who'd just stepped in the room.

Emma.

Christ, his stomach clenched so tightly at the sight of her he thought he was going to empty it. Reject all the alcohol he'd consumed when what he'd really wanted was to inhale her. She was the only one who ever chased away the darkness.

Emma.

He needed her, to turn to her instead of alcohol. But tonight it hurt too badly to look at her, it hurt too fucking much. The thought of a world—his world—without her in it, damn near doubled him over.

She crossed the room, Gare a few paces behind. Even Gary knew something was wrong and had changed allegiances. They all knew. Though she'd yet to say a fucking thing.

Not that he'd given her a chance. Any time Emma started talking like she had something important to tell him, something life altering, Joe changed the subject. Convinced himself if she never gave voice to it, he wouldn't have to deal with the cold hard reality that stared him in the face. It had worked, too. Until she'd blindsided him today with something he'd never seen coming. A declaration of love.

Fuck. What happened to the days when alcohol wiped away all feeling?

Oh, yeah, it never really had.

Goddamnit.

"Joe."

Emma stepped before him and it was all he could do not to pull her into his arms and beg her to tell him he was wrong. That it was all a nightmare he'd yet to wake from. All of it but her love for him—*that* he wanted to absorb into his bloodstream with a desperation he'd never before experienced.

Her eyes darted to the bottle in his hand, then the woman at his side. Pain filled her. He could see it reflected back at him even as he was incapable of doing anything about it. Maybe the alcohol had done more than he thought. His limbs no longer listened to the commands from his brain.

"This again?" she whispered. "You're back to the drinking, surrounding yourself with these people who don't even know you?"

He didn't want to be here. *Save me, Em.*

"What's the matter? Did I scare the shit out of you in the bus today? Make you feel something you don't know how to deal with?"

Yes. Damnit, why couldn't he answer her? She deserved better than this. Better than him. He was no good, the asshole she'd called him from the beginning.

Emma sighed. "Jesus, Joe."

When the nameless blonde shifted closer, brushing up against him, he startled. Hers wasn't the touch he wanted. She wasn't the woman he needed.

"Back off," Emma told her and Joe smiled.

At least he thought he did. Why did the alcohol have to hit him now?

Gary stepped in and moved the woman away.

Emma inched closer, pressed in tighter. She placed her hand in the center of his chest, smoothed it down to settle atop his abs.

Joe sucked a breath. Even with the cloud of alcohol his body recognized her, welcomed her. His heartrate accelerated. His breathing shallowed.

"There's no use denying it." Her voice dropped to a pitch meant for his ears only. "It's in your swift intake of air when I touch you, the way your hand always drops to my hip and you ease me closer. I don't think you even realize you do it, but it's there. All I have to do is get just close enough..."

She shifted and sure as shit, his hand fell to her hip, his breath hiccupped and he pulled her even closer. The noise of the room faded until all he could see and hear was her.

"You've got a belly full of fear mixed with a big ball of emotion swimming around in you right now, don't you, Joe? And it frightens you so bad, you're willing to push me away rather than having to deal with it."

He didn't want to push her away. He wanted to go back in time, to before the weight loss and dark circles, before he loved her so much he feared for the man he'd become when she left him.

"You'll fall back on old habits, the whiskey, the groupies? The people who allow you to hide from life, who accept this hollowed out version of the man you really are? You're drinking because you think it will take the edge off. But it won't. You know it won't."

He did and it wouldn't.

Her eyes teared, and fuck if his didn't, too. Yet, he couldn't seem to do anything but stand there and bear witness to her pain.

"You'll wake up tomorrow and what you're feeling right now will still be there." She smoothed her hand back up his chest, settled it atop his heart. "Only I won't be. I'll be gone."

Panic drove the air from his lungs, left him struggling for breath.

"You follow through with this and I'm leaving you, Joe. I won't let you hurt me this way and I sure as hell won't watch you fall back into the shit."

She stepped away from him. Far enough his hand dropped to his side.

The ache in his chest grew.

"Do you know how many people would give anything for what you have? Not the fame or wealth—the opportunity to wake up tomorrow healthy, pain free and with a future stretching out before them?"

There it was. The truth he'd been struggling to ignore. She was talking about herself. How she would give anything for what he had.

"Emma, please."

She continued to step away from him, a tear sliding down her cheek. When she spoke, her voice cracked and she dropped it low enough he had to strain to catch the words. "When you're gone and people remember you, what will they say about you? That you were happy, generous and kind? That you loved big? Or that you were the drunken singer in a rock band?"

Emma turned on her heel and walked away. The noise of the room returned so quickly it was painful.

Son of a bitch.

Gary materialized in front of him. "You're just going to let her walk? What the fuck, Joe?" Gary unclipped the radio from his belt and slapped it in the center of Joe's chest. "That little voice in your head that says you don't deserve Emma?"

"Yeah?"

"I'm beginning to think it may be right."

Joe knew it was.

Gary stepped away, the radio clattering to the floor between them, and Joe scowled. "Where are you going"

"Where you should be going. To reassure that beautiful woman you're not the insensitive ass you appear to be."

EMMA BOLTED OUT of the room and headed straight for the back exit. Immediate escape was the only answer. If she could get the hell away from there, maybe she could find a nice quiet place to break down. Then she could figure out her next step. Decide where to go. There were really only two options—stay or go. But neither was pain free. Not anymore.

A sleek black Escalade sat idling just outside the exit. The rear door opened and Vivian Johnson stepped out. She took one look at Emma's face and her gaze skittered away.

Perfect. Not like Emma wanted to talk anyway. She made a beeline for the bus and almost made it before her tears turned to sobs.

Knees weak, she grabbed hold of the door handle. Her arms shook, her whole body shook, and there was no way to know whether it was from heightened emotion or something worse. Closing her eyes, she pressed her forehead to the door and waited for the trembling to pass.

"Emma?"

"You're talking to the wrong girl, Gary. You need to be over there by the Escalade."

"No. I don't."

A deep breath helped, but not nearly enough. She opened her eyes, swiped at her cheeks, but didn't take her forehead off the bus. The stainless steel exterior felt too good against her overheated skin.

A tissue appeared in her peripheral vision. "You and your damn pockets," she mumbled and accepted it.

"Come with me."

Any other time, she would have challenged him and his commanding tone, even if just in fun. Tonight she didn't have the energy. The stabbing pain at the back of her head that never seemed to go away, combined with her inability to control her emotions today, sapped all of her strength. "I have to figure out what I'm going to do."

He softened his voice. "Not just yet, you don't."

"I'm not going back inside."

"Neither am I."

Her arms no longer shook. With everything else that had gone down, at least she had that. Emma faced Gary.

The Escalade pulled away, but he just looked at her, his dark eyes filled with enough concern it was evident even in the low light. He held out his hand. "Walk with me?"

She hesitated, giving the SUV one more glance. "There's still time to stop her."

He sighed, hand still held out for her. "I've made my choice, Emma."

Damnit. She'd just gotten her tears under control and he was going to kick start them again. "Yeah, the wrong one."

His phone alerted as she placed her hand in his and they started walking. Using his free hand, he slipped his cell from his pocket, checked the message then promptly powered it down.

Emma shifted her hold from Gary's hand to just above his elbow. "I've never seen you turn off your phone before."

He shrugged. "I'm off the clock tonight."

"Ha! You're never off the clock."

"It'll do him some good to sit and fret."

Joe.

The muscles under her hand tightened. "If he wants to know where you are, he can contact you," Gary growled.

"That'll be difficult since my cell is sitting on the bus with a dead battery."

He glanced down at her as they waited for the intersection to clear so they could cross the street. "Do you want to go back?"

"No." She shook her head then followed it with a shrug. "I don't know what I want."

What a joke. She knew exactly what she wanted and it wasn't to be walking through the city, no matter how warm and beautiful the weather. Sure, this was her nightly ritual, to spend some time beneath the stars after far too much of it trapped indoors. But tonight, what she wanted more than anything was Joe—holding her, whispering reassurances to her.

Loving her.

Since it was no longer that simple, she settled for a walk with Gare. He didn't feel the need to fill the silence with talk and she was glad for that. Especially, when time passed and her throat began to burn again. Tears started down her face.

"Stupid," she muttered, using both hands to wipe her cheeks. "This is so damn stupid. And so is he."

Gary offered her another tissue. "He's getting smarter."

"Yeah? How do you figure?"

They stopped in front of a high-rise while Gary powered up his phone and sent a text. Once he was done, he dropped the phone back into his pocket and looked down at her. "He's with you now."

She chuckled, or tried to. It came out more as an exhalation of air. "I suppose you heard all of that back there?"

His gaze darted to the building's glass front. "I heard nothing you don't want me to have heard."

"You hear everything."

He smiled.

It was a moment before she realized he wasn't smiling at her comment, but at a man walking toward them from inside the building—a security guard. He stood about six or seven inches shorter than Gary, but was damn near as big in muscle. His hair was brown, cut short and thinning a bit on top. He had a hard look to him, until he smiled. Then his face softened.

He smiled as he swung the door open and motioned them inside. Gary took her elbow, guiding her into the building before releasing her.

The moment the door clicked shut the security guard stuck out his hand. "Garrison, you son of a bitch! How the hell are you?"

Garrison?

"Pretty good, Matheson, you?"

The men did that whole 'handshake that becomes a brief hug followed by a thump on the back' thing. They whopped each other pretty good, too. Like it was some sort of unspoken test to see who would cry uncle first.

Emma rolled her eyes.

"Not bad," Matheson replied. "Not bad at all. Damn it was good to hear from you today. Is this your girl?" His smile remained, as he looked her over with a keen eye. The perusal took seconds, but being on the receiving end left Emma feeling like he hadn't missed a thing and, if pushed, could recall in detail something as insignificant as the shape and color of the earring in her tragus.

Gary shook his head. "Joe's."

Matheson raised a brow. "He know you swept her away tonight?"

"He does."

Even though Matheson checked her over again, there was something about him that put Emma at ease. Maybe it was the smile. Or the fact that Gary obviously liked and trusted the man.

"Joe know you made her cry?" Matheson asked, puffing up.

Suddenly what she liked about the man became clear. He had the same fierce warrior vibe as Gary. Something that brought her comfort at a time when she was feeling fragile.

Gary frowned. His body went taut.

Emma knew what that meant. He was about to go big scary ogre on her.

"Whoa, whoa, okay, too much testosterone in the room right now. Let's take it down a notch." She kept her gaze on Matheson, while patting Gary on the arm. "Joe made me cry."

"Ah." Matheson pulled a set of keys out of his pocket. "So my man Gare was the one to swoop in and save the day." He nodded and turned for the bank of elevators at his back. "This way."

Emma looked up at Gary. "Where are we going?"

"Trust me," he replied, and motioned for her to go before him.

They stepped into the elevator farthest right, thankfully one with a view.

Matheson stuck a key in the panel and pressed a couple buttons, then stepped back out. "Enjoy."

The doors closed and the elevator rose.

Emma faced the glass wall and the view of the city. "How do you know that man?"

"He's an old friend of mine."

She'd already figured that out. "A friend from your military days." Emma didn't state it as a question. He was just going to deny it anyway, like he always did.

"Yes."

Startled, she faced him. "You're no longer evading. That's bad, isn't it? Next, you're going to tell me you really were S.A.S."

He just looked at her.

The elevator continued to rise. Higher and higher, past all the floors designated on the panel, before it stopped and the doors opened.

Gary stepped out and crossed a landing to an outer door directly opposite.

Emma followed. "Is that why you brought me here? You're not going to pull some double-o-seven move and toss me from the roof are you?"

"That's British Secret Service."

"Whatever."

"Your imagination is terrifying." With a shake of his head, he pushed the door open. "I brought you here because you needed to get away from the bullshit at the arena. And because I figured you would like the place."

The night breeze kissed her cheeks as she stepped through the door and onto the roof. Not just any high-rise roof, though. This one had been turned into a garden. Flowering plants and small trees surrounded her, welcomed her into their comforting embrace. Cushioned chairs were scattered about the space, along with tables lit with solar lamps. But the best thing about it was, this high above the city, the air wasn't tainted with exhaust.

"It's beautiful." And obviously meant for another woman. Next to the table sitting in the center of the garden, sat an ice bucket and a bottle of wine. Emma ran a fingertip around the rim of the bucket. "Gare—"

"Don't."

"I feel bad. You were planning to bring Vivian here, weren't you?"

He shrugged. "It's not a big deal."

"How can you say that?" He'd set it up ahead of time, called a friend and, most likely called in a favor. All to impress a beautiful woman who'd caught his eye. He certainly couldn't have imagined being here with her instead. "I'll leave and you can—"

"Sit down, Emma."

She mirrored his pose, crossing her arms. "You do know I'm not afraid of you, no matter what tone you take with me."

"No? Just a few moments ago you thought I was going

to toss you off the roof." His dimple made an appearance as he smiled then sank into the seat nearest him. "Please. Is that better? Stop worrying about who I planned to bring here. You're who I brought, so sit down, *please*, and enjoy."

"Fair enough." She chose the seat across from him and sat. "But if you think you'll still get to use those condoms I know you have stashed in one of your pockets, think again. I mean, I love you and all, but it's more of a brother-sister thing."

"Shit."

"Maybe cousins—just not the kissing kind."

"You are too much," he mumbled, rubbing the back of his neck. "You know that?"

Emma smiled and looked up at the night sky. It was clear, the moon but a sliver.

"At least you're back to goading me." His voice softened. "I like that better than the tears. Witnessing a woman's tears makes me want to…"

"Punch people?" she suggested. A plane moved through her field of vision, most likely coming from Denver International Airport. It's destination a mystery, she began mentally guessing where it could be heading. "You're a natural born protector, that's why you can't stand tears."

They lapsed into silence. One she eventually broke. "I knew what I was getting into with him."

"Joe? I believe you did."

"I've never worn blinders about what his life was like."

"That's good."

She straightened, feeling the ache behind her ribs that made its presence known whenever she thought of Joe and that damn bottle of whiskey. With a shake of her head, she focused on Gary, who sat with his hands clenched together between his knees, brow furrowed as he stared back at her. "How do you do it?"

His frown deepened at the hitch in her voice. "Do what?"

"Watch him drink his life away?"

"I've been with Joe for seven years."

She nodded. "He told me."

Gary unclenched and clenched his hands. "Joe was a different person back then. Reckless, sure, but not self-destructive. He was happy, a pleasure to be around. Loved the music, the life, and it showed." Gary stood, walked around to the back of his chair and curled his fingers into the cushion. "Gradually, over the last two years, that all changed, until he became the man you met."

"The accomplished drinker."

"I was going to say narcissistic asshole."

Emma chuckled.

Gary shrugged. "Since he met you, he has become more and more the man he was when he hired me. Joe saw something in you that first night. I don't know what it was—I don't really care—I just know, the moment he laid eyes on you, you were it for him."

Great, the lump was back in her throat.

"You took his life, shook it up and rearranged it. You leave him not knowing if he's coming or going. It's good for him."

"Is it? He's drinking again."

Gary let the silence hang between them a minute then blew a breath. "What happened today?"

"What do you mean?"

"You know what I mean. In the tour bus, after the incident with the motorbike. What did you say that sent him into a tailspin?" He was quiet another moment then rubbed the back of his neck. "I think he turned to alcohol tonight for the same reasons he's been turning to it for years now—to quiet the demons. The thing is, once you came along, he gave up the booze and turned to you. Why not tonight? What happened that caused him to panic?"

She choked a laugh. It sounded more like a sob. "I'm in love with him."

Gary didn't even blink. "That's what you told him?"

"Yes."

"That would do it." He released his hold on the cushion and straightened, pinning her in place with his gaze. "I thought perhaps you finally told him you're sick."

"What?!"

"You're sick, aren't you? All the signs are there."

"I'm exhausted, sure. This life is—"

Gary stopped her words with a lift of his hand. Then he returned to his seat across from her, his mouth flat and his features tight. "My real name is Tobias, Tobias Garrison. I joined the British Army at eighteen, and was selected for Special Air Service—S.A.S.—at twenty-two. In the military, they call you by your last name, Garrison, which became Gare to my friends, then—"

"Gary."

"Yes."

So she'd been right about all of it. His military background, his name.

"Your turn, Emma."

She sat up and offered her hand in introduction. "Emma Mae Travers."

Instead of shaking her hand, he sandwiched it in both of his. "And?"

A tear escaped.

"Fuck!" He launched to his feet, paced away then returned. "Have you told him?"

Emma shook her head, swiped the tear from her cheek.

"He knows. And he's scared shitless."

"So am I," she whispered.

"Jesus. You have to tell him. Why haven't you already?"

She didn't mean to look into his eyes, but felt the need to know. What she discovered solidified her fear. "That look. That one you're wearing is why I haven't. I can't bear to see that look on his face."

He scrubbed his hand over his cheeks like he could wash the pity from his eyes. It didn't work.

"So instead of telling him, you'll run away?"

"He's killing himself. Sliding back into the—"

"And you honestly believe that is going to stop if you leave him?" He was so upset he shook. "Or is it just that *you* won't have to watch? What about the rest of us, Emma? What about me?"

She had seen Gary angry and happy, even intimidating. This was new. She didn't know what to do with distraught Gary. She looked away. Needed to look away. Then kicked her own ass and walked over to him.

Emma placed her hand in the center of his chest, the way she did with Joe when she wanted him to listen. "This ends badly no matter what. That hit me the other day when I looked at him and realized I love him. Not the star-struck crap I felt when I met him. Not the half-assed love that brought me to him. I love him, Tobias."

"You think I don't?" He covered her hand with his. "If you walk away now, he'll backslide. There will be no stopping it."

"God." She dropped her forehead to rest alongside their hands. "I never meant for this to happen."

"It did happen. Now you have to deal with it. We all do."

"And if I stay and tell him and he regresses anyway?"

"That's always a possibility, isn't it? However, I can guarantee what will happen if you walk without telling him. Joe will blame himself."

She felt his hand brush her back lightly before settling.

"You brought him this far, Emma. He didn't want to be in there tonight, with the whiskey and the women. He wanted you. Tell me you could see that."

She'd seen a man who'd gotten spooked and didn't know how to handle it. A man she was sure felt the same way about her as she felt about him, but had been too afraid to deal with it. If he knew about her illness, and it seemed they all did, then the wild fear she'd witnessed in his eyes took on a whole new meaning.

She lifted her head and met Gary's gaze.

A muscle ticked in his jaw. "You need to be honest with him and see this through to its natural conclusion— whatever that may be."

May 16

You can't stop your body from failing you.

I've learned that the hard way. No matter how well you treat yourself, how strictly you play by the rules or even if you never do, when it's your time to go, nothing you do can stop it.

I spoke with Alison today. Let her know that I'll be home soon. It's almost my time.

She said she would have everything ready.

She knows how important this is to me, so I know she will.

Poor Al. I'm going through so much personally that sometimes I forget what this must be like for her. I try to imagine, if the roles were reversed, how I would feel having to make preparations for her death.

Thank God she has Kevin. He'll be strong for her when she can't be. He'll hold her when I no longer can. He's a good man.

Al deserves a good man.

Number of days since I decided to live: 86

Number of days since I met Joe: 43

Current level of panic: 7/10

EIGHTEEN

May 20

E MMA'S HEAD THROBBED by the time they returned to the arena and she climbed the bus steps. Gary had made some excuse about needing to check in with his team then ran off. She had no idea if it was the truth or just his way of giving her and Joe a bit of privacy. Either way, she was happy to have it.

Joe sat on the larger of the two couches, arms resting on the table before him, right hand curled around his favorite mug—the blue and white one with the word 'wanker' across the front. The mug always made her smile and tonight was no exception.

He wore jeans and nothing else. One look at him and her heart took off on a run. Her throat tightened. "Joe."

His eyes never left her face as he stood, closed the space between them and slowly pulled her in. His warmth enveloped her as he snugged her against his body, tucking her head beneath his chin. "I'm sorry, Sunshine. So damn sorry."

This was where she wanted to be. Right here, wrapped in his arms. She pressed her nose into his throat and inhaled him. Just him, no telltale scent of whiskey. He couldn't have consumed much more after she'd left because he appeared to be sober now.

"I went looking for you," he said, drawing a deep breath. "When I couldn't find you, I thought you'd left me. I panicked. Started texting and calling Gary, but—"

"He turned his phone off."

Joe muttered a curse. "Of course, he did."

"Why, Joe?" She pulled back until she could look into his eyes. "The whiskey. The silence. Tell me why."

"Em…"

She cupped his face with one hand and made him look at her. "Give me the truth, please."

"I had to see if I could go back to it." He didn't take his gaze off her and his eyes were filled with pain and sadness. "If I could survive having nothing but that…once you're gone."

Oh, God. Her breath stuttered, heart lodged in her throat. She shifted, pulled away from him and he let her. Gary's words popped into her head. "You didn't want to be there."

Joe shook his head. "I hate that place and that man I used to be. You make me want more, Em. You are the first person in a very long time to make me want to be better. When I'm with you, I forget."

"Forget what?" she whispered.

"That I'm not good enough for you."

"How can you say that? How can you even think that?" Sweet Jesus, he wasn't the one pretending to be something he wasn't. Keeping secrets, hiding the truth because the pain of losing him scared her as much as the thought of how little time she had left.

She looked everywhere but at him. That damn mug, the floor. Her throat tightened, tears burned the backs of her eyes.

The Monster in her head roared.

Emma rubbed the back of her neck, soothing the beast. She looked back at Joe, found his dark eyes on her. "You are better than the people you surround yourself with lead you to believe."

"I'm not."

Damnit. She pushed back her own pain and focused on his. "Is this why you keep them around? Because you honestly believe you're not good enough?" Needing to touch him, she settled her hand over a hard pec. "Of course you feel unimportant when none of them gives you anything in return. But it's not true. It's a falsehood. You *are* important. You *are* special—but not because of the reasons they all feed you. Not just because you can play a guitar and sing."

"Emma."

She trembled as desperation welled up within her. "Listen to me. Hear what I'm saying to you. You need to get rid of the leeches. Get rid of all the toxic shit. Live your life. Stop being the rock star you think everyone wants you to be. Be the man I know you to be. The man in this room, right now, is who you are. *This* man is the man I love."

He shook his head and she stopped the action by cupping his cheeks. She shifted closer, close enough his hand dropped to her hip and he released a sigh as he pulled her in.

"I love you." The desperate edge left her voice as she softened against him. "The man who danced with me beneath the stars even though you can't dance for shit."

He chuffed a laugh.

"Who kisses me senseless to distract me from my fear whenever we're in an elevator."

"It's not like that's a hardship."

"You were in the midst of an interview the other day,

actually in the process of answering a question when you grabbed me. I think the interviewer swallowed his tongue and you didn't even blink. You just pulled me into your arms the moment those doors closed. In the middle of something that should have taken most of your attention, you were still thinking of me. No matter how you feel about yourself, I'm telling you that's something special."

His hands slid over her body, one cupping the back of her head, the other slipping beneath her shirt to settle against the bare skin at the base of her spine. "I'm always thinking of you, Sunshine. I love you."

Oh, God. He'd given her the words. Emotion clogged her throat. Tears spilled from her eyes. Emma pressed her face against his chest.

"Em? What did I say? Shit. I take it back."

"You better not," she said, her words muffled.

"Don't cry, Em. Please."

The tremor in his voice made her cry harder.

"I'm not good with tears. I'll do anything. I'll...sing that stupid song you love so much."

Then he was. His voice pitched just for her. "It's too late, to save myself from falling."

"Stop," she whispered.

"I took a chance and you changed my way of life."

"That's not how it goes."

"But you misread my meaning—"

"No, I didn't." She pulled her face out of his chest, leaned in and kissed him, because she had a feeling if he finished the verse she wouldn't be able to stop crying.

"What? You don't like my singing?"

"I love your singing." She smiled, threaded her hands into his hair and kissed him again.

Kissed him until he was cupping her face in his big hands while his thumbs wiped the tears from her cheeks. "It's a stupid song."

"It's a beautiful song."

"You're beautiful." He pressed a kiss to one swollen eye then the other. "My ray of sunshine. Stay with me after the tour. Come with me to England."

No. She backed up as panic surged.

"I'll take you for a ride in my Koenigsegg. We'll dance through the halls of my house in Prestbury."

"Joe, I…can't. I won't be…"

Pain flashed in his eyes. "Don't leave me, Em," he said softly, much too softly. "You're my salvation."

It was too much. What she'd done to him. The pain her silence had caused them both. She sobbed and The Monster used her weakness to take a stronger hold.

"Joe." It was hard to talk, damn near impossible to get the words out. "You have to see in yourself what I see. You have to save yourself. I won't always be here with you."

He pushed his over-long hair from his face, his eyes pleading. "Don't say it."

The pain in her head intensified—became a living thing with a pulse all its own. Her arms shook uncontrollably. Worse, so much worse than ever before.

"Joe, I—" Her vision blurred. Her heart galloped at a terrifying rate.

Her doctor had warned this would happen. That, one day, the pain would become too much to bear. That it would most likely occur during a time of stress or physical exertion. Yet it still couldn't touch the pain in her heart. The ache for the man who was in his own personal hell. Who knew what she was going to say to him and it hurt him so badly, he all but vibrated with it.

The room spun. She was the one vibrating.

"No," she whispered.

"Em?"

"No. Not now." A deep breath did nothing. She pushed the words out, needing to give voice to them before the seizure took hold. "I've kept something from you, Joe. I'm sorry."

His image faded as everything went dark.

JOE SAT AT the head of the emergency room bed and stared into the eyes of the most beautiful woman he'd ever met. The one who'd worked her way into his life, his heart, and changed his world. Drove away the darkness. Saved him. He looked into her eyes and swore to do anything to save her. He'd give up his fame, his fortune, give it all away. As long as it meant keeping Emma in his life.

None of those things mattered. Not if she was gone.

Watching her collapse had to be the scariest event he'd ever witnessed. She'd been shaking, crying, then, down she went. Thank Christ, he'd managed to grab her before she hit her head on the floor. Even so, she'd been out for at least thirty minutes. As long as it had taken for him to pull on a shirt and stuff his feet into shoes while Gary carried her to the car, held her for the ride to the hospital then brought her inside.

Joe hadn't wanted to let go of her, but Gare had insisted, snatching her off the floor while mumbling about not needing the publicity should someone get a photo of Joe carrying an unconscious woman off his tour bus.

As if Joe gave a flying fuck about bad publicity. All he

cared about was the health of the woman who'd finally come to about sixty seconds ago, curling her fingers into the front of his shirt as she did. Her eyes held a mixture of pain and fear, and he couldn't stop touching her. Stroking her hair away from her face. Reassuring them both.

"What were you doing when she passed out?" the doctor asked. He didn't yet seem aware that Emma had regained consciousness and Joe didn't feel the need to tell him.

He kept his focus on Emma instead of the man asking the questions. "I'd just told her I love her. She was crying, trying to tell me something. Something I didn't want to hear."

"What—"

"She gets headaches. They incapacitate her."

"Is she on any medication?"

"For the headaches, yes. She injects it."

"Do you know the name of the medication?"

He'd read the name once or twice, but couldn't recall it. "I don't know."

Emma remained silent. A tear slipped from the corner of her eye, and he brushed it away with his thumb.

"Her arms tremble." He talked to her as much as the doctor, needing her to know. "They start to shake for no apparent reason. She thinks I don't notice, but I've known all along."

"How often does this happen? How long do the tremors last?"

"One or two times a day anymore. Thirty to sixty seconds. A few minutes at most."

Releasing his shirt, Emma linked her fingers with his.

Joe closed his eyes and absorbed. "It started again right before she passed out. Worse than ever before. Her whole body shook."

"She had a seizure," the doctor speculated.

Another tear slipped free, sliding down her temple and into her hair.

He lowered his voice, chasing the tear with the backs of his fingers, stroking her cheek with his free hand. "I didn't want to hear what you needed to tell me, Emma."

The doctor looked up from his notes. "Ms. Travers."

Joe kept talking. "If you didn't say it, I could go on pretending I didn't see it."

"Ms. Travers, if you can answer a few questions for me, we can figure out a way to best treat you."

"My—" She cleared her throat. "My medical charts—"

"Are not here," the man interrupted.

Her eyes slid closed, and she took a deep breath. Then one more before opening them again. "There's a thumb drive in my bags. My medical records are on it."

The doctor shifted closer, clearly shocked. "You keep your medical records with you?"

"I was planning a trip overseas." Emma closed her eyes again. She turned her head until her face was partially covered by Joe's hand resting on her pillow. "Can you turn down the lights, please?"

When the doctor didn't move quickly enough, Joe did. He crossed the room and flicked off the overhead lights.

Emma sighed audibly.

The doctor flipped a different switch and a light beneath the cabinet over the sink flickered to life, keeping the room from total darkness.

"Ms. Travers."

"Call Doctor Daniel Hollister at the Cleveland Clinic." Emma linked her fingers with Joe's the moment he returned to his spot back at the head of her bed.

"I'll do that. Until then, if you can answer a few questions, I can better decide how to treat your pain."

"I don't want anything."

The doctor sighed. "With your level of pain—"

"No. Call Doctor Daniel Hollister. He'll tell you."

"What will he tell me Ms. Travers?"

She ignored the doctor and looked into Joe's eyes.

"Em?"

"I have cancer."

Joe went still for a beat as his body struggled to absorb the shock. Then he was on his feet so fast the metal stool he'd been sitting on skidded across the floor with a metallic screech. He barely registered Emma's jolt of pain as he backed away from her, as if physical distance could soften the blow he knew she was about to deliver. He kept moving, until there was nowhere else to run, the wall literally stopping his escape.

"A brain tumor."

His knees gave and he slid down the wall.

"Glioblastoma Multiforme."

The words meant nothing to him, but the doctor shifted his feet and sighed.

Joe rested his elbows on his knees and stared at the floor as pain burned through him. The sound of someone gasping for breath reverberated in a room otherwise silent. It was a moment before he realized the noise came from him.

"There's nothing you can do for me. Do you understand?" Emma whispered.

Joe prayed she wasn't talking to him because he didn't understand. He never would.

"Nothing except give us some privacy. Please."

He heard a rustling and knew the doctor had moved. The door opened then swung shut. He remained on the floor, dropping his head back against the wall and closing his eyes. Tensed his muscled and waited for the next blow.

"I should have told you," Emma whispered.

"I didn't want to know."

"I was afraid. I'm still afraid. I didn't want you to pity me."

She'd said that once before. In the beginning.

"I knew I would love you. I was already half in love with you when I hopped a plane to Baton Rouge. But I never imagined you would love me."

"What did you think we were doing here?"

"I thought you would get bored and move on."

He chuffed a laugh. As if he could ever get bored of her. She excited him in every way possible—physically, mentally and emotionally.

"I should have stayed away from you."

If she had, where would he be? Drunk and buried in some faceless female in a desperate attempt to drown out the darkness.

Instead of filled with panic that, without her, his life might just go back to that. "There are treatments, clinical trials or something."

"No."

"I have a fuck lot of money, Em. I can—"

"You can't," she said softly, and much too closely. "I'm sorry."

He opened his eyes and she was there. Kneeling in front of him in that damn hospital gown that made her seem even more pale and fragile. The hand with her I.V. in the back of it was curled around the I.V. stand, her other pushed his hair back away from his face. Wiped away tears he hadn't realized he was shedding.

"I'm sorry," she repeated softly.

As she crawled between his knees and curled up against his chest, he wrapped his arms around her and sighed. Even gutted, her touch managed to bring him a bit of peace.

"I was afraid to be alone, too weak to stay away from you. You make me feel like I did before my diagnosis. Before there was a monster in my head slowly killing me."

"God, Em."

"I tried to tell you in Chicago."

Her tears soaked the fabric of his shirt. "I know."

"Then again in—"

"I know. I wouldn't let you."

"I should have anyway. I should have told you I'm dying."

A giant weight pressed down on him. Breathing became impossible.

"Please," he begged. "Please stop talking."

His ears rang. His fingers went numb.

There was no escaping the cold hard reality any longer. Emma wasn't just sick. She was dying.

As gently as he could, Joe wrapped her tighter, pulled her closer.

He buried his face in her hair and broke.

THIRTY MINUTES LATER, Joe still sat on the floor, Emma on his lap, asleep in his arms. A nurse had come in about ten minutes earlier, shot him a disapproving glance then answered his questions. She hadn't been back.

He should probably think about getting Emma onto the

bed but he didn't move. The risk of waking her or, worse, hurting her, was too great. He was so physically and emotionally drained, he wasn't sure he could stand with her in his arms.

"I'm not staying here," she said softly.

The whisper of her voice startled him. He hadn't realized she was awake.

"No one can make me. Not even you."

The body beneath his hands tensed. Her breaths quickened. Panic sounded in her voice. "They're going to want to admit me, lock me in a room and—"

"They want to make you comfortable," he soothed.

She trembled, crying. Once her tears started, they hadn't stopped, even as she dozed. The nurse said it was from the pain. All he knew was it tore him in half. He had to make her feel better, help her in whatever way he could. If that meant letting them give her something, he would. Not that he had the power to make any medical decisions for her, but he could allay her fears. Do his best to keep her calm while he helped her to see that she needed the pain medication. He couldn't stand her suffering.

"They want to pump me full of drugs." Her hand fisted his shirt. Her voice bordered on hysteria. "You don't understand. They'll turn me into a drooling mass of human flesh with no idea what day it is or even where I am. I'm not going out like that, Joe."

"It's okay, Sunshine."

"It's not. I don't want to die here. I want to go home. I want to be in my own bed."

The door swung open and the nurse stepped in, a small tray in hand. She set the tray near the sink then slipped a pair of nitrile gloves from the box hung on the wall. Once the gloves were in place, she approached them, reaching for Emma's wrist—the one with the identification bracelet they'd given her upon arrival.

"I don't want this."

When the nurse walked away without comment, Emma's hand tightened on his shirt. She locked her gaze with his. "I don't want this. They can't—"

"Em."

She couldn't get any closer but she tried anyway, grasping at his arms, his shirt. "No," she whispered. "No. Please, I don't want this."

Fuck. He wasn't strong enough for this. She was nearly out of her mind with fear.

"What are you giving her?" he asked the nurse as she swiped an alcohol swab over a hub about half way up the I.V. tubing, then inserted the needle of the syringe and pushed the medication into the line.

"She needs rest."

"NO!"

Joe cupped Emma's face and looked into her eyes. She was terrified, softly begging him to not let them drug her, but it was already too late. The medication was doing its job. Her limbs grew lax, her breathing leveled out.

Her panic remained. "I don't want this," she whispered.

Then she was out cold.

"It really is the best thing for her." The nurse stated, disposing of the needle and her gloves. "I can't imagine the amount of pain she must be in."

There was physical pain and there was emotional pain. The doctor was focusing on the physical. But watching Emma panic over the thought of being knocked out and made comfortable had Joe focusing on the emotional. "Is my friend still outside the door?"

"You mean your bodyguard? The younger nurses are whispering about you being pretty famous."

He didn't comment.

"Yes, he's still there."

"Send him in please."

Joe tried to snug Emma closer, hold her as she rested, but it was near impossible. Whatever she'd been given, she was like a rag doll. Even asleep, she was never this limp. They'd done exactly as she'd warned they would—drugged her out of her mind. Turned her into a drooling mass of human flesh.

Gary stepped in and leaned against the closed door. He took one look at Emma and scrubbed his hand over his face. "What did they do to her? I could hear her begging... Fuck."

Visibly uncomfortable, Gary paced. Something Joe had never seen him do in all the years he'd known him. He was always too controlled for such a show of emotion.

"She doesn't want to be here," Joe told him.

"Who would?" He rolled his shoulders, shook out his arms, all the time moving back and forth in the confined space, his actions reminding Joe of how he loosened up before sparing. "Is this really what you want for her?"

Gary's anger was unmistakable, as was his intent. His fist was going to connect with something. Joe wondered who the winner was going to be—his face or the wall.

"I don't want any of this for her." He gave his friend complete honesty, knowing Gary cared for Emma, too. "If I could trade places with her, I wouldn't hesitate."

"Goddamnit." Gary let out a slow, careful breath then leaned against the door again. His gaze returned to Emma.

"When I go, I want my eyes wide open so I can stare death in the face while I flip him the bird."

"Christ, Gare."

"I don't want to be so stoned that I never see him coming. No way Emma wants that either. This isn't about you, Joe."

"How the fuck isn't it about me? I only just found her and now..." Now he had to let her go. *Her* way. Even if it meant he had to watch her suffer. "I need some air. Is the car still here?"

"It is."

"You'll stay with Emma?"

"Yes."

They both looked down at her and Joe's gut tightened. He traced the backs of his fingers over the tearstains on her cheeks and frowned. "Take her."

Gary scooped her up and gently placed her on the bed. He covered her with the blanket then held out a key card. "Kirk had Marvin check us into a hotel for the night. The car service knows which one."

Joe took the card. "I have to speak with her doctor then make a few calls. Someone should let her friend Alison know what's happened."

Gary nodded.

"Stay with Emma. She's going to want to leave." God, he wanted out of this damn tiny box with no windows. It was suffocating. No wonder Em didn't want to stay here. But she needed to, at least for now. "I don't care what you have to do, she stays here."

"Joe."

Joe stopped with his hand on the door. He turned to Gary. "She is the only thing that matters."

Gary tipped his head in acknowledgement. "I agree."

"From now on, your job is to protect her. Even if that means keeping her here when she wakes up and tries to leave. Got it?"

"You realize I have zero chance of getting her to listen to me. And I won't use force."

Of course, he wouldn't, but Gare was right. No one made Emma do anything she didn't want to do. It was one of the things Joe loved most about her, even when it frustrated the hell out of him. "Let her know I'll be back. I have to…"

"Make some calls. I got it. Try to get some rest will you? You look as bad as she does."

Joe glanced at Emma. He wanted to crawl into the bed with her, wrap his arms around her and hold her. But that wouldn't help her. He had to find some way to help her.

"Joe?"

"Yeah?"

"Go. She won't miss you. Not until the drugs wear off."

"I have to help her," he whispered.

"Go."

May 19

There are a lot of things about being diagnosed with cancer that make you feel like you have no control.

Death is not one of them.

I can choose the way I die.

At the very least where I die.

Whether it's in a sterile, lifeless hospital room or, my own home.

I choose home.

In my own bed.

Centered in my glass room.

My gaze on the world I leave behind.

Number of days since I decided to live: 89

Number of days since I met Joe: 46

Current level of panic: 6/10

NINETEEN

"I'M SORRY," THE emergency department doctor said softly.

God, Joe was sick of hearing those words. Emma was sorry, the doctor was sorry. Hell, even the damn nurses were sorry. If one more person told him they were 'sorry' he was going to beat the shit out of them. "There has to be someone, somewhere who can help her. An operation?"

"Mr. Campbell, surgery is not an option. The disease is too advanced. I'm sor—"

"Will you stop saying that? Stop telling me how bloody sorry you are and tell me what I can do to help her!"

In direct correlation to Joe raising his voice, the doctor lowered his. "You can convince her to stay here, were we can manage her pain."

"She doesn't want that."

"I'm not sure we should be considering her wishes at this time."

Unable to summon even the most basic of manners, Joe stared at him and snarled. "Why the fuck not?"

"Her disease is most likely impairing her judgement."

The man had no idea how close he was to having his head taken off. "And what is to blame for impairing yours?"

"Mr. Campbell, I understand this is a stressful time for

you—"

"Believe me, you have no idea."

"—but making threats against me is not a good idea."

He hadn't made any threats against the man. Not yet. "Did you call her regular doctor?"

"I did."

"What did her doctor tell you?"

The emergency room physician sighed. "That she would never agree to remain here."

"She won't." At least the guy in Cleveland seemed to have a decent understanding of Emma and her wishes. "She wants to go home."

"Back to Cleveland Clinic."

"*Home.* She wants to go home."

"I really don't recommend that. Glioblastoma Multiforme is said to be excruciatingly painful."

As if Joe hadn't already figured that out. "How long does she have? Is managing her pain going to make the time she has any longer?"

"No, but it will make her more comfortable."

Joe thought back to the condition she'd been in as he'd walked out of her room. "You mean you'll knock her on her ass. Pump her full of enough drugs to render her unconscious. That's your plan for pain management?"

The doctor pulled back, clearly shocked.

"How much time does Emma have?" Joe repeated.

"A few days. Two weeks at most."

Bile crawled up the back of his throat, the need to vomit nearly overwhelming. He swallowed it back down. "No more drugs, do you hear me?"

"Mr. Campbell, you don't have the authority to make—"

Joe slammed his hands atop the man's desk and leaned in. "No, but I've got enough money to have a shit storm rain down on this hospital if you don't follow the wishes of your patient. If Emma says no, the answer is no."

JOE HAD TO stop at the bus on his way to the hotel. He needed find both Emma's mobile and the thumb drive she'd spoken of. The question was, where the hell were the buses?

Luckily, a quick text to Kirk gained him the answer so he didn't have to contact Marvin.

Joe climbed the steps, walked into the front lounge and swore, his mug in pieces at his feet. The last place he remembered it being was on the table as Emma had returned. With everything that had happened since, obviously it remained atop that table, unnoticed by Clay, until the bus pulled out of the arena and the mug had landed on the floor.

Joe cleaned up the mess, then gathered his and Emma's things. There was no way of telling when they'd get back here so he may as well take all of it to the hotel. Her cell phone and thumb drive in his pocket, he glanced at her laptop then took a seat at the table.

He booted the computer and popped in the thumb drive. Emma's medical records weren't hard to find. They were the only item on the storage device. Launching a web browser, he logged onto his email and attached the file, entering the recipient's address from memory before sending it into cyber space.

That was the easy part.

Christ, he wished he had something to calm his nerves. But his something was in the local emergency room in a medically induced fog. Staring down at his phone, he dialed the number of the only physician he knew well enough to talk to about this.

"It's four in the morning, Campbell," Dominic snarled. Dom, not Rebecca. "What the fuck you doing calling my woman? Is there something I need to know about the two of you?"

Joe smiled for the first time in what felt like days, even though it had only been hours. One thing he could always count on from Dom was the rash of verbal shit he dished out at the start of every phone conversation.

Joe welcomed the distraction. "Yeah. Between shows, I routinely jump a flight to California. Your girl and I double up your pain pills and shag on your bed."

Dom huffed. "Wait. Am I on the bed with you?"

Joe shrugged, even though Dom couldn't see him through the phone. "Of course. Where the fuck else would you be?"

"You bloody bastard. I'm gonna kick your arse."

"Dream on, old man. You couldn't take me on your best day let alone when you're still recovering."

Dom laughed. "Harsh. You're fucking harsh, you know that?"

"Put your beautiful fiancée on, will you? Harsh is having to deal with you after the night I've had." He'd done his best to keep up the social niceties—or his and Dom's version of them—but there was no way Dom could've missed the hitch in his voice.

"Joe?"

"Please Dom, not now."

"Sure."

Dominic and Rebecca's hushed conversation came through the phone. Joe tried not to listen.

"Joe? What's wrong?"

What was it about a friendly female voice when a person was at their lowest? "Rebecca." Her name was all he managed without taking a deep breath to center himself. "I emailed you a file I need you to look at. It's important."

"Sure, let me find it. Although I don't know what I could possibly do to..."

Silence.

"Are you still there?" Joe asked.

"These are medical records." And she wasn't happy about it. That much was evident in her tone.

"They are."

"Whose are these? Wait. It doesn't matter because unless your name is Emma Travers I can't even look at this. It's against HIPPA regulations. I'm not her doctor and you aren't—"

"I don't give a fuck about regulations, Rebecca," he growled. Shit, he needed to calm down. "I'm sorry, I..." He was falling apart and she was worried about rules and regulations. "We're in Denver and Emma's...in hospital. She won't care if you see her records, Rebecca. I can promise you that. I...really need someone to talk to about this. Someone I trust."

Rebecca's voice softened. "She's important to you."

"Emma is everything. I know you understand that." She would, because she'd just gotten *her* everything back. Dominic was growing stronger every day and the joy in both of their voices, the fact they'd found each other again after years apart... "You understand, Rebecca."

"I do," she whispered. "I'll call you back."

"I have to make a few calls. I'll ring you in, say, an hour?"

"Sure."

He rang off.

JOE'S CONVERSATION WITH Emma's friend Alison didn't go much smoother. Once she'd gotten over the shock of him calling her, that awkward moment where she was rendered speechless just by him saying her name, things got really uncomfortable.

"Where's Emma?" Alison asked, her voice tinged with fear. "Why didn't *she* call me?"

"She's in hospital. The emergency department."

"And you left her there?"

Joe pulled the phone away from his ear—a protective maneuver against her screech of alarm.

"What were you thinking?"

He waited to make sure she was finished before replying. "She's not alone. A friend is with her."

"But not *you*."

"I had a few calls to make. This one, for instance. Her mobile was still on the bus so I had to leave her." He sighed. "I'll be back before her meds wear off."

"God, she'll hate that." It was Alison's turn to sigh. "You better hope you are because she won't stay there. The minute they wear off enough for her to fight the effects, Emma will be out of there. You know that about her, right? You must. She'll crawl out of that hospital naked if she has to. She hates those places."

"Fuck. She's probably devising her escape plan already." Joe scrubbed his hand over his face. He was so exhausted, his eyes were at half-mast.

"How long ago did you leave her?"

There was that tone again. The one that let him know if she were in the room with him, she would strip the flesh from his body for leaving Emma.

"It's okay. Gary would call if she was awake."

"Big scary ogre, Gary?"

"What? Christ, is that what she calls him?"

Alison chuckled. "She told me he acts like a big scary ogre, but he's really just a cream puff."

Joe chuckled. He wondered how Gare would feel about being labeled a cream puff. Of course, knowing Emma, she'd already called him one to his face.

"Joe? How are *you* doing? I know this is new to you." she said gently. "The last time Emma and I spoke, she still hadn't told you. I assume you're pretty angry."

"I don't think I've worked through any of this enough to find anger." She was surprisingly easy to talk to when she wasn't screeching at him. He told her what, until that moment, he'd only told Emma. "I love her."

"Of course, you do," Alison said with a laugh that quickly turned to a sob. "What's not to love about Em?"

○━━

NO MATTER HOW he wished it, Joe still wasn't numb. In fact, he was one giant raw nerve, skating dangerously close to the line. One wrong move, one more shitty phone conversation, and he was going to lose it and break something.

A very real possibility since he'd yet to ring Rebecca back.

This was why he stood at the window, doing his best to find calm. He needed to talk to Rebecca before returning to the hospital, and was running out of time. The sun had already begun to rise. Emma would be awake soon. Awake, and wondering why he wasn't with her.

A ring sounded from behind him. Joe glanced over his shoulder and noticed it was the laptop—Rebecca, requesting a video chat. He sighed then rubbed his hand over the back of his neck. The very last thing he wanted was to have a visual to go along with this conversation.

Joe crossed the room and accepted the chat. He refused to sit, choosing instead to lean with his hands atop the table.

Dom's face popped on the screen. "Joe."

"Hey." Dom looked good. Way better than the last time Joe had seen him—pale and drawn and lying in the intensive care unit.

"You look like shit." Dom's image grew as if he was leaning closer to the camera. "What can I do, Joe? Tell me, and I will."

His voice said it all. Joe knew before Rebecca even joined the conversation that she wouldn't be able to offer him hope.

Damnit. His throat burned. Joe closed his eyes against the truth.

"Get out of here, Dom. Go."

He didn't need to see to know Rebecca was shoving Dom off screen.

With a deep breath for courage, Joe opened his eyes. Then quickly averted his gaze. "They say it's a brain tumor. Something called—"

"Glioblastoma Multiforme, yes."

"Tell me what to do, Rebecca," he said on a strangled whisper.

"Look at me, Joe."

"Don't! Goddamnit, don't use that tone." The one that told him he was screwed. Joe looked into her eyes and his heart stopped. The pain was all encompassing. "You know people. Tell me who to call, where to take her to get help. There's got to be someone—"

"According to her records she's been through chemo and radiation therapy. She opted out of treatment in February when her doctor told her it wasn't stopping progression."

"She should have told me. Six weeks ago when…"

"You didn't know? Jesus." With tears in her eyes, Rebecca shook her head. "You couldn't have helped her then, either. It wouldn't have made a difference."

Except in his life. If she'd told him she had cancer, there was no guarantee he wouldn't have walked away from her and never looked back. Never known the joy of loving her.

Or the pain of losing her. "I can't…I only just found her."

"I'm so sorry."

Fuck, he was tired of hearing that. "How long does Emma have?"

"There's no way for me to—"

"Guess, Rebecca." Joe raked his hand through his hair. He swallowed back emotion, desperately trying to compartmentalize what he was feeling. "You're a doctor." She was a genius from what he'd heard. Literally. "Just take a guess. Please."

Rebecca studied him for a minute. "Does she suffer from headaches and nausea? Has she had any blackouts?"

"Yes."

"Seizures?"

"All of that."

Rebecca drew a deep breath and released it on a sigh. "What does the staff doctor say?"

"He wants to admit her. Pump her full of meds and make her comfortable." He swore colorfully. "Fucker's already medicated her after Emma said no."

The news pissed Rebecca off. She straightened in her seat, her color rising. "That is completely unethical. Is Emma still at this hospital?"

"Yeah, and she hates it. She's never tolerated being locked inside for too long. Not the bus, the arena or a hotel. She always has to get outside." Joe swallowed hard. "I have to get her out of there."

Her gaze full of comfort and understanding, she said, "yes, you do."

"I've been waiting…hoping for something. A miracle, I guess. It's not coming, is it?"

"She probably only has a few days…a week, maybe." Her voice cracked. "It's hard to say."

God, it hurt. It hurt so damn bad, he couldn't breathe. "I have more money than any man needs for ten lifetimes and what good does it do me if I can't save the woman I love?"

Rebecca started to cry. A tear streaked down her face then another. Dom re-appeared, swiping the backs of his fingers down her cheek, tucking a strand of her hair behind her ear.

It was too much. Just too fucking much. These people who meant the world to him, aching along with him. Joe pushed away from the table as pain tore a hole inside of him.

The door to his room clicked and swung open.

He scrubbed his hands over his face, surprised to find his cheeks damp, then faced the door and froze.

"Emma."

How the fuck? She wouldn't know what hotel the band

had checked into, what room he was in. Unless... *Gary. Of course.*

"Sunshine, why aren't you in hospital?"

She crossed to him, the pain in her eyes less than he'd witnessed last night. She was no longer crying. However, her right arm trembled slightly as she cupped his face and ran her thumb over his cheek. "I left."

"You left?"

She glanced down at her damp thumb, her expression concerned. "I can't breathe in that place. I checked myself out. It's time for me to go home. I want to go home, Joe."

Heart stuck in his throat, he could only nod.

Emma shifted her gaze from him to the computer.

Joe followed her line of sight. "Guys, this is Emma. Em, I know you recognize the old man. The lovely woman next to him is his fiancée, Rebecca."

"Hello," Rebecca said in greeting.

Dominic flashed his most charming smile. "She's way too pretty for you, Campbell. What does she see in you?"

Emma smiled back. "So, is it a British thing or a rock god thing?"

"What?" Dom asked.

"The exceptional good looks and charm."

Joe chuffed. "You find that ugly bastard attractive?"

Emma's gaze returned to him. She ran her thumb over the strip of hair below his bottom lip. "Nowhere near as attractive as you."

"Of course not. Who is?" he teased.

The smile she gave him was so close to its usual intensity, a lump formed in his throat. Christ, she was beautiful.

"I'm going to bed. You'll come sing me to sleep?"

"If that's what you want."

She leaned in until her mouth hovered just above his. "I also want you naked."

Joe settled his hand on her waist and brushed a kiss to her lips. "Then that's how you'll have me, Sunshine."

With one last look at the laptop, Emma walked away.

His smile vanished.

"Joe." Rebecca's voice trembled. "What are you going to do?"

Tears were in her eyes when he looked to the screen, so he glanced away, back in the direction Emma had disappeared. "I'm taking her home."

"If there's anything you need," Dom said quietly, the teasing note no longer in his voice. "Just call."

Joe nodded and disconnected. He went in search of Emma and found her sitting on the side of the bed.

Credit card in one hand and cell phone in the other, she spoke softly with whoever was on the other end of the line. "I need a jet. Denver, Colorado to Cleveland, Ohio. One passenger."

"I'm going with you."

She startled, her eyes meeting his. "No. You have to—"

"I'm going with you," he repeated, stepping farther into the room and stripping his shirt off. "You and me, Sunshine."

Her eyes filled with tears. "I'll call back," she whispered into her phone then disconnected. "You don't want any part of this, Joe."

He didn't bother to deny it. He didn't *want* any part of it. He *needed* to be a part of it.

Joe toed off his shoes, bent at the waist and pulled off his socks.

Emma continued to stare down at her phone. "There

will be seizures and blackouts. My personality may change."

"You mean like the glorious mood swings yesterday?" He shrugged and stripped out of his jeans. "Piece of cake."

She laughed then froze. Her gaze moved over him from head to toe and back again. As her tongue darted across her lips, he damn near groaned. "Why are you stripping? Are you trying to distract me from this conversation?"

Hell, if he had thought of it, he probably would have. "Is it working?"

"You are a gorgeous man, you know that?" Her fingers brushed his abs and he sucked in a breath. "Of course, you do. I could see it in your eyes the night we met. You knew how gorgeous you were and how quickly you could have me naked."

He took her hands and eased her to her feet. "If you remember, I never did get you naked that night." Grasping her shirt by the bottom edge, he pulled it over her head and off. "I never even got a kiss from you."

"Is that what you want now?" she asked, stroking her palm over his cock. "A kiss?"

"Christ," he hissed, suddenly painfully erect. Circling his fingers around her wrist, he moved her hand to his chest. "This isn't about sex, Sunshine. You asked for me naked. I aim to please."

"I asked for you naked because... Never mind." She shook her head then released the button and lowered the zip on her jeans, sitting on the edge of the bed to finish removing them.

"Hey." What was this? Emma never had a problem speaking her mind. Joe tucked a finger beneath her chin and tipped her head up. The tears in her eyes tore at him. "Talk to me."

"I know I look terrible. Too thin and—"

"You're beautiful."

"Yet you don't want to make love to me."

Her hands were on the move again, dancing across his flesh, leaving a trail of heat in their wake. "I do. God, I do. What I don't want is to hurt you."

When she tugged his wrist, he sank to his knees before her.

She cupped his face in her hands, smoothed her thumbs over his cheeks. "The only way you hurt me is if you turn me away. I need this, Joe. I need you inside of me, one more time, before I leave."

He kissed her softly. Then again, not so softly. "You're not going home alone. Do you hear me?" Crawling onto the bed, Joe rolled her beneath him, supporting his weight with his elbows on either side of her face. "Christ, do you really expect me to walk away and continue with the tour like you don't matter?"

She sighed and pressed her face into his neck, her hands sliding down his back as she wiggled closer.

"I love you, Emma. I'm staying with you until the end."

May 23

I've missed my hometown. With all the places I've traveled these past few weeks on the road with Joe, all the beautiful cities and towns, there's still nothing like coming home.

The weather is beautiful. The sun is shining, birds are singing and the spring flowers are all in bloom. I sit outside and soak it in as much as possible, Joe at my side. Never more than an arm's length away.

I know he's afraid. Afraid to sleep. To let me out of his sight for more than a few moments at a time.

I'm afraid, too. Afraid to linger for too long, drawing out his suffering.

Loss is an inevitable part of life.

So is love.

I love Joe enough I don't want to extend his pain.

It's time to give in to The Monster.

Time to say good-bye.

Number of days since I decided to live: 93
Number of days since I met Joe: 50
Current level of panic: 8/10

TWENTY

May 24

"ALISON?" EMMA OPENED her eyes, blinking until the room came into focus. The lights were low and she could just make out her friend sitting in a chair near the dresser. "How long was I out?"

She hated losing time, but there was no stopping it. No staying awake no matter how hard she tried. When her body decided to sleep, which was pretty much constantly anymore, she slept.

"Only an hour," Alison replied. "Can I get you anything? Something to drink, maybe?"

Emma shook her head and pressed her fingers against her eyes. "Where's Joe?" Sleeping she hoped.

Al moved closer, crossing the room to sit on the end of the bed. "Last I knew, he was in the living room arguing with someone named Marvin."

"Fucking asshole," Emma muttered then cringed. Alison wasn't much for swearing and the f-bomb was her least favorite word. "Sorry."

A slow smile curved Al's lips. "No, from what I heard, he is definitely a fucking asshole."

"Wow. We need to document this occasion. You just said fucking."

She chuckled. "Stop."

Emma tried to sit up, but her body wasn't cooperating. That was one of the most frustrating things about all of this. The fact that her body no longer listened to the commands she sent it. Being damn near helpless was worse than the pain that never let up.

Alison shifted. "Can I—"

"No. I've got this." She could do it, damnit. Once situated, Emma sighed. "You can get me my journal and cell phone."

"Sure." Alison's eyes were warm and full of concern as she handed the items over. "Anything else?"

"Yes." Emma closed her hand over the key around her neck. "Help me take my necklace off."

Instead, Al visibly swallowed and stepped back. Apprehension filled her gaze.

The alarmingly quick rate at which she was failing had both Alison and Joe wearing that same look most of the time. But, no matter how many times she'd seen it, the look still filled Emma with misery. "Please."

She could feel the tremble in Alison's hands as she unhooked the clasp. As soon as it was free, Emma placed it atop the journal in her lap. "Al—"

Alison was back to shaking her head.

"Al, look at me." Emma waited until she did. "Go find Joe. Keep him busy, okay? I need fifteen minutes alone."

"What are you going to do?"

Emma placed her hand on Alison's arm. "Fifteen minutes, then you come back alone. I need to talk to you."

It was clear Alison didn't want to, but she agreed and walked out of the room.

Emma opened her journal and draped her necklace between the pages. She took a moment to stare down at the key, recalling the conversation she and Joe had shared the night before.

They'd been in her bed, laying face to face, Joe touching her. He touched her all the time anymore—brushed his fingers down her cheeks, her arms. Stroked her back. If he wasn't touching her, he was singing to her. Softly, almost as if the act brought him the same comfort it brought her.

Last night, he'd been silent, just looking at her as he absently traced the backs of his fingers over her collarbone...

"I don't think your angel was offering you a key," he said softly.

"No?"

"I think she was telling you that you *were the key. That you still had something left to do."*

"What's that?"

"Unlock my heart," he whispered. *"You made me a better man, Emma."*

There was no disguising the tears his words caused. She didn't try to swipe them away as she pressed her lips to his. "Promise me you won't go back. You'll stay in the light, even when I'm no longer with you."

"God, Em."

"Please. I have to know you'll be okay. You're my forever, Joe. I'm just not yours."

Emma picked up her pen, the blank page daunting. She didn't know what to say to him, had no idea where to begin. There weren't enough words to express what the time she'd spent with Joe meant to her. Not enough hours left in the day.

After a few false starts, she decided that the words were already there—in her previous entries, the sketches and mementos tucked between the pages. Instead of trying to retell the story, she went with what it meant to have him with her right now. And what she wanted for him in the future.

When she was done, she closed the journal, securing it with the leather tie. Then she swiped her tears away and pulled herself together. There was one final thing she had to do.

Gary answered on the first ring. "Emma?"

"He's going to need you."

Silence.

"Hello?"

"I'm here." His voice broke. "I'm here, Em. We all are. Here, in Cleveland."

"Good," she whispered. "Tobias?"

"I've always hated that name. It doesn't sound so bad coming from you." He sucked an audible breath then let it out slowly. "People don't come much better than you, Emma. I'm going to miss you."

She already missed him. Missed the way his dimple flashed when he smiled. The combined look of frustration and affection he'd give her when she teased. "Don't let him fall back into the darkness. Promise me. Promise you'll keep him in the light."

"I promise."

"It won't be long now."

"Damnit. Goddamnit."

The tears in his voice tore at her. So strong and tough, but with a heart of gold. "It was nice knowing you, Tobias."

"Believe me, the pleasure was all mine."

Emma still clutched the phone in her hand when Alison returned.

Al took one look at her and burst into tears.

"Come here," Emma whispered, patting the side of the bed. "I need you to do something for me."

Even though she shook her head in the negative, Al stepped closer and sat.

Her hands shook as Emma reached out, the knife-sharp pain in her skull excruciating.

Alison held hers clenched together in her lap. Emma took one and turned it palm up. She placed her journal in Al's upturned hand, held it there with her own on top. "After I'm gone, you'll give this to Joe."

"Emma." Her name was barely a whisper of sound.

"You still have Gary's number, right?"

Alison nodded.

"After I'm gone, the very first thing you do is call Gary. Joe's going to need him. Got it?"

"Yes."

"Then you give this to Joe. You make sure he gets this. No matter whatever else happens, you give this to Joe. Do you understand?"

Another nod.

"Say it Al. I need to hear you say it."

Alison wiped her hand beneath her nose and sniffed. "No matter what, I make sure Joe gets your journal."

Emma breathed a sigh of relief. She closed her eyes, knowing she wasn't going to be able to hold out against The Monster much longer. "Now," she said, cupping Alison's face in her hands, looking deep into her eyes. "You're going to stop crying."

"You can't make me."

She softened her voice. "No, I can't. But I can make you leave."

"No."

"Yes. Get off this bed and go home to Kevin. Tell that dear, sweet man you love him. Do it for me. Then continue to tell him every day for the rest of your long life together. Do it now, Alison."

She nodded, but didn't move. "I love you, Emma."

"I love you, too."

JOE STOOD IN Emma's glass room staring at the lights of the city. Not far away, much closer than he ever imagined, stood the arena. Literally, only minutes from the condo. There was a performance going on. He didn't know who was there, but semis and tour buses filled the back parking lot. They made him think of the last time he'd been in this city, in that very lot, kissing Emma for the first time. How his pulse had tripped at the first brush of her finger across his lips. How damn good it felt to lift her into his arms and pin her against the bus.

How long ago was that now? He didn't know. Had no idea how many days he'd even been in this city, as one had blurred into the next until time seemed to stand still. Only it didn't. Or if it did, it was just his time because Emma...Emma was growing weaker by the moment.

Damnit. He pressed his forehead to the glass, closed his eyes, and damn near missed it when Alison darted out of Emma's room. The energy shift in the air and a sound too much like a sob had him turning in time to see her pull open the door. With tears in her eyes, tears streaming down her face, she glanced at him then left.

He found Emma curled in a ball on her bed. Her mobile phone was clutched in one hand, the other covered her eyes as she sobbed.

"Sunshine."

His voice only seemed to make her cry harder. Not knowing what else to do, Joe climbed under the covers with her. He removed the phone from her fingers and snugged her close.

"Don't cry, Em. Please don't cry."

She shifted, tucking her head beneath his chin and pressing her face to his neck.

"It's okay," he soothed. "I've got you."

He placed his hand against the back of her neck, fingers moving over the muscles, easing the tension. Damned if he knew whether it did anything to ease the pain, but she sighed. Her body relaxed against his.

It didn't take long for him to realize he couldn't feel the chain of her necklace. "Em, where's your key?"

Her only response was a shake of her head.

An odd sense of loss filled him.

"You always smell so good." She spoke in a whisper. The tremor in her body sounded in her voice.

"So you keep telling me."

"Don't let go of me."

"I won't, Sunshine. I won't let go."

She drifted to sleep in under ten minutes.

Joe was still holding her an hour later when her breathing shifted and grew erratic. The trembling in her limbs increased tenfold and a soft whimper escaped. He continued holding her as he began to sing—something that often soothed her, even in sleep.

Tonight it didn't work.

This was it.

He could tell by the way she breathed, how her body

would stop for a bit before starting back up with a gasp of air that jolted him every time. She was slipping away and there wasn't a damn thing he could do about it. Nothing, but not let go of her as he sang her that stupid, beautiful song she loved so much.

Her lungs stopped and he held his breath, willed her to stay with him. Just a little longer. He wasn't ready. Would never be ready to let her go.

Her body jerked, sucking in a deep breath, and so did he. Her eyes opened. "Joe?"

Not the soft sound of his name on her lips like he'd heard so often. This one was full of pain and fear. As if she didn't think she would find him.

"I'm here, Sunshine. I'm right here."

She reached for him, cupped his cheek in her trembling hand.

Joe covered her hand with his.

"I love you," she whispered. "I love you, Joe."

Tears spilled down his face. "I love you, Sunshine."

Then she was gone.

JOE WAS IN a fog—his limbs heavy, weighted down, useless—and it hadn't taken a drop of alcohol to get here.

Just Emma's death.

She was gone. Lost to him.

He was suffocating. Smothered by pain and loss.

"It's about damn time you showed your face around here, Joe." Marvin was raging, going on and on about canceled shows and lost revenue.

He didn't give a shit about Joe's loss.

"You're playing in Reno tomorrow. Do you hear me?

Forget the girl."

"What the fuck is wrong with you, Marvin?" Gary yelled.

What was wrong with Marvin? Joe expected this shit from Marvin. What he'd never expected was Gary to just offer him up on a platter. Gare, his closest friend, the man hired to protect him, had done exactly that—tossed him, broken and bleeding, to the sharks.

And like any shark who smelled blood in the water, Marvin was in a frenzy.

"You're playing, and you'll give the best damn performance of your life or—"

"Get out," Joe growled. Marvin was poking at raw wounds. Wounds made all the worse by Gary's betrayal. "Get the fuck out, now. Both of you."

Gary glanced in his direction then did the intelligent thing and took Marvin by the arm. "Come on, Marv."

"I'm not going anywhere," Marvin argued. "You need to get him together, Gare. Pack his shit and haul his ass to the airport because we're flying—"

The coffeemaker smashed against the wall, missing Marvin's face by a hair.

Christ, that felt good. Joe grabbed the next closest thing, his acoustic guitar. How the fuck it had found its way into this room, he didn't know. Most likely a plant from Marv— a reminder to get back to work. The guitar followed the coffeemaker.

It didn't supply the same satisfying crash of destruction, but it required both men take evasive maneuvers. That was gratifying.

Gary and Marvin vacated—pretty fucking quickly, too—as he plucked the lamp off the side table. The television came next, then the mirror in the bathroom. Joe tore the room apart, piece by piece. Destroyed anything and everything he could get hands on. Not stopping until he'd exhausted all options.

Expecting hotel security any moment, he collapsed in the chair. Jesus, he'd lost it. Tears streamed from his eyes, snot ran down his face. He was a fucking mess.

Pulling a shirt from the bag near his feet, he scrubbed his face.

At the floor, near his feet, rested Emma's journal, knocked there during his frenzy. The tie had come loose, allowing a chain to slip free. A silver chain.

Heart in his throat, he snatched up the leather book. He slid his fingers into the page that held the chain and flipped the book open. His name, written in Emma's delicate script, topped the page. In the center, lay her key.

A tremble worked through his body. His hands shook as he cupped the key in his palm and brought it to his lips. Joe breathed in, looking for her scent, knowing he wouldn't find it on a small piece of silver. He clipped the chain around his neck and sighed. Then read the missive she'd left him.

Joe,

If you are reading this, it means my time has come. I can't know what you're feeling right now, but I imagine it is close to the ache in my chest as I write these last words to you. I asked Alison to give you my journal with the hope that it brings you a measure of peace. That you read my thoughts and know just how much joy you brought me. How very much I loved you.

You told me last night I was the key that unlocked your heart and turned you into a better man. What I didn't say, and I need you to know, is you were my key, too. My key to happiness. Our time together may have seemed too short for you, but for me it was a lifetime. One you filled with music and dancing, laughter and love.

Your lifetime is waiting for you. And if there's one last thing I can ask, it's to not forget what I worked so hard to show you. Life is beautiful – but no one comes out of it alive. So live each day as if it's your last. Walk in the sunshine. Dance beneath the stars. Laugh hard and long and never, ever forget how very special you are.

You are good enough.
I love you.

When he was done, he read the words again. Then he closed the book and reopened it at the beginning.

February 15
I dreamt of an angel last night…

Joe had no idea how much time passed before he reached the end. When he did, he could only sit in shock. Her words, her journal, that when started she'd meant only for herself, told the story of a woman who'd made the decision to face life with her eyes wide open. A woman who, by some mysterious stroke of fate, not only found and fell in love with him, she'd sacrificed herself for him. All so she could teach him what he'd been missing while walking around in an alcohol induced stupor.

Christ. What was he supposed to do with this knowledge?

He closed the book and waited for his old friend darkness to return. But all that greeted him was the echo of silence. The crippling pain of loss.

He glanced around at the destruction that was his room—it mirrored his soul.

He looked at Emma's journal, her final words. Her plea to him to never forget how to live. She'd given up everything for him. The least he could do was let her know she'd taught him well. He knew where to find the light, and it wasn't in this room.

It sure as fuck wasn't in that arena they wanted him to return to.

Carefully, he tucked everything back into the journal, tied it and placed it in his duffle. He added his wallet, passport, mobile phone and charger then zipped it closed. Pushing his arms into his black leather jacket, he grabbed his bag and walked out the door without a backward glance.

GARY STARED AT what was left of Joe's hotel room and the rock that had sat in his gut all day grew exponentially. He'd made a mistake. He shouldn't have brought Joe back to this. The numb look on his best friend's face as he'd scooped him off the floor of Emma's condo told the story. Joe was in no shape to be thrown back into the thick of things. Gary had fucked up.

Big-time.

But the pain of loss that filled Joe, filled him, too. He'd cared for Emma. Loved her, in his own way. God, just thinking about her made him want to break down. She'd gone so quickly. One day tossing jabs at him and smiling in that way only she could. A few later...gone.

Damn, it hurt. It hurt so fucking bad. And she was just

his friend.

Emma was Joe's light.

Gary couldn't begin to imagine what Joe was going through. The crippling pain he must feel. Yet what had he done? Sure as shit, not the job he was paid to do. He hadn't protected Joe from Marvin's bullshit.

Now Joe was gone. One look at the destruction before him and Gary knew it.

Joe had walked.

Desperate to stop him, Gary took off at a jog, down three flights of stairs, across the lobby and out the front door, bursting onto the sidewalk in time to find Joe climbing into a taxi.

"Joe!"

Joe froze, but didn't turn back. "Tell Marvin he's fired," he said, voice filled with anger and heartache.

Happily. "And me?" Gary asked, knowing he deserved the same fate.

Joe hung his head. He didn't answer.

Goddamnit, he had to fix this. Seven years of friendship was washing away before his eyes and damned if Gary know how to fix it. "Where are you going?"

"I need to go for a walk."

Watch for more books in the Blind Man's Alibi series coming soon.

About the Author

The youngest of four, Sarah Grimm can't remember a time when she wasn't writing. In fact, her siblings believe she began writing in utero to pass the time. As a child, Sarah wrote constantly, littering the house with bulging spiral notebooks and ignoring the ribbing of her mother and sister who routinely said 'romances?' in a somewhat scornful tone. Sarah is a Romance Through the Ages award winner for Best Contemporary Romance, a RONE Awards finalist, and a Gayle Wilson Award of Excellence finalist.

Visit her online at:
www.sarahgrimm.com

Other Books by Sarah Grimm

Not Without Risk

After Midnight (Black Phoenix #1)

Midnight Heat (Black Phoenix #2)